THE MASTER
OF APPLEBY

MORE WILDSIDE CLASSICS

THE MASTER OF APPLEBY

FRANCIS LYNDE

WILDSIDE PRESS

THE MASTER OF APPLEBY

This edition published in 2006 by Wildside Press, LLC.
www.wildsidepress.com

CHAPTER I

IN WHICH I WHET MY FATHER'S SWORD

The summer day was all but spent when Richard Jennifer, riding express, brought me Captain Falconnet's challenge.

'Twas a dayfall to be marked with a white stone, even in our Carolina calendar. The sun, reaching down to the mountain-girt horizon in the west, filled all the upper air with the glory of its departing, and the higher leaf plumes of the great maples before my cabin door wrought lustrous patterns in gilded green upon a zenith background of turquoise shot with crimson, like the figurings of some rich old tapestries I had once seen in my field-marshal's castle in the Mark of Moravia.

Beyond the maples a brook tinkled and plashed over the stones on its way to the near-by Catawba; and its peaceful brawling, and the evensong of a pair of clear-throated warblers poised on the topmost twigs of one of the trees, should have been sweet music in the ears of a returned exile. But on that matchless bride's-month evening of dainty sunset arabesques and brook and bird songs, I was in little humor for rejoicing.

The road made for the river lower down and followed its windings up the valley; but Jennifer came by the Indian trace through the forest. I can see him now as he rode beneath the maples, bending to the saddle horn where the branches hung lowest; a pretty figure of a handsome young provincial, clad in fashions three years behind those I had seen in London the winter last past. He rode gentleman-wise, in small-clothes of rough gray woolen and with stout leggings over his hose; but he wore his cocked hat atilt like a trooper's, and the sword on his thigh was a good service blade, and no mere hilt and scabbard for show such as our courtier macaronis were just then beginning to affect.

Now I had known this handsome youngster when he was but a little lad; had taught him how to bend the Indian bow and loose the reed-shaft arrow in those happier days before the tyrant Governor Tryon turned hangman, and the battle of the Great Alamance had left me fatherless. Moreover, I had drunk a cup of wine with him at the Mecklenburg Arms no longer ago than yesterweek—this to a renewal of our early friendship. Hence, I must needs be somewhat taken aback when he drew rein at my doorstone, doffed his hat with a sweeping bow worthy a courtier of the great Louis, and said, after the best manner of Sir Charles Grandison:

"I have the honor of addressing Captain John Ireton, some-time of his Majesty's Royal Scots Blues, and late of her Apostolic Majesty's Twenty-ninth Regiment of Hussars?"

It was but an euphuism of the time, this formal preamble, declaring that his errand had to do with the preliminaries of a private quarrel between gentlemen. Yet I could scarce restrain a smile. For these upcroppings of courtier etiquette have ever seemed to march but mincingly with the free stride of our western backwoods. None the less, you are to suppose that I made shift to match his bow in some fashion, and to say: "At your service, sir."

Whereupon he bowed again, clapped hat to head and tendered me a sealed packet.

"From Sir Francis Falconnet, Knight Bachelor of Beaumaris, volunteer captain in his Majesty's German Legion," he announced, with stern dignity.

Having no second to refer him to, I broke the seal of the cartel myself. Since my enemy had seen fit to come thus far on the way to his end in some gentlemanly manner, it was not for me to find difficulties among the formalities. In good truth, I was overjoyed to be thus assured that he would fight me fair; that he would not compel me to kill him as one kills a wild beast at bay. For certainly I should have killed him in any event: so much I had promised my poor Dick Coverdale on that dismal November morning when he had choked out his life in my arms, the victim first of this man's treachery, and, at the last, of his sword. So, as I say, I was nothing loath, and yet I would not seem too eager.

"I might say that I have no unsettled quarrel with Captain Falconnet," I demurred, when I had read the challenge. "He spoke slightingly of a lady, and I did but—"

"Your answer, Captain Ireton!" quoth my youngster, curtly. "I am not empowered to give or take in the matter of accommodations."

"Not so fast, if you please," I rejoined. "I have no wish to disappoint your principal, or his master, the devil. Let it be tomorrow morning at sunrise in the oak grove which was once my father's wood field, each man with his own blade. And I give you fair warning, Master Jennifer; I shall kill your bullyragging captain of light-horse as I would a vermin of any other breed."

At this Jennifer flung himself from his saddle with a great laugh.

"If you can," he qualified. "But enough of these 'by your leave, sirs.' I am near famished, and as dry as King David's bottle in the smoke. Will you give me bite and sup before I mount and ride again? 'Tis a long gallop back to town on an empty stomach, and with a gullet as dry as Mr. Gilbert Stair's wit."

Here was my fresh-hearted Dick Jennifer back again all in a breath; and I made haste to shout for Darius, and for Tomas to take his horse, and otherwise to bestir myself to do the honors of my poor forest fastness as well as I might.

Luckily, my haphazard larder was not quite empty, and there were presently a bit of cold deer's to eat and some cakes of maize bread baked in the ashes to set before the guest. Also there was a cup of sweet wine, home-pressed from the berries the Indian scuppernong, to wash them down. And afterward, though the evening was no more than mountain-breeze cool, we had a hand-ful of fire on the hearth for the cheer of it while we smoked our reed-stemmed pipes.

It was over the pipes that Jennifer unburdened himself of the gossip of the day in Queensborough.

"Have you heard the newest? But I know you haven't, since the post-riders came only this morning. The war has shifted from the North in good earnest at last, and we are like to have a taste of the harryings the Jerseymen have had since '76. My Lord Corn-wallis is come as far as Camden, they say; and Colonel Tarleton has crossed the Catawba."

"So? Then Mr. Rutherford is like to have his work cut out for him, I take it."

Jennifer eyed me curiously. "Grif Rutherford is a stout Indian fighter; no West Carolinian will gainsay that. But he is never the man to match Cornwallis. We'll have help from the North."

"De Kalb?" I suggested.

Again the curious eyeshot. "Nay, John Ireton, you need not fear me, though I am just now this redcoat captain's next friend. You know more about the Baron de Kalb's doings than anybody else in Mecklenburg."

"I? What should I know?"

"You know a deal—or else the gossips lie most recklessly."

"They do lie if they connect me with the Baron de Kalb, or with any other of the patriot side. What are they saying?"

"That you come straight from the baron's camp in Virginia—to see what you can see."

"A spy, eh? 'Tis cut out of whole cloth, Dick, my lad. I've never took the oath on either side."

He looked vastly disappointed. "But you will, Jack? Surely, you have not to think twice in such a cause?"

"As between King and Congress, you mean? 'Tis no quarrel of mine."

"Now God Save us, John Ireton!" he burst out in a fine fervor of youthful enthusiasm that made him all the handsomer, "I had never thought to hear your father's son say the like!"

I shrugged.

"And why not, pray? The king's minion, Tryon, hanged my father and gave his estate to his minion's minion, Gilbert Stair. So, in spite of your declarations and your confiscations and your laws against alien landholders, I come back to find myself still the son of the outlawed Roger Ireton, and this same Gilbert Stair firmly lodged in my father's seat."

Jennifer shrugged in his turn.

"Gilbert Stair—for sweet Madge's sake I'm loath to say it— Gilbert Stair blows hot or cold as the wind sets fair or stormy. And I will say this for him: no other Tryon legatee of them all has steered so fine a course through these last five upsetting years. How he trims so skilfully no man knows. A short month since, he had General Rutherford and Colonel Sumter as guests at Appleby Hundred; now it is Sir Francis Falconnet and the British light-horse officers who are honored. But let him rest: the cause of independence is bigger than any man, or any man's private quarrel, friend John; and I had hoped—"

I laid a hand on his knee. "Spare yourself, Dick. My business in Queensborough was to learn how best I might reach Mr. Rutherford's rendezvous."

For a moment he sat, pipe in air, staring at me as if to make sure that he had heard aright. Then he clipt my hand and wrung it, babbling out some boyish brava that I made haste to put an end to.

"Softly, my lad," I said; "'tis no great thing the Congress will gain by my adhesion. But you, Richard; how comes it that I find you taking your ease at Jennifer House and hobnobbing with his Majesty's officers when the cause you love is still in such desperate straits?"

He blushed like a girl at that, and for a little space only puffed the harder at his pipe.

"I did go out with the Minute Men in '76, if you must know, and smelt powder at Moore's Creek. When my time was done I would have 'listed again; but just at that my father died and the Jennifer acres were like to go to the dogs, lacking oversight. So I came home and—and—"

He stopped in some embarrassment, and I thought to help him on.

"Nay, out with it, Dick. If I am not thy father, I am near old enough to stand in his stead. 'Twas more than husbandry that rusted the sword in its scabbard, I'll be bound."

"You are right, Jack; 'twas both more and less," he confessed, shamefacedly. "'Twas this same Margery Stair. As I have said, her father blows hot or cold as the wind sets, but not she. She is the fiercest little Tory in the two Carolinas, bar none. When I had got Jennifer in order and began to talk of 'listing again, she flew into a pretty rage and stamped her foot and all but swore that Dick Jennifer in buff and blue should never look upon her face again with her good will."

I had a glimpse of Jennifer the lover as he spoke, and the sight went somewhat on the way toward casting out the devil of sullen rage that had possessed me since first I had set returning foot in this my native homeland. 'Twas a life lacking naught of hardness, but much of human mellowing, that lay behind the home-coming; and my one sweet friend in all that barren life was dead. What wonder, then, if I set this frank-faced Richard in the other Richard's stead, wishing him all the happiness that poor Dick Coverdale had missed? I needed little: would need still less, I thought, before the war should end; and through this love-match my lost estate would come at length to Richard Jennifer. It was a meliorating thought, and while it held I could be less revengeful.

"Dost love her, Dick?" I asked.

"Aye, and have ever since she was in pinafores, and I a hobbledehoy in Master Wytheby's school."

"So long? I thought Mr. Stair was a later comer in Mecklenburg."

"He came eight years ago, as one of Tryon's underlings. Madge was even then motherless; the same little wilful prat-a-pace she has ever been. I would you knew her, Jack. 'Twould make this shiftiness of mine seem less the thing it is."

"So you have stayed at home a-courting while others fought to give you leisure," said I, thinking to rally him. But he took it harder than I meant.

"'Tis just that, Jack; and I am fair ashamed. While the fighting kept to the North it did not grind so keen; but now, with the red-coats at our doors, and the Tories sacking and burning in every settlement, 'tis enough to flay an honest man alive. God-a-mercy, Jack! I'll go; I've got to go, or die of shame!"

He sat silent after that, and as there seemed nothing that a curst old campaigner could say at such a pass, I bore him company.

By and by he harked back to the matter of his errand, making some apology for his coming to me as the baronet's second.

"'Twas none of my free offering, you may be sure," he added. "But it so happened that Captain Falconnet once did me a like turn. I had chanced to run afoul of that captain of Hessian pigs, Lauswoulter, at cards, and Falconnet stood my friend—though now I bethink me, he did seem over-anxious that one or the other of us should be killed."

"As how?" I inquired.

"When Lauswoulter slipped and I might have spitted him, and didn't, Falconnet was for having us make the duel *à outrance*. But that's beside the mark. Having served me then, he makes the point that I shall serve him now."

"'Tis a common courtesy, and you could not well refuse. I love you none the less for paying your debts; even to such a villain as this volunteer captain."

"True, 'tis a debt, as you say; but I like little enough the manner of its paying. How came you to quarrel with him, Jack?"

Now even so blunt a soldier as I have ever been may have some prickings of delicacy where the truth might breed gossip—gossip about a tale which I had said should die with Richard Coverdale and be buried in his grave. So I evaded the question, clumsily enough, as has ever been my hap in fencing with words.

"The cause was not wanting. If any ask, you may say he trod upon my foot in passing."

Jennifer laughed.

"And for that you struck him? Heavens, man! you hold your life carelessly. Do you happen to know that this volunteer captain of light-horse is accounted the best blade in the troop?"

"Who should know that better than—" I was fairly on the brink of betraying the true cause of quarrel, but drew rein in time. "I care not if he were the best in the army. I have crossed steel before—and with a good swordsman now and then."

"Anan?" said Jennifer, as one who makes no doubt. And then: "But this toe-pinching story is but a dry crust to offer a friend. You spoke of a lady; who was she? Or was that only another way of telling me to mind my own affairs?"

"Oh, as to that; the lady was real enough, and Falconnet did grossly asperse her. But I know not who she is, nor aught about her, save that she is sweet and fair and good to look upon."

"Young?"

"Aye."

"And you say you do not know her? Let me see her through your eyes and mayhap I can name her for you."

"That I can not. Mr. Peale's best skill would be none too great for the painting of any picture that should do her justice. But she is small, with the airs and graces of a lady of the quality; also, she has witching blue eyes, and hair that has the glint of summer sunshine in it. Also, she sits a horse as if bred to the saddle."

To my amazement, Jennifer leaped up with an oath and flung his pipe into the fire.

"Curse him!" he cried. "And he dared lay a foul tongue to her, you say? Tell me what he said! I have a good right to know!"

I shook my head. "Nay, Richard; I may not repeat it to you, since you are the man's second. Truly, there is more than this at the back of our quarrel; but of itself it was enough, and more than enough, inasmuch as the lady had just done him the honor to recognize him."

"His words—his very words, Jack, if you love me!"

"No; the quarrel is mine."

"By God! it is not yours!" he stormed, raging back and forth before the fire. "What is Margery Stair to you, Jack Ireton?"

I smiled, beginning now to see some peephole in this millstone of mystery.

"Margery Stair? She is no more than a name to me, I do assure you; the daughter of the man who sits in my father's seat at Appleby Hundred."

"But you are going to fight for her!" he retorted.

"Am I? I pledge you my word I did not know it. But in any case I should fight Sir Francis Falconnet; aye, and do my best to kill him, too. Sit you down and fill another pipe. Whatever the quarrel, it is mine."

"Mayhap; but it is mine, too," he broke in, angrily. "At all events, I'll see this king's volunteer well hanged before I second him in such a cause."

"That as you choose. But you are bound in honor, are you not?"

"No." He filled a fresh pipe, lighted it with a coal from the hearth, and puffed away in silence for a time. When he spoke again it was not as Falconnet's next friend.

"What you have told me puts a new face on the matter, Jack. Sir Francis may find him another second where he can. If he has aught to say, I shall tell him plain he lied to me about the quarrel, as he did. Now who is there to see fair play on your side, John Ireton?"

At the question an overwhelming sense of my own sorry case grappled me. Fifteen years before, I had left Appleby Hundred and my native province as well befriended as the son of Roger Ireton was sure to be. And now—

"Dick, my lad, I am like to fight alone," said I.

He swore again at that; and here, lest I should draw my loyal Richard as he was not, let me say, once for all, that his oaths were but the outgushings of a warm and impulsive heart, rarely bitter, and never, as I believe, backed by surly rancor or conscious irreverence.

"That you shall not, Jack," he asserted, stoutly. "I must be a-gallop now to tell this king's captain to look elsewhere for his next friend; but to-morrow morning I'll meet you in the road between this and the Stair outlands, and we'll fare on together."

After this he would brook no more delay; and when Tomas had fetched his horse I saw him mount and ride away under the low-hanging maples—watched him fairly out of sight in the green and gold twilight of the great forest before turning back to my lonely hearth and its somber reminders.

I stirred the dying embers, throwing on a pine knot for better light. Then I took down my father's sword from its deer-horn brackets over the chimney-piece, and set myself to fine its edge and point with a bit of Scotch whinstone. It was a good blade; a true old Andrea Ferara got in battle in the seventeenth century by one of the Nottingham Iretons.

I whetted it well and carefully. It was not that I feared my enemy's strength of wrist or tricks of fence; but fighting had been my trade, and he is but a poor craftsman who looks not well to see that his tools are in order against their time of using.

CHAPTER II

WHICH KNITS UP SOME BROKEN ENDS

It was in the autumn of the year '64, as I was coming of age, that my father made ready to send me to England. Himself a conscience exile from Episcopal Virginia, and a descendant of those Nottingham Iretons whose best-known son fought stoutly against Church and King under Oliver Cromwell, he was yet willing to humor my bent and to use the interest of my mother's family to enter me in the king's service.

Accordingly, I took ship at Norfolk for "home," as we called it in those days; and, after a stormy passage and overmuch waiting as my cousins' guest in Lincolnshire, had my pair of colors in the Scots Blues, lately home from garrison duty in the Canadas.

Of the life in barracks of a young ensign with little wit and less wisdom, and with more guineas in his purse than was good for him, the less said the better. But of this you may like to know that, what with a good father's example, and some small heritage of Puritan decency come down to me from the sound-hearted old Roundhead stock, I won out of that devil's sponging-house, an army in the time of peace, with somewhat less to my score than others had to theirs.

It was in this barrack life that I came to know Richard Coverdale and his evil genius, the man Francis Falconnet. Coverdale was an ensign in my own regiment, and we were sworn friends from the first. His was a clean soul and a brave; and it was to him that I owed escape from many of the grosser chargings on that score above-named.

As for Falconnet, he was even then a ruffler and a bully, though he was not of the army. He was a younger son, and at that time there were two lives between him and the baronetcy; but with a mother's bequeathings to purchase idleness and to gild his iniquities, he was a fair example of the *jeunesse dorée* of that England; a libertine, a gamester, a rakehell; brave as the tiger is brave, and to the full as pitiless. He was a boon companion of the officers' mess; and for a time—and purpose—posed as Coverdale's friend, and mine.

Since I would not tell my poor Dick's story to Richard Jennifer, I may not set it down in cold words here for you. It was the age-old tragic comedy of a false friend's treachery and a woman's weakness; a duel, and the wrong man slain. And you may know this; that Falconnet's most merciful role in it was the part he played one chill November morning when he put Richard Coverdale to the wall and ran him through.

As you have guessed, I was Coverdale's next friend and second in this affair, and but for the upsetting news of the Tryon tyranny in Carolina,—news which reached me on the very day of the meeting,—I should there and then have called the slayer to his account.

How my father who, Presbyterian and Ireton though he was, had always been of the king's side, came to espouse the cause of the "Regulators," as they called themselves, I know not. In my youthful memories of him he figures as the feudal lord of his own domain, more absolute than many of the petty kinglings I came afterward to know in the German marches. But this, too, I remember; that while his rule at Appleby Hundred was stern and despotic enough, he was ever ready to lend a willing ear to any tale of oppression. And if what men say of the tyrant Tryon's tax-gatherers and law-court robbers be no more than half truth, there was need for any honest gentleman to oppose them.

What that opposition came to in '71 is now a tale twice told. Taken in arms against the governor's authority, and with an estate well worth receiving, my father had little justice and less mercy accorded him. With many others he was outlawed; his estates were declared forfeit; and a few days later he, with Benjamin Merrill and four more captivated at the Alamance, was given some farce of a trial and hanged.

When the news of this came to me you may well suppose that I had no heart to continue in the service of the king who could sanction and reward such villainies as these of the butcher William Tryon. So I threw up my lieutenant's commission in the Blues, took ship for the Continent, and, after wearing some half-dozen different uniforms in Germany, was lucky enough to come at length to serviceable blows under my old field-marshal on the Turkish frontier.

To you of a younger generation, born in the day of swift mail-coaches and well-kept post-roads, the slowness with which our laggard news traveled in that elder time must needs seem past belief. It was early in the year '79 before I began to hear more than vague camp-fire tales of the struggle going on between the colonies and the mother country; and from that to setting foot once more upon the soil of my native Carolina was still another year.

What I found upon landing at New Berne and saw while riding a jog-trot thence to the Catawba was a province rent and torn by partizan warfare. Though I came not once upon the partizans themselves in all that long faring, there were trampled fields and pillaged houses enough to serve as mile-stones; and in my native Mecklenburg a mine full charged, with slow-match well alight for its firing.

Charleston had fallen, and Colonel Tarleton's outposts were already widespread on the upper waters of the Broad and the Catawba. Thus it was that the first sight which greeted my eyes when I rode into Queensborough was the familiar trappings of my old service, and I was made to know that in spite of Mr. Jefferson's boldly written Declaration of Independence, and that earlier casting of the king's yoke by the patriotic Mecklenburgers themselves, my boyhood home was for the moment by sword-right a part of his Majesty's province of North Carolina.

You are not to suppose that these things moved me greatly. As yet I was chiefly concerned with my own affair and anxious to learn at first hands the cost to me of my father's connection with the Regulators.

Touching this, I was not long kept in ignorance. Of all the vast demesne of Appleby Hundred there was no roof to shelter the son of the outlawed Roger Ireton save that of this poor hunting lodge in the mighty forest of the Catawba, overlooked, with the few run-away blacks inhabiting it, in the intaking of an estate so large that I think not even my father knew all the metes and bounds of it.

I shall not soon forget the interview with the lawyer in which I was told the inhospitable truth. Nor shall I forget his truculent leer when he hinted that I had best be gone out of these parts, since it was not yet too late to bring down the sentence of outlawry from the father to the son.

It was well for him that I knew not at the time that he was Gilbert Stair's factor. For I was mad enough to have throttled him where he sat at his writing table, matching his long fingers and smirking at me with his evil smile. But of this man more in his time and place. His name was Owen Pengarvin. I would have you remember it.

For a week and a day I lingered on at Queensborough, for what I knew not, save that all the world seemed suddenly to have grown stale and profitless, and my life a thing of small account. One day I would be minded to go back to my old field-marshal and the keeping of the Turkish border; the next I would ride over some part of my stolen heritage and swear a great oath to bide till I should come to my own again. And on these alternating days the storm of black rage filled my horizons and I became a derelict to drive on any rock or shoal in this uncharted sea of wrath.

On one of these gallops farthest afield I chanced upon the bridle-path that led to our old hunting lodge in the forest depths.

Tracing the path to its end among the maples I found the cabin, so lightly touched by time that the mere sight of it carried me swiftly back to those happy days when my father and I had stalked the white-tailed deer in the hill glades beyond, with this log-built cabin for a rest-camp. I spurred up under the low-hanging trees. The door stood wide, and a thin wreath of blue smoke curled upward from the mouth of the wattled chimney.

Then and there I had my first welcome home. Old black Darius—old when I had last seen him at Appleby Hundred, and a very grandsire of ancients now—was one of the runaways who made the forest lodge a refuge. He had been my father's body-servant, and, notwithstanding all the years that lay between, he knew me at once.

Thereupon, as you would guess, I came immediately into some small portion of my kingdom. Though Darius was the patriarch, the other blacks were also fugitives from Appleby Hundred; and for the son of Roger Ireton there was instant vassalage and loyal service. But best of all, on my first evening before the handful of fire in the great fire-place, Darius brought me a package swathed in many wrappings of Indian-tanned deerskin. It contained my father's sword, and, more precious than this, a message from the dead. My father's farewell was written upon a leaf torn from his journal, and was but a hasty scrawl. I here transcribe it.

My Son:
    I know not if this will ever come into your hands, but it and my sword shall be left in trust with the faithful Darius. We have made our ill-timed cast for liberty and it has failed, and to-morrow I and five others are to die at the rope's end. I bequeath you my sword—'tis all the tyrant hath left me to devise—and my blessing to go with it when you, or another Ireton, shall once more bare the true old blade in the sacred cause of liberty.
        Thy father,
            Roger Ireton.

You may be sure I conned these few brave words till I had them well by heart; and later, when my voice was surer and my eyes less dim, I summoned Darius and bade him tell me all he knew. And it was thus I learned what I have here set down of my father's end.

The next day, all indecision gone, I rode to Queensborough to ascertain, if so I might, how best to throw the weight of the good old Andrea into the patriot scale, meaning to push on thence to

Charlotte when I had got the bearings of the nearest patriot force.

'Twas none so easy to learn what I needed to know; though, now I sought for information, a curious thing or two developed. One was that this light-horse outpost in our hamlet was far in advance of the army of invasion—so far that it was dangersomely isolated, and beyond support. Another was the air of secrecy maintained, and the holding of the troop in instant readiness for fight or flight.

Why this little handful of British regulars should stick and hang so far from Lord Cornwallis's main, which was then well down upon the Wateree, I could not guess. But for the secrecy and vigilance there were good reasons and sufficient. The patriot militia had been called out, and was embodying under General Rutherford but a few miles distant near Charlotte.

I had this information in guarded whispers from mine host of the tavern, and was but a moment free of the tap-room, when I first saw Margery Stair and so drank of the cup of trembling with madness in its lees. She was riding, unmasked, down the high road, not on a pillion as most women rode in that day, but upon her own mount with a black groom two lengths in the rear. I can picture her for you no better than I could for Richard Jennifer; but this I know, that even this first sight of her moved me strangely, though the witching beauty of her face and the proudness of it were more a challenge than a beckoning.

A blade's length at my right where I was standing in front of the tavern, three redcoat officers lounged at ease; and to one of them my lady tossed a nod of recognition, half laughing, half defiant. I turned quickly to look at the favored one. He stood with his back to me; a man of about my own bigness, heavy-built and well-muscled. He wore a bob-wig, as did many of the troop officers, but his uniform was tailor-fine, and the hand with which he was resettling his hat was bejeweled—overmuch bejeweled, to my taste.

Something half familiar in the figure of him made me look again. In the act he turned, and then I saw his face—saw and recognized it though nine years lay between this and my last seeing of it across the body of Richard Coverdale.

"So!" thought I. "My time has come at last." And while I was yet turning over in my mind how best to bait him, the lady passed out of earshot, and I heard him say to the two, his comrades, that foul thing which I would not repeat to Jennifer; a vile boast with which I may not soil my page here for you.

"Oh, come, Sir Frank! that's too bad!" cried the younger of the twain; and then I took two strides to front him fairly.

"Sir Francis Falconnet, you are a foul-lipped blackguard!" I said; and, lest that should not be enough, I smote him in the face so that he fell like an ox in the shambles.

CHAPTER III

IN WHICH MY ENEMY SCORES FIRST

True to his promise, Richard Jennifer met me in the cool gray birthlight of the new day at a turn in the river road not above a mile or two from the rendezvous, and thence we jogged on together.

After the greetings, which, as you may like to know, were grateful enough on my part, I would fain inquire how the baronet had taken his second's defection; but of this Jennifer would say little. He had broken with his principal, whether in anger or not I could only guess; and one of Falconnet's brother officers, that younger of the twain who had cried shame at the baronet's vile boast, was to serve in his stead.

It was such a daydawn as I have sometimes seen in the Carpathians; cool and clear, but with that sweet dewy wetness in the lower air which washes the over-night cobwebs from the brain, and is both meat and drink to one who breathes it. On the left the road was overhung by the bordering forest, and where the branches drooped lowest we brushed the fragrance from the wild-grape bloom in passing. On the right the river, late in flood, eddied softly; and sounds other than the murmuring of the waters, the matin songs of the birds, and the dust-muffled hoof-beats of our horses there were none. Peace, deep and abiding, was the key-note of nature's morning hymn; and in all this sylvan byway there was naught remindful of the fierce internecine warfare aflame in all the countryside. Some rough forging of this thought I hammered out for Jennifer as we rode along, and his laugh was not devoid of bitterness.

"Old Mother Nature ruffles her feathers little enough for any teapot tempest of ours," he said. "But speaking of the cruelties, we provincial savages, as my Lord Cornwallis calls us, have no monopoly. The post-riders from the south bring blood-curdling stories of Colonel Tarleton's doings. 'Tis said he overtook some of Mr. Lincoln's reinforcements come too late. They gave battle but faint-heartedly, being all unready for an enemy, and presently threw down their arms and begged for quarter—begged, and were cut down as they stood."

"Faugh!" said I. "That is but hangman's work. And yet in London I heard that this same Colonel Tarleton was with Lord Howe in Philadelphia and was made much of by the ladies."

Jennifer's laugh was neither mirthful nor pleasant.

"'Tis a weakness of the sex," he scoffed. "The women have a fondness for a man with a dash of the brute in him."

I laughed also, but without bitterness.

"You say it feelingly. Do you speak by the book?"

"Aye, that I do. Now here is my lady Madge preaching peace and all manner of patience to me in one breath, and upholding in the next this baronet captain who, though I would have seconded him at a pinch, is but a pattern of his brutal colonel."

I put two and two together.

"So Falconnet is on terms at Appleby Hundred, is he?"

"Oh, surely. Gilbert Stair keeps open house for any and all of the winning hand, as I told you."

The thought of this unspoiled young maiden having aught to do with such a thrice-accursed despoiler of women made my blood boil afresh; and in the heat of it I let my secret slip, or rather some small part of it.

"Sir Francis had ever a sure hand with the women," I said; and then I could have bitten my masterless tongue.

"So?" queried Jennifer. "Then this is not your first knowing of him?"

"No." So much I said and no more.

We rode on in silence for a little space, and then my youthling must needs break out again in fresh beseechings.

"Tell me what you know of him, and what it was he said of Madge," he entreated. "You can't deny me now, Jack."

"I can and shall. It matters not to you or to any what he is or has been."

"Why?"

"Because, as God gives me strength and skill, I shall presently run him through, and so his account will be squared once for all with all men—and all women, as well."

"God speed you," quoth my loyal ally. "I knew not your quarrel with him was so bitter."

"It is to the death."

"So it seems. In that case, if by any accident he—"

I divined what he would say and broke in upon him.

"Nay, Dick; if he thrusts me out, you must not take up my quarrel. I know not where you learned to twirl the steel, or how, but you may be sure he would spit you like a trussed fowl in the first bout. I have seen him kill a man who was reckoned the best short sword in my old regiment of the Blues."

"Content yourself," said my young Hotspur, grandly. "If you spare him he shall answer to me for that thing he said of Madge Stair; this though I know not what it was he said."

I smiled at his fuming ardor, and glancing at the pair of pistols hanging from his saddle-bow, asked if he could shoot.

"Indifferent well."

"Then make him challenge you and choose your own weapon. 'Tis your only hope, and poor enough at that, I fear. I have heard he can clip a guinea at ten paces."

From that we fell silent again, being but a little way from the rendezvous, and so continued until, at a sudden turn in the road, we came in sight of a rude barricade of felled trees barring the way. Jennifer saw it first and pulled up short, loosing his pistols in their cases as he drew rein.

"'Ware the wood!" he said sharply, and none too soon, for even as he spoke the glade at our left filled as by magic with a motley troop deploying into the road as to surround us.

"Now who are these?" I asked; "friends or foes?"

"Foes who will hang you in your own halter strap; Jan Howart's Tories—the same that burned the Westcotts in their cabin a fortnight since. Will your horse take that barricade, think you?"

"Aye,—standing, if need be."

"Then at them, in God's name. Charge!"

It needed but the word and we were in the thick of it. I remembered my old field-marshal's maxim, *Von Feinden umringt, ist die Zeit zu zerschmettern*; and truly, being so plentifully outnumbered, we did strike both first and hard.

A line of the ragged horsemen strung itself awkwardly across the road to guard the flimsy barricade, and at this we charged, stirrup to stirrup. In the dash there was a scattering volley from the wood, answered instantly by the bellowings of Jennifer's great pistols; and then we came to the steel.

It was my first fleshing of the good old Andrea, and a better balanced blade I had never swung in hand-to-hand mellay. As we closed with the half-dozen defenders of the barrier, Jennifer reined aside to give me room to play to right and left, and in the midst of it went nigh to death because he held his hand to watch a cut and double thrust of mine.

"Over with you!" I shouted, pricking the man who would have mowed him down with a great scythe handled as a sword.

Our horses took the barrier in a flying leap, straining themselves for the race beyond. When we had pulled them down to a foot pace we were safely out of rifle shot and there was space to count the cost.

There was no cost worth counting. A saddle horn bullet-shattered for me, and the back of Jennifer's sword hand scored lightly across by another of the random missiles summed up our woundings. Dick whipped out his kerchief to twist about the scored hand, while I glanced back to see if any Tory cared to follow.

"Lord, Jack! I owe you one to keep and one to pay back," quoth my youngster, warmly. "I never saw a swordsman till this day!"

"Mere tricks, Dick, my lad; I have had fifteen years in which to learn them. And these were but country yokels armed with farming tools. The two with swords had little wit to use them."

"Oh, come!" said he. "I know a pretty bit of sword play when I see it. If we come whole out of this adventure with the baronet you shall teach me some of these 'mere tricks' of yours."

I promised, glancing back toward the dust-veiled barrier in the distance.

"Dick, you passed this way an hour ago; was that breastwork in the road then?"

"Not a stick of it."

"Then we may dare say our volunteer captain fights unwillingly."

"How so?" he demanded, being much too straightforward himself to suspect duplicity in others.

"'Tis plain enough. This was a trap, meant to stop or delay us, and I'll wager high it was the baronet who set and baited it. It would please him well to be able to say what our failure to come would give him warrant for. Let us gallop a bit, lest we be late and so play into his hand."

Jennifer smiled grimly and gave his horse the rein. "I think you'd charge the Fall of Man to him if that would give you better leave to kill him. I'd hate to own you for my enemy, John Ireton."

For all our swift speeding we were yet a little late at the rendezvous under the tall oaks. When we came on the ground the baronet was walking up and down arm in arm with his second, a broad-shouldered young Briton, fair of skin and ruddy of face.

If Falconnet had set the Tory trap for us he veiled his disappointment at its failure. His face, dark and inscrutable as it always was, was made more sinister by the plasters knitting up his broken cheek, but I was right glad to make sure that my blow had spared his eyes. Richly as he deserved his fate, I thought it would be ill to think on afterward that I had had him at a disadvantage of my own making.

There was little time wasted in the preliminaries. When Falconnet saw us he dropped his second's arm and began to make ready. I gave my sword to Jennifer, and the seconds went apart together. There was some measuring and balancing of weapons, and then Richard came back.

"The baronet's sword is a good inch longer than yours in the blade, and is somewhat heavier. Tybee has brought a pair of French short-swords which he offers. Will you change your terms?"

"No; I am content to fight with my own weapon."

Jennifer nodded. "So I told him." And then: "There was no surgeon to be had in town, Dr. Carew having gone with the Minute Men to join Mr. Rutherford. Tybee says 'tis scarce in accordance with the later rulings to fight without one."

"To the devil with their hairsplittings!" said I. "Let us have done with them and be at it."

Falconnet was removing his coat, and I stripped mine. The seconds chose the ground where the turf was short and firm, and yet yielding enough to give good footing. We faced each other, my antagonist baring an arm which, despite the bejeweled hand, was to the full as big-muscled as my own. My glance went from his weapon, a rather heavy German blade, straight and slender-pointed, to his face. He was smiling as one who strives to make the outer man a mask to cover all emotion, and the plasters on his cheek drew the smile into a grimace that was all but devilish.

The seconds fell back, but when Jennifer would have given the signal I stopped him.

"One moment, if you please. Sir Francis Falconnet, you know me?"

The thin-lidded eyes were veiled for an instant, and then he lied smoothly.

"Your pardon, Captain Ireton; I have not that honor."

"'Tis a small matter, but you do lie this morning as basely as you lied to Richard Coverdale nine years agone," said I; and then I signed Jennifer to give the word.

"Attention, gentlemen! On guard!"

My enemy's sword leaped to meet mine, and at the same instant I heard another click of steel betokening that the seconds had fallen to in a bit of by-play between themselves, as was then the fashion. After that I heard nothing for a time save the sibilant whisperings of the Ferara and the German long-sword, and saw nothing save the fierce eyes glaring at me out of the midst of the plaster-marred smile.

Recreant though he was, I must do my adversary the justice to say that he was a skilful master of fence, agile as a French dancer, and withal well-breathed and persevering. Twice, nay, thrice, before I found my advantage he had pricked me lightly with that extra inch of slender point. But when I had fairly felt his wrist I knew that his heavier weapon would shortly prove his undoing;

knew that the quick parry and lightning-like thrust would presently lag a little, and then I should have him.

Something of this prophecy of triumph he must have read in my eyes, for on the instant he was up and at me like a madman, and I had my work well cut out to hold him at the blade's length. I was so holding him; was, in my turn, beginning to press him slowly, when there came a drumming of hoofbeats on the soft turf, and then a woman's cry.

I looked aside, and to my dying day I shall swear that my antagonist did likewise. What I saw was Mistress Margery Stair riding down upon us at a hand-gallop, and I lowered my point, as any gentleman would.

In the very act—'twas while Jennifer was clutching at her bridle rein to stay her from riding fair between us—I felt the hot-wire prick of the steel in my shoulder and knew that my enemy had run me through as I stood.

Of what befell afterward I have but dim memories. There were more hoof-tramplings, and then I felt the dewy turf under my hands and soft fingers tremblingly busy at my neckerchief. Then I saw swimmingly, as through a veil of mist, a woman's face just above my own, and it was full of horror; and I heard my enemy say: "'Twas most unfortunate and I do heartily regret it, Mr. Jennifer. I saw not why he had lowered his point. Can I say more?"

How Richard Jennifer made answer to this lie I know not; nor do I know aught else, save by hear-say, of any further happening in that grassy glade beneath my father's oaks. For the big German blade was a shrewd blood-letter, and I fell asleep what time my lady was trying to stanch with her kerchief the ebbing tide of life.

CHAPTER IV

WHICH MAY BE PASSED OVER LIGHTLY

When I came back to some clearer sensing of things, I found myself abed in a room which was strange and yet strangely familiar. Barring a great oaken clothes-press in one corner, a raree-show of curious china on the shelves where the books should have been, and the face of an armored soldier staring down at me from its frame over the chimney piece, where I should have looked to see my mother's portrait, the room was a counterpart of my old bedchamber at Appleby Hundred. There was even a faint odor of lavender in the bed-linen; and the sense of smell, which hath ever a better memory than any other, carried me swiftly back to my boyhood, and to the remembrance that my mother had always kept a spray or two of that sweet herb in her linen closet.

At the bedside there was a claw-footed table, which also had the look of an old friend; and on it a dainty porringer, filled with cuttings of fragrant sweetbriar. This was some womanly conceit, I said to myself; and then I laughed, though the laugh set a pair of wolf's jaws at work on my shoulder. For you must know that I had lived the full half of King David's span of three-score and ten years, and more, and what womanly softness had fallen to my lot had been well got and paid for.

I closed my eyes the better to remember what had befallen, and when I opened them again was fain to wonder if the moment of back-reaching stood not for some longer time. In the deep bay of the window was a great chair of Indian wickerwork, and I could have sworn it had but now been empty. Yet when I looked again a woman sat in it.

Now of a truth I had seen this woman's face but twice; and once it wore a smile of teasing mockery and once was full of terror; but I thought I should live long and suffer much before the winsome challenging beauty of it would let me be as I had been before I had looked upon it.

She knew not that I was awake and slaking the thirst of my eyes upon the sweetness of her, and so I saw her then as few ever saw her, I think, with the womanly barriers of defense all down. 'Tis a hard test, and one that makes a blank at rest of many a face beautiful enough in action; but though this lady's face was to the full as changeful as any April sky, it was never less than triumphantly beautiful.

I had said her eyes were blue, but now they were deep wells

reflecting the soft gray of the clouded sky beyond the window-panes. I had made sure that her lips lent themselves most readily to mocking smiles scornful of any wit less trenchant than her own; but now these mocking lips were pensive, and with the rounded cheek and chin gave her the look of a sweet child wanting to be kissed. I had said her hair was bright in the sunlight, and so, indeed, it was; but lacking the sun it still held the dull luster of burnished copper in its masses, and her simple, care-free dressing of it at a time when *les grandes dames* were frizzing and powdering and adding art to art to mar the woman's crown of glory, gave her yet more the look of a child.

Lastly, I had called her small, and certainly her figure was girlish beside those grenadier dames of Maria Theresa's court to whom my old field-marshal had once presented me. But when she rose and went to stand in the window-bay I marked this; that not any duchess or margravine of them all had a more queenly bearing, or, with all their stays and furbelows, could match her supple grace and lissom figure.

What with the blood-lettings and the wound fever, coupled with the subtle witchery of her presence thus in my sick room, it is little to be wondered at that a curious madness came over me, or that I forgot for the moment the loyalty due to my dear lad. Could I have stood before her and, reading but half consent in the deep-welled eyes, have clipt her in my arms and laid my lips to hers, I would have run to pay the price, in earth or heaven or hell, I thought, deeming the fierce joy of it well worth any penalty.

At this I should have stirred, I suppose, for she came quickly and stood beside me.

"You have slept long and well, Captain Ireton," she said; and in all the thrilling joy of her nearer presence I found space to mark that her voice had in it that sweet quality of sympathy which is all womanly. "They say I am good only to fetch and carry—may I fetch you anything?"

I fear the madness of the moment must still have been upon me, for I said: "Since you are here yourself, dear lady, I need naught else."

At a flash I had my whipping in a low dipped curtsy and a mocking smile like that she had flung to Falconnet.

"*Merci! mon Capitaine,*" she said; and for all my wincings under the sharp lash of her sarcasm I was moved to wonder how she had the French of it. And then she added: "Is it the custom for Her Apostolic Majesty's officers to come out of a death-swound only to pay pretty compliments?"

"'Twas no compliment," I denied; and, indeed, I meant it.

Then I asked where I was, and to whom indebted, though I had long since guessed the answer to both questions.

In a trice the mocking mood was gone and she became my lady hostess, steeped to her finger-tips in gracious dignity.

"You are at Appleby Hundred, sir. 'Twas here they fetched you because there was no other house so near, and you were sorely hurt. Richard Jennifer and my black boy made a litter of the saddle-cloths, and with Sir Francis and Mr. Tybee to help—"

I think she must have seen that this thrust was sharper than that of the German long-sword, for she stopped in mid-sentence and looked away from me. And, surely, I thought it was the very irony of fate that I should thus be brought half dead to the house that was my father's, with my enemy and his second to share the burden of me.

"But your father?" I queried, when the silence had grown over-long.

"My father is away at Queensborough, so you must e'en trust yourself to my tender mercies, Captain Ireton. Are you strong enough to have your wound dressed?"

She asked, but waited for no answer of mine. Summoning a black boy to hold the basin of water, she fell to upon the wound-dressing with as little ado as if she had been a surgeon's apprentice on a battle-field, and I a bloodless ancient too old to thrill at the touch of a woman's hands.

"Dear heart! 'tis a monstrous ugly hurt," she declared, replacing the wrappings with deft fingers. "How came you to go about picking a quarrel with Sir Francis?"

"'Twas not of my seeking," I returned, and then I could have cursed my foolish tongue.

"Is that generous, Captain Ireton? We hear something of the talk of the town, and that says—"

"That says I struck him without sufficient cause. I am content to let it stand so."

"Nay, but you should not be content. Is there not strife enough in this unhappy land without these causeless bickerings?"

Here was my lady turned preacher all in a breath and I with no words to answer her. But I could not let it go thus.

"I knew Sir Francis Falconnet in England," said I, hoping by this to turn her safe aside.

"Ah; then there was a cause. Tell it me."

"Nay, that I may not."

Though she was hurting me sorely in the wound-dressing, and knew it, she laughed.

"'Tis most ungallant to deny a lady, sir. But I shall know

without the telling; 'twas about a woman. Tell me, Captain Ireton, is she fair?"

Seeing that her mood had changed again, I tried to give her quip for jest; but what with the pain of the sword-thrust and the sweet agony of her touches I could only set my teeth against a groan. She went on drawing the bandagings, little heedful how she racked me, I thought; and yet when all was done she stood beside me all of a tremble, as any tender-hearted woman might.

"There," she said; "'tis over for a time, and I make no doubt you are glad enough. Now you have nothing to do save to lie quiet till it heals."

"And how long will that be, think you?"

"We shall see; a long time, I hope. You shall be punished properly for your hot temper, I promise you, Captain Ireton."

With that she left me and went to stand in the window-bay; and from lying mouse-still and watching her over-steadily I fell asleep again. When I awoke the day was in its gloaming and she was gone.

After this I saw her no more for six full circlings of the clock-hands, and grew fair famished for a sight of her sweet face. But to atone, she, or some messenger of Richard Jennifer's, brought me my faithful Darius, and he it was who fetched me my food and drink and dressed my wound. From him I gleaned that the master of Appleby Hundred had returned from Queensborough, and that there were officers in red coats continually going back and forth, always with a hearty welcome from Gilbert Stair.

Now, though the master of my stolen heritage had little cause to love me, I thought he had still less to fear me; so it seemed passing strange that he came not once to my bedchamber to pass the time of day with his unbidden guest, or to ask how he fared. But in this, as in many other things, I reckoned without my enemy, though I might have known that Sir Francis would be oftenest among the red-coated officers coming and going.

But stranger than this, or than my lady's continued avoidance of me, was the lack of a visit from Richard Jennifer. Knowing well my dear lad's loyalty to the patriot cause, I could only conjecture that he had finally broken Margery's enforced truce to go and join Mr. Rutherford's militia, which, as Darius told me, was rallying to attack a Tory stronghold at Ramsour's Mill.

With this surmise I was striving to content myself on that evening of the third day, when Mistress Margery burst in upon me, bright-eyed and with her cheeks aflame.

"Captain Ireton, I will know the true cause of this quarrel which, failing in yourself, you pass on to Richard Jennifer!" she cried. "Was it not enough that you should get yourself half slain, without sending this headstrong boy to his death?"

Now in all my surmisings I had not thought of this, and truly if she had sought far and wide for a whip to scourge me with she could have found no thong to cut so deep.

"God help me!" I groaned. "Has this fiend incarnate killed my poor lad?"

"No, he is not dead," she confessed, relenting a little. "But he has the baronet's bullet through his sword-arm for the sake of your over-seas disagreement with Sir Francis."

I could not tell her that though my quarrel with this villain was but the avenging of poor Dick Coverdale's wrongs, Richard Jennifer's was for the baronet's affront to her. So I bore the blame in silence, glad enough to be assured that my dear lad was only wounded.

"Why don't you speak, sir?" she snapped, flying out at me in a passion for my lack of words.

"What should I say? I have not forgot that once you called me ungenerous."

"You should defend yourself, if you can. And you should ask my pardon for calling my father's guest hard names."

"The last I will do right heartily. 'Twas but the simple truth, but it was ill-spoken in your presence, Mistress Stair."

At this she laughed merrily; and in all my world-wanderings I had never heard a sound so gladsome as this sweet laugh of hers when she would be on the forgiving hand.

"Surely any one would know you are a soldier, Captain Ireton. No other could make an apology and renew the offense so innocently in the same breath." Then her mood changed again in the dropping of an eyelid, and she sighed and said: "Poor Dick!"

As ever when she was with me, my eyes were devouring her; and at the sigh and the trembling of the sweet lips in sympathy I found that curious love-madness coming upon me again. Then I saw that I must straightway dig some chasm impassable between this woman and me, as I should hope to be loyal to my friend. So I said: "He loves you well, Mistress Margery."

She glanced up quickly with a smile which might have been mocking or loving; I could not tell which it was.

"Did he make you his deputy to tell me so, Captain Ireton?"

Now I might have known that she was only luring me on to some pitfall of mockery, but I did not, and must needs burst out in some clumsy disclaimer meant to shield my dear lad. And in the midst of it she laughed again.

"Oh, you do amuse me mightily, *mon Capitaine*," she cried. "I do protest I shall come to see you oftener. Tis as good as any play!"

"Saw you ever a play in this backwoods wilderness?" I asked, glad of any excuse to change the talk and keep her by me.

"No, indeed. But you are not to think that no one has seen the great world save only yourself, Captain Ireton. What would you say if I should tell you that I, too, have seen your London, and even your Paris?"

Here I must blunder again and say that I had been wondering how else she came by the Parisian French; but at this her jesting mood vanished suddenly and she spoke softly.

"I had it of my mother, who came of the Huguenots. She spoke it always to me. But my father speaks it not, and now I am losing it for want of practice."

How is it that love transforms the once contemptible into a thing most highly to be prized? My eight years of campaigning on the Continent had given me the French speech, or so much of it as the clumsy tongue of me could master, and I had always held it in hearty English scorn. Yet now I was eager enough to speak it with her, and to take as my very own the little cry of joy wherewith she welcomed my hesitant mouthing of it.

From that we fell to talking in her mother's tongue of the hardships of those same Huguenot *émigrés*; and when I looked not at her I could speak in terms dispassionate and cool of this or aught else; and when I looked upon her my heart beat faster and my blood leaped quickly, and I knew not always what it was I said.

After a time—'twas when Darius fetched me my supper and the candles—she went away; and so ended a day which saw the beginning of a struggle fiercer than any the turbaned Turk had ever given me. For when I had eaten, and was alone with time to think, I knew well that I loved this woman and should always love her; this in spite of honor, or loyalty to Richard Jennifer, or any other thing in heaven or earth.

CHAPTER V

HOW I LOST WHAT I HAD NEVER GAINED

Though I dared not hope she would keep her promise and was sometimes so sorely beset as to tremble at her coming, Margery looked in upon me oftener, and soon there grew up between us a comradeship the like of which, I think, had never been between a woman loved and a man who, loving her, was yet constrained to play the part of her true lover's friend.

If I played this part but stumblingly; if at times the madness of my passion would not be denied the look or word or hand-clasp not of poor cool friendship; I have this to comfort me: that in after time, when my dear lad came to know, he forgave me freely—nay, held me altogether blameless, as I was not.

Of what these looks and words and hand-clasps meant to Margery I had no hint. But in my hours of sanity, when I would pass these slippings in review, I could recall no answering flash of hers to salt the woundings of the conscience-whip. So far from it, it seemed, as this sweet comradeship budded and blossomed on the stock of a better acquaintance, she came to hold me more as if I were some cross between a father or an elder brother, and some closer confidant of her own sex.

You are not to understand that she was always thus, nor overoften. More frequently that side of her which I soon came to call the mother's was turned to me, and I was made to stand a target for her wit and raillery. But she was ever changeful as a child, and in the midst of some light jesting mood would sober instantly and give my age its due.

In some of these, her soberer times, I felt her lean upon me as my sister might, had I had one; at others she would frankly set me in her father's place, declaring I must tell her what to say or do in this or that entanglement. Again, and this came oftener as our friendship grew, she would talk to me as surely woman never talked to any but a kinsman, telling me naïvely of her conquests, and sparing no gallant of them all save only Richard Jennifer.

And of Dick and his devotion she spoke now and then, as well, though never mockingly, as of the others. Nay, once when I pressed her on this point, asking her plainly if my dear lad had not good cause to hope, she would only smile and turn her face away, and say that of all the men she knew the hopeful ones pleased her best. So I was thus assured that if it were a scale for love to tip, my lady's heart would fall to Richard.

Now I took this to be a hopeful sign, that she would tell me freely of these her little heart affairs; and seeing her so safe upon the side of friendship, held the looser rein upon my own un-chartered passion. So long as I could keep my love well masked and hidden what harm could come to her or any if I should give it leave to live in prison? None, I thought; and yet at times was made a very coward by the thought. For love, like other living things, will grow by what it feeds upon, and once full-grown, may haply come to laugh at bonds, however strong or cunningly devised.

With such a fever in my veins it was little wonder that my wound healed slowly. As time passed by, with never a word of news from the world without—if Margery knew aught of the fighting she would never lisp a syllable to me—and with Gilbert Stair still keeping churlishly beyond the sight or sound of me, I fretted sorely and would be gone.

Yet this was but a passing mood. When Margery was with me I was not ill-content to eat the bread of sufferance in her father's house, and angry pride had scanty footing. But when she was away this same pride took sharp revenges, getting me out of bed to bully Darius into dressing me that I might foot it up and down the room while I was still unfit for any useful thing.

One morning in the summer third of June my lady came early and surprised me at this business of pacing back and forth. Whereat she scolded me as was her wont when I grew restive.

"What weighty thing have you to do that you should be so fierce to be about it, Monsieur Impetuous?" she cried. "*Fi donc!* you'd try the patience of a saint!"

"Which you are not," I ventured. "But truly, Margery, I am growing stronger now, and the bed does irk me desperately, if you must know. Besides—"

"Well, what is there else besides? Do I not pamper you enough?"

I laughed. "I'll say whatever you would have me say—so it be not the truth."

"I'll have you say nothing until you sit down."

She pushed the great chair of Indian wickerwork into place before the window-bay, and when I was at rest she drew up a low hassock and sat at my feet.

"Now you may go on," she said.

"You have not told me what you would have me say."

"The truth," she commanded.

"'What is truth,' said jesting Pilate,'" I quoted. "Why do you suppose my Lord Bacon thought the Roman procurator jested at such a time and place?"

"You are quibbling, Monsieur John. I want to know why you are so impatient to be gone."

"Saw you ever a man worthy the name who could be content to bide inactive when duty calls?"

"That is not the whole truth," she said, half absently. "You think you are unwelcome here."

"'Twas you said that; not I. But I must needs know your father will be relieved when he is safely quit of me."

"'Twas you said that, not I, Monsieur John," she retorted, giving me back my own words. "Has ever word been brought you that he would speed your parting?"

"Surely not, since I am still here. But you must know that I have never seen his face, as yet."

"And is that strange? You must not forget that he is Gilbert Stair, and you are Roger Ireton's son."

"I am not likely to forget it. But still a word of welcome to the unbidden guest would not have come amiss. And it was none of my seeking—this asylum in his house."

"True; but that has naught to do with any coolness of my father's."

"What is it, then?—besides the fact that I am Roger Ireton's son?"

"I think 'twas what you said to Mr. Pengarvin."

"That little smirking wretch? What has he to say or do in this?"

She looked away from me and said: "He is my father's factor and man of affairs."

"Ah, I have always to be craving your pardon, Margery. But I said naught to this parchment-faced—to this Mr. Pengarvin, that might offend your father, or any."

"How, then, will you explain this, that you swore to drive my father from Appleby Hundred as soon as ever you had raised a following among the rebels?"

"'Tis easily explained: this thrice-accursed—oh, pardon me again, I pray you; I will not name him any name at all. What I meant to say was that he lied. I made no threats to him; to tell the plain truth, I was too fiercely mad to bandy words with him."

"What made you mad, Monsieur John?"

"'Twas his threat to me—to taint me with my father's outlawry. Do you greatly blame me, Margery?"

"No."

Thereat a silence came and sat between us, and I fell to loving her the more because of it; but when she spoke I always loved her more for speaking.

"My father has had little peace since coming here," she said, at length. "He is old and none too well; and as for king and Congress, asks nothing but his right to hold aloof. And this they will not give him."

Remembering what Jennifer had told me of Gilbert Stair's trimming, I smiled within.

"That is the way of all the world in war-time, *ma petite*. A partizan may suffer once for all, but both sides hold a neutral lawful prey."

'Twas as the spark to tinder; my word the spark and in her eyes the answering flash.

"I tell him so!" she cried. "I tell him always that the king will have his own again. But still he halts and hesitates; and when these rebels come and quarter on us—"

I fear she must have seen my inward smile this time, for she broke off in the midst, and I made haste to forestall her flying out at me.

"Oh, come, my dear; you should not be so fierce with him when you yourself have brought a rebel to his house to nurse alive."

She looked me fairly in the eye. "You should be the last to remind me of my treason, Monsieur John."

"Then you are free to call it treason, are you, Margery?" I said.

She looked away from me again. "How can it well be less than treason?" Then suddenly she turned and clasped her hands upon my knee. "You must not be too hard upon me, Monsieur John. I've tried to do my duty as I saw it, and I have asked no questions. And yet I know much more than you have told me."

"What do you know?"

"I know your wound has been your safety. If you should leave this room and house to-day you would never wear the buff and blue again, Captain Ireton."

"You mean they would hang me for a spy. Will you believe me, Margery, if I say I have not yet worn the buff and blue at all?"

"*Oh!*" The little exclamation was of pure delight. "Then they were all mistaken? You are no rebel, after all?"

Was ever man so tempted since the fall of Adam? As I have writ it down for you in measured words, I was no more than half a patriot at this time. And love has made more traitors than its opposites of lust or greed. In no uncertain sense I was a man without a country; and this fair maiden on the hassock at my feet was all the world to me. I saw in briefer time than any clock hands ever measured how much a yielding word might do for me; and then I thought of Richard Jennifer and was myself again.

"Nay, little one," I said; "there has been no mistake. For their own purposes my enemies have passed the word that I am here as the Baron de Kalb's paid spy. That is no mistake; 'tis a lie cut out of whole cloth. I came here straight from New Berne, and back of that from London and the Continent, and scarcely know the buff and blue by sight. But I am Carolina born, dear lady; and this King George's governor hanged my father. So, when God gives me strength to mount and ride—"

"Now who is fierce?" she cried. And then, like lightning: "Will you raise a band of rebels and come and take your own again?"

"You know I will not," I protested, so gravely that she laughed again, though now there were tears, from what well-spring of emotion I knew not, in her eyes.

"Oh, mercy me! Have you never one little grain of imagination, Monsieur John? You are too monstrous literal for our poor jesting age." Then she sobered quickly and added this: "And yet I fear that this is what my father fears."

I did not tell her that he might have feared it once with reason, or that now the houseless dog she petted should have life of me though mine enemy should sick him on. But I did say her father had no present cause to dread me.

"He thinks he has. And surely there is cause enough," she added.

I smiled, and, loving her the more for her fairness, must smile again.

"Nay, you have changed all that, dear lady. Truly, I did at first fly out at him and all concerned for what has made me a poor pensioner in my father's house—or rather in the house that was my father's. But that was while the hurt was new. I have been a soldier of fortune too long to think overmuch of the loss of Appleby Hundred. 'Twas my father's, certainly; but 'twas never mine."

"And yet—and yet it should be yours, John Ireton." She said it bravely, with uplifted face and eloquent eyes that one who ran might read.

"'Tis good and true of you to say so, little one; but there be two sides to that, as well. So my father's acres come at last to you and Richard Jennifer, I shall be well content, I do assure you, Margery."

She sprang up from her low seat and went to stand in the window-bay. After a time she turned and faced me once again, and the warm blood was in cheek and neck, and there was a soft light in her eyes to make them shine like stars.

"Then you would have me marry Richard Jennifer?" she asked.

'Twas but a little word that honor bade me say, and yet it

choked me and I could not say it.

"Dick would have you, Margery; and Dick is my dear friend—as I am his."

"But you?" she queried. "Were you my friend, as well, is this as you would have it?"

My look went past her through the lead-rimmed window-panes to the great oaks and hickories on the lawn; to these and to the white road winding in and out among them. While yet I sought for words in which to give her unreservedly to my dear lad, two horsemen trotted into view. One of them was a king's man; the other a civilian in sober black. The redcoat rode as English troopers do, with a firm seat, as if the man were master of his mount; but the smaller man in black seemed little to the manner born, and daylight shuttled in and out beneath him, keeping time to the jog-trot of his beast.

I thought it passing strange that with all good will to answer her, these coming horsemen seemed to hold me silent. And, indeed, I did not speak until they came so near that I could make them out.

"I am your friend, Margery mine; as good a friend as you will let me be. And as between Richard Jennifer and another, I should be a sorry friend to Dick did I not—"

She heard the clink of horseshoes on the gravel and turned, signing to me for silence while she looked below. The window over-hung the entrance on that side, and through the opened air-case-ment I heard some babblement of voices, though not the words.

"I must go down," she said. "'Tis company come, and my father is away."

She passed behind my chair, and, hearing her hand upon the latch, I had thought her gone—gone down to welcome my enemy and his riding mate, the factor. But while I was cursing my un-ready tongue and repenting that I had not given her some small word of warning, she spoke again.

"You say 'Richard Jennifer or another.' What know you of any other, Monsieur John?"

"Nay, I know nothing save what you have told me; and from that I have been hoping there was no other."

"But if I say there may be?"

My heart went sick at that. True, I had thought to give her gen-erously to Dick, whose right was paramount; but to another—

"Margery, come hither where I may see you." And when she stood before me like a bidden child: "Tell me, little comrade, who is that other?"

But now her mood was changed again, and from standing

sweet and pensive she fell a-laughing.

"What impudence!" she cried. "*Ma foi*! You should borrow Père Matthieu's cassock and breviary; then, mayhap, I might confess to you. But not before."

But still I pressed her.

"Tell me, Margery."

She tossed her head and would not look at me. "Dick Jennifer is but a boy; suppose this other were a man full-grown."

"Yes?"

"And a soldier."

The sickness in my heart became a fire.

"O Margery! Don't tell me it is this fiend who came just now!"

All in a flash the jesting mood was gone, but that which took its place was strange to me. Tears came; her bosom heaved. And then she would have passed me but I caught her hands and held them fast.

"Margery, one moment: for your own sweet sake, if not for Dick's or mine, have naught to do with this devil's emissary of a man. If you only knew—if I dared tell you—"

But for once, it seemed, I had stretched my privilege beyond the limit. She whipped her hands from my hold and faced me coldly.

"Sir Francis says you are a brave gentleman, Captain Ireton, and though he knows well what you would be about, he has not sent a file of men to put you in arrest. And in return you call him names behind his back. I shall not stay to listen, sir."

With that she passed again behind my chair, and once again I heard her hand upon the latch. But I would say my say.

"Forgive me, Margery, I pray you; 'twas only what you said that made me mad. 'Tis less than naught if you'll deny it."

I waited long and patiently, and thought she must have gone before her answer came. And this is what she said:

"If I must tell you then;'tis now two weeks and more since Sir Francis Falconnet asked me to marry him. I—I hope you do feel better, Captain Ireton."

And with these bitterest of all words to her leave-taking, she left me to endure as best I might the hell of torment they had lighted for me.

CHAPTER VI

SHOWING HOW RED WRATH MAY HEAL A WOUND

It was full two days after the coming of the baronet and the factor-lawyer Pengarvin before I saw my lady's face near-hand again, and sometimes I was glad for Richard Jennifer's sake, but oftener would curse and swear because I was bound hand and foot and could not balk my enemy.

I knew Sir Francis and the lawyer still lingered on at Appleby Hundred—indeed, I saw them daily from my window—and Darius would be telling me that they waited upon the coming of some courier from the south. But this I disbelieved. Some such-like lie the baronet might have told, I thought; but when I saw him walk abroad with Margery on his arm, pacing back and forth beneath the oaks and bending low to catch her lightest word with grave and courtly deference that none knew better how to feign, I knew wherefore he stayed—knew and raged afresh at my own impotence, and for the thought that Margery was wholly at the mercy of this devil.

Yours is a colder century than was ours, my dears. Your art has tempered love and passion into sentiment, and hate you have learned to call aversion or dislike. But we of that simple-hearted elder time were more downright; and I have writ the word I mean in saying that my love was at the mercy of this fiend.

I know not how it is or why, but there are men who have this gift—some winning way to turn a woman's head or touch her heart; and I knew well this gift was his. 'Twas not his face, for that was something less than handsome, to my fancy; nor yet his figure, though that was big and soldierly enough. It was rather in some subtlety of manner, some power of simulation whereby in any womanly heart he seemed to stand at will for that which he was not.

As I have said, I knew him well enough; knew him incapable of love apart from passion, and that to him there was no sacredness in maiden chastity or wifely vows. So he but gained his end he cared no whit what followed after; ruin, broken hearts, lost souls, a man slain now and then to keep the scale from tipping—all were as one to him, or to the Francis Falconnet I knew.

And touching marriage, with Margery or any other, I feared that love would have no word to say. Passion there might be, and that fierce desire to have and wear which burns like any miser's fever in the blood; but never love as lovers measure it. Why, then, had he proposed to Margery? The answer did not tarry. Since he was now but a gentleman volunteer it was plain that he had squandered his estate, and so might brook the marriage chain if it were linked up with my father's acres.

It was a bait to lure such a gamester strongly. As matters stood with us in that wan summer of exhaustion and defeat, the king's cause waxed and grew more hopeful day by day. And in event of final victory a landless baronet, marrying Margery's dower of Appleby Hundred, might snap his fingers at the Jews who, haply, had driven him forth from England.

And as for Margery? Truly, she had told me, or as good as told me, that her maiden love had pledged itself a pawn for Jennifer's redeeming. But there be other things than love to sway a woman's will. This volunteer captain with the winning way was of the *haute noblesse*, and he could make her Lady Falconnet. Moreover, he was with her day by day; and you may mark this as you will; that a present suitor hath ever the trump cards to play against the absent lover.

So, brooding over this, I wore out two most dismal days—the first in many I had had to pass alone. But on the morning of the third the sky was lightened, though then the light was but a flash and darkness followed quickly after. She came again and brought me a visitor; it was this same Father Matthieu with whom she had jestingly compared me, and lest I should take my punishment too lightly, stayed but to make the good priest known to me.

Now I was born and bred an heretic, by any papist's reckoning, but I have ever held it witless in that man who lets a creed obstruct a friendship. Moreover, this sweet-faced cleric was the friendliest of men; friendly, and yet the wiliest Jesuit of them all, since he read me at a glance and fell straightway to praising Margery.

"A truly sweet young demoiselle," he said, by way of foreword, no sooner was the door closed behind her, and while he preached a sermon on this text I grew to know and love him.

He was a little man, as bone and muscle go, with deep-set eyes, and features kind and mild and fine as any woman's; some such face as Leonardo gave St. John, could that have been less youthful. I could not tell his order, though from his well-worn cassock girded at the waist with a frayed bit of hempen cord he might have been a Little Brother of the Poor. But this I noted; that he was not tonsured, and his white hair, soft and fine as Margery's, was like an aureole to the finely chiseled features. As missionary men of any creed are apt, he looked far older than he really was; and when he came to tell me of his life among the Indians, it was patent how the years had multiplied upon him.

I listened, well enough content to learn him better by his own report.

"But you must find it thankless work; this gospeling in the wilderness," I ventured, when all was said. "'Tis but a hermit's life for any man of parts; and after all, when you have done your utmost, your converts are but savages, as they were."

At this he smiled and shook his head. *"Non, Monsieur,* not so. You are a soldier and can not see beyond your point of sword. *Mais, mon ami,* they have souls to save, these poor children of the forest, and they are far more sinned against than sinning. I find them kind and true and faithful; and some of them are noble, in their way."

I laughed. "I've read about those noble ones," I said. "'Twas in a book called 'Hakluyt's Voyages.' Truly, I know them not as you do, for in my youth I knew them most in war. We called them brave but cruel then; and when I was a boy I could have shown you where, within a mile of this, they burned poor Davie Davidson at the stake."

"Ah, yes; there has been much of that," he sighed. "But you must confess, Captain Ireton, that you English carry fire and sword among them, too."

From that he would have told me more about the savages, but I was interested nearer home. As I have said, I was like any prisoner in a dungeon for lack of news, and so by degrees I fetched him round to telling me of what was going on beyond my window-sight of lawn and forest.

Brave deeds were to the fore, it seemed. At Ramsour's Mill, a few miles north and west, some little handful of determined patriots had bested thrice their number of the king's partizans, and that without a leader bigger than a county colonel. Lord Rawdon, in command of Lord Cornwallis's van, had come as far as Waxhaw Creek, but, being unsupported, had withdrawn to Hanging Rock. Our Mr. Rutherford was on his way to the Forks of Yadkin to engage the Tories gathering under Colonel Bryan. As yet, it seemed, we had no force of any consequence to take the field against Cornwallis, though there were flying rumors of an army marching from Virginia, with a new-appointed general at its head.

On the whole it was the king's cause that prospered, and the rising wave of invasion bade fair to inundate the land. So thought my kindly gossip; and, having naught to gain or lose in the great war, or rather having naught to lose and everything to gain, whichever way these worldly cards might run, he was a fair, impartial witness.

As you may well suppose, this news awoke in me the lust of battle, and I must chafe the more for having it. And while my visitor talked on, and I was listening with the outward ear, my brain was busy putting two and two together. How came it that the British outpost still remained at Queensborough, with my Lord Rawdon withdrawn and the patriot home guard well down upon its rear? Some urgent reason for the stay there must be; and at that I remembered what Darius had told me of its captain's waiting for some messenger from the south.

I scored this matter with a question mark, putting it aside to think on more when I should be alone. And when the priest had told me all the news at large, we came again to speak of Margery.

"I go and come through all this borderland," he said, when I had asked him how and why he came to Appleby Hundred, "but it was mam'selle's message brought me here. She is my one ewe lamb in all this region, and I would journey far to see her."

I wondered pointedly at this, for in that day the West was fiercely Protestant and the Mother Church had scanty footing in the borderland.

"But Mistress Margery is not a Catholic!" said I.

His look forgave the protest in the words.

"Indeed, she is, my son. Has she not told you?"

Now truly she had not told me so in any measured word or phrase; and yet I might have guessed it, since she had often spoken lovingly of this same Father Matthieu. And yet it was incredible to me.

"But how—I do not understand how that can be," I stammered. "Surely, she told me she was of Huguenot blood on the mother's side, and that is—"

The missionary's smile was lenient still, but full of meaning.

"Not all who wander from the Catholic fold are lost forever, Captain Ireton. The mother of this demoiselle lived all her life a Protestant, I think, but when she came to die she sent for me. And that is how her child was sent to France and grew up convent-bred. Monsieur Stair gave his promise at the mother's death-bed, and though he liked it not, he kept it."

"Aha, I see. And for this single lamb of your scant fold you brave the terrors of our heretic backwoods? It does you credit, Father Matthieu. The war fills all horizons now, mayhap, but I have seen the time in Mecklenburg when your cassock would have been a challenge to the mob."

His smile was quite devoid of bitterness. "The time has not yet passed," he said, gently. "I have been six weeks on the way from

Maryland hither, hiding in the forest by day and faring on at night. Indeed, I was in hiding on a neighboring plantation when our demoiselle's messenger found me."

This put me keen upon remembering what had gone before; how he had said at first that she had sent for him. I thought it strange, knowing how perilous the time and place must be for such as he. But not until he rose and, bidding me good day, left me to myself, did I so much as guess the thing his coming meant. When I had guessed it; when I put this to that—her telling me Sir Francis had proposed for her, and this her sending for the priest— the madness of my love for her was as naught compared to that anger which seized and racked me.

I know not how the hours of this black day were made to come and go, grinding me to dust and ashes in their passage, yet leaving me alive and keen to suffer at the end.

A thousand times that day I lived in torment through the scene in which the priest had doubtless come to play his part of joiner. The stage for it would be the great room fronting south; the room my father used to call our castle hall. For guests I thought there would be space enough and some to spare, for, as you know, our Mecklenburg was patriot to the core. But as to this, the bride-groom's troopers might fill out the tale, and in my heated fancy I could see them grouped beneath the candle-sconces with belts and baldrics fresh pipe-clayed, and shakos doffed, and *sabretaches* well in front. "A man full-grown—a soldier," she had said; and trooper-guests were fitting in such case.

From serving in a Catholic land I knew the customs of the Mother Church. So I could see the priest in cassock, alb and stole as he would stand before some makeshift altar lit with candles. And as he stands they come to kneel before him; my winsome Margery in all her royal beauty, a child to love, and yet an empress peerless in her woman's realm; and at her side, with his knee touching hers, this man who was a devil!

What wonder if I cursed and choked and cursed again when the maddening thought of what all this should mean for my poor wounded Richard—and later on, for Margery herself—possessed me? In which of these hot fever-gusts of rage the thought of inter-ference came, I know not. But that it came at length—a thought and plan full-grown at birth—I do know.

The pointing of the plan was desperate and simple. It was nei-ther more nor less than this: I knew the house and every turn and passage in it, and when the hour should strike I said I should go down and skulk among the guests, and at the crucial moment find or seize a weapon and fling myself upon this bridegroom as he should kneel before the altar.

With strength to bend him back and strike one blow, I saw not why it might not win. And as for strength, I have learned this in war: that so the rage be hot enough 'twill nerve a dying man to hack and hew and stab as with the strength of ten.

Although it was most terribly over-long in coming, the end of that black day did come at last, and with it Darius to fetch my supper and the candles. You may be sure I questioned him, and, if you know the blacks, you'll smile and say I had my labor for my pains—the which I had. His place was at the quarters, and of what went on within the house he knew no more than I. But this he told me; that company surely was expected, and that some air of mystery was abroad.

When he was gone I ate a soldier's portion, knowing of old how ill a thing it is to take an empty stomach into battle. For the same cause I drank a second cup of wine,—'twas old madeira of my father's laying-in,—and would have drunk a third but that the bottle would not yield it.

It was fully dark when I had finished, and, thinking ever on my plan, would strive afresh to weld its weakest link. This was the hazard of the weapon-getting. With full-blood health and strength I might have gone bare-handed; but as it was, I feared to take the chance. So with a candle I went a-prowling in the deep drawers of the old oaken clothes-press and in the escritoire which once had been my mother's, and found no weapon bigger than a hairpin.

It was no great disappointment, for I had looked before with daylight in the room. Besides, the wine was mounting, and when the search was done the hazard seemed the less. So I could rush upon him unawares and put my knee against his back, I thought the Lord of Battles would give me strength to break his neck across it.

At that I capped the candles, and, taking post in the deep bay of the window, set myself to watch for the lighting of the great room at the front. This had two windows on my side, and while I could not see them, I knew that I should see the sheen of light upon the lawn.

The night was clear but moonless, and the thick-leafed masses of the oaks and hickories rose a wall of black to curtain half the hemisphere of starry sky. As always in our forest land, the hour was shrilly vocal, though to me the chirping din of frogs and insects hath ever stood for silence. Somewhere beyond the thicket-wall an owl was calling mournfully, and I bethought me of that superstition—old as man, for aught I know—of how the hooting of an owl betokens death. And then I laughed, for surely death would come to one or more of those beneath my father's roof within the compass of the night.

Behind the close-drawn curtain, though I could see it not, the virgin forest darkened all the land; and from afar within its secret depths I heard, or thought I heard, the dismal howling of the timber wolves. Below, the house was silent as the grave, and this seemed strange to me. For in the time of my youth a wedding was a joyous thing. Yet I would remember that these present times were perilous; and also that my bridegroom captained but a little band of troopers in a land but now become fiercely debatable.

It must have been an hour or more before the sound of distance-muffled hoofbeats on the road broke in upon the chirping silence of the night. I looked and listened, straining eye and ear, hearing but little and seeing less until three shadowy horsemen issued from the curtain-wall of black beneath my window.

It was plain that others watched as well as I, for at their coming a sheen of light burst from the opened door below, at which there were sword-clankings as of armed men dismounting, and then a few low-voiced words of welcome. Followed quickly the closing of the door and silence; and when my eyes grew once again accustomed to the gloom, I saw below the horses standing head to head, and in the midst a man to hold them.

"So!" I thought; "but three in all, and one of them a servant. 'Twill be a scantly guested wedding." And then I raged within again to think of how my love should be thus dishonored in a corner when she should have the world to clap its hands and praise her beauty.

At that, and while I looked, the lawn was banded farther on by two broad beams of light; and then I knew my time was come.

Feeling my way across the darkened chamber I softly tried the door-latch. It yielded at the touch, but not the door. I pulled and braced myself and pulled again. 'Twas but a waste of strength. The door was fast with that contrivance wherewith my father used to bar me in what time I was a boy and would go raccooning with our negro hunters. My enemy was no fool. He had been shrewd enough to lock me in against the chance of interruption.

I wish you might conceive the helpless horror grappling with me there behind that fastened door; but this, indeed, you may not, having felt it not. For one dazed moment I was sick as death with fear and frenzy and I know not what besides, and all the blackness of the night swam sudden red before my eyes. Then, in the twinkling of an eye, the madness left me cool and sane, as if the fit had been the travail-pain of some new birth of soul. And after that, as I remember, I knew not rage nor haste nor weakness—knew no other thing save this; that I had set myself a task to do and I would do it.

My window was in shape like half a cell of honeycomb, and close beside it on the outer wall there grew an ancient ivy-vine which more than once had held my weight when I was younger and would evade my father's vigilance.

I swung the casement noiselessly and clambered out, with hand and foot in proper hold as if those youthful flittings of my boyhood days had been but yesternight. A breathless minute later I was down and afoot on solid ground; and then a thing chanced which I would had not. The man whom I had called a servant turned and saw me.

"Halt! Who goes there?" he cried.

"A friend," said I, between my wishings for a weapon. For this servant of my prefigurings proved to be a trooper, booted, spurred and armed.

"By God, I think you lie," he said; and after that he said no more, for he was down among the horses' hoofs and I upon him, kneeling hard to scant his breath for shoutings.

It grieves me now through all these years to think that I did kneel too hard upon this man. He was no enemy of mine, and did but do—or seek to do—his duty. But he would fight or die, and I must fight or die; and so it ended as such strivings will, with some grim crackling of ribs—and when I rose he rose not with me.

With all the fierce excitement of the struggle yet upon me, I stayed to knot the bridle reins upon his arm to make it plain that he had fallen at his post. That done, I took his sword as surer for my purpose than a pistol; and hugging the deepest shadow of the wall, approached the nearer window. It was open wide, for the night was sultry warm, and from within there came the clink of glass and now a toast and now a trooper's oath.

I drew myself by inches to the casement, which was high, finding some foothold in the wall; and when I looked within I saw no wedding guests, no priest, no altar; only this: a table in the midst with bottles on it, and round it five men lounging at their ease and drinking to the king. Of these five two, the baronet and the lawyer, were known to me, and I have made them known to you. A third I guessed for Gilbert Stair. The other two were strangers.

CHAPTER VII

IN WHICH MY LADY HATH NO PART

Seeing that I had taken a man's life for this, the chance of looking in upon a drinking bout, you will not wonder that I went aghast and would have fled for very shame had not a sudden weakness seized me. But in the midst I heard a mention of my name and so had leave, I thought, to stay and listen.

It was one of the late-comers who gave me this leave; a man well on in years, grizzled and weather-beaten; a seasoned soldier by his look and garb. Though his frayed shoulder-knot was only that of a captain of foot,'twas plain enough he ranked his comrade, and the knight as well.

"You say you've bagged this Captain Ireton? Who may he be? Surely not old Roger's son?"

"The same," said the baronet, shortly, and would be filling his glass again. He could always drink more and feel it less than any sot I ever knew.

"But how the devil came he here? The last I knew of him—'twas some half-score years ago, though, come to think—he was a lieutenant in the Royal Scots."

Mine enemy nodded. "So he was. But afterward he cut the service and levanted to the Continent."

The questioner fell into a muse; then he laughed and clapped his leg.

"Ecod! I do remember now. There was a damned good mess-room joke about him. When he was in the Blues they used to say his solemn face would stop a merry-making. Well, after he had been in Austria a while they told this on him; that his field-marshal had him listed for a majority, and so he was presented to the empress. But when Maria Theresa saw him she shrieked and cried out, '*Il est le père aux têtes rondes, lui-même! Le portez-vous dehors!*' So he got but a captaincy after all; ha! ha! ha!"

Now this was but a mess-room gibe, as he had said, cut out of unmarred cloth, at that. Our Austrian Maria ever had a better word than "roundhead" for her soldiers. But yet it stung, and stung the more because I had and have the Ireton face, and that is unbeloved of women, and glum and curst and solemn even when the man behind it would be kindly. So when they laughed and chuckled at this jest, I lingered on and listened with the better grace.

"What brought him over-seas, Sir Francis?" 'Twas not the

grizzled jester who asked, but the younger officer, his comrade.

Falconnet smiled as one who knows a thing and will not tell, and turned to Gilbert Stair.

"What was it, think you, Mr. Stair?" he said, passing the question on.

At this they all looked to the master of Appleby Hundred, and I looked, too. He was not the man I should have hit upon in any throng as the reaver of my father's estate; still less the man who might be Margery's father. He had the face of all the Stairs of Ballantrae without its simple Scottish ruggedness; a sort of weasel face it was, with pale-gray eyes that had a trick of shifty dodging, and deep-furrowed about the mouth and chin with lines that spoke of indecision. It was not of him that Margery got her firm round chin, or her steadfast eyes that knew not how to quail, nor aught of anything she owed a father save only her paternity, you'd say. And when he spoke the thin falsetto voice matched the weak chin to a hair.

"I? Damme, Sir Francis, I know not why he came—how should I know?" he quavered. "Appleby Hundred is mine—mine, I tell you! His title was well hanged on a tree with his damned rebel father!"

A laugh uproarious from the three soldiers greeted his petulant outburst; after which the baronet enlightened the others.

"As you know, Captain John, Appleby Hundred once belonged to the rebel Roger Ireton, and Mr. Stair here holds but a confiscator's title. 'Tis likely the son heard of the war and thought he stood some chance to come into his own again."

"Oh, aye; sure enough," quoth the elder officer, tilting his bottle afresh. And then: "Of course he promptly 'listed with the rebels when he came? Trust Roger Ireton's son for that."

My baronet wagged his head assentingly to this; then clinched the lie in words.

"Of course; we have his commission. He is on De Kalb's staff, 'detached for special duty.'"

"A spy!" roared the jester. "And yet you haven't hanged him?"

Sir Francis shrugged like any Frenchman. "All in good time, my dear Captain. There were reasons why I did not care to knot the rope myself. Besides, we had a little disagreement years agone across the water; 'twas about a woman—oh, she was no mistress of his, I do assure you!"—this to quench my jester's laugh incredulous. "He was keen upon me for satisfaction in this old quarrel, and I gave it him, thinking he'd hang the easier for a little blooding first."

Here the factor-lawyer cut in anxiously. "But you will hang

him, Sir Francis? You've promised that, you know."

I did not hate my enemy the more because he turned a shoulder to this little bloodhound and quite ignored the interruption.

"So we fought it out one morning in Mr. Stair's wood-field, and he had what he came for. Not to give him a chance to escape, we brought him here, and as soon as he is fit to ride I'll send him to the colonel. Tarleton will give him a short shrift, I promise you, and then"—this to the master of Appleby Hundred—"then your title will be well quieted, Mr. Stair."

At this the weather-beaten captain roared again and smote the table till the bottles reeled.

"I say, Sir Frank, that's good—damned good! So you have him crimped here in his own house, stuffing him like a penned capon before you wring his neck. Ah! ha! ha! But 'tis to be hoped you have his legs well tied. If he be any son of my old mad-bull Roger Ireton, you'll hardly hang him peacefully like a trussed fowl before the fire."

The baronet smiled and said: "I'll be your warrant for his safety! We've had him well guarded from the first, and to-night he is behind a barred door with Mr. Stair's overseer standing sentry before it. But as for that, he's barely out of bed from my pin-prick."

Having thus disposed of me, they let me be and came to the graver business of the moment, with a toast to lay the dust before it. It was Falconnet who gave the toast.

"Here's to our bully redskins and their king—How do you call him, Captain Stuart? Ocon—Ocona—"

"Oconostota is the Chelakee of it, though on the border they know him better as 'Old Hop.' Fill up, gentlemen, fill up; 'tis a dry business, this. Allow me, Mr. Stair; and you, Mr.—er—ah—Pengarden. This same old heathen is the king's friend now, but, gentlemen all, I do assure you he's the very devil himself in a copper-colored skin. 'Twas he who ambushed us in '60, and but for Attakullakulla—"

"Oh, Lord!" groaned Falconnet. "I say, Captain, drown the names in the wine and we'll drink them so. 'Tis by far the easiest way to swallow them."

By this, the grizzled captain's mention of the old Fort Loudon massacre, I knew him for that same John Stuart of the Highlanders who, with Captain Damaré, had so stoutly defended the frontier fort against the savages twenty years before; knew him and wondered I had not sooner placed him. When I was but a boy, as I could well remember, he had been king's man to the Cherokees; a sort of go-between in times of peace, and in the border wars a man the Indians feared. But now, as I was soon to learn, he was a man for us to fear.

"'Tis carried through at last," he went on, when the toast was drunk. And then he stopped and held up a warning finger. "This business will not brook unfriendly ears. Are we safe to talk it here, Mr. Stair?"

It was Falconnet who answered.

"Safe as the clock. You passed my sentry in the road?"

"Yes."

"He is the padlock of a chain that reaches round the house. Let's have your news, Captain."

"As I was saying, the Indians are at one with us. 'Twas all fair sailing in the council at Echota; the Chelakees being to a man fierce enough to dig the hatchet up. But I did have the devil's own teapot tempest with my Lord Charles. He says we have more friends than enemies in the border settlements, and these our redskins will tomahawk them all alike."

I made a mental note of this and wondered if my Lord Cornwallis had met with some new change of heart. He was not oversqueamish as I had known him. Then I heard the baronet say:

"But yet the thing is done?"

"As good as done. The Indians are to have powder and lead of us, after which they make a sudden onfall on the over-mountain settlements. And that fetches us to your part in it, Sir Frank; and to yours, Mr. Stair. Your troop, Captain, will be the convoy for this powder; and you, Mr. Stair, are requisitioned to provide the commissary."

There was silence while a cat might wink, and then Gilbert Stair broke in upon it shrilly.

"I can not, Captain Stuart; that I can not!" he protested, starting from his chair. "'Twill ruin me outright! The place is stripped,—you know it well, Sir Francis,—stripped bare and clean by these thieving rebel militia-men; bare as the back of your hand, I tell you! I—"

But the captain put him down in brief.

"Enough, Mr. Stair; we'll not constrain you against your will. But 'tis hinted at headquarters that you are but a fair-weather royalist at best—nay, that for some years back you have been as rebel as the rest in this nesting-place of traitors. As a friend—mind you, as a friend—I would advise you to find the wherewithal to carry out my Lord's commands. Do you take me, Mr. Stair?"

The trembling old man fell back in his chair, nodding his "yes" dumbly like a marionette when the string has been jerked a thought too violently, and his weasel face was moist and clammy. I know not what double-dealing he would have been at before this, but it was surely something with the promise of a rope at the publishing of it.

So he and his factor fell to ciphering on a bit of paper, reckoning ways and means, as I took it, while Falconnet was asking for more particular orders.

"You'll have them from headquarters direct," said Stuart. "Oconostota will furnish carriers, a Cherokee escort, and guides. The rendezvous will be hereabouts, and your route will be the Great Trace."

"Then we are to hold on all and wait still longer?"

"That's the word: wait for the Indians and your cargo."

Falconnet's oath was of impatience.

"We've waited now a month and more like men with halters round their necks. The country is alive with rebels."

Whereupon Captain Stuart began to explain at large how the northern route had been chosen for its very hazards, the better to throw the partizans off the scent. I listened, eager for every word, but when the horses stirred behind me I was set back upon the oft-recurrent under-thought of how the gloom did also hide a silent figure lying prone, with the three bridle reins knotted round its wrist.

But though the unnerving under-thought would not begone, the scene within the great room held me fast by eye and ear. The master and his factor sat apart, their heads together over the knotty problem of subsistence for the convoy troop. At the table-end, with the bottle gurgling now at one right hand and now at another, the three king's men drank confusion to the rebels, and in the intervals discussed the powder-convoy's route across the mountains. The senior plotter had some map or chart of his own making, and he was pricking out on it for Falconnet the route agreed upon in council with the Cherokees.

At this cool outlaying of the working plan, some proper sense of what this plot of savage-arming meant to every undefended cabin on the frontier seized and thrilled me. I knew, as every border-born among us knew, the dismal horrors of an Indian massacre; and this these men were planning was treacherous murder on an unwarned people. All was to be done in midnight secrecy. Supplied with ammunition, the Cherokees, led by this Captain Stuart or some other, were first to fall upon the over-mountain settlements. These laid waste, the Indians were to form a junction with the army of invasion, and so to add the torch and tomahawk and scalping knife to British swords and muskets.

It was a plot to make the blood run cold in my veins, or in the veins of any man who knew the cruel temper of these savages; and when I thought upon the fate of my poor countrymen beyond the mountains, I saw what lay before me.

The settlers must be warned in time to fight or fly.

But while I listened, with every faculty alert to reckon with the task of rescue, I take no shame in saying that the problem balked me. Lacking the strength to mount and ride in my own proper person, there was nothing for it but to find a messenger; and who would he be in a region at the moment distraught with war's alarums, and needing every man for self-defense?

At that, I thought of Jennifer. True, he was wounded, too; but he would know how best to pass the word to those in peril. I made full sure he'd find a way if I could reach him; and when I had it simmered down to this, the problem simplified itself. I must have speech with Dick before the night was out, though I should have to crawl on hands and knees the half-score miles to Jennifer House.

Having decided, I was keen to be about it while the night should last—the friendly darkness, and some fine flush of excitement which again had come at need to take the place of healthful vigor. But when I would have quit the window to begone upon my errand a sober second thought delayed me. If my simple counterplot should fail, some knowledge of the powder-convoy's route would be of prime importance. Lacking the time to warn the overmountain men, the next best thing would be to set some band of patriot troopers upon the trail and so to overtake the convoy. Nay, on this second thought's rehearsing the last expedient seemed the better of the two, since thus the plot would come to naught and we would be the gainers by the capture of the powder.

So now you know why I should stick and hang by toe and finger-tip and glare across the little space that gaped between my itching fingers and the bit of parchment passed from hand to hand around the table's end. If I could make a shift to rob them of this map—

It was a desperate chance, but in the frenzy of the moment I resolved to take it. Their placings round the table favored me. Gilbert Stair and the lawyer sat fair across from me, but they were still intent upon their figurings. Of the trio at the table's end, the baronet and the captain had their backs to me. The younger officer sat across, and he was staring broadly at my window, though with wine-fogged eyes that saw not far beyond the bottleneck, I thought.

My one hope hinged upon the boldness of a dash. If I could

spring within and sweep the two candlesticks from the table, there was a chance that I might snatch the parchment in the darkness and confusion and escape as I had come.

So I began by inches to draw me up and feel for some better launching hold. But in the midst, for all my care and caution, I slipped and lost my grip upon the casement; lost that and got another on the wooden shutter opened back against the outer wall, and then went down, pulling the shutter from its rusted hinges in crashing clamor fit to rouse the dead.

As if they were quick echoes, other crashings followed as of chairs flung back; and then the window just above me filled with crowding figures. I marvel that I had the wit to lie quiet as I had fallen, but I had; and those above, looking from a lighted room into the belly of the night, saw nothing. Then Captain Stuart shouted to his dragoon horse-holder.

"Ho! Tom Garget; this way, man!" he cried; and when he had no answer, put a leg across the window seat to clamber out. 'Twas in the very act, while I was watching catlike every movement, that I saw the precious scrap of parchment in his hand.

Here was the chance I had prayed for. Tom Garget's sword had clattered down beside me, and with it I sprang afoot and cut a whizzing circle by my doughty captain's ear that made him cringe and gasp and all but tumble out upon me. The bit of parchment fluttered down and in a trice I had it safe.

You may think small of me, if so you must, my dears, when I confess what followed after. No man is braver than his opportunity, and I had little stomach for a fight with three unwounded men. Hence it was narrowed now to a bold sortie for the horses, and this I made while yet the captain hung in air and sought his foothold.

With all my breathless haste it was not done too soon, nor soon enough. When I had quickly freed a horse from the dead hand that held it tethered, and was making shift to climb into the saddle, they thronged upon me; the captain from his window, the others pouring hotly through the gaping doorway.

I made shift to get astride the horse, to prick the poor beast with the point of sword, and so to break away in some brief dash beneath the oaks. But it was a chase soon ended. As I remember, I was reeling in the saddle what time the foremost of them overtook me. I held on grimly till the horse pursuing lapped the one I rode by head, by neck and presently by withers. Then I turned and would be making frantic-feeble passes with the sword at the man upon his back.

It was my plotting captain who rode me thus to earth; and

when I thrust he laughed and swore, and turned the blade aside with his bare hand. Then, pressing closer, he struck me with his fist, and thereupon the night and all its happenings went blank as if the blow had been a cannon shot to crush my skull.

CHAPTER VIII

IN WHICH I TASTE THE QUALITY OF MERCY

Two ways there be to fetch a stunned man to his senses, as they will tell you who have seen the rack applied: one is to slack the tension on the cracking joints and minister cordials to the victim; the other to give the straining winch a crueller twist. It was not the gentler way my captors took, as you would guess; and when I came to know and see and feel again a pair of them were kicking me alive, and I was sore and aching from their buffetings.

How long a time came in between my futile dash for liberty and this harsh preface to their dragging of me back to the manor house, I could not tell. It must have been an hour or more, for now a gibbous moon hung pale above the tree-tops, and all around were bivouac fires and horses tethered to show that in the interval a troop had come and camped.

The scene within the great fore-room of the house had been shifted, too. A sentry was pacing back and forth before the door— a Hessian grenadier by the size and shako of him; and when the two trooper bailiffs thrust me in, and I had winked and blinked my eyes accustomed to the candle-light, I saw the table had been swept of its bottles and glasses, and around it, sitting as in council, were some half-score officers of the British light-horse with their colonel at the head.

As it chanced, this was my first sight near at hand Of that British commander whose name in after years the patriot mothers spoke to fright their children. He did not look a monster. As I recall him now, he was a short, square-bodied man, younger by some years than myself, and yet with an old campaigner's head well set upon aggressive shoulders. His eyes were black and ferrety; and his face, well seasoned by the Carolina sun, was swart as any Arab's. A man, I thought, who could be gentle-harsh or harsh-revengeful, as the mood should prompt; who could make well-turned courtier compliments to a lady and damn a trooper in the self-same breath.

This was that Colonel Banastre Tarleton who gave no quarter to surrendered men; and when I looked into the sloe-black eyes I saw in them for me a waiting gibbet.

"So!" he rapped out, when I was haled before him. "You're the spying rebel captain, eh? Are you alive enough to hang?"

His lack of courtesy rasped so sorely that I must needs give place to wrath and answer sharply that there was small doubt of it, since I could stand and curse him.

He scowled at that and cursed me back again as heartily as any fishwife. Then suddenly he changed his tune.

"They tell me you were in the service once and left it honorably. I am loath to hang a man who has worn the colors. Would it please you best to die a soldier's death, Captain Ireton?"

I said it would, most surely.

He said I should have the boon if I would tell him what an officer on the Baron de Kalb's staff should know: the strength of the Continentals, the general's designs and dispositions, and I know not what besides. I think it was my laugh that made him stop short and damn me roundly in the midst.

"By God, I'll make you laugh another tune!" he swore. "You rebels are all of a piece, and clemency is wasted on you!"

"Your mercy comes too dear; you set too high a price upon it, Colonel Tarleton. If, for the mere swapping of a rope for a bullet, I could be the poor caitiff your offer implies, hanging would be too good for me."

"If that is your last word—But stay; I'll give you an hour to think it over."

"It needs not an hour nor a minute," I replied. "If I knew aught about the Continental army—which I do not—I'd see you hanged in your own stirrup-leather before I'd tell you, Colonel Tarleton. Moreover, I marvel greatly—"

"At what?" he cut in rudely.

"At your informant's lack of invention. He might have brought me straight from General Washington's headquarters while he was about it. 'Twould be no greater lie than that he told you."

He heard me through, then fell to cursing me afresh, and would be sending an aide-de-camp hot-foot for Falconnet.

While the messenger was going and coming there was a chance for me to look around like a poor trapped animal in a pitfall, loath to die without a struggle, yet seeing not how any less inglorious end should offer. The eye-search went for little of encouragement; there was no chance either to fight or fly. But apart from this, the probing of the shadows revealed a thing that set me suddenly in a fever, first of rage, and then of apprehension.

As I have said, this gathering-room of our old house was in size like an ancient banquet hall. It had a gable to itself in breadth and height, and at the farther end there was a flight of some few steps to reach the older portion of the house beyond. The upper end of this low stair pierced the thick wall of the older house, and in the shadows of the niche thus formed I saw my lady Margery.

She was standing as one who looks and listens; and my rage-fit blazed out upon the descrying of a shadowy figure of a man behind her; a man I guessed in jealous wrath to be the baronet—a reasonless suspicion, since the volunteer captain would certainly have made his presence known when his colonel had called for him. But while my heart was yet afire my lady moved aside as if to have a better sight of us below; and then I saw it was the priest behind her.

While I was watching her, and we were waiting yet upon the aide-de-camp's return, there was a stir without, and when it reached the door the sentry challenged. Some confab followed, and I overheard enough to tell me that a scouting party had come in, bringing a prisoner. The colonel bade me stand aside, and passed the word to fetch the prisoner before him. When the thing was done I set my teeth upon a groan. For it was Richard Jennifer.

Luckily, he did not single me out among the bystanders, being fresh come from the night without to the glare of candle-light within; and while the swart-faced colonel plied him with questions I had a chance to look him up and down. Though his arm was still in its sling, he was seemingly the better of his wound. There was a glow of health and strength returning in cheek and eye, and I thought him handsomer than ever what time he stood forth boldly and fronted down the bullying colonel.

Knowing the Jennifer stock and its fine scorn of subterfuge, I feared it would go hard with Richard; and so, indeed, it had gone, lacking a word in season from an enemy. When Tarleton would have made him choose between the taking of the king's oath and captivity in the hulks at Charleston, a burly Hessian captain at the table spoke the word in season.

"*Verdammt!* mine Colonel; I vill know dis Mr. Yennifer. He is a prave yoong schalavags, and he is not gone out mit der rebels. Give him to me for mine plunders."

The colonel laughed and showed his teeth. Having one man to hang he could afford to be lenient with another.

"What will you do with him, Captain Lauswoulter? By the look of him he'd make but indifferent sausage-meat."

"Vat shall I do mit him? I shall make him mine best bows and send him home, py Gott! Ve did had some liddle troubles mit der cards, and ven mine foot was slipped on dis *verdammt* grease-grass, he did not run me t'rough so like he might."

"Oh; an affair of honor? Well, we'll count that in his favor. Take him away, Trelawny, and quarter yourself and twenty men upon him at Jennifer House. You have your parole, Mr. Jennifer; but by the Lord, if you break it by so much as a wink or a nod,

Trelawny will hang you to your own ridge-pole."

Given a hearing, Jennifer would have spoiled it all by swearing hotly he had given no parole, but at the word the colonel roared him down like a bull of Bashan, and in the hubbub my brave lad was hustled out.

Though I was full to bursting with my news there was nothing I could do; and when it was fairly over and he was gone, I was right glad he had not seen me. For I knew well his steel-true loyalty, and that at sight of me in trouble he would have lost his slender chance of guarded liberty, and with it my last hope of sending word across the mountains; though, as for that, the hope was well-nigh dead at any rate.

While Jennifer's guard and quota were mounting at the door the aide-de-camp returned, and that without the baronet. I caught but here and there a word of his report; enough to gather that the captain-knight was not yet in from posting out the sentries.

I made no doubt his absence was designed. He would have Margery believe that he had spared me honorably as an enemy wounded, and so had left me to the tender mercies of his colonel, well assured that Tarleton would not spare me. And this the colonel did not mean to do, as I was now to hear in brief.

"You put a bold front on, Captain Ireton, but 'tis to no purpose, this time," he began. "'Tis charged against you that you rode here from the baron's camp with your commission in your pocket, and came and went within our lines like any other spy. You are a soldier, sir, and you know that's hanging. Yet I will hear you if you've anything to say."

I made so sure that I should hang in any case that it seemed foolish to answer, and so I saved my breath. Withal he was the terror of our Southland, this tyrant colonel gave me time to consider; and while he waited, grim and silent, the candles on the table guttered and ran down, and the dim light failed till I could no longer see the face of her I loved framed in the archway of the stair.

I thought it hard that I had seen my last of her sweet face thus through thickening shadows, as a dream might fade. Nevertheless, I would be glad that I had seen her thus, since otherwise, I thought, I must have gone without this last or any other sight of her.

It was while I was still straining my eyes for one more glimpse of her, and while the court room silence deepened dense upon us like the shadows, that Colonel Tarleton signed to those who guarded me. A hand was laid upon my shoulder, but when I would have turned to go with them a woman's cry cut sharp into the stillness. Then, before any one could say a word or think a thought, my dauntless little lady stood beside me, her eyes alight and all her glorious beauty heightened in a blaze of generous emotion.

"For shame! Colonel Tarleton," she cried. "Do you come thus into my father's house and take a wounded guest and hang him? You say he is a spy, but that he can not be, for he has lain abed in this same house a month or more. You shall not hang him!"

At this there was a mighty stir about the table, as you may guess; and some would smile, and some would snuff the candles for a better sight of her sweet face. And through it all, the while my heart went near to bursting at this fresh proof of her most fearless loyalty, I ground my teeth in wrath that all those men should look their fill and say by wink and nod and covert smile that this were somewhat more than hostess loyalty.

But it was the colonel's mocking smile that lashed me sharpest; his smile and what he said; and yet not that so much as what he left to be inferred.

"Ha! How is this, Mistress Margery? Do you keep open house for the king's enemies? That spells treason, my dear young lady, and hath an ugly look for you, besides."

"It should have no look at all, save that of hospitality, sir," she countered, bravely. "Surely I may plead for justice to a wounded man who was, and is, my father's guest?"

"And yet he is a spy, and spies must hang."

"He is no spy."

The colonel's bow made but a mock of true politeness.

"You should not make me contradict a lady, Mistress Margery. 'Tis evident you have not all his confidence. He was captured red-handed in the act at yonder window, listening to that which he may never know and live to prate about. Besides, he killed a sentry for his chance to listen, and for that I'd hang him if he were my own father's guest."

So much he said as mild as if he had not left his reading of the law to figure in our annals as King George's butcher. Then in a sudden gust of rage he turned upon the priest, cursing him brutally and threatening vengeance for his bringing of the lady to the court room.

My brave one stood a moment, shocked as she had warrant for. Then, before the priest or I or any one could stop her, she ran to throw herself upon her knees at Colonel Tarleton's feet—to kneel and plead for me as I would gladly have died a thousand deaths rather than have her plead; for life for me, or if not that, at least for some brief respite that the priest might shrive me.

And in the end she won the respite, though I did think it far too dearly bought. When he granted it the colonel lifted her and took her hand, bowing low over it with courtly deference. "For your sake, Mistress Margery, it shall be put off till morning," he said; then gave the order: At dawn they would march me out and hang me, and I would best be ready. For later than the sunrise of a new day the king himself might not delay my taking off.

"You know too much, my cursing Captain," was his parting word. "Were it not for Mistress Margery and my promise, you should not keep the breath to tell it over night."

CHAPTER IX

HOW A GOLDEN KEY UNLOCKED A DOOR

Having my dismissal and reprieve I was remanded to the custody of that young Lieutenant Tybee whom you have met and known as Falconnet's second in the duel. Interpreting his orders liberally, he suffered me to keep my own room for the night. I had expected manacles and a roommate guard at the least, but my gentlemanly jailer spared me both. When he had me safe above-stairs, he barred the door upon me, set a sentry pacing back and forth in the corridor without, and another to keep an eye upon the window from below, and so left me.

There was no great need for either sentry, or for bolts and bars. What with the night's adventures and my scarce-healed wound, I was far sped on that road which ends against the blind wall of exhaustion, as you may well suppose. For while a man may borrow strength of wine or rage or passion, these lenders are but pitiless usurers and will demand their pound of flesh; aye, and have it, too, when all the principal is spent.

So, when Tybee barred the door and left me with a single candle to my lighting, I was fain to fall upon the bed in utter weariness, thinking that the respite bought by my sweet lady's humbling was more dearly bought than ever, and that the truest mercy would have been the rope and tree without this interval of waiting.

To me in this grim Doubting Castle of despair the priest came. He was a good man and a true, this low-voiced missioner to the savages, and he would be a curster man than I who failed to give him his due meed of praise and love. For in this dismal interval of waiting, with death so sure and near that all the air was growing chill and lifeless at its presence, he was a ready help in time of need. If I were "heretic" to him, I swear I knew it not for aught he said or did; and though I trusted that when my time was come I should stand forth with some small simple-hearted show of courage, yet when he went away I felt I was the stronger for his coming. And this, mark you, though I was still unshriven, and he had never named the churchly rite to me.

When he was gone I fell to wearing out the time afoot; and, lest you think me harder than I was, it may be said that while I did not make confession to the kindly priest, I hope I tried to make my peace with God in some such simpler fashion as our forebears did. 'Twas none so great a matter, for one who lives a soldier's life must needs be ripe for plucking hastily.

But in the final casting of accounts there was an item written down in red, and one in black, and these would not be scored across for all the travail of a soul departing. The one in black was bitter sorrow for the fate from which I might not live to save my loved one; the one in red was this; that I should die and carry hence the knowledge that might else nip the Indian onfall in the bud.

No sooner was the priest away than I began to upbraid myself because I had not told him of this British-Indian murder plan. And yet on second thought 'twas clear that it had been but a poor shifting of the burden to weaker shoulders; and thankless, too, for Tarleton would be sure to put him on the question-rack to make him tell of all that passed between us.

As I had let him go, he would have naught to tell, and so was safe, where otherwise he might be hanged or buried in the hulks for knowing what I knew. No, it were best he knew it not; but how was I to rid me of this burden?—of this and of that other laid upon me for my love?

The question asked itself a many a time, and was as often answerless, before there came a stir without and voices in the corridor. It was the changing of the guard, I guessed, and so it proved, since presently I heard the clanking of the officer's sword, and double footfalls minishing into silence.

The sentry newly come paced back and forth to a low-hummed quick-step of his own, bestirring himself as one who, roused but now from sleep, would wake himself and be alert. He made more noise than did the other, and that is why I marked it when the footfalls ceased abruptly. A moment afterward the bar was lifted cautiously from its socket, the latch clicked gently, and the door swung open. I looked, and must needs look again to make assurance sure. For on the threshold stood my lady Margery, and just behind her some broad figure of a woman whom I knew for her stout Norman tiring-maid.

She gave me little time for any word of welcome or of deprecation. While still I stood amazed she dragged the woman in with her and closed the door. At that I found my tongue.

"Margery! Why have you come?" I spoke in French, and she was quick to lay a finger on her lip.

"Speak to me in English, if you please," she whispered. "Jeanne knows nothing, and she need not know. But you ask why I come: could I do less than come, dear friend?"

I had always marveled that she could be so mocking hard at times, and at other times—as now—so soft and gentle. And though I thought it cruel that I should have to fight my battle for the losing of her over again, I had not the heart to chide her.

"You could have done much less, dear lady," I said, taking her hands in mine; "much less, and still be blameless. You have done too much for me already. I would you had not done so much, I would to God I had been hanged before you went upon your knees to that—"

She freed one hand and laid a finger on my lip—nay, it was her palm, and if I took a dying man's fair leave and kissed it softly, I think she knew it not.

"Hush!" she commanded. "Is this a time to harbor bitter thoughts? I thought you might have other things to say to me, Monsieur John."

"There is no other thing that I may say."

"Not anything at all?"

"Naught but a parting hope for you. I hope you will be true and loyal to yourself, Margery *mia*."

"To myself? I do not understand."

"I think you do—I think you must."

"But I do not."

I turned it over more than once in my mind if I should tell her all I had feared; should tell her how I came to kill a man and was fair set to kill another had I found a wedding afoot in the great fore-room. I could not bring myself to do it, and yet I thought it would go hard with me if I should leave her still unwarned.

"If I should try to make you understand, you will be angry, as you were before."

The wicker chair was close beside the table and she sat down. And when she spoke she had her hands tight-clasped across her knee and would not look at me.

"Is it—about—Sir Francis?"

"It is," said I, pausing once more upon the brink of full confession.

She waited patiently for me to speak further; waited and let me fight it out in slow pacings up and down before her chair. Without, the night was calm and still, and through the opened casement came the measured beat of footfalls on the gravel where the outer sentry kept his watch beneath the window. Within, the single candle battled feebly with the gloom and lighted naught for me save my dear lady's face, pensive now and saintly sweet as it had been that morning when I had dwelt upon it the while she knew it not. And in the background stood the sleepy tire-woman, giving no sign of life save now and then a tortured yawn behind her hand.

I think my lady must have known how hard it was for me to

speak, for, when the silence had grown overlong, she said, gently: "I bought these flying minutes of the sentry, Monsieur John. Will you not use them?"

"If I should say the thing I ought to say, you'll think the minutes dearly bought, I fear."

"No, that I shall not, if it will ease your mind."

"Then tell me why you sent for Father Matthieu."

The light was dim, as I have said, yet I could see the faint flush spread from neck to cheek.

"You are not of the Church, Monsieur John. You would not understand if I should tell you."

"I think I understand without your telling. You said Sir Francis Falconnet had asked for you."

"'Twas you who drove me to say it."

"Because I tried to warn you?"

"Because you would be vengeful when you should have been forgiving."

"'Twas not revenge, just then, though while I live I shall have ample cause to hate this man."

"What was it, then?"

"It was love; love for you, and—and Richard Jennifer."

She rose, and I could see her eyes ashine for all the half-gloom of the candle-light.

"You are a loyal friend!" she said, and there was that within the words to make me glad, whatever fate the dawn should have in store for me. "You always think of others first; you think of others now, when—when death—Oh, Monsieur John! what can I do for you? Say quick! The man is coming to the door!"

"Now I have told you this, there is but one other thing, Margery dear; one little thing that will not let me die in peace. If I might have ten words with Richard Jennifer—"

She left me in a fever-flutter of excitement, whipped to the door, and had a word with him who stood without. I heard the chink of coin, and then she hastened back to me, all eagerness and tremulous impatience.

"Tell me—tell me instantly what I must do. I am not afraid. Shall I ride down to Jennifer House and fetch Dick here?"

"He is a prisoner, and if he were not, they would not let him see me. Besides, I would not let you go on such an errand. And yet—God help me, Margery! there is many an innocent life hanging on this; the lives of helpless women and little children. Have you ever a messenger to send, a man who will risk his life and can be trusted fully?"

"Yes, yes!" she cried. "Write it down for me and Dick shall

have it. Quick; for Our Lady's sake, be quick about it! *O Sancta Maria, mater. Dei—*"

The low impassioned chant of the Roman litany was ringing in my ears as I sat down to the table to write my message to Richard Jennifer. There were quills and an ink-pot at hand, but no paper. I felt mechanically in my pocket and found, not some old letter, as I hoped, but the crumpled parchment map snatched and hidden when Captain Stuart had winced and dropped it at the bidding of the whistling sword about his ears.

How it was they had not searched me for it, I know not; though haply the captain did not guess how he had lost it. Be that as it might, I had it safe, and Dick should have it safe, and use it, too, to some good purpose, as I fondly hoped.

You'd hardly think from the slow and clumsy spinning of this tale that I could crowd the narrative of all that I had seen and heard into a niggard three-score words or less. But this I did, writing them upon the margin of the captain's map, and noting in an added line the pricking out of the powder convoy's route. And while my pen was looping on the flourish to my name, my eager little lady seized the pounce-box, sanded me the heavy trailings of the quill, snatched and hid the parchment in her bosom, and was gone.

And but for this; that I heard the door-latch click behind her, and then the heavy wooden bar fall into place, I might have thought the happenings of the hour the unsubstantial fancies of a dream.

CHAPTER X

HOW A FORLORN HOPE CAME TO GRIEF

Although I could not hope to know the outcome of this desperate cast to speed the warning to the over-mountain settlements—could never live to know it, as I thought—I screened the candle and stood beside the open window, not to see or hear, but rather from the lack of sight or sound to gather some encouragement. For sure, I reasoned, if Margery's messenger should fail to pass the sentries there would be clamor enough to tell me of it.

So while the minutes of this safety-silence multiplied and there was space for sober after-thought, I fell to casting up the chances of success. Now that Margery was gone, and with her all the fine enthusiasm that such devoted souls as hers do always radiate, it was plain enough that nothing less than a miracle could bring success. Tarleton's Legion was made up of veterans schooled well in border warfare, and though the bivouac seemed but a camp of motionless figures fast manacled in sleep—I could see them strewn like dead men round the smoldering fires—I made no doubt the sentries were alert and wakeful. How then was any messenger of Margery's to pass the lines, or, passing them, to come at Jennifer, who by this time would be at Jennifer House, a prisoner in all but name?

Chewing such wormwood thoughts as these, I watched and listened while the measured minutes, circling slow on leaden wings, pecked at my heart in passing, and despair, cold like a winter fog, had chilled me to the bone. For now it came to me that while I would be saving life, mayhap I had been periling it again. There was small doubt that if the messenger were taken with my letter, his life would pay the forfeit. And if the fear of death should make him tell who sent him and to whom he was sent,—I had been careful so to word the letter as to shield my correspondent,—both Margery and Dick would be involved.

'Tis worthy of remark how, building on the simplest supposition, we seldom prophesy aright. For all my fine-spun theories the manner of the thing that happened was all unlike the forecast. Suddenly, and in silence, out of the ghostly shadows of the trees and into the wan moonlight of the open space beneath my window, with neither shout nor crash of sentry-gun to give me warning, came three figures riding abreast—a man in trooper trappings on either hand, and on the led horse sandwiched in between, a woman.

You may believe my heart went cold at the sight. I knew at once what she had done—this fearless maid who would be loyal to her friend at any cost. Having no messenger she could trust—she knew it well when she had promised me—she had taken the errand upon herself, braving a hazard that would have daunted many a man.

I thought the worst had surely now befallen, and wished a hundred times that I had died before it came to this. But there was worse in store. Her captors passed the word while yet I looked and choked with rage and grief; and then the bivouac buzzed alive, and men came running, some with arms and some with torches, these last to flash the light upon her and to jeer and laugh. At length—it seemed an age to me—an officer appeared to flog the rabble into order; then she was taken from her horse and led into the house.

Anon the windows of the great fore-room flung bands of yellow torchlight out upon the lawn, and I knew that Tarleton's court was set again. At that the pains of hell gat hold upon me and I did pray as I had never prayed before that God would grant me this one boon—to stand beside her in this time of trial; to give me tongue of eloquence to tell them all that she was innocent; to give me breath to swear she knew not why she went, or what the message was she carried.

Yours is a skeptic age, my dears, and you have learned to scoff at things you do not understand. But, so long as I shall live, I must believe that agonizing plea was answered. While yet the anguish of it wrung my soul there came a hasty trampling in the corridor, the sentry's challenge, and then a quick unbarring of the door. I turned upon my heel to face a young ensign come with two men at his back to take me to the colonel.

They bound me well and strongly with many wrappings of stout cord before they led me down. Nor must you think me broken-spirited because I let them. In any other cause but this I hope I should have fought to die unmanacled; but now I suffered gladly this little, seeing I had made my dear lady suffer so greatly.

When we were come into the room below they let me stand beside her, as I had prayed God they might; and when I stole a glance at her I was fain to think my coming gave her courage and support. For you must know the place was fair alive with men, and flaring light with torches; and they had never offered her a chair.

The colonel stood apart, the center of a group of officers, and Falconnet was with him. Hovering on the edges of the group, as if afraid to show themselves too boldly in such a coil, were Gilbert Stair and that smooth parchment-visaged knave, his factor. The while they thrust me forth to take my place at Margery's side, the good old priest came and would have joined us; but they would not suffer him.

So we two stood alone together as we had stood before; but now my lady's eyes were downcast, and her lips and cheeks were pale. Yet she was more beautiful than I had ever seen her—so beautiful that I would swear the sum of all the precious gifts in God's great universe might be expressed for me in this; that I might die to save her from this shame and agony.

When my guards had thrust me forward, the colonel made short work of our fresh offense.

"'Twas a dastard's trick, my Captain—this tangling of the lady in your treason," he began. "How did you get your speech with her?"

"That is none of your affair, Colonel Tarleton," I retorted boldly, thinking that with such a man the shortest word were ever the best. "Yet I may say that the lady knew not what she did, nor why. As for my getting speech with her, she was not any way to blame. I tampered with your sentry."

"By God, you lie!" was his comment on this. "She might have tampered with the guard and so got leave to keep a midnight tryst with you, but not you." And then to my poor frighted love: "Have you no shame, Mistress Margery Stair?"

Now I have said that she was changeful as any child or April sky, but never had I seen her pass from mood to mood as she did then. One moment she stood a woman tremulous and tearful as any woman caught in desperate deed; the next she became a goddess vilified, and if her look had been a dagger I think her flashing eyes had killed him where he stood.

"You've found a way to make me speak, sir, and I wish you joy of it. 'Twas I who bribed your sentry, and I did go to Captain Ireton's room."

The colonel laughed and shot a gibe sharp at my enemy.

"How is this, Sir Francis. Did I not tell you you had thrust an inch or so too high? By God, sir, I think you will come over-late, if ever you do come at all. This captain-emeritus hath forestalled you beautifully."

As more than once before in this eventful night, the air went flaming red before my eyes and helpless wrath came uppermost. I saw no way to clear her, and had there been the plainest way, dumb rage would still have held me tongue-tied. So I could only mop and mow and stammer, and, when the words were found, make shift to blunder out that such an accusation did the lady grievous wrong; that she had come attended and at my beseeching, to take a message from a dying man to one who was his friend.

For my pains I had a brutal laugh in payment; a laugh that, starting with the colonel, went the rounds in jeering grins of incredulity. And on the heels of it the colonel swore afresh, cursing me for a clumsy liar.

"A likely story, that!" he scoffed. "Next you will say she knew not what this message was."

"I said it once. She knew not what the message was, nor why I sent it."

I felt her eyes upon me as I spoke, and turned to find them full of tearful pleading. "Oh, tell the truth!" she whispered. "Don't you see? He has the letter!"

I looked, and sure enough he held it in his hand; and then I understood the flash of irony in the sloe-black eyes of him.

"You lie clumsily, Captain Ireton, though it is a gentlemanly lie and does you honor. But we have trapped you fairly and you may as well make a clean breast of it. Your mistress knew very well what you would have her do, and since she is your mistress, went to do it."

While he was speaking I had a thought white-hot from some forge-fire of inspiration—a thought to tip an arrow of conviction and set it quivering in the mark. I would not stop to measure it; to look aside at her or any other lest one brief glance apart should send the arrow wavering from its course. So I looked the colonel boldly in the eye and drew the bow and sped the shaft.

"You think no other than a mistress would have done this, Colonel Tarleton—that it was done for love? Well, so it was; but with the love there went a duty."

"A duty, say you? How is that?"

I bowed as best I might, being so tightly bound; then fixed his eye again.

"You had forgot that honor is not wholly dead, sir. This lady is my wife."

CHAPTER XI

HOW A LIE WAS MADE THE VERY TRUTH

For some small instant I dared not loose my eye-grip on the colonel, to glance aside at Falconnet, or Gilbert Stair, or at the woman close beside me. If I had flinched or wavered, or let an eyelid droop but by the thickness of a hair, this keen-eyed colonel would have been upon me to cut the ground beneath my feet and leave me dangling by the lie.

But as it was, I faced him down; and winning him, won all. There was a muttered oath from Falconnet, a tremulous cry of rage from where her father stood; and then I sought my lady's eyes to read my sentence in them.

She gave me but a glance, and though I tried as I had never tried before to read her meaning it was hid from me. But this I marked; that she did draw aside from me, and that her face was cold and still, and that her lips were pressed together as if not all nor any should ever make her speak again.

At this sharp crisis, when a look or word would cost me more than death and my dear lady her honor, it was the colonel who, all unwittingly, stood my friend. A breath of doubt upon my lie and we were lost; and once I thought he would have breathed it. But he did not. Instead, he broke out in a laugh, with a gibe flung first at Gilbert Stair and then at Falconnet.

"God save us! I give you joy, Mr. Stair, and you, Sir Francis. These two have duped you bravely. By heavens! Sir Frank; 'twas you who should have had the sword thrust in the duel. In that event you might have stood in Captain Ireton's shoes, and so had the priest fetched for your benefit." Then he turned to Margery with a bow that had no touch of mockery in it. "I crave your pardon, Madam; I knew not you were pleading for your husband's life an hour ago. It grieves me that I may not spare him to you longer than the night, but war is cruel at its best."

She stood like any statue done in cold Carrara while he spoke; and when she made no sign he gave the word to recommit me.

"Take him away, Lieutenant Tybee, and see he has a bribe-proof man this time to keep him company. Madam Ireton, I'll put you on your honor: you may have access to him, but there must be no messages carried in or out. To your quarters, gentlemen. We must ride far and hard to-morrow."

When his final word had set her free, my frozen maiden came to life and ran to throw herself in helpless sobbings, not upon her father, as you would think, but upon the good priest. And it was Father Matthieu who led her, still crying softly, out of the throng and up the low stair; and now I marked that all the rough soldiery stood aside and made way for her with never a man among them to scoff or sneer or point a gibe.

At her going, Tybee drew his sword and cut the cord that bound me.

"These youngling cubs are over-cautious, Captain Ireton. We shall not make it harder for each other than we must," he said, with bluff good nature. And then: "Will you lead the way to your room, sir?"—this to give the youngling cub another lesson, I suppose.

I walked beside him to the stair, and when I stumbled, being weak and spent, he took my arm and steadied me, and I did think it kindly done. At my own door he gave me precedence again, saying, with a touch of the grateful Old World courtesy, "After you, sir," and standing aside to let me enter first. When we were both within he touched upon the colonel's mandate.

"I must obey my orders, Captain Ireton, but by your good leave I shall not lock you up with any trooper; I'll stay with you myself."

I thought this still more kindly than aught he had done before, and so I told him. But he put it off lightly.

"'Tis little enough any one can do for you, my friend, but I will do that little as I can. You are like to have a visitor, I take it; if you have, I'm sure 'twill be a comfort if your body-guard can be stone blind and deaf."

So saying, he dragged the big wicker chair into the window-bay, planted himself deep within it with his back to all the room, and so left me to my own devices.

Being spent enough to sleep beneath the shadow of a gibbet, I threw myself full-length upon the bed and was, I think, adrift upon the ebb tide of exhaustion and forgetfulness when once again the shifting of the wooden door-bar roused me. I rose up quickly, but Tybee was before me. There was some low-voiced conference at the door; then Tybee came to me.

"'Tis Mr. Gilbert Stair," he said. "He has permission from the colonel and insists that he must see you *solus*. I'll take your word and leave you, if you like."

At first I hung reluctant, wanting little of the host who came so late to see his guest. Then, as if a sudden flash of lightning had revealed it, I realized, as I had not before, how I had set the feet of my dear lady in a most hideous labyrinth of deception; how this lie that I had told to bridge a momentary gap must leave her neither maid nor widow in the morning.

"Yes, yes; for God's sake let him in, Mr. Tybee!" I burst out. "I am fair crazed with weariness, and had forgot. 'Tis most important, I do assure you."

The thing was done at once, and before I knew it I was alone with the old man who, though he was my supplanter, was also Margery's father. He entered cautiously, shielding his bedroom candle with his hand and peering over it to make me out, as if his venturing in were not unperilous. And I marked that when he put the candle down upon the table, he edged away and felt behind him for the door as if to make sure of his retreat in case of need.

"Sit down, Captain Ireton; sit down, I beg of you," he said, in his thin, rasping treble. And when I had obeyed: "I think you must know what I've come for, Captain Ireton?"

I said I could guess; and he began again, volubly now, as if to have it over in the shortest space.

"'Twas not a gentlemanly thing for you to do, Captain Ireton—this marrying of a foolish girl out of hand while you were here a guest; and as for the priest that did it, I—I'll have him hanged before the army leaves, I promise you. But now 'tis done, I hope ye're prepared to make the best of it?"

I saw at once that his daughter had not yet confided in him; that he was still entangled in my lie. So I thought it well to probe him deeper while I might.

"What would you call 'the best' if I may ask?" said I, growing the cooler with some better seeing of the way ahead.

"The marriage settlements!" he cried shrilly, coming to the point at once, as any miser would. "'Tis the merest matter of form, as ye may say, for your title to Appleby Hundred is well burnt out, I promise you. But for the decent look of it you might make over your quitclaim to your wife."

"Aye, truly; so I might."

"And so you should, sir; that you should, ye miserable, spying runag"—he choked and coughed behind his hand and then began again without the epithets. "'Tis the very least ye can do for her now, when you have the rope fair around your curs—ahem—your—your rebel neck. Only for the form's sake, to be sure, ye understand, for she'd inherit after you in any case."

I saw his drift at last, and, not caring to spare him, sped the shaft of truth and let it find the joint in his harness.

"'Tis as you say, Mr. Stair. But as it chances, Mistress Margery is not my wife."

If I had flung the candle at him where he stood fumbling behind him for the door-latch,'twould not have made him shrink or dodge the more.

"Wha—what's that ye say?" he piped in shrillest cadence. "Not married? Then you—you—"

"I lied to save her honor—that was all. A wife might do the thing she did and go scot free of any scandal; but not a maid, as you could see and hear."

For some brief time it smote him speechless, and in the depth of his astoundment he forgot his foolish fear of me and fell to pacing up and down, though always with the table cannily between us. And as he shuffled back and forth the thin lips muttered foolish nothings, with here and there a tremulous oath. When all was done he dropped into a chair and stared across at me with leaden eyes; and truly he had the look of one struck with a mortal sickness.

"I think—I think you owe me something now beyond your keeping, Captain Ireton," he quavered, at length, mumbling the words as do the palsied.

"Since you are Margery's father, I owe you anything a dying man can pay," said I.

"Words; empty words," he fumed. "If it were a thing to do, now—"

"You need but name the thing and I will do it willingly."

Instead of naming it he shot a question at me, driving it home with certain random thrustings of the shifty eyes.

"Who is your next of kin, Captain Ireton?"

"Septimus, of the same name, master of Iretondene, on the James River, and a major in the Virginia line," I answered, wondering how my cousin once removed should figure in the present coil. But Gilbert Stair's next question dispelled the mystery.

"If you should die intestate, this Septimus would be your heir?"

"As next of kin, I should suppose he would. But I have nothing to devise."

"True; and yet"—he paused again as if the wording of it were not easy.

"Be free to speak your mind, Mr. Stair," said I.

"'Tis this," he cried, gathering himself as with an effort. "You've claimed my daughter as your wife before them all, and when you die to-morrow morning you'll leave her neither wife nor maid. I think—I think you'd best make that lie of yours the truth."

If one of his thin hands that clutched the chair arms had pressed a secret spring and loosed a trap to send me gasping down an oubliette, I should have been the less astounded. Indeed, for some short space I thought him mad; yet, on second thought, I saw the method in his madness. Could Margery be brought to view it calmly, this was a sword to cut the knot of all entanglements.

As matters stood, the world would call her widow at my death; and since a woman is first of all the keeper of her own good name, she would never dare aver the truth. So in common justice she should own the name the world would call her by. Again, as matters stood, no wrong could come of it to her, or Richard Jennifer, or any. Dick would love her none the less because a dying man had given her his name for some few hours. And if, at any future time, the Ireton title should revive and this poor double-dealing miser should be forced to quit his hold on Appleby Hundred, my father's acres would be hers in her own right. One breach in all this sudden-builded wall I saw, but could not mend it. With the Ireton acres hers by double right, the baronet would press his suit with greater vigor than before. But as to this, no further act of mine could help or hinder; and if I died her husband she would in decency delay a while.

So summing up in far less time than it has cost to write it out for you, I gave my host his answer.

"I told you you might name the deed, and I would do it, Mr. Stair. If you can make your daughter understand—"

"The jade will do as she is bid," he cut in wrathfully. "If she will drag my good name in the mire, I'm damned if she sha'n't pay the scot. And now about the settlements, Captain Ireton; you'll be making her legatee residuary?"

At this I saw his drift again, most clearly; that he would never stickle for his daughter's honor, but for the quieting of his title to my father's lands—a title that my cousin Septimus might dispute. It was enough to set me obstinate against him; but I constrained myself to think of Margery and Richard Jennifer, and not at all of this poor petty miser.

"I'll sign a quitclaim in her favor, if that is what you mean," I said. "But 'tis a mere pen-scratch for the lawyers to haggle over. As you said a while ago, the wife will be the husband's heir-at-law, in any event."

"True; but we'd best be at it in due and proper form." He rose and hobbled to the door and was so set upon haste that his shaking hand played a rattling tattoo on the latch. "I—I'll go and have the papers drawn, and you will sign them, Captain Ireton; I have your passed word that you will sign them?"

"Aye; they shall be signed."

He went away at that, and Tybee entered. Much to my comfort, the lieutenant asked no questions; so far from it, he crossed the room without a word, flung himself into the great chair and left me to my own communings.

These were not altogether of assurance. Though I had promised readily enough to make my lie a truth, I saw that all was yet contingent upon my lady's viewing of the proposal. That I could win her over I had some hope, if only they would leave the task for me. But there was room to fear that this poor miser father would make it all a thing of property and so provoke her to resistance. And, notwithstanding what he said—that she would do as she was bid—I thought I knew her temper well enough to prophesy a hitch. For I made sure of one thing, that if she put her will against the world, the world would never move her.

'Twas past midnight, with Tybee dozing in his chair, when next I heard some stirrings in the corridor. As before, it was the lifting of the wooden bar that roused my friendly guard, and when he went to parley at the door I stood apart and turned my back.

When I looked again my company was come. At the table, busied with a parchment that might have been a ducal title deed for size, stood Gilbert Stair and the factor-lawyer, Owen Pengarvin. A little back of them the good old Father Matthieu had Margery on his arm. And in the corner Tybee stood to keep the door.

I grouped them all in one swift eye-sweep, and having listed them, strove to read some lessoning of my part in my dear lady's face. She gave me nothing of encouragement, nor yet a cue of any kind to lead to what it was that she would have me say or do. As I had seen it last, under the light of the flaring torches in the room below, her face was cold and still; and she was standing motionless beside the priest, looking straight at me, it seemed, with eyes that saw nothing.

It was the factor-lawyer who broke the silence, saying, with his predetermined smirk, that the parchment was ready for my signature. Thinking it well beneath me to measure words with this knavish pettifogger, I looked beyond him and spoke to his master.

"I would have a word or two in private with your daughter before this matter ripens further, Mr. Stair," I said.

My lady dropped the priest's arm and came to stand beside me in the window-bay. I offered her a chair but she refused to sit. There was so little time to spare that I must needs begin without preliminary.

"What has your father told you, Margery?" I asked.

"He tells me nothing that I care to know."

"But he has told you what you must do?"

"Yes." She looked with eyes that saw me not.

"And you are here to do it of your own free will?"

"No."

"Yet it must be done."

"So he says, and so you say. But I had rather die."

"'Tis not a pleasing thing, I grant you, Margery; notwithstanding, of our two evils it is by far the less. Bethink you a moment: 'tis but the saying of a few words by the priest, and the bearing of my name for some short while till you can change it for a better."

Her deep-welled eyes met mine, and in them was a flash of anger.

"Is that what marriage means to you, Captain Ireton?"

"No, truly. But we have no choice. 'Tis this, or I must leave you in the morning to worse things than the bearing of my name. I would it had not thus been thrust upon us, but I could see no other way."

"See what comes of tampering with the truth," she said, and I could see her short lip curl with scorn. "Why should you lie and lie again, when any one could see that it must come to this—or worse?"

"I saw it not," I said. "But had I stopped to look beyond the moment's need and seen the end from the beginning, I fear I should have lied yet other times. Your honor was at stake, dear lady."

"My honor!"—this in bitterest irony. "What is a woman's honor, sir, when you or any man has patched and sewed and sought to make it whole again? I will not say the word you'd have me say!"

"But you must say it, Margery. 'Tis but the merest form; you forget that you will be a wife only in name. I shall not live to make you rue it."

"You make me rue it now, beforehand. *Mon Dieu!* is a woman but a thing, to stand before the priest and plight her troth for 'merest form'? You'll make me hate you while I live—and after!"

"You'd hate me worse, Margery dear, if I should leave you drowning in this ditch. And I can bear your hatred for some few hours, knowing that if I sinned and robbed you, I did make restitution as I could."

She heard me through with eyelids down and some fierce storm of passion shaking her. And when she answered her voice was low and soft; yet it cut me like a knife.

"You drive me to it—listen, sir, *you drive me to it*! And I have said that I shall hate you for it. Come; 'tis but a mockery, as you say; and they are waiting."

I sought to take her hand and lead her forth, but this she would not suffer. She walked beside me, proud and cold and scornful; stood beside me while I sat and read the parchment over. It was no marriage settlement; it was a will, drawn out in legal form. And in it I bequeathed to Margery Ireton as her true jointure, not any claim of mine to Appleby Hundred, *but the estate itself.*

I read it through as I have said, and, looking across to these two plotters, the miser-master and his henchman, smiled as I had never thought to smile again.

"So," said I; "the truth is out at last. I wondered if the confiscation act had left you wholly scatheless, Mr. Stair. Well, I am content. I shall die the easier for knowing that I have lain a guest in my own house. Give me the pen."

'Twas given quickly, and I signed the will, with Tybee and the lawyer for the witnesses; Margery standing by the while and looking on; though not, I made sure, with any realizing of the business matter.

When all was done the priest found his book, and we stood before him; the woman who had sworn to hate, and the man who, loving her to full forgetfulness of death itself, must yet be cold and formal, masking his love for her dear sake, and for the sake of loyalty to his friend. And here again 'twas Tybee and the lawyer who were the witnesses; the one well hated, and the other loved if but for this; that when the time came for the giving of the ring, he drew a gold band from his little finger and made me take and use it.

And so that deed was done in some such sorry fashion as the time and place constrained; and had you stood within the four walls of that upper room you would have thought the chill of death had touched us, and that the low-voiced priest was shriving us the while we knelt to take his benediction. All through this farce—which was in truth the grimmest of all tragedies—my lady played her part as one who walks in sleep; and at the end she let her father lead her out with not a word or look or sign to me.

You'd guess that I would take it hard—her leaving of me thus, as I made sure, for all eternity; and I did take it hard. For when the strain was off, and there was no one by to see or hear save my good-hearted death-watch, I must needs go down upon my knees beside the bed in childish weakness, and sob and choke and let the hot tears come as I had not since at this same bedside I had knelt a little lad to take my mother's dying love.

CHAPTER XII

HOW THE NEWS CAME TO UNWELCOME EARS

Though all the western quarter of the sky was night-black and spangled yet with stars, the dawn was graying slowly in the east when Tybee roused me.

"They have not come for you as yet," he said; "so I took time by the forelock and passed the word for breakfast. It heartens a man to eat a bite and drink a cup of wine just on the battle's edge. Will you sit and let me serve you, Captain Ireton?"

"That I will not," said I; adding that I would blithely share the breakfast with him. Whereat he laughed and clipt my hand, and swore I was a true soldier and a brave gentleman to boot.

So we sat and hobnobbed at the table; and Tybee lighted all the remnant candle-ends, and broached the wine and pledged me in a bumper before we fell to upon the cold haunch of venison.

My summons came when we had shared the heel-tap of the bottle. It was my toast to this kind-hearted youngster, and we drained it standing what time the stair gave back the tread of marching men. Tybee crashed his glass upon the floor and wrung my hand across the table.

"Good by, my Captain; they have come. God damn me, sir, I'll swear they might do worse than let you go, for all your spying. You've carried off this matter with the lady as a gentleman should, and whilst I live, she shall not lack a friend. If you have any word to leave for her—"

I shook my head. "No," said I; then, on second thought: "And yet there is a word. You saw how I must see the matter through to shield the lady?"

"Surely; 'twas plain enough for any one to see."

"Then I shall die the easier if you will undertake to make it plain to Richard Jennifer. He must be made to know that I supplanted him only in a formal way, and that to save the lady's honor."

The lieutenant promised heartily, and as he spoke, the oaken bar was lifted and my reprieve was at an end.

Having the thing to despatch before they broke their fast, my soldier hangmen marched me off without ado. The house and all within it seemed yet asleep, but out of doors the legion vanguard was astir, and newly kindled camp-fires smoked and blazed among the trees. In shortest space we left these signs of life behind, and I began to think toward the end.

'Tis curious how sweet this troubled life of ours becomes when that day wakes wherein it must be shuffled off! As a soldier must, I thought I had held life lightly enough; nay, this I know; I had often worn it upon my sleeve in battle. But now, when I was marching forth to this cold-blooded end without the battle-chance to make it welcome, all nature cried aloud to me.

The dawn was not unlike that other dawn a month past when I had ridden down the river road with Jennifer; a morning fair and fine, its cup abrim and running over with the wine of life. I thought the cool, moist air had never seemed so sweet and fra-grant; that nature's garb had never seemed so blithe. There was no hint nor sign of death in all the wooded prospect. The birds were singing joyously; the squirrels, scarce alarmed enough to scamper out of sight, sat each upon his bough to chatter at us as we passed. And once, when we were filing through a bosky dell with softest turf to muffle all our treadings, a fox ran out and stood with one uplifted foot, and was as still as any stock or stone until he had the scent of us.

A mile beyond the outfields of Appleby Hundred we passed the legion picket line, and I began to wonder why we went so far; wondered and made bold to ask the ensign in command, turning it into a grim jest and saying I misliked to come too weary to my end.

The ensign, a curst young popinjay, as little officer cubs are like to be, answered flippantly that the colonel had commuted my sentence; that I was to be shot like a soldier, and that far enough afield so the volleying would not wake the house.

So we fared on, and a hundred yards beyond this point of question and reply came out into an open grove of oaks: then I knew where they had brought me—and why. 'Twas the glade where I had fought my losing battle with the baronet. On its far-ther confines two horses nibbled rein's-length at the grass, with Falconnet's trooper serving-man to hold them; and, standing on the very spot where he had thrust me out, my enemy was waiting.

'Twas all prearranged; for when the ensign had saluted he marched his men a little way apart and drew them up in line with muskets ported. But at a sign from Falconnet, two of the men broke ranks and came to strap me helpless with their belts. I smiled at that, and would not miss the chance to jeer.

"You are a sorry coward, Captain Falconnet, as bullies ever are," I said. "Would not your sword suffice against a man with empty hands?"

He passed the taunt in silence, and when the men had left me, said: "I have come to speed your parting, Captain Ireton. You are a thick-headed, witless fool, as you have always been; yet since you've blundered into serving me, I would not grudge the time to come and thank you."

"I serve you?" I cried. "God knows I'd serve you up in collops at the table of your master, the devil, could I but stand before you with a carving tool!"

He laughed softly. "Always vengeful and vindictive, and always because you must ever mess and meddle with other men's concerns," he retorted. "And yet I say you've served me."

"Tell me how, in God's name, that I may not die with that sin unrepented of."

"Oh, in many small ways, but chiefly in this affair with the little lady of Appleby."

"Never!" I denied. "So far as decent speech could compass it, I have ever sought to tell her what a conscienceless villain you are."

He laughed again at that.

"You know women but indifferently, my Captain, if you think to breach a love affair by a cannonade of hard words. But I am in no humor to dispute with you. You have lost, and I have won; and, were I not here to come between, you'd look your last upon the things of earth in shortest order, I do assure you."

"You?—you come between?" I scoffed. "You are all kinds of a knave, Sir Francis, but your worst enemy never accused you of being a fool!"

There was a look in his eyes that I could never fathom.

"You are bitter hard, John Ireton—bitter and savage and unforgiving. You knew the wild blade of a half-score years ago, and now you'd make the grown man pay scot and lot for that same youngster's misdeeds. Have you never a touch of human kindliness in you?"

To know how this affected me you must turn back to that place where I have tried to picture out this man for you. I said he had a gift to turn a woman's head or touch her heart. I should have said that he could use this gift at will on any one. For the moment I forgot his cool disposal of me in the talk with Captain Stuart; forgot how he had lied to make me out a spy and so had brought me to this pass.

So I could only say: "You killed my friend, Frank Falconnet, and—"

"Tush!" said he. "That quarrel died nine years ago. Your reviving of it now is but a mask."

"For what?" I asked.

"For your just resentment in sweet Margery's behalf. Believe it or not, as you like, but I could love you for that blow you gave me, John Ireton. I had been losing cursedly at cards that day, and mine host's wine had a dash of usquebaugh in it, I dare swear. At any rate, I knew not what it was I said till Tybee said it over for me."

"But the next morning you took a cur's advantage of me on this very spot and ran me through," I countered.

"Name it what you will and let it go at that. There was murder in your eye, and you are the better swordsman. You put me upon it for my life, and when you gave me leave, I did not kill you, as I might."

"No; you reserved me for this."

He took a step nearer and seemed strangely agitated.

"You forced my hand, John Ireton," he said, speaking low that the others might not hear. "You had her ear from day to day and used your privilege against me. As an enemy who merely sought my life for vengeance's sake I could spare you; but as a rival—"

I laughed, and sanity began to come again. "Make an end of it," I said. "I'd rather hear the muskets speak than you."

For reply he took a folded paper from his pocket and spread and held it so that I might read. It was a letter from my Lord Cornwallis, directing Captain Falconnet to send his prisoner, Captain John Ireton, sometime lieutenant in the Royal Scots Blues, under guard to his Lordship's headquarters in South Carolina.

"Can you read it?" he asked.

I nodded.

"Well, this supersedes the colonel's sentence. If I say the word to Ensign Farquharson you will be remanded."

"To be shot or hanged a little later, I suppose?"

"No. Have you any notion why my Lord Charles is sending for you?"

"No," said I, in my turn; and, indeed, I had not.

"He knows your record as an officer, and would give you a chance to 'list in your old service."

"I would not take it—at your hands or his."

"You'd best take it. But in any event, you'll have your life and honorable safe-conduct beyond the lines."

"Make an end," I said again. "I understand you will obey his Lordship's order, or disregard it, as your own interest directs. What would you have me do?"

"A very little thing to weigh against a life. Mr. Gilbert Stair is my very good friend."

I let that go uncontradicted.

"His title to the estate is secure enough, as you know, but you can make it better," he went on.

This saying of his told me what I had only guessed: that as yet he had not been admitted into Gilbert Stair's full confidence; also, that he had no hint of what had taken place in my chamber some hour or two past midnight. At that, a joy fierce like pain came to thrill me.

"Go on," said I.

"Your route to Camden lies through Charlotte. Your guard will give you time and opportunity to execute a quitclaim in Mr. Stair's favor."

"Is that all?" I asked.

"No; after that our ways must lie apart—or yours and Margery's, at all events. Give me your word of honor that you relinquish any claim you have, or think you have, upon her, and I pass this letter on to the ensign."

"And if I refuse?"

He came so near that I could see the lurking devil in his eyes.

"If you refuse? Harken, John Ireton; if you had a hundred lives to thrust between me and the thing I crave, I'd take them all." So much he said calmly; then a sudden gust of passion seized him, and for once, I think, he spoke the simple truth. "God! I'd sink my soul in Calvin's hell to have her!"

I could not wholly mask the smile of triumph that his words evoked. This fox of maiden vineyards was entrapped at last. I saw the fire of such a passion as such a man may know burning in his eyes; and then I knew why he was come upon this errand.

"So?" said I. "Then Mistress Margery sent you here to save me?" 'Twas but a guess, but I made sure it hit the truth.

He swore a sneering oath. "So the priest carried tales, did he? Well, make the most of it; she would not have her father's guest taken from his bed and hanged like a dog."

I smiled again. "'Twas more than that: she would even go so far as to beg her husband's life a boon from that same husband's mortal enemy."

"Bah!" he scoffed. "That lie of yours imposed upon the colonel, but I had better information."

"A lie, you say? True, 'twas a lie when it was uttered. But afterward, some hour or so past midnight, by the good help of Father Matthieu, and with your Lieutenant Tybee for one witness and the lawyer for another, we made a sober truth of it."

I hope, for your own peace of mind, my dears, that you may never see a fellow human turn devil in a breath as I did then. His man's face fell away from him like a vanishing mask, and in the place of it a hideous demon, malignant and murderous, glared upon me. Twice his hand sought the sword-hilt, and once the blade was half unsheathed. Then he thrust his devil-face in mine and hissed his parting word at me so like a snake it made me shudder with abhorrence.

"You've signed your own death warrant, you witless fool! You'd play the spoil-sport here as you did once before, would you? Curse you! I wish you had a hundred lives that I might take them one by one!" Then he wheeled sharp upon his heel and gave the order to the ensign. "Belt him to the tree, Farquharson, and make an end of him. I've kept you waiting over-long."

They strapped me to a tree with other belts, and when all was ready the ensign stepped aside to give the word. Just here there came a little pause prolonged beyond the moment of completed preparation. I knew not why they waited, having other things to think of. I saw the firing line drawn up with muskets leveled. I marked the row of weather-beaten faces pillowed on the gun-stocks with eyes asquint to sight the pieces. I remember counting up the pointing muzzles; remember wondering which would be the first to belch its fire at me, and if, at that short range, a man might live to see the flash and hear the roar before the bullets killed the senses.

But while I screwed my courage to the sticking place and sought to hold it there, the pause became a keen-edged agony. A glance aside—a glance that cost a mightier effort than it takes to break a nightmare—showed me the ensign standing ear a-cock, as one who listens.

What he heard I know not, for all the earth seemed hushed to silence waiting on his word. But on the instant the early morning stillness of the forest crashed alive, and pandemonium was come. A savage yell to set the very leaves a-tremble; a crackling volley from the underwood that left a heap of writhing, dying men where but now the firing squad had stood; then a headlong charge of rough-clad horsemen—all this befell in less than any time the written words can measure.

I sensed it all but vaguely at the first, but when a passing horseman slashed me free I came alive, and life and all it meant to me was centered in a single fierce desire. Falconnet had escaped the fusillade; was making swiftly for his horse, safe as yet from any touch of lead or steel. So I might reach and pull him down, I cared no groat what followed after.

It was not so to be. In the swift dash across the glade I went too near the shambles in the midst. The corporal of the firing squad, a bearded Saxon giant, whose face, hideously distorted, will haunt me while I live, lay fairly in the way, his heels drumming in the death agony, and his great hands clutching at the empty air.

I leaped to clear him. In the act the clutching hands laid hold of me and I was tripped and thrown upon the heap of dead and dying men, and could not free myself in time to stop the baronet.

I saw him gain his horse and mount; saw the flash of, his sword and the skilful parry that in a single parade warded death on either hand; saw him drive home the spurs and vanish among the trees, with his horse-holding trooper at his heels.

And then my rescuers, or else my newer captors, picked me up hastily; and I was hoisted behind the saddle of the nearest, and so was borne away in all the hue and cry of a most unsoldierly retreat.

CHAPTER XIII

IN WHICH A PILGRIMAGE BEGINS

As you have guessed before you turned this page, the men who charged so opportunely to cut me out of peril were my captors only in the saving sense.

Their overnight bivouac was not above a mile beyond the glade of ambushment. It was in a little dell, cunningly hid; and the embers of the camp-fires were still alive when we of the horse came first to this agreed-on rallying point.

Here at this rendezvous in the forest's heart I had my first sight of any fighting fragment of that undisciplined and yet unconquerable patriot home-guard that even in defeat proved too tough a morsel for British jaws to masticate.

They promised little to the eye of a trained soldier, these border levies. In fancy I could see my old field-marshal,—he was the father of all the martinets,—turn up his nose and dismiss them with a contemptuous "*Ach! mein Gott!*" And, truly, there was little outward show among them of the sterling metal underneath.

They came singly and in couples, straggling like a routed band of brigands; some loading their pieces as they ran. There was no hint of soldier discipline, and they might have been leaderless for aught I saw of deference to their captain. Indeed, at first I could not pick the captain out by any sign, since all were clad in coarsest homespun and well-worn leather, and all wore the long, fringed hunting shirt and raccoon-skin cap of the free borderers.

Yet these were a handful of the men who had fought so stoutly against the Tory odds at Ramsour's Mill, their captain being that Abram Forney of whom you may read in the histories; and though they made no military show, they lacked neither hardihood nor courage, of a certain persevering sort.

"Ever come any closter to your Amen than that, stranger?" drawled one of them, a grizzled borderer, lank, lean and weather-tanned, with a face that might have been a leathern mask for any hint it gave of what went on behind it. "I'll swear that little whip'-snap' officer cub had the word 'Fire' sticking in his teeth when I gave him old Sukey's mouthful o' lead to chaw on."

I said I had come as near my exit a time or two before, though always in fair fight; and thereupon was whelmed in an avalanche of questions such as only simple-hearted folk know how to ask.

When I had sufficiently accounted for myself, Captain Forney—he was the limber-backed young fellow I had ridden behind—gripped my hand and gave me a hearty welcome and congratulation.

"My father and yours were handfast friends, Captain Ireton. More than that, I've heard my father say he owed yours somewhat on the score of good turns. I'm master glad I've had a chance to even up a little; though as for that, we should both thank the Indian." At which he looked around as one who calls an - eye-muster and marks a missing man. "Where is the chief, Ephraim?"—this to the grizzled hunter who was methodically reloading his long rifle.

"He's back yonder, gathering in the hair-crop, I reckon. Never you mind about him, Cap'n. He'll turn up when he smells the meat a-cooking, immejitly, *if* not sooner."

Here, as I imagine, I looked all the questions that lacked answers; for Captain Forney took it in hand to fit them out with explications.

"'Tis Uncanoola, the Catawba," he said; "one of the friendlies. He was out a-scouting last night and came in an hour before day-break with the news that Colonel Tarleton was set upon hanging a spy of ours. From that to our little ambushment—"

"I see," said I, wanting space to turn the memory leaves. "This Catawba: is he a man about my age?" Captain Forney laughed. "God He only knows an Indian's age. But Uncanoola has been a man grown these fifteen years or more. I can recall his coming to my father's house when I was but a little cadger."

At that, I remembered, too; remembered a tall, straight young savage, as handsome as a figure done in bronze, who used some-times to meet me in the lonelier forest wilds when I was out a-hunting; remembered how at first I was afraid of him; how once I would have shot him in a fit of boyish race antipathy and sudden fright had he not flung away his firelock and stood before me defenseless.

Also, I recalled a little incident of the terrible scourge in '60 when the black pox bade fair to blot out this tribe of the Catawbas; how when my father had found this young savage lying in the forest, plague-stricken and deserted by all his tribesmen, he had saved his life and earned an Indian friendship.

"I know this Uncanoola," I said. "My father befriended him in the plague of '60, and was never sorry for it, as I believe." Then I would ask if these Catawbas had ranged themselves on the patriot side, a question which led the young militia captain to give me the news at large while his borderers were breaking camp and making their hasty preparations for the day's march.

"'Tis liberty or death with us now; we've burnt our bridges

behind us," he said, when he had confirmed the tidings I had had the day before from Father Matthieu. "And since here in Carolina we have to fight each man against his neighbor, 'tis like to go hard with us, lacking help from the North."

"Measured by this morning's work, Captain Forney, these irregulars of yours seem well able to give a good account of themselves," I ventured.

He shook his head doubtfully. He was but a boy in years, but war is a shrewd schoolmaster, and this youth, like many another on the fighting frontier, had matriculated early.

"You've seen us at our best," he amended. "We can ambush like the Indians, fire a volley, yell, charge—and run away."

"What's that ye're saying, youngster?" The grizzled hunter had finished reloading his rifle, and, lounging in earshot with all the freedom of the border, would take the captain up sharply on this last.

"You heard me, Eph Yeates," replied my young captain, curtly.

The old man leaned his rifle against a tree, spat on his hands, cut a clumsy caper in air, and gave tongue in a yell that should have been heard by Tarleton's men at Appleby.

"By the eternal 'coonskins! I can gouge the eye out of ary man that says Eph Yeates carn't stand up fair and square and whop his weight in wildcats; and I can do it now, *if* not sooner!" he shrilled. "Come on, you pap-eating, apron-stringed, French-daddied—"

Where the blast of vituperative insult would have spent itself in natural course we were not to know, for in the midst another of the borderers, a wiry little man in greasy deerskin, came up behind the capering ancient, whipped an arm around his neck, and in a trice the two went down, kicking, scratching, buffeting and mauling, as like to a pair of battling bobcats as was ever seen.

For a moment I thought my youngster would let them have it out to the finish, but he did not. At his order some of the others pulled the twain apart, reluctantly, I fancied; and when the thing was done the old man caught up his rifle and strode away in blackest wrath without a look behind him.

Captain Forney shrugged and spread his hands as his French father might have done.

"Now you know wherein our weakness lies, Captain Ireton," he said. "There goes as true a man and as keen a shot as ever pulled trigger. Let him fight in his own way, and he'll take cover and name his man for every bullet in his pouch. But as for yielding to decent authority, or standing against trained troops in open field—" He shrugged again and turned to tighten his saddle-girth.

"I see," said I. Then I asked him of his plans and intendings, and was told that he and his handful were a-march to join General Rutherford, who was gone to the Forks of Yadkin to break up some Tory embodiment thereabouts.

"You have your work cut out to dodge the British light-horse, Captain Forney," said I; capping the venture by telling him what little I knew of Tarleton's dispositions, and also of the Indian-arming plot I had overheard.

"We'll dodge the redcoats, never you fear; we're at our best in that," he rejoined, carelessly. "And as to the Cherokee upstirring, that's an old story. The king's men have tried it twice and they have not yet caught Jack Sevier or Jimmie Robertson a-napping. Ease your mind on that score, Captain Ireton, and come along with us, if you have nothing better to do. I can promise you hard living, and hard fighting enough to keep it in countenance."

At this I was brought down to some consideration of the present and its demands. As fortune's wheel had twirled, I had my life, to be sure; but by the having of it was made the basest traitor to my friend—to Jennifer, and no whit less to Margery.

'Twas out of any thought that I should take the field against the common enemy, leaving this tangled web of mystery and misery behind. In sheerest decency I owed it first to Jennifer to make a swift and frank confession of the ill-concluded tale of happenings. That done, I owed it equally to him and Margery to find some way to set aside the midnight marriage.

So I fell back upon my wound for an excuse, telling the captain that I was not yet fit to take the field—which was true enough. Whereupon he and his men set me well beyond the danger of immediate pursuit and we parted company.

When I was left alone I had no plan that reached beyond the day's end. Since to go to Jennifer House by daylight would be to run my neck afresh into the noose, I saw nothing for it but to lie in hiding till nightfall. The hiding place that promised best was the old hunting lodge in the forest, and thitherward I turned my face.

It was a wise man who said that he who goes with heavy heart drags heavy feet as well; but while I live I shall remember how that saying clogged the path for me that morning, making the shrub-sweet summer air grow thick and lifeless as I toiled along. For sober second thought, and the unnerving reaction which comes upon the heels of some sharp peril overpast, left me aghast at the coil in which a tricky fate had entangled me.

The second thought made plain the dispiteous hardness of it all, showing me how I had reasoned like a boy in planning for retrieval. Would Jennifer believe my tale, though I should swear it out word for word on the Holy Evangelists? I doubted it; and striving to see it through his eyes, was made to doubt it more. For death should have been my justifier, and death had played me false.

As for setting the midnight marriage aside, I made sure the lawyer tribe could find a way, if that were all. But here there was a loyal daughter of the Church to reckon with. Loathing her bonds, as any true-hearted maiden must, would Margery consent to have them broken by the law? I knew well she would not. Though our poor knotting of the tie had been little better than a tragic farce, it lacked nothing of force to bind the tender conscience of a woman bred to look upon the churchly rite as final.

So, twist and turn it as I might, the coil was desperate; and as I strode on gloomily, measuring this the first stage in a pilgrimage I had never thought to make, a fire of sullen anger began to smoke and smolder within me, and I could find it in my heart to curse the cruel kindness of my rescuers; to sorrow in my inmost soul that they had come between to make a living recreant of one who would fain have died an honest man.

CHAPTER XIV

HOW THE BARONET PLAYED ROUGE-ET-NOIR

The sun was well above the tree-tops, and the morning was abroad for all the furred and feathered wood-folk, when I forsook the Indian path to make a prudent circle of reconnaissance around the cabin in the maple grove.

Happily, there was no need for the cautionary measure. The hunting lodge was undiscovered as yet by any enemy; and when I showed myself my poor black vassals ran to do my bidding, weeping with childish joy to have me back again.

Since old Darius was still at Appleby Hundred, Tomas ranked as majordomo; and I bade him post the blacks in a loosely drawn sentry line about the cabin, this against the chance that Falconnet might stumble on the place in searching for me. For I made no doubt his Tory spies would quickly pass the word that I was not with Abram Forney's band, and hence must be in hiding.

When all was done I flung myself upon the couch of panther-skins, hoping against hope that sleep might come to help me through the hours of waiting. 'Twas a vain hope. There was never a wink of forgetfulness for me in all the long watches of the summer day, and I must lie wide-eyed and haggard, thinking night would never come, and making sure that fate had never before walled a man in such a dungeon of despair.

There was no loophole of escape with honor; The heavens were brass, with all the horizons narrowed to a bounding wall to hem me in on every side. There was no sally-port in all this wall save one—the one that death had promised to open at the dawn. The promise had been broken. True, death had thrust the key within the lock, and I had heard the grating of the bolts; and yet the key had been withdrawn and I was left a prisoner of life.

There was no hope of other outlet. Now there was space to view it calmly, I saw how foolish was the thought that Margery would connive at any breaking of the marriage bond. She would bear my name, and hate me for the giving of it; would go on hating me, I thought, to all eternity; but she would never take her freedom back again, save at a dead man's hands.

It was thus that each fresh scanning of the prison wall that shut me in this dungeon of dishonor fetched me once and again to this one sally-port of death. And when it came to this; that I had searched in vain for other outlet, you will not think it strange that I sat down in spirit at this postern to see if I might open it with my own hands.

It was not love of life that made me hesitate. At two-score years he who has lived at all has lived his best; and if he live beyond the turning point of youthful ardor he must beg the grace of younger men to linger yet a little longer on the stage which once was his and now is theirs.

No, it was not any love of life for life's own sake that held me back. 'Twas rather that the Ireton blood is linked up with that thing we call a conscience, a heritage from those simple-hearted ancestors to whom the suicide was a soul accurst—a soul impenitent, whose very outer husk of flesh and bones they used to bury at the crossing of the ways, with a sharpened stake to pinion it.

'Twas this ancestral conscience made me cowardly; and when the sight of my father's sword—Darius had rescued and restored it to its place upon the chimney-breast—would set me thinking of the Israelitish king, and how, when all was lost, he fell upon his blade and died, this horror of the suicide came to give me pause.

Besides, that way to right the double wrong was not so clear as it might seem. As matters stood, my living for the present was Margery's best safeguard. Till she became my widow and my heir-at-law, the mercenary baronet would play his cards to win her honorably. I doubted not he'd make hot love to her; but while she stayed a wife, and was not yet a widow, he'd keep his passion decently in bounds, if only for the better compassing of his end.

But from this horn of the dilemma I slipped to fall upon the other. If my living on as Margery's husband was her safety for the time, it was an offering of idol-meats upon the altar of my dear lad's friendship. What would he think of me? How could I go about to make it plain that I had robbed him for his own honor's sake?—that it was not I but fate that was to blame?

These questions came up answerless, like deep-sea plummets where no bottom is. I saw the way no farther on than this; that I must go straightway to Jennifer and tell him all. Beyond that point the darkness was Egyptian, and I could only hope that tricky fate would turn again and blot me out, and make it plain to Richard, and to my dear lady, that love, and not base treachery, had set me on to do as I had done.

In some such dismal grindings of the mill of thought the hours of waiting were outworn at length; and when the sun was dipping to the mountains in the west I rose and washed me in the brook, and afterward constrained myself to eat what Tomas had prepared for me.

The sunset glow was fading in the upper air, and underneath the canopy of leaves the wood was darkening on to twilight, when

I made ready to be gone. Because I thought I might have need of it before the night was done, I buckled on the heirloom sword; and telling Tomas and the other blacks for their own safety to keep an alarm guard waking through the night, I sallied forth upon my errand.

I've wished a thousand times, as I sit here before the fire and jot these memories down in crabbed black on white, that I could conjure up for you some speaking picture of this scene primeval in which the story moves.

True, its hills and valleys are the same; the river keeps its course; and in the west the mountain sky-line is unchanged. But here similitude is at an end. You've hacked the virgin forest into shapes and fringes where once it was an ample mantle seamed only by the rivers, and frayed here and there at distant intervals by the settler's ax.

Beneath this mantle lay a world unlike the world you know. Plunged in its furtive depths you felt the spell of nature's mystery upon you; the mystery of the hoary wood, age-old, steeped in the nepenthe of the centuries. In brightest summer day, which, in these forest aisles, became a misty green translucence, the silence, the vastness, the solitude laid each a finger on you, bidding you go softly all the way. But in the twilight hour the real held still more aloof, and all the shadows bristled with dim fantastic shapes to awe and affright the alien-born.

I was not alien-born. From earliest childhood I had known and loved these forest solitudes. Yet now, as when I was a little lad, the twilight shadows awed me. Here it was a gnarled and twisted tree-trunk so like a crouching panther that I sprang aside and had the steel half out before the clearer vision came. There it was the figure of a man gliding stealthily from tree to tree, it seemed; keeping even pace with me as if with sinister intent.

I pushed on faster, drawing the sword to keep me better company, though inwardly I scoffed and jeered at this new twittering of the nerves. What threat was there for me in silent shadows in the wood? The dogs I had to fear were bred in British kennels, and there was never any lack of clamor when they were beating up a cover.

Yet this persistent shadow clung upon my footsteps until from casting furtive glances sidewise I came to holding it craftily in the tail of my eye. 'Twas surely moving as I moved, and surely drawing nearer. I picked a time and place, measured my distance, and darting suddenly aside, sent home a thrust which should have pinned the phantom to a tree.

"Ugh! What for Captain Long-knife want kill the tree?"

The voice came from behind, and when I wheeled again my shadow was become incarnated in flesh and blood; a stalwart Indian, naked to the belt, standing so near he could have pricked me with his scalping knife.

It was God's mercy that by some swift intuition I knew him for the friendly Catawba. It is an ill thing to take a frighted man unawares.

"Uncanoola?" said I.

He nodded. "Where 'bouts Captain Long-knife going?"

I told him briefly; whereat he shook his head.

"No find Captain Jennif' this way; find him *that* way," pointing back along the path.

"How does the chief know that? Has he seen him?" Though my long exile had well-nigh cost me the trick of it, I made shift to drop into the stately Indian hyperbole.

"Wah! Uncanoola has seen the Great Water: that make him have long eyes—see heap things."

"Will the Catawba tell the friend whose life he saved what he has seen?"

"Uncanoola see heap things," he repeated. "See Captain Jennif' so"—he threw himself flat upon the ground and pictured me a fugitive crawling snake-like through the underwood. "Bime-by, come to river and find canoe—jump in and paddle fas'; bime-by, 'gain, stop paddling and laugh and shake fist this way, and say 'God-damn.'"

By this I knew that Jennifer had escaped; nay, more; had somehow learned of my escape and was seeking me.

"Is that all the chief saw?" I asked.

"Ugh! See heap more things: see one thing white squaw no let him tell Captain Long-knife. Maybe some time tell, anyhow."

"The white squaw?" said I. "Who is she?"

The Catawba laughed, an Indian laugh, silent and suppressed; a mere shaking of the ribs.

"No can tell that, neither, too," he said. Then, with a swift dart aside from the subject: "Captain Long-knife care much 'bout black dogs yonder?"

I knew he meant the negroes at the hunting lodge.

"The white man cares for the black as a kind master should," I returned.

The Indian spat upon the ground in token of his hatred and contempt for all the black skins in his fatherland. I never understood this bitter race antipathy between the red and black, but 'tis a tale well written out in many a bloody massacre of that earlier day.

"The wolves will kill all the black dogs and drink their blood before the moon is awake. Uncanoola has spoken."

I sheathed my sword and turned to take the backward trace.

"Captain Long-knife will go and fight for his black dogs with wool on their heads?" he queried.

"If need be," I asserted.

"Wah!" he ejaculated, and at the word was gone as if the earth had swallowed him.

I lost no time in indecision. Since Jennifer was abroad, I had no business at the plantations; and if Tomas and the other refugees were like to come to harm, I could do no less than hasten back to warn or help them.

So I retraced my steps, hurriedly, as the business urged; and saw no more shadows in the ancient wood—in truth, had much ado to see the single step ahead, so thickly did the darkness gather in those skyless depths.

I was breasting the last low hill, was come so near that I could hear the murmur of the river, when in the farthest hazy vista of the tree-tops a softened glow appeared, changing the black to green and then to red. 'Twas like the childish Africans, I said, to draw a secret sentry line for safety's sake, and then to build a fire to advertise it far and wide. Truly, the Catawba's wolves might find an easy—

A chattering scream of agony sent shrill and sharp upon the stillness of the night halted me and broke the gibing comment in the midst. I stood and listened. The cry rang out again; then I loosed the Andrea in its scabbard and fell a-running, though the half-healed wound scanted me sorely of the breath I wanted.

The cabin clearing, or rather the thinned-out grove which stood in lieu thereof, was but a niggard acre hemmed in on every side, save that toward the river, by the virgin forest. For cover there were holly thickets here and there, and into one of these I plunged, creeping on hands and knees to gain a hidden viewpoint.

The scene in the little clearing was one to brand itself in lasting shapes upon the memory. A brush heap newly kindled gave out a dusky glow flaring in waves of smoky red against the overarching foliage. The open space around the cabin was alive with half-naked savages running to and fro; and in the gloom beyond the fire I saw a shadowy horseman backed by others still more phantom-like.

There was no mystery about it. My enemy had come with sleuth-hound Indians at his back to run me down. The savages were, no doubt, that band of over-mountain Cherokees pledged by their chief to pilot the powder convoy; and by their help the baronet had tracked me.

This was the first thought, caught at in passing; but when I came to look again I saw what had been done. Sprawled on the ground before the burning brush pile, his wrinkled face a hideous mask of suffering, with the eyeballs starting from their sockets in the death-wrench, lay my faithful Darius.

By what inhuman tortures they had made him point the way, or how or why they slew him at the last, I know not, but I made sure it was his death-scream that had halted me and set the stillness of the forest alive with ghastly echoes.

At sight of the stiffening body of the faithful slave you may suppose my blood ran cold and hot by turns, and that his blood cried out for vengeance from the sod that soaked it up. With ten years more of youth and less of age I might have tried to hew my way to Falconnet's stirrup, and so to square accounts with him. But had I been a-mind to rush upon the stage without my cue, another climax in the ghastly tragedy forbade it.

This climax turned upon the capture of my horse-boy, Tomas. The other blacks, it seemed, had made good their escape; but Tomas, lagging behind through fear or foolishness, had given these copper-colored devils leave to run him down and drag him back into the fire light, with yells of savage triumph.

They flung him down upon his knees beside the captain's horse, and though I caught but here and there a word above the frenzied yipping of the Indians, it was plain the baronet was asking him of me.

I could not hear the black boy's gibbering answers, but that he would not tell them what they wished to know—could not, indeed, since I had left no word behind to track me by—was quickly evident. A cord was found, and while I crouched behind the holly screen, aghast and helpless as one against two-score or more, they looped him by the thumbs and swung him up to dangle from a maple bough a musket's length or such a matter before the cabin door.

He bore the torture patiently, as some poor dumb beast suffering at the hand of man, and would not part his lips for all the captain's curses. But this was only the merciful beginning. With yells of savage fury the Indians carried brands to make a slow fire at his feet; and, lest that should not be enough, a brace of them climbed to the roof, tore off the splits for kindling, and set the cabin wall alight behind him.

You may thank God, my dears, that you are living in a kindlier age. Mayhap the savage, now a-march toward the setting sun, is still as pitiless as he was; but not in any corner of the world, I think, would Anglo-Saxon men, wearing the king's or any other uniform, be witnesses unmoved of such a devil's carnival of torment as this that made me nauseate with horror.

As with the stretching of the cord the wretched black spun slowly round and round before the growing blaze, his cries were something terrible to hear. And when the fire light played upon his face it was a sight to freeze the blood: the eyes shut tight against the shriveling heat, the cracking lips drawn back, the black skin changing to a dry and sickly brown. And ever and anon between the shrieks the parched lips shaped a plea: "O Massa! Massa Cap'm! shoot po' nigga and let um die!"

This plea for cruel kindness cut me to the marrow of my bones; and lacking means to save his life, I thought I might at least make shift to try to put him out of misery.

The enemy's dispositions favored me. The savages, drunk with lust of blood, leaped and danced around their victim. Falconnet sat his horse apart beneath the maples, and with his body-guard of troopers, was well within the borderland of lurid shadow where the fire light mingled with the night.

I crept away and made a swift detour to the right to come behind the rearmost horseman of the troop. As his ill luck would have it, his horse, affrighted at the firelit pandemonium, was in the act of wheeling to run away. Being cumbered with a musket, the man made clumsy work of handling his mount, and when the beast came down in a snorting tremble to rear afresh at sight of me, the man flung away the musket and drew his sword.

In cooler blood I might have given him his soldier's chance, but here again it was another's life or mine. Even so, I might have fought him fair, had he but held his tongue and fought in silence. But this he would not, so I had to quiet him or have the others about my ears upon his shoutings.

That done, I snatched the musket that had cost the man his life, and, staying not to see what should befall, ran back to cover. In the interval of weapon-getting the fire against the cabin wall had gnawed its way from log to log and now was lapping with its yellow tongues beneath the eaves. But lest the victim should not suffer long enough, the Indians were at work in yelling frenzy, flogging the blaze with green branches broken from the trees so that the fire itself should not be merciful.

I waited till the slowly spinning figure of the black should turn and make a mark I could not miss. The pause gave space for some swift steadying of the nerves, but with the colder thought it also brought a fierce and terrible temptation. The finger on the musket's trigger held a life in pawn, and I might pick and choose and say what life I'd take.

I glanced aside at Falconnet. He was a fairer mark than my poor Tomas, and by the laws of God and man had earned his death. The tortured slave had little time to suffer at the worst, and with the bullet that would give him surcease I could well avenge him. More than this; that bullet planted in my enemy's heart would save my lady Margery harmless, leaving me free to go to my own place and so to right the wrong that I had done.

All in the pivoting instant of the pause the musket swung slowly round as of its own volition, and through its sights I saw the slashings, gold on red, across the breasting of his captain's riding coat. One little crooking of the trigger-finger and the lead had gone upon its errand. But at the balancing instant that piteous cry was lifted once again: "O Massa! Massa Cap'm! God 'a' mussy—shoot po' nigga and let 'um die!"

I did as any other man would do, as you have guessed. The great king's musket swept another arc, and roared and belched and spat its messenger of death; and my poor Tomas had the boon he prayed for.

And then, as if the musket flash and roar had been a lodestone and these fierce Cherokees so many bits of steel to cluster thick upon it, I was surrounded in the twinkling of an eye, and whizzing hatchets and rifle bullets whining sibilant were but an earnest of the fate I had invited.

CHAPTER XV

IN WHICH A HATCHET SINGS A MAN TO SLEEP

In such a coil as this I'd looped about me there was nothing for it, as it seemed, but to draw the steel and die as a soldier should. So I broke cover on the forest side of the holly thicket with a yell as fierce as theirs, and picked a tree to set my back against, and ran for it.

I never reached the tree. In mid career, when all the Cherokee wolf pack was bursting through the holly tangle at my heels, two men, a white man and an Indian, ran in ahead, as I supposed to cut me off. Just then the dry roof of the hunting lodge roared aflame, reddening the forest far and near. The light was at my back and on the faces of the two who ran to meet me. A great sob swelled in my throat and choked me, but I ran the faster. For these were my dear lad and the friendly Catawba, charging gallantly to cover my retreat.

It was a ready help in time of need. They ran in bravely, the chief ahead, twirling his tomahawk for the throw, with Dick a pace to right and rear, his two great pistols brandished and the grandsire of all the broadswords dangling by a thong at his wrist.

"Follow the chief!" he shouted in passing; and at the word the Catawba stopped short, sent his hatchet whistling into the yapping pack behind me, and swerved to run aside and point the way for me.

Left to myself, I hope I should have had the grace to stand with Jennifer. But at the turning point of indecision the quick-witted Indian read my thought, and snatching the sword from my hand, gave me no choice but to follow him.

So I ran with him; but as I fled I looked behind and saw a sight to put the ancient hero tales to the blush. One man against two-score my brave Dick stood, while through the underwood the mounted soldiery came to make the odds still greater.

He never flinched for all the hurtling missiles sent on ahead to cut him down, nor gave a glance aside to where the horsemen were deploying to surround him. As I looked, the two great pistols belched in the very faces of the nearest Cherokees; and in the momentary check the firearms made, the basket-hilted claymore went to work, rising and falling like a weaver's beam.

I saw no more; but some heart-bursting minutes later, when Jennifer came racing on behind to share the flight his heroic stand had made a possibility, the swelling sob choked me once again;

and when I thought of what this his rescue of me meant to him, I could have blubbered like a boy.

But there was little time or space to give remorse an inning. The Cherokees, checked but for the moment, were storming hotly at our heels. And as we ran I heard the shouted command of Falconnet to his mounted men: "A rescue! Right oblique, and head them in the road! Gallop, you devils!"

We ran in Indian file, I at the chief's heels and Jennifer at mine. I followed the Catawba blindly; and being as yet little better than half a man in breath and muscle, was well-nigh spent before we crashed down through a tangled briar thicket into the river road.

We were in time, but with no fraction of a minute to spare. We could hear the *pad-pad-pad* of the light-footed runners close upon us, following now by the noise we made; and on our left the air was trembling to the thunder of the mounted men coming at a break-neck gallop down the road.

"Thank God!" says Richard, with a quick eyeshot to right and left in the lesser gloom of the open. "I was afeard even the chief might miss the place in the dark. Down the bank to the river!— quick, man, and cautious! If they smell us out now, we're no better than buzzard-meat!" And when we reached the water's edge: "You taught me how to paddle a pirogue, Jack; I hope you haven't lost the knack of it yourself."

"No," said I; and the three of us slid the hollowed log into the stream.

We were afloat in shortest order, holding the canoe against the current by clinging to the overhanging trees that fringed the bank; yet with paddles poised for a second dash for freedom should the need arise. I should have dipped forthwith to save the precious minutes, but Jennifer stayed me.

"Hist!" he whispered. "Hold steady and listen. They can not see us from above; mayhap we've thrown them off the scent."

I thought it most unlikely; but his guess was right and mine was wrong. Though any of these savages could lift a trail in daylight, following it at top speed like a trained blood-hound, yet now the darkness baffled them.

So there was some running to and fro in the road above our heads, and then the troopers galloped down. Followed hastily a labored confab through the linguister, broken in the midst by a fury of hot oaths from Falconnet; and then the chase swept on toward the plantations, and we were left to make their losing of us sure by whatsoever means we chose.

We paddled slowly up stream in silence, keeping well within

the blacker shadow of the tree fringe. When we came opposite the glowing ruins of the hunting lodge, Jennifer backed upon his paddle.

"You'll go ashore?" said he.

I said I would, adding: "They have slaughtered poor old Darius, and I am loath to leave his bones for the buzzards to pick."

He made no comment other than to swear in sympathy. When the pirogue grounded, the Indian was out like a cat, to vanish phantom-wise among the trees. I followed in some clumsier fashion, leaving Jennifer to keep the canoe; but half way up the hill he joined me, and would not turn back for all my urging. "No; hang me if I'll let you out of eye-grip again," was all he would say; and so we went together, and were together at the seeing of what the glowing ember-heap would show us.

Poor Tomas had his sepulture already. His cord had burned in two and let him down so close beside the cabin wall that all the blazing debris from the overhanging eaves had made his funeral pile. Darius lay as I had last seen him; and him we buried in the maize clearing at the back, with the ember glow for funeral lights.

It was a chanceful thing to do. Since the Cherokees had left their dead and wounded, and Falconnet the body of his trooper who had yielded me the musket, there was small doubt they would return. Yet we had time to dig a shallow grave for my old henchman; to dig and fill it up again; and afterward to make a circuit round the burning pile to reach the river side once more.

When we had launched the canoe, and were afloat and ready for the start, the Catawba was still missing.

"Where is the chief, think you?" I asked; but Dick's answer, if, indeed, he gave me any, was lost in a chorus of ear splitting yells rending the silence of the night like demon cries. Then a single ululation, long drawn and fair blood chilling, answered back, and Jennifer swept the pirogue stern to strand with a quick paddle stroke.

"That last was Uncanoola's war cry; they've doubled back in time to catch him at it!" he cried. "Stand by to drive her when I give the word! Here he comes!"

Down the sloping hillside, looking, in the red glow of the ember heap, more like a flying demon than a man, came the Catawba, one hand gripping the scalping-knife, the other flung aloft to flaunt his terrible trophies in sight of his pursuers. They were so close upon him that waiting promised death for all of us; so Jennifer dipped again to send the canoe a broad jump from the bank.

"Ready!" he cried. "He'll take the water like a fish, and we can pick him up afterward—*Now!*"

I heard the clean-cut dive of the Indian, and struck the paddle deep to balance Jennifer's stroke. But as I bent to put my back into it, some flying missile caught me fair behind the ear, and but for Jennifer's quick wit I should have swamped the crazy shallop. In a flash he jerked me flat between his knees and sent the pirogue with a mighty thrust beyond the zone of fire light.

At that, though all the sense was beaten out of me, I was alive enough to hear the savage yells of disappointed rage behind us; these and the spitting crackle of a dozen rifles fired at random in the darkness. But afterward all sounds, save the rhythmic dip and drip of Jennifer's paddle, faded on the sense of hearing till, as it would seem, this gentle monody of dipping blade and tinkling drops became a crooning lullaby to blot out all the years that lay between, and make me once again a little child sinking asleep in my young mother's arms.

CHAPTER XVI

HOW JENNIFER THREW A MAIN WITH DEATH

'Tis a sure mark of healthful sleep that it never makes account of time. No odds how long the night, 'tis but a moment from the lapse of consciousness to its recovery in the morning. But this deep sleep that crept upon me as I lay in the pirogue, listening to the tinkling drip from Jennifer's paddle, was not of healthful weariness; and when I came awake from it there was a dim and troubled vista of vague and broken dreams to measure off the longest night I could ever remember.

The place of this awakening was a burrow in the earth. My bed of bearskins over fragrant pine-tufts was spread upon the ground, and by the flickering light of a handful of fire I could see the earth walls of the burrow, which were worn smooth as if the place had been the well-used den of some wild creature. But overhead there was the mark of human occupancy, since the earth-arch was sooted and blackened with the reek of many fires.

When I stirred there was another stir beyond the handful of fire, and Jennifer came to kneel beside me, taking my hand and chafing it as a tender-hearted woman might, and asking if I knew him.

"Know you? Why should I not?" I said, wondering why the words took so many breaths between.

"O Jack!" was all I had in answer; but when he had found a tongue to babble out his joy, I learned the why and wherefore. Once more grim death had reached for me, lying await in the twirled tomahawk that set me dreaming of my mother's lap and lullaby. For a week I had lain here upon the bed of pine-tufts, poised upon the brink of the death pit with only my dear lad to hold and draw me back.

"A week?" I queried, when he had named the interval. "And you have been here all the time?"

"I've never left you, save to forage for the pot," he admitted. "I dared not leave you, Jack."

"But where are we?" I would ask.

"In a den on the river's edge, a mile or more above your sacked cabin. 'Tis some dodge-hole hollowed out by the Catawbas long ago and shared since by them and the bears, judging from the stinking reek of it. Uncanoola steered me hither the night of the raid."

"Then the chief came off safely?" I said, falling into a dumb and impotent rage that the saying of two words should scant me so of strength to say a third.

"Right as a trivet—scalps and all," laughed Jennifer. "He'll be the envy of every warrior in the tribe when he vaunts himself at the Catawbas' council fire."

I let it rest a while at that, casting about for words to shape a hungrier question.

"Have you no news?" I asked, at length.

"Little or none," he answered shortly.

"But you have had some word—some news—from Appleby Hundred?" I stammered feebly.

"Nothing you'd care to hear," he rejoined, evasively, I thought. "'Tis as you left it, save that Tarleton whipped away to the south again as suddenly as he came, and our cursing baronet has made the manor house his headquarters in fact, lodging himself and all his troop on Mr. Stair. From his lying quiet and keeping the Cherokees in tow, there will be some deviltry afoot, I'll warrant."

I knew that Falconnet was waiting for the powder cargo, but another matter crowded this aside.

"But—but Margery?" I queried, on sharpest tenter-hooks to know how much or little he had heard.

I thought his brow darkened at the question, but mayhap it was only a shadow cast by the flickering fire. At any rate, he laughed hardily.

"She is well—and well content, I dare swear. 'Twas only yesterday I saw her taking the air on the river road, with Falconnet for an escort. You told me once he had a sure hand with the women and it made me mad; but, truly, I have come to think you drew it mild, Jack."

Now though I could ply a decent ready blade, or keep a firing line from lurching at a pinch, I had not learned to put a snaffle on a blundering tongue, as I have said before.

"Damn him as you please, Dick, and he'll warrant it. But you must not judge the lady over harshly, nor always by appearances. She may have flouted you as a boyish lover, and yet I think—"

I stopped in sheer bewilderment, shot through and through with keenest agonies of remorseful recollection. For at the moment I had clean forgot the gulf impassable I had set between these two. So I would have lapsed into shamed silence, but Jennifer would not suffer it.

"Well, what is it that you think?" he demanded.

"I think—nay, I may say I know that she thinks well of you, Dick," I blundered on, seeing no way to put him off.

He gripped my hand, and in his eyes there was the light of the old love reawakening.

"Don't lift me up to fling me down again, Jack! How can you know what she thinks of me?" he broke in, eagerly.

I should have told him then all there was to tell. He had been thrice my savior, and his heart was soft and malleable on the side of friendship. I knew it—knew that the pregnant moment for full confession had arrived; and yet I could not force my tongue to shape the words. Indeed, I saw more clearly than before that never any word of mine could make him understand that I was not a faithless traitor in intention. So I paltered with the truth, like any wretched coward of them all.

"You forget that I have come to know her well," I said. "I was a month or more under the same roof with her, and in that time she told me many things."

Now, this witless speech was no better than a whip to flog him on.

"What things?" he questioned, promptly.

"Oh, many things. She spoke often of you."

"What did she say of me, Jack? Tell me what she said," he begged. "It can make no difference now; she is less than nothing to me—nay,'tis even worse than that, since she would play Delilah if she could. But oh, Jack, I love her!—I should love her if I stood on the gallows and she stood by to spring the drop and turn me off!"

Truly, if the lash of remorse had lacked its keenest thong, this passionate outburst of his would have added it. None the less, I must needs be weaker than water and fall back another step and put him off.

"Another time, Richard. I am strangely unnerved and dizzy-headed now. By and by, when I am stronger, I will tell you all."

Taking a reproach where none was meant, he sprang up with a self-aimed malison upon his lack of care for me, stirred the fire alive and brewed me a most delicious-smelling cup of broth. And afterward, when I had drunk the broth with some small beckonings of returning appetite, he spread his coat to screen me from the fire light and would have driven me to sleep again.

"At any rate, you shall not talk," he promised. "If you are wakeful I will talk to you and tell you what little I have gleaned about the fighting."

His news was chiefly a later repetition of Father Matthieu's and Captain Abram Forney's, but there was this to add: the Congress had appointed the Englishman, Horatio Gates, chief of the army in the South, and this new leader was on his way to take command.

De Kalb, with the Maryland and Delaware lines and Colonel Armand's legion, was encamped on Deep River, waiting for the newly-appointed general; and Caswell and Griffith Rutherford, with the militia, were already pressing forward to some handgrips with my Lord Cornwallis in the South.

Nearer at hand, the partizan war-fire flamed afresh wherever a Tory company met a patriot, and there were wicked doings, more like savage massacres than fair-fought battles of the soldier sort.

When he had made an end of his small war budget, I set him on to tell me how he came to be at hand to help me so in the nick of time on the night of the cabin sack.

"'Twas partly chance," he said. "A redcoat troop had me in durance at Jennifer House, and while they affected to hold me at parole, I never gave consent to that, and so was kept a prisoner. They shut me in the wine-bin with a guard, and when the fellow was well soaked and silly, I bound and gagged him and broke jail. I took the river for it, meaning to outlie until the hue and cry was over; and just at dusk Uncanoola dropped upon me and told me of your need. From that to helping him cut you out of your raffle with the Cherokees was but a hand's turn in the day's work."

"A lucky turn for me," I said; and then at second thought I would deny the saying, though not for him to hear. But this was dangerous ground again, and I clawed off from it like a desperate mariner tempest-driven on a lee shore; asking him how he had learned the broadsword play, and where he got the antique claymore.

He laughed heartily, and more like my care-free Dick, this time.

"Thereby hangs a tale. I told you how I was out with the Minute Men in '76 at Moore's Creek, where we fought the Scotchmen. It was our first pitched battle, and I opine it smelled somewhat of severity on both sides—no quarter was asked, and the Tory MacDonalds fought like fiends for King George, small cause as they had to love the House of Hanover."

"How was that?" I would ask, being as little familiar with the low country settlements as any native-born Carolinian could be.

"They were expatriates for the Pretender's sake, many of them. Mistress Flora's husband was one of the prisoners we took. But, as I was saying, they were Tories to a man, and they fought wickedly. When it was over, the prisoners would have fared hardly but for a woman. In the thick of the fight, Mistress Mary Slocumb, of Dobbs, whose husband was with us, came storming down upon the field, having rode a-gallop some forty-odd miles because she dreamed her goodman was killed. She begged for the prisoners, and so Caswell hanged only those who were blood guilty—these and the house burners. A raw-boned piper named M'Gillicuddy fell to my lot, and he is now my majordomo at Jennifer House; as honest a fellow as ever skirled a pibroch."

"That was like you," I said; "to make a friend and retainer out of your prisoner. And so this Highland piper has been your fencing master, has he?"

"'Twas he taught me what little I know of the claymore play; and this stout old blade is his. 'Tis as good as a woodman's ax when you have the knack of swinging it."

"Truly," said I. "Also, you seemed to have the knack, and the strength as well, in spite of the crippled arm you were carrying in a sling the night before when they haled you into Colonel Tarleton's court at Appleby."

"A little ruse of war," he said, laughing and making a fist to show me his arm was strong and sound again. "'Twas M'Gillicuddy put me up to it, saying they would be like to deal the gentler with a wounded man. But how came you to know?"

Here was another chance to tell him what he should be told, but the words would not say themselves.

"I stood within arm's reach of you that night," said I; and from that I hastened swiftly through the story of my trial as a spy and what it came to in the morning, and never mentioned Margery's part in it at all.

"You have a bitter enemy in Frank Falconnet," was his comment, when I had made an end of this recounting of my adventures. "He knows you are in hiding hereabouts, and has been scouring the neighborhood well for you—or, more belike, for both of us."

"How do you know this?" I asked.

"I have both seen and heard. This den of ours opens on the river's edge, and, two days since, his Indians came within an ace of nabbing me. 'Twas just at dusk, and I made out to dodge them by doubling past in the canoe."

"But you say you have heard, as well?"

"Yes."

"How?"

"Don't ask me, Jack."

I said I had no right to ask more than he chose to tell; and at this he blurted out an oath and let me have the sharp-edged truth.

"Falconnet has an ally whose wit is shrewder than his. Can you guess who it is?"

"No."

"'Tis this same Madge Stair you have been defending, Jack," he said, bitterly. "It seems that Falconnet made sure we had both gone to join the army, which was but natural. If she were less than the spiteful little Tory vixen that she is, she would have been content to let it rest so. But she would not let it rest so. With her own lips she assured Falconnet he still had us to reckon with; nay, more—she made a boast of it that we would never go so far away from her."

Weak and fever-shaken as I was, I yet made shift to get upon my elbow feebly fierce, denouncing it hotly for a lie.

"Who slandered her like this, Dick? Put a name to the cur, and as I live and get my strength again, I'll hunt him down and choke him with that lie!"

"Nay," he objected soberly; "that would be my quarrel, were there ever a peg to hang a quarrel on. But it came by a sure hand, and one that is friendly enough to all concerned. An old free borderer, Ephraim Yeates by name, brought me the tale. He had been spying round at Appleby Hundred, wanting to know, for some purpose of his own, why the redcoats and Cherokees were hanging on so long; and this much he overheard one night when he was outlying under the window of the withdrawing-room. He says she was in a pretty passion at the baronet's slackness, stamping her foot at him and lashing him with the taunt that he was afeard of one or both of us."

I fell back on the bearskins to shut my eyes and call up all the might of love to grapple with this fresh misery. It was in this fierce conflict of faith against apparent fact that I descried the parting of the ways for the lover and the husband.

Jennifer believed this most incredible thing, and yet he loved her—would go on loving her, as he had said, in spite of all. That was the lover's road, and I could never bear him company on it. Could I believe her so pitiless cruel as this, I made sure no husband-love could live beyond that moment of conviction.

But at this perilous pass the husband's road ran truer than the lover's. Richard believed her capable of this hard-hearted thing and went on loving her blindly in spite of it. But as for me, I said I would never give belief an inch of standing-room; that had I stood in Ephraim Yeates's shoes, having the witness of my own eyes and ears, I would still have found excuse and exculpation for her.

I stole a glance at Jennifer. He was sitting with his face in his hands, a silent figure of a strong man humbled. He had called her a Delilah, and the green withes of her binding cut sore into the flesh.

"You say you love her, Dick; can you believe her capable of

this, and yet go on loving her?" I asked.

He let me see his face. It was haggard and grief-marred.

"I'd pay the devil's own price could I say 'no' to that, Jack. But I can not."

"Then I swear I love her better than you do, Richard Jennifer. She hates me well—God knows she has good cause to hate me fiercely; yet I would trust her with my life."

I looked to see him pin me down at this; and though the words had fairly shaped and said themselves, I laid fast hold of my courage and was prepared to make them good. But he would only smile and draw the bearskin cover over me, tucking me in as tenderly as a mother, and saying very gently:

"So she has bewitched you, too; and now there are two poor fools of love instead of one. But you are stronger than I, Jack. You will break the spell and put it down and live beyond it, and that I never shall—God help me!" And with that, he went to his own bed beside the fire, telling me I must lie quiet and try to sleep.

I did lie quiet, but sleep came not, nor did I woo it. For long past the time when I could hear his measured breathing, I lay awake to plan how I might draw the baronet's man-hunt to myself, and so free my loyal Richard of the peril that by rights was mine.

CHAPTER XVII

SHOWING HOW LOVE TOOK TOLL OF FRIENDSHIP

For some few days after Jennifer's narrow escape at the entrance to our hiding place, the Cherokees were hot upon our scent, quartering the forest on both banks of the river, determined, as it seemed, to hunt or starve us out.

It was in this time of siege that I came to know, as I had not known before, the depth and tenderness of my dear lad's love for me. While the life-tide was at its ebb and I was querulous and helpless weak, he was my leech and nurse and heartening friend in one. And later, when the tide was fairly turned and I had found my soldier's appetite again, he spent many of the nights abroad and never let me guess what risks he ran to fetch me dainties from the outer world.

In this night raiding no danger was too great to hold him back from serving me. Once, when we were washing down our evening meal of meat and maize cake with plain cold water, I mourned the good wine idling in its bin at Jennifer House. At that, without a word to me, he took the whole night for a perilous adventure and fetched a dozen bottles of the Jennifer port to make me choke and strangle at the thought of what its bringing had cost in toil and hazard.

Another time I spoke of English beef, saying how it would rebuild a man at need—how it had made the English soldier what he is. Whereupon, as before, my loving forager took a hint where none was intended; was gone the night long, and slaughtered me some Tory yearling,—'twas Mr. Gilbert Stair's, I mistrusted, though Dick would never name the owner, and so I had a sirloin to my breakfast.

In these and many other ways he spent himself freely for love of me. If he had been a younger brother of my own blood the common parentage could not have made him tenderer.

'Twas not the mere outgushing of a nature open-armed to make a bosom friend of all the world; nor any feminine softness on his part. If I have drawn him thus my pen is but a clumsy quill, for he was manly-rough and masterful, with all the native strength and vigor of the border-born.

But on the side of love and friendship no woman ever had a truer heart, a keener eye or a lighter hand. And in a service for friend or mistress he would spend himself as recklessly as those old knights you read about who made a business of their chivalry.

With his daily offerings of unselfishness to shame me, you may be sure that I was flayed alive; self-flogged like a miserable monk, with all the woundings of the whip well salted by remorse. As you have guessed, I had not yet summoned up the courage to tell him how I had staked his chance of happiness upon a casting of the die of fate—staked and lost it. Now that it was gone, I saw how I had missed the golden opportunity; how I had weakly hesitated when delay could only make the telling harder.

By tacit consent we never spoke of Margery. Richard's silence hung upon despair, I thought; and as for mine, since the husband's road and the lover's lay so far apart, I could not bring myself to speak of her. But she was always first in my thoughts in that time of convalescence, as I made sure she was in his; and at the last the hidden thing between us was brought to light.

It was on a night some three weeks or more after my fever turn. Our larder had run low again, and Jennifer had spent the earlier hours of the night abroad—to little purpose, as it chanced. 'Twas midnight or thereabouts when he came swearing in to tell me that the Tories were out again to harry our side of the river afresh, and to make a refugee's begging of a bag of meal a thing of peril.

"They'll starve us out in shortest measure at this rate," he prophesied. "They have trampled down all the standing corn for miles around, and this morning they burned the mill. 'Tis our notice to quit, and we'd best take it. There has been fighting to the south of us—a plenty of it—at Rocky Mount and Hanging Rock, and elsewhere, and every man is needed. If you are strong enough to stand the march, we'll run the gantlet down the river in the pirogue and cut across from the lower ford to join Major Davie or Mr. Gates."

I said I was fit enough, and would do whatever he thought best. And then I took a step upon the forbidden ground.

"Falconnet is still at Appleby Hundred?" I said.

He nodded.

"And you will join the army at the front and leave Margery to his tender mercies?"

His laugh was bitter; so bitter that I scarce knew it for Richard Jennifer's.

"Mistress Margery Stair is well, and well content, as I told you once before. She has no wish for you or me, unless it be to see us well hanged."

"Nay, Richard; you judge her over-harshly. I fear you do not love her as her lover should."

"Say you so? Listen: to-night I got as far as the manor house, being fool enough to risk my neck for another sight of her. God help me, Jack! I had it. They have scraped together all the Tory riff-raff this side of the river—Falconnet and the others—and are holding high revel at Appleby. Since it is still our true-blue border-land, they are scant enough of women of their own kidney, and I saw Madge dancing like any light o' love with every jackanapes that offered."

"In her father's house she could not well do less," I averred, cut to the heart, as he was, and yet without his younger lover's jealousy to make me unjust.

"Or more," he added, savagely. "'Tis as I say; she lacks nothing we can give her, and we'd as well be off about our business."

I think he never had it in his heart to leave her in any threat of danger. But from his point of view there was no danger threatening her save that which she seemed willing enough to rush upon—a life of titled misery as Lady Falconnet. I saw how he would see it; saw, too, that his was the saner summing of it up. And yet—

He broke into my musings with a pointed question. "What say you, Jack? 'Tis but a little whiffet of a Tory jade who cares not the snap of her finger for either of us. The night is fine and dark. Shall we float the canoe and give them all the slip?"

This was how it came to turn upon a "yes" or "no" of mine. I hesitated, I know not why. In the little pause the fire burned low between us, and the shadows deepened in the burrow cavern until they strangled the eye as mephitic vapors scant a man of breath. The silence, too, was stifling. There was no sound to breach it save the gurgling murmur of the river, and this was subdued and inter-mittent like the death-rattle in the throat of the dying.

I've always made a scoff of superstition, and yet, my dears, a thousand questions in this life of ours must hang answerless to the crack of doom if you deny it standing-room. I knew no more than I have set down here of Margery's besetment; nay, I had every reason Richard Jennifer had to believe that she was well and well content, lacking nothing, save, mayhap, the freedom to marry where she chose.

And yet, out of the stifling silence there came a sudden cry for help; a cry voiceless to the outward ear, but sharp and piercing to that finer inward sense; a cry so real that I would start and listen, marveling that Jennifer made no sign of having heard it.

In the harkening instant there was a faint twang like the thrumming of a distant harp string, and then the grave-like silence was rent smartly by the whistling hiss of an arrow, the shaft passing evenly between us and scattering the handful of fire where it struck.

Jennifer came alive with a start, leaping up with a malediction between his teeth upon our dallying.

"Too late, by God!" he cried. "They've trapped us like a pair of blind moles!" And with that he caught up the ancient broadsword, only to swear again when he found no room to swing it in.

Having the handier weapon, I slipped out before him, creeping on hands and knees till I could see the leafy screen at the den's mouth, and the shimmering reflection of the stars upon the water beyond it. There was no sight nor sound of any enemy, and the canoe lay safe as Jennifer had left it.

To make assurance sure, I would have scrambled to the bank above; but at the moment Jennifer hallooed softly to me, and so I crept back into the burrow.

"See here," he said, excitedly. "What a devil will you make of this?"

He had drawn the scattered embers together, fanning them ablaze again, and had sought and found the arrow. It was a blunt-head reed and no war shaft. And around the middle of it, tightly wrapped and tied with silken threads, was a little scroll of parchment.

"'Tis the Catawba's arrow," said Jennifer, though how he knew I could not guess; and then he cut the threads to free the scroll.

Unrolled and spread at large, the parchment proved to be that map of Captain Stuart's that I had found and lost again. And on the margin of it was my note to Jennifer, written in that trying moment when the bribed sentry waited at the door and my sweet lady stood trembling beside me, murmuring her "Holy Marys."

"Read it," said I. "It explains itself. Tarleton had laid me by the heels to wait for the hangman, and I would have passed the word about the Indian-arming on to you. But my messenger was over-hauled, and—"

"Yes, yes," he broke in; "I've spelled it out. But this line added at the bottom—surely, that is never your crabbed fist. By heaven! 'tis in Madge's hand!"

He knelt to hold it closer to the flickering firelight, and we deciphered it together. It was but a line, as he had said, with neither greeting nor leave-taking, address nor signature.

"If this should come into the hands of any true-hearted gentleman"—here was a blot as if the pen had slipped from the fingers holding it; and then, in French, the very wording of the inarticulate cry that had come to me out of the darkness and silence: *"A moi! pour l'amour de Dieu!"*

We fell apart, each to his own side of the handful of embers.

"You make it out?" said I, after a moment of strained silence.

He nodded. "She has prattled the parlez-vous to me ever since we were boy and maid together."

A full minute more of the threatening silence, and at the end of it we were glaring at each other like two wild creatures crouching for the spring.

It was Jennifer who spoke first. "'Twas meant for me," he said; and his voice had the warning of a mastiff's growl in it.

"No!" said I, curtly.

"I say it was!"

"Then you say the thing which is not."

Had I been Richard Jennifer, I know not what bitter reproach I should have found to hurl at the man who had thrice owed his life to me. But he said no word of what had gone before.

"You may give me the lie, if you like, John Ireton; I shall not strike you." He said it slowly, but his face was gray with anger. Then he added, hotly: "You know well that word was meant for me!"

At this—God forgive me!—my jealous wrath broke bounds and I cursed him for a beardless coxcomb who must needs think he stood alone in the eye of every woman he should meet. "She needs a man!" I raged, lost now to every sense of decent justice, "a man, I say! And to whom would she send if not to her—"

I choked upon the word. He had risen with me, and we stood face to face in that grim earth-womb, snarling fiercely at each other across the narrow firelit space; two men with every tie to knit us close together, and yet—God save us all!—a pair of wild beasts strung up to the killing pitch because, forsooth, we must needs front each other across a deadline drawn by the finger of a woman!

God knows what would have come of all this had my dear lad been as fierce a fool as I. 'Twas his good common sense that saved us both, I think, for when the savage rival madness was at its height he turned away, swearing we were the very pick and choice of a world of asses to stand thus feeling for each other's throats when, mayhap, the lady needed both of us.

This brought me to my senses at a gallop, as you would guess; to them and to the lighting of the conscience fire within whereon to grill the wicked heart that but now had thirsted for a brother's blood.

"Now God have mercy on us both!" I groaned. "Forgive me, Dick, if you can; I was as mad as any Bedlamite. If I have any claim on her, 'tis not of her good will, you may be sure. You have the baronet to fear—not me."

He shook his head and pointed to the parchment—to the line in French.

"Francis Falconnet was under the same roof with her—or at least in easy call—when she wrote that, Jack. He is no longer my rival—nor yours."

His word set me thinking, and I would fall to picking out the strands that jealous wrath had woven for me into the web of happenings. Setting aside the story brought by Ephraim Yeates, there was no certain proof that she had ever favored the Englishman; nay, more, till I had come to be madly jealous of Falconnet, I had made sure that Jennifer was the favored one.

At this, as one sees a landscape struck out clear and vivid by the lightning's flash, I saw the true meaning of the word the hunter had brought—saw it and went upon my knees to grope blindly for the sword I had let fall when Dick had found the arrow.

"What is it, Jack?" he asked, gently.

"My sword!" I gasped. "We should have been half-way there by this. Yeates was misled. 'Tis Falconnet she fears. She was at bay—hark you, at bay and fair desperate. That word of hers to the baronet was her poor pitiful defiance built on her trust in us, and we have lain here—"

He found the sword and thrust it into my hand, crying:

"Come on! You can strew the dust and ashes on me later. You said you loved her the better, and I do believe it now, Jack! You trusted her, as I did not. We'll fight as one man to cut her out of this coil, whatever it may be; and after that is done I'll make my bow and leave you a fair field."

"Nay, nay; that you shall not, Dick," I began; but he was half-way through the narrow passage to the open, trailing the ancient broadsword and the bearskin from his bed; and I was fain to follow quickly, leaving the protest all unfinished.

CHAPTER XVIII

IN WHICH WE HEAR NEWS FROM THE SOUTH

As near as might be guessed, it wanted yet an hour or two of daybreak when we made a landing within the boundaries of Appleby Hundred, and beached and hid the pirogue in the bushes.

Of the down-stream flitting through the small hours of the warm midsummer night there is no sharp-etched picture on the memory page. As I recall it, no spoken word of Jennifer's or mine came in to break the rhythm of the hasting voyage. Our paddles rose and fell, dipping and sweeping in unison as if we two, kneeling in bow and stern, were separate halves of some relentless mechanism driven by a single impulse. Overhead the starlit dome circled solemnly to the right or left to match the windings of the stream. On each hand the tree-fringed shores sped backward in the gloom; and beneath the light shell of poplar wood that barely kissed the ripples in passing, the river lapped and gurgled, chuckling weirdly at the paddle plungings, and swirling aft in the longer reaches to point at us down the lengthening wake with a wavering finger silver-tipped in the wan starlight.

With the canoe safely hidden at the landing place, which was some little distance from that oak grove where I had twice kept tryst with death, we set out for the manor house, skulking Indian fashion through the wood; and, when we reached the in-fields, looking momently to come upon a sentry.

Thinking the approaches from the road and river would be better guarded than that from the wood, we skirted a widespread thicket tangle, spared by my father twenty years before to be a grouse and pheasant cover, and fetching a compass of half a mile or more across the maize fields, came in among the oaks and hickories of the manor grounds.

Still there was no sight nor sound of any enemy; no light of candles at the house, or of camp-fires beneath the trees.

A little way within the grove, where the interlacing tree-tops made the darkness like Egyptian night, Jennifer went on all fours to feel around as if in search of something on the sward. Whereat I called softly to know what he would be at.

He rose, muttering, half as to himself: "I thought I'd never be so far out of reckoning." Then to me: "A few hours since, the Cherokees were encamped just here. You are standing in the ashes of their fire."

"So?" said I. "Then they have gone?"

"Gone from this safely enough, to be sure. They have been gone some hours; the cinders are cold and dew wet."

"So much the better," I would say, thinking only that now there would be the fewer enemies to fight.

He clipt my arm suddenly, putting the value of an oath into his gripping of it.

"Come awake, man; this is no time to be a-daze!" His whisper was a sharp behest, with a shake of the gripped arm for emphasis. "If the Indians are gone, it means that the powder train has come and gone, too."

"Well?" said I.

I was still thinking, with less than a clod's wit, that this would send the baronet captain about his master's business, and so Margery would have surcease of him for a time, at least. But Jennifer fetched me awake with another whip-lash word or two.

"Jack! has the night's work gone to your head? If Falconnet has got his marching orders you may be sure he's tried by hook or crook to play 'safe bind, safe find,' with Madge. By heaven! 'twas that she was afeard of, and we are here too late! Come on!"

With that he faced about and ran; and forgetting to loose his grip on my arm, took me with him till I broke away to have my sword hand free. So running, we came presently to the open space before the house, and, truly, it was well for us that the place was clean deserted; for by this we had both forgot the very name of prudence.

Jennifer outran me to the door by half a length, and fell to hammering fiercely on the panel with the pommel of his broad-sword.

"Open! Mr. Stair; open!" he shouted, between the batterings; but it was five full minutes before the fan-light overhead began to show some faint glimmerings of a candle coming from the rooms beyond.

Richard rested at that, and in the pause a thin voice shrilled from within.

"Be off, you runagates! Off, I say! or I fire upon ye through the door!"

Giving no heed to the threat, Dick set up his clamor again, calling out his name, and bidding the old man open to a friend. In some notching of the hubbub I heard the unmistakable click of a gun-flint on steel. There was barely time to trip my reckless batterer and to fall flat with him on the door-stone when a gun went off within, and a handful of slugs, breaching the oaken panel at the height of a man's middle, went screeching over us.

Before I knew what he would be at, Richard was up with an oath, backing off to hurl himself, shoulder on, against the door. It gave with a splintering crash, letting him in headlong. I followed less hastily. It was as black as a setter's mouth within, the gun fire having snuffed the old man's candle out. But we had flint and steel and tinder-box, and when the punk was alight, Jennifer found the candle under foot and gave it me. It took fire with a fizzing like a rocket fuse, and was well blackened with gunpowder. When the flint had failed to bring the firing spark, the old man had set his piece off with the candle flame.

We found him in the nook made by the turn of the stair, flung thither, as it seemed, by the recoil of the great bell-mouthed blunderbuss which he was still clutching. The fall had partly stunned him, but he was alive enough to protest feebly that he would take a dozen oaths upon his loyalty to the cause; that he had mistook us for some thieving marauders of the other side; craftily leaving cause and party without a name till he should have his cue from us.

Whereupon Richard loosed his neckcloth to give him better breathing space, and bidding me see if the revelers had left a heel-tap of wine in any bottle nearer than the wine cellar, lifted the old man and propped him in the corner of the high-backed hall settle.

The wine quest led me to the banqueting-room. Here disorder reigned supreme. The table stood as the roisterers had left it; the very wreck and litter of a bacchanalian feast. Bottles, some with the necks struck off, were scattered all about, and the floor was stained and sticky with spilt wine and well sanded with shattered glass.

I found a remnant draining in one of the broken bottles, and a cup to pour it in; and with this salvage from the wreck returned to Jennifer and his charge. The old man had come to some better sensing of things,—he had been vastly more frightened than hurt, as I suspected,—and to Richard's eager questionings was able to give some feebly querulous replies.

"Yes, they're gone—all gone, curse 'em; and they've taken every plack and bawbee they could lay their thieving hands upon," he mumbled. "'Tis like the dogs; to stay on here and eat and drink me out of house and home, and then to scurry off when I'm most like to need protection."

"But Madge?" says Richard. "Is she safe in bed?"

"She's a jade!" was all the answer he got. Then the old man sat up and peered around the end of the settle to where I stood, cup and bottle in hand. "'Tis a Christian thought," he quavered. "Give me a sup of the wine, man."

I served him and had a Scottish blessing for my wastefulness, because, forsooth, the broken bottle spilt a thimbleful in the pouring. I saw he did not recognize me, and was well enough content to let it rest thus.

Richard suffered him to drink in peace, but when the cup was empty he renewed his asking for Margery. At this the master of the house, heartened somewhat by my father's good madeira, made shift to get upon his feet in some tremulous fashion.

"Madge, d'ye say? She's gone; gone where neither you nor that dour-faced deevil that befooled us all will find her soon, I promise you, Dickie Jennifer!" he snapped; and I gave them my back and stumbled blindly to the door, making sure his next word would tell my poor wronged lad all that he should have learned from never any other lips but mine own. But Richard himself parried the impending stroke of truth, saying:

"So she is safe and well, Mr. Stair, 'tis all I ask to know."

"She is safe enough; safer by far than you are at this minute, my young cock-a-hoop rebel, now that the king—God save him!—has his own again."

I turned quickly on the broad door-stone to look within. Out of doors the early August dawn was graying mistily overhead, but in the house the sputtering tallow dip still struggled feebly with the gloom. They stood facing each other, these two, my handsome lad, the pick and choice of a comely race, looking, for all his toils and vigils, fresh and fit; and the old man in his woolen dressing-gown, his wig awry, and his lean face yellow in the candle-light.

"How is that you say, Mr. Stair?" says Dick. "The king—but that is only the old Tory cry. There will never be a king again this side of the water."

The old man reached out and hooked a lean finger in the lad's buttonhole. "Say you so, Richard Jennifer? Then you will never have heard the glorious news?" This with a leer that might have been of triumph or the mere whetting of gossip eagerness—I could not tell.

"No," says Richard, with much indifference.

"Hear it, then. 'Twas at Camden, four days since. They came together in the murk of the Wednesday morning, my Lord Cornwallis and that poor fool Gates. De Kalb is dead; your blethering Irishman, Rutherford, is captured; and your rag-tag rebel army is scattered to the four winds. And that's not all. On the Friday, Colonel Tarleton came up with Sumter at Fishing Creek and caught him napping. Whereupon, Charlie McDowell and the over-mountain men, seeing all was lost, broke their camp on the Broad and took to their heels, every man jack of them for himself. So ye see, Dickie Jennifer, there's never a cursed corporal's guard left in either Carolina to stand in the king's way."

He rattled all this off glibly, like a child repeating some lesson got by heart; but when I would have found a grain of comfort in the hope that it was a farrago of Falconnet's lies, Jennifer made the truth appear in answer to a curt question.

"'Tis beyond doubt?—all this, Mr. Stair?"

The old loyalist—loyalist now, if never certainly before—sat down on the settle and laughed; a dry wizened cackle of a laugh that sounded like the crumpling of new parchment.

"You'd best be off, light foot and tight foot, Master Richard, lest you learn shrewdly for yourself. 'Tis in everybody's mouth by this. There were some five-and-forty of the king's friends come together here no longer ago than yestere'en to drink his Majesty's health, and eh, man! but it will cost me a pretty penny! Will that satisfy ye?"

"Yes," said Jennifer, thinking, mayhap, as I did, that nothing short of gospel-true news would have sufficed to unlock this poor old miser's wine cellar.

"Well, then; you'd best be off while you may; d'ye hear? I bear ye no ill-will, Richard Jennifer; and if Mr. Tarleton lays hold of you, you'll hang higher than Haman for evading your parole, I promise you. We'll say naught about this rape of the door-lock, though 'tis actionable, sir, and I'll warn you the law would make you smart finely for it. But we'll enter a *nolle prosequi* on that till you're amnestied and back, then you can pay me the damage of the broken lock and we'll cry quits."

At this my straightforward Richard snorted in wrathful derision. However much he loved the daughter, 'twas clear he had small regard for the father.

"Seeing we came to do you a service, Mr. Stair, I think we may set the blunderbuss and the handful of slugs over against the smashed door. And that fetches me back to our errand here. You say Madge is safe. Does that mean that you have spirited her away since last night?"

"Dinna fash yoursel' about Madge, Richard Jennifer. She's meat for your betters, sir!" rasped the old man, lapsing into the mother tongue, as he did now and then in fear or anger.

"Still I would know what you mean when you say she is safe," says Richard, whose determination to crack a nut was always proportioned to the hardness of the shell.

Gilbert Stair cursed him roundly for an impertinent jackanapes, and then gave him his answer.

"'Tis none of your business, Dickie Jennifer, but you may

know and be hanged to you! She rode home with the Witherbys last night after the rout, and will be by this safe away in t'other Carolina where your cursed Whiggeries darena lift head or hand."

"Of her own free will?" Dick persisted.

"Damme! yes; bag, baggage, serving wench and all. Now will you be off about your business before some spying rascal lays an information against me for harboring you?"

Richard joined me on the door-stone. The dawn was in its twilight now, and the great trees on the lawn were taking gray and ghostly shapes in the dim perspective.

"You heard what he had to say?" said he.

I nodded.

"It seems we have missed our cue on all sides," he went on, not without bitterness. "I would we might have had a chance to fire a shot or two before the ship went down."

"At Camden, you mean? That's but the beginning; the real battles are all to be fought yet, I should say."

He shook his head despondently. "You are a newcomer, Jack, and you know not how near outworn the country is. Gilbert Stair has the right of it when he says there will be nothing to stop the redcoats now."

I called to mind the resolute little handful under Captain Abram Forney, one of many such, he had told me, and would not yield the point.

"There will be plenty of fighting yet, and we must go to bear a hand where it is needed most," said I. "Where will that be, think you? At Charlotte?"

He looked at me reproachfully.

"This time 'tis you who are the laggard in love, John Ireton. Will you go and leave Mistress Margery wanting an answer to her poor little cry for help?"

I shrugged. "What would you? Has she not taken her affair into her own hands?"

"God knows how much or little she has had to say about it," said he. "But I mean to know, too, before I put my name on any company roll." We were among the trees by this, moving off for safety's sake, since the day was coming; and he broke off short to wheel and face me as one who would throttle a growling cur before it has a chance to bite. "We know the worst of each other now, Jack, and we must stand to our compact. Let us see her safe beyond peradventure of a doubt; then I'm with you to fight the redcoats single-handed, if you like. I know what you will say— that the country calls us now more than ever; but there must needs be some little rallying interval after all this disaster, and—"

"Have done, Richard," said I. "Set the pace and mayhap I can keep step with you. What do you propose?"

"This; that we go to Witherby Hall and get speech with Mistress Madge, if so be—"

"Stay a moment; who are these Witherbys?"

"A dyed-in-the-wool Tory family seated some ten miles across the line in York district. True, 'tis a rank Tory hotbed over there, and we shall run some risk."

"Never name risk to me if you love me, Richard Jennifer!" I broke in. "What is your plan?"

His answer was prompt and to the point. "To press on afoot through the forest till we come to the York settlement; then to borrow a pair of Tory horses and ride like gentlemen. Are you game for it?"

I hesitated. "I see no great risk in all this, and whatever the hazard, 'tis less for one than for two. You'd best go alone, Richard."

He saw my meaning; that I would stand aside and let him be her succor if she needed help. But he would not have it so.

"No," he said, doggedly. "We'll go together, and she shall choose between us for a champion, if she is in the humor to honor either of us. That is what 'twill come to in the end; and I warn you fairly, John Ireton, I shall neither give nor take advantage in this strife. I said last night that I would stand aside, but that I can not—not till she herself says the killing word with her own lips."

"And that word will be—?"

"That she loves another man. Come; let us be at it; we should be well out of this before the plantation people are astir."

CHAPTER XIX

HOW A STUMBLING HORSE BROUGHT TIDINGS

Having a definite thing to do, we set about it forthwith, taking to the fields and making a wide circuit around the manor house and the quarters where the blacks were already stirring, to come out to the river and so to cross in our canoe.

The morning, soft and warm enough, threatened now to break the fair weather promise of the starlit night. Away in the east a heavy cloud bank curtained off the sunrise, and in the fields the few dry maize blades left by the partizan harriers were whispering to the gusts.

In the great forest all was yet dim and shadowy, and silent as the grave but for the whispering murmur of the rising wind in the higher tree-tops; a sound so like the babbling of brooks as most cunningly to deceive the ear and make it set the eye at work to look for water where there was none.

Not to take a certain hazard for the sake of better speed, we shunned the road, and for the first hour or so were not greatly hindered by keeping to the forest paths. In vast areas this virgin wood was free of undergrowth, open and park-like as a well-kept grove. Fireside tradition on the border tells how the Indians kept the forest clear by yearly burnings of the smaller growth; this for the better hunting of the deer. I vouch, not for the truth of this accounting for the fact, but for the fact itself. For endless miles between the watercourses these park-like stretches covered hill and dale; a vast mysterious temple of God's own building, its naves and choirs and transepts columned by the countless trees, with all their leafy crowns to interlace and form the groined arches overhead.

Through these pillared aisles we tramped abreast, shunning the road, as I have said, yet holding it parallel with our course where its direction served. In the open vistas we had frequent glimpses of it, winding, at feud with all the points of the compass, among the trees. But farther on we came into the lower land of a creek bottom, and here a thickset undergrowth robbed us of any view and made the march a toilsome struggle with the bushes.

It was in the densest of this underwood, when we could hear the purring of the stream ahead, that Jennifer stopped suddenly and began to sniff the air.

"Smoke," he said, briefly, in answer to my query. "A camp-fire, with meat abroil. Never tell me you can't smell it."

I said I could not—did not, at all events.

"Then you are not as sharp set for breakfast as I am. Call up your woodcraft and we'll stalk it." And, suiting the action to the word, he dropped noiselessly on hands and knees to inch his way cautiously out of the thicket.

I followed at his heels, marveling at his skill in threading the maze with never a snapped twig to betray him. For though I have called him a youthling, he came of great, square-shouldered English stock, and was well upon fourteen stone for weight. Yet upon occasion, as now, he could be as lithe and cat-like as an Indian, stealthy in approach and tiger-strong to spring.

In due time our creeping progress brought us out of the thicket on the brink of the higher creek bank. Just here the stream ran in a shallow ravine with shelving banks of clay, and on its hither margin was a bit of grassy intervale big enough for a horse to roll upon. Though it was sadly out of season, the carcass of a deer, fresh killed, hung upon a branch of the nearest tree, with a rifle leaning against the trunk as if to guard it. In the middle of the bit of sward a tiny camp-fire burned; and at the fire, squatting with their backs to us and each toasting a cut of the deer's meat on a forked stick, were two men.

One of these men would pass by courtesy as a white. His hunting-shirt and leggings were of deer skin, well grimed and greasy, with leather fringes at the seams of leg and sleeve. For all the summer heat, he wore a cap fashioned of raccoon-skin with the fur on; and for this great cap his iron-gray hair, matted and unkempt, served as a fringe to keep the other tasselings in countenance. The hunting-shirt was belted at the waist, and in the belt was thrust a sheathless knife huge enough to serve a butcher's purpose. From two leather thongs crossed upon his shoulders hung the powder-horn and bullet-pouch; and these, with the knife and rifle, summed up his accoutrements.

The other was a red man, and his attire was simpler. Like all our southern Indians, he went naked to the waist; but the savage's love of ornament showed forth in the fringe of colored porcupine quills on his leggings and in his raven hair bestuck with feathers. For arms he had an arsenal in his belt; two great pistols, a tomahawk, and the scalping-knife, this last smaller than the white man's carving tool, but far more vicious looking.

For a moment or two we crouched irresolute on the brink of the ravine, neither of us recognizing the two below. Then my young rashling must needs let out a yell.

"Now, by all that's lucky!" he cried, and would have leaped to his feet. But at the instant the earth-edge gave way under him, and he was sent tumbling with the small landslide of clay down upon the twain at the fire.

It went within a trembling hair's-breadth of a tragedy. The two at the fire sprang up as one man; and the bound that set the hunter afoot brought his long rifle to his shoulder. But that the Indian was the quicker, Richard's life would have paid the penalty of his slip, I think. At the trigger-pulling instant the Catawba thrust the thick of his hand between stone and steel, and the flint bit, harmless for Jennifer, into the palm of the Indian.

"Wah!" he ejaculated, in his soft guttural. "No want kill Captain Jennif', hey?"

Ephraim Yeates lowered his weapon and released the pinched hand held fast by the gun-flint.

"Well, I'm daddled, fair and square, Cap'n Dick!" he declared. "Jest one more shake of a dead lamb's tail, and I'd 'a' had ye on my mind, sartain sure! I allowed ye knowed better than to come whammling down that-away behint a man whilst he's a-cooking his ven'son."

Dick laughed and called to me to follow as I could. And his answer to the old borderer was no answer at all.

"'Tis to be hoped you and the chief don't mean to be niddering with that deer's meat. We were guessing but a half-hour back, Captain Ireton and I, whether or no we'd have to take up belt-slack for our breakfast."

At the word the Catawba whipped out his knife and fell to work hospitably on the meat supply. Meanwhile I came upon the scene, something less hurriedly than Richard. Ephraim Yeates looked me up and down with a sniff for my foreign-cut coat, another for my queue, and a third for the German ritter-boots I wore.

"Umph!" said he. "Now if here ain't that there dad-blame' Turkey-fighter again! What almighty cur'is things the good Lord do let loose on a stiff-necked and rebellious gineration!" Then to me, most pointedly: "Say, Cap'n; the big woods ain't no fitting place for such as you, ez I allow. Ye mought be getting them purty boots o' your'n all tore up on the briars."

He ended with a dry little laugh not unlike Mr. Gilbert Stair's parchment crackle; and, being his guest for the nonce, I laughed with him.

"Have your joke and welcome, Mr. Yeates," said I. "I am too near famished to quarrel with my chance of breakfast."

Much to my astoundment he flung his raccoon-skin cap into the air, spat upon his hands and began that insane war-dance of his.

"Whoop!" he yelled. "No band-box dandy from the settle-mints ever sot out to call me 'Mister' and got away alive to brag on't! Ketch hold, you infergotten, Turkey-fighting, silver-buttoned jack-a-dandy till I dip ye in the creek and soak a flour-ration 'r two out 'n that there pig-tail top-knot o' your'n! *Yip-pee!*"

By this Jennifer was trying, as well as a man bent double with laughter might, to interpose in the interest of peace and amity; and even the stoical Catawba was all a-grin. So, seeing I was like to lose countenance with all of them, I watched my chance, and closing with my capering ancient, gave him a hearty wrestler's hug.

For all he was so gaunt and thin, and full twenty years or more my senior, he was a pretty handful. 'Twas much like trying to catch a fall out of some piece of steel-wired mechanism. None the less, after some wild stampings and strivings in which the old man all but made good his promise to put me in the creek, I took him unawares with a Cornishman's trick—a cross-buttock shifted suddenly to a shoulder-lift—which sent him flying overhead to land all abroad in the soft clay of the landslide.

The effect of this little triumph was magical and wholly un-looked for. When he had gathered himself and set his limbs in order, Ephraim Yeates sat up and thrust out a claw-like hand.

"Put it there, stranger," he said. "I reckon ez how that settles it. Old Eph Yeates'll share fair, powder and lead, parched corn *and* pan-meat with the man that can flop him that-away. Whilst ye're a-needing a friend in the big woods—a raw-meat-eating Injun-skinner that can jest or'narily whop his weight in wildcats—why, old Eph's your man; from now on, *if* not sooner." And in this wise began an alliance the like of which, for true-blue loyalty on this old borderer's part, these colder-hearted times of yours, my dears, will never see.

As you would guess, I gripped the hand of pledging most heartily, pulling the old man to his feet and protesting it was but a trick he would never let another play on him. And then we four fell upon the deer's meat which was by this time—not cooked, to be sure, but seared a little on the outside in true hunter fashion.

While we ate, Richard spoke freely of our intendings; and in return Ephraim Yeates was able to confirm Mr. Gilbert Stair's war news to the letter. For all his Tory bias and prejudice, it seemed that Margery's father had spoken by the book. Gates' army was crushed and scattered to the four winds; Thomas Sumter's free-lances had been attacked, worsted and driven, with the leader himself so sorely wounded that he was carried from the field in a blanket slung between the horses of two of his men; and, as was to be expected, the Tories were up and arming in all the north country. Truly, the prospect was most gloomy and the outlook for the patriot cause was to the full as desperate as King George himself could wish.

"But you, Ephraim, and the chief, here; are you two running away like all the others?" Richard would ask.

The old hunter growled his denial between the mouthfuls of scarce-warmed meat. "I reckon ez how 'tis t'other way 'round; we're sort o' camping on the redcoats' trail, ez I allow. Ain't we, Chief, hey?"

The Catawba's assent was a guttural "Wah!" and Ephraim Yeates went on to explain.

"Ye see, 'tis this-away. You took a laugh out'n me, Cap'n Dick, for spying 'round on that there Britisher hoss-captain and his redskins; but 'long to'ards the last I met up with a thing 'r two wo'th knowing. 'Twas a powder and lead cargo they was a-waiting for; and they're allowing to sneak it through the mountings to the overhill Cherokees."

"Well?" says Dick.

The old man cut another slice of the venison and took his time to impale it on the forked toasting stick.

"Well, then I says to the chief, here, says I, 'Chief, this here's our A-number-one chance to spile the 'Gyptians; get heap gun, heap powder, heap lead, heap scalp.' The chief, he says, 'Wah!'— which is good Injun-talk for anything ye like,—and so here we are, hot-foot on the trail o' that there hoss-captain and his powder varmints."

"Alone?" said I, in sheer amazement at the brazen effrontery of this chase of half a hundred well-armed men by two.

The old hunter chuckled his dry little laugh. "We ain't sich tarnation big fools ez we look, Cap'n John. There's a good plenty of 'em to wallop us, ez I'll allow, if it come to fighting 'em fair and square. But there'll be some dark night 'r other whenst we can slip up on 'em and raise a scalp 'r two and lift what plunder we can tote; hey, Chief?"

But now Richard would inquire what time in the night the powder convoy left Appleby Hundred, and if Gilbert Stair's York District guests had traveled with it. To these askings Yeates made answer that Falconnet and his troop, with the Cherokee contingent, had taken the road at midnight, or thereabouts; and that the Witherbys, with Mistress Margery riding her own black mare, and her maid on a pillion behind a negro groom, had passed some two hours later.

This was as we had hoped it might be; but when Dick's satisfaction would have set itself in words, the old hunter made a sudden sign for silence and quickly flung himself full length to lay his ear to the ground. Whereat we all began likewise to listen, but I, for one, heard nothing till Yeates said: "A hoss; a-taking the back track like old Jehu the son of Nimshi was a-giving him the whip and spur," and then we all marked the distant drumming of hoofbeats.

The old borderer sprang afoot, kicked the fire into the stream, and caught up his rifle. "Let's be a-moving," he said. "We must make out to stop that there hoss-galloper at the ford and find out what-all he's a rip-snorting that-away for."

The road crossing of the stream was but a little way above our breakfast camp; and we were out of the thicket in time to see the horseman, a negro clinging with locked arms to the neck of his mount, come tearing down to the ford. At sight of us, or else because he would not take the water at full speed, the horse reared, pawed the air, and fell clumsily, carrying his skilless rider with him.

We picked the black up and soused him in the stream till he found his tongue; and the first wagging of that useful member gave us news to fire the blood in our veins—in Jennifer's and mine, at any rate.

"Yah!" he screamed, choking out the muddy creek water that had well-nigh strangled him. "Yah! red debbil Injins kill ebbery-body and tote off Mistis Marg'y and dat Jeanne 'ooman! Dat's what dey done!"

CHAPTER XX

IN WHICH WE STRIVE AS MEN TO RUN A RACE

It was some time before the affrighted black could give us any connected account of what had befallen; and when at length the story was told, all save the principal fact of the carrying off of Mistress Margery and her maid was hazy enough.

Pruned down to the simple statement of the fact, and with all the foolish terror chatterings weeded out, his news came to this: the party of homing revelers had been ambushed and waylaid at the fording of a creek some miles to the southward, and in the mellay the young mistress and her tire-woman had been captured.

So far as any actual witness of the eye went, the negro had seen nothing. There had been a volley fire from the thicket-belly of black darkness, a swarming attack to a chorus of Indian yells, shouts from the men, shrieks from the women, confusion worse confounded in which the newsbearer himself had been unhorsed and trodden under foot. After which he knew no more till some one—his master, as he thought—kicked him alive and bade him mount and ride post-haste on the backward track to Appleby Hundred, crying the news as he went that Mistress Margery Stair and her maid had been kidnapped by the Indians.

Pinned to the mark and questioned afresh, the slave could not affirm of his own knowledge that any one had been killed outright. Pinned again, it proved to be only a guess of his that the one who had given him his orders was his master. In the darkness and confusion he could make sure of nothing; had made sure of nothing save his own frenzy of terror and the wording of the message he carried.

When we had quizzed him empty we hoisted him upon his beast and sent him once more a-gallop on the road to Appleby Hundred. That done, a hurried council of war was held in which we four fell apart, three against one. Jennifer was for instant pursuit, afoot and at top speed; and Ephraim Yeates and the Catawba, abandoning their own emprise apparently without a second thought, sided indifferently with him. For my part, I was for going back to prepare in decent order for a campaign which should promise something more hopeful than the probability of speedy exhaustion, starvation and failure.

We grew hot upon it, Richard and I; he with a young lover's unrecking rashness, and I with an old campaigner's foresight to make me stubborn; and Ephraim Yeates and the Catawba drew aside and let us have it out. Dick argued angrily that time was the all-important item, and was not above taunting me bitterly, flinging the reproach of cold-blooded age in my face and swearing hotly that I knew not so much as the alphabet of love.

The taunts were passed in silence, since I would set them over against the irrevocable wrong I had done him, saying in my heart that nothing he could say or do should again tempt me to give place to the devil of jealous wrath.

But when he would give me space I set the hopelessness of pursuit, all unprepared as we were, in plainest speech. The chase might well be a long one, and we were but scantily armed and without provisions. The hunter's rifle must be our sole dependence for food, and in the summer heat we would be forced to kill daily. On the other hand, with horses, a bag of corn apiece, firearms and ammunition, we should be in some more hopeful case; and, notwithstanding the delay in starting, could make far better speed.

For all the good it did I might have spared my pains and saved my breath. Jennifer broke me in the midst, crying out that I was even now killing the precious minutes; and so our ill-starred venture had its launching in the frenzied haste that seldom makes for speed. One small concession I wrung out of his impatience—this with the help of Yeates and the Catawba. We went back to the breakfast camp, rekindled the fire, and cooked what we could keep and carry of the venison.

In spite of this delay it was yet early in the forenoon of that memorable Sunday, the twentieth of August, when we set our faces southward and took up the line of march to the ford of the ambushment. By now the sky was wholly overcast, and the wind was blowing fresher in the tree-tops; but though as yet the storm held off, the air was the cooler for the threatened rain and this was truly a blessing, since the old hunter put us keen upon our mettle to keep pace with him.

We marched in Indian file, Ephraim Yeates in the lead, Uncanoola at his heels, and the two of us heavier-footed ones bringing up the rear. Knowing the wooded wilderness by length and breadth, the old man held on through thick and thin, straight as an arrow to the mark; and so we had never a sight of the road again till we came out upon it suddenly at the ford of violence.

Here I should have been in despair for the lack of any intelligible hint to point the way; and I think not even Jennifer, with all his woodcraft, could have read the record of the onfall as Yeates and the Catawba did. But for all the overlapping tangle of moccasin and hoof prints neither of these men of the forest was at fault, though ten minutes later even their skill must have been baffled, inasmuch as the first few spitting raindrops were pattering in the tree-tops when we came upon the ground.

"That's jest about what I was most afeard of," said the borderer, with a hasty glance skyward. "Down on your hunkers, Chief, and help me read this sign afore the good Lord takes to sending His rain on the jest and the unjest," and therewith these two fell to quartering all the ground like trained dogs nosing for a scent.

We stood aside and watched them, Richard and I, realizing that we were of small account and should be until, perchance, it should come to the laying on of hearty blows. After the closest scrutiny, which took account of every broken twig and trampled blade of grass, this prolonged until the rain was falling smartly to wash out all the foot-prints in the dusty road, Yeates and the Indian gave over and came to join us under the sheltering branches of an oak.

"'Tis a mighty cur'is sign; most mighty cur'is," quoth the hunter, slinging the rain-drops from his fur cap and emptying the pan of his rifle, not upon the ground, as a soldier would, but saving every precious grain. "Ez I allow, I never heerd tell of any Injuns a-doing that-away afore; have you, Chief? hey?"

The Catawba's negative was his guttural "Wah," and Ephraim Yeates, having carefully restored the final grain of the priming to his powder-horn, proceeded to enlighten us at some length.

"Mighty cur'is, ez I was a-saying. Them Injuns fixed up an ambush*ment*, blazed in a volley at the clostest sort o' range, and followed it up with a tomahawk and knife rush,—lessen that there Afrikin was too plumb daddled to tell any truth, whatsomedever. And, spite of all this here rampaging, they never drawed a single drop o' blood in the whole enduring scrimmage! Mighty cur'is, that; ain't it, now? And that ain't all: some o' them same Injuns, or leastwise one of 'em, was a-wearing boots with spurs onto 'em. What say, Chief?"

Uncanoola held up all the fingers of one hand and two of the other. "Sebben Injun; one pale-face," he said, in confirmation.

I looked at Richard, and he gave me back the eyeshot, with a hearty curse to speed it.

"Falconnet!" said he, by way of tail-piece to the oath; and I nodded.

"'Twas that there same hoss-captain, sure enough, ez I reckon," drawled Yeates. "Maybe one o' you two can tell what-all he mought be a-driving at."

Jennifer shook his head, and I, too, was silent. 'Twas out of all reason to suppose that the baronet would resort to sheer violence and make a terrified captive of the woman he wanted to marry. It was a curious mystery, and the hunter's next word involved it still more.

"And yit that ain't all. Whilst some o' the Injuns was a-whooping it up acrost the creek, a-chasing the folks that was making tracks for their city o' refuge, t'others run the two gals off into the big woods at the side o' the road. Then Mister Hoss-Captain picks up the Afrikin, chucks him on a hoss and sends him a-kiting with his flea in his ear; after which he climbs *his* hoss and makes tracks hisself—not to ketch up with the gals, ez you mought reckon, but off yon way," pointing across the creek and down the road to the southward.

Jennifer heard him through, had him set it all out again in plainest fashion, and after all could only say: "You are sure you have the straight of it, Eph?"

The borderer appealed to Uncanoola. "Come, Chief; give us the wo'th of your jedgment. Has the old Gray Wolf gone stun-blind? or did he read them sign like they'd ort to be read?"

"Wah! the Gray Wolf has sharp eye—sharp nose—sharp tongue, sometime. Sign no can lie when he read 'um."

Jennifer turned to me. "What say you, Jack? 'Tis all far enough beyond me, I'll confess."

I was as much at sea touching the mystery as he was; yet the thing to do seemed plain enough.

"Never mind the baronet's mystery; 'tis Mistress Margery's hazard that concerns us," I would say. And then to Ephraim Yeates: "Will this rain kill the trail, think you?"

He shook his head dubiously. "I dunno for sartain; 'twill make a heap o' differ' if they was anyways anxious to hide it. Ez it starts out, with the women a-hossback, 'tis plain enough for a blind man to lift on the run."

"Then let us be at it," said I. "We can very well afford to let the mystery untangle itself as we go." And with this the pursuit began in relentless earnest.

The trail of the two horses ridden by Margery and her woman cut a right angle with the road, turning northwest along the left bank of the stream; and, despite the rain, which was now pouring steadily even in the thick wood, the hoof-prints were so plainly marked that we could follow at a smart dog-trot.

In this speeding the old hunter and the Indian easily out-wearied Jennifer and me. They both ran with a slow swinging leap, like the racking gait, half pace, half gallop, of a well-trained troop horse. Mile after mile they put behind them in these swinging bounds; and when, well on in the afternoon, we stopped to eat a snack of the cold meat and to slake our thirst at one of the many rain pools, I was fain to follow Jennifer's lead, throwing myself flat on the soaking mold to pant and gasp and pay off the arrears of breathlessness.

This breathing halt was of the briefest; but before the race began again, Ephraim Yeates took time to make a careful scrutiny of the trail, measuring the stride of the horses, and looking sharply on the briars for some bit of cloth or other token of assurance. When we came up with him he was mumbling to himself.

"Um-hm; jes' so. They was a-making tracks along hereaway, sartain, sure; larruping them hosses to a keen jump, lickity-split. Now, says I to myself, what's the tarnation hurry? Ain't they got all the time there is to get where they're a-going, immejitly, *if* not sooner?" Then he turned upon me. "Cap'n John, can't you and the youngster lay your heads side and side and make out what-all this here hoss-captain mought be up to? It do look like he had some sort o' hatchet to grind, a-sending that Afrikin back to raise a hue and cry, and then a-letting his Injuns leave a trail like this here that any tow-head boy from the settlemints could follow at a canter."

Richard said he could never guess the meaning of it all; and my mind was to the full as blank as his. I made sure some deep-laid plot was at the bottom of the mystery; but we had measured many weary miles in the wilderness, and the plotter's trap had been fairly baited, set and sprung, before the lightning flash of explication came to show us all its devilish ingenuity.

But now "Forward," was the word, and we fell in line again, and again the tireless running of the two guides stretched and held us on the rack of weariness. Happily for us two who were out of training, the rainy-day dusk came early; and though Yeates and the Indian, running now with their bodies bent double and their noses to the ground, held on long after Richard Jennifer and I were bat-blind for any seeing of the hoof-prints, the end came at length and we bivouacked as we were, fireless, and with the last of the cooked ration of deer's meat for a scanty supper.

After the meal, which was swallowed hastily in the silence of utter fatigue, we scooped a hollow in a last year's leaf bed and lay down to sleep, wet to the skin as any four half-drowned water rats, and to the full as miserable.

Fagged as I was, 'twas a long time before sleep came to make me forget; a weary interval fraught with dismal mental miseries to march step and step with the treadmill rackings of the aching muscles. What grievous hap had befallen my dear lady? and how much or how little was I to blame for this kidnapping of her by my relentless enemy? Was it a sharp foreboding of some such resort to savage violence that had tortured her into sending the appeal for help?

With this, I fell to dwelling afresh upon the wording of her message, hungering avidly for some hint to give me leave to claim it for my own. Though I made sure she did not love me,—had never loved me as other than a make-shift confidant, whose face and age would set him far beyond the pale of sentiment,—yet I had hoped this friendship-love would give her leave to call upon me in her hour of need.

Was I the one to whom her message had been sped? Suddenly I remembered what Richard had said; that the arrow was the Catawba's. If Uncanoola were the bearer of the parchment, he would surely know to whom he had been sent.

His burrow in the leaf bed chanced to be next to mine, and I could hear his steady breathing, light and long-drawn, like that of some wild creature—as, truly, he was—sleeping with all the senses alert to spring awake at a touch or the snapping of a twig. A word would arouse him, and a single question might resolve the doubt.

I thought of all this, and yet, when I would have wakened the Indian, a shaking ague-fit of poltroon cowardice gave me pause. For while the doubt remained there was a chance to hope that she had sent to me, making the little cry for help a token, not of love, perchance, but of some dawning of forgiveness for my desperate wronging of her. And in that hesitant moment it was borne in upon me that without this slender chance for hope I should go mad and become a wretched witling at a time when every faculty should be superhuman sharp and strong for spending in her service.

So I forebore to wake the Indian; and following out this thought of service fitness, would force myself to go to sleep and so to gather fresh strength for the new day's measure.

CHAPTER XXI

HOW WE KEPT LENTEN VIGILS IN TRINITYTIDE

'Twould weary you beyond the limit of good-nature were I to try to picture out at large the varied haps and hazards of our wanderings in the savage wilderness. For the actors in any play the trivial details have their place and meaning momentous enough, it may be; yet these are often wearisome to the box or stall yawning impatiently for the climax.

So, if you please, you are to conceive us four, the strangest ill-assorted company on the footstool, pushing on from day to day deeper and ever deeper into the pathless forest solitudes, yet always with the plain-marked trail to guide us.

At times the march measured a full day's length amid the columned aisles of the forest temple through lush green glades dank and steaming in the August heat, or over hillsides slippery with the fallen leaves of the pine-trees. Anon it traced the crooked windings of some brawling mountain stream through thicket tangles where, you would think, no woman-ridden horse could penetrate.

One day the sun would shine resplendent and all the columned distances would fill with soft suffusings of the gray and green and gold, with here and there a dusky flame where the sweet-gum heralded the autumn, whilst overhead the leafy arches were fine-lined traceries and arabesques against the blue. But in the night, mayhap, a dismal rain would come, chill with the breath of the nearing mountains; and then the trees turned into dripping sprinkling-pots to drench us where we lay, sodden already with the heaviness of exhaustion.

Since the hasting pursuit was a thing to tap the very fountain-head of fortitude and endurance, we fared on silent for the better part; and in a little time the hush of the solitudes laid fast hold of us, scanting us of speech and bidding us go softly. And after this the march became a soundless shadow-flitting, and we a straggling file of voiceless mechanisms wound up and set to measure off the miles till famine or exhaustion should thrust a finger in among the wheels and bid them stop forever.

This was the loom on which we wove the backward-reaching web of strenuous onpressing. But through that web the scarlet thread of famine shuttled in and out, and hunger came and marched with us till all the days and nights were filled with cravings, and we recked little of fair skies or dripping clouds, or aught besides save this ever-present specter of starvation.

You will not think it strange that I should have but dim and misty memories of this fainting time. Of all privations famine soonest blunts the senses, making a man oblivious of all save that which drives him onward. The happenings that I remember clearest are those which turned upon some temporary bridging of the hunger gulf. One was Yeates's killing of a milch doe which, with her fawn, ran across our path when we had fasted two whole days. By this, a capital crime in any hunter's code, you may guess how cruelly we were nipped in the hunger vise. Also, I remember this: as if to mock us all the glades and openings on the hillsides were thicketed with berry bushes, long past bearing. And, being too late for these, we were as much too early for the nuts of the hickory and chestnut and black walnut that pelted us in passing.

The doe's meat, coming at a time of sharpest need, set us two days farther on the march; and when that was spent or spoiled we did as we could, being never comfortably filled, I think, and oftener haggard and enfeebled for the want of food. Since we dared not stop to go aside for game, the Catawba would set overnight snares for rabbits; and for another shift we cut knobbed sticks for throwing and ran keen-eyed along the trace, alert to murder anything alive and fit to eat. In this haphazard hunting nothing ever fell to Jennifer's skilless clubbing, or to mine; but the old borderer and the Indian were better marksmen, and now and then some bird or squirrel or rabbit sitting on its form came to the pot, though never enough of all or any to more than sharpen the famine edge of hunger.

For all the sharp privations of the forced march there was no hint on any lip of turning back. With Margery's desperate need to key us to the unflinching pitch, Richard and I would go on while there was strength to set one foot before the other. But for the old borderer and the Indian there was no such bellows to blow the fire of perseverance. None the less, these two did more than second us; they set the strenuous pace and held us to it; the Catawba Spartan-proud and uncomplaining; the old hunter no whit less tireless and enduring. At this far-distant day I can close my eyes and see the gaunt, leather-clad figure of Ephraim Yeates, striding on always in the lead and ever pressing forward, tough, wiry and iron to endure, and yet withal so elastic that the shrewdest discouragement served only to make him rebound and strike the harder. Good stuff and true there was in that old man; and had Richard or I been less determined, his fine and noble heroism in a cause which was not his own would have shamed us into following where he led.

We had been ten days in this starving wilderness, driving onward at the pace that kills and making the most of every hour of daylight, before Yeates and the Indian began to give us hope that we were finally closing in upon our quarry.

The dragging length of the chase grew upon two conditions. From the beginning the kidnappers were able to increase their lead by stretching out the days and borrowing from the nights; also, they were doubtless well provisioned, and they had horses for the captives and their impedimenta. But as for us, we could follow only while the daylight let us see the trail; and though we ran well at first, the lack of proper food soon took toll of speed.

So now, though the hoof prints grew hourly fresher, and we were at last so close upon the heels of the kidnappers that their night camp-fires were scarcely cold when we came upon them, we ran no longer—could hardly keep a dogged foot-pace for the hunger pains that griped and bent us double.

The tenth day, as I well remember, was furnace-hot, as were all the fair-weather days of that never-to-be-forgotten summer, with a still air in the forest that hung thick and lifeless like the atmosphere of an oven; this though we were well among the mountains and rising higher with every added mile of westering.

The sun had passed the meridian, and we were toiling, sweaty-weak, up a rock-strewn mountain side, when a thing occurred to rouse us roughly from the famine stupor and set us watchfully alert. In the steepest part of the ascent where the wood, scanted of rooting ground by the thickly sown strewing of boulders, was open and free of undergrowth, Ephraim Yeates halted suddenly, signed to us with upflung hand, and dropped behind a tree as one shot; and in the same breath the Catawba, running at Yeates's heels, lurched aside and vanished as if the earth had gaped and swallowed him.

A moment later the twang of a bow-string buzzed upon the breathless noontide stillness, and Jennifer clutched and dragged me down in good time to let the arrow whistle harmless over us. Then, like a distorted echo of the buzzing bow-string, the sharp crack of the old borderer's rifle rang out smartly, setting the cliff-crowned mountain side all a-clamor with mocking repetitions.

"Missed him, slick and clean, by the eternal coon-skin!" growled the marksman, sitting up behind his tree to reload. "That there's what comes o' being so dad-blame' hongry that ye can't squinch fair atween the gun-sights. I reckon ez how ye'd better hunker down and lie clost, you two. 'Twouldn't s'prise me none if that redskin had a wheen more o' them sharp-p'inted sticks in his—The Lord be praised for all His marcies! the chief's got him!"

But Uncanoola had not. He came in presently, his black eyes snapping with disappointment, saying in answer to Yeates's question that the yell had been his own; that his tomahawk had sped no truer than the old borderer's bullet.

"Chelakee snake heap slick: heap quick dodge," was all we could get out of him; and when that was said he squatted calmly on a flat stone and fell to work grinding the nick out of the edge of the mis-sped hatchet.

This incident told us plainly enough that the kidnappers were now but a little way ahead, and that their rear-guard scouts were holding us well in hand. So from that on we went as men whose lives are held in pawn by a hidden foe, looking at every turn for an ambushment. Nevertheless, we were not waylaid again; and when at length the long hot afternoon drew to its close with the mountain of peril well behind us, we had neither seen nor heard aught else of the Cherokees.

That night we camped, fireless and foodless, on the banks of a swift-flowing stream in a valley between two great mountains. We reached this stream a little before dark, and since the trail led straight into the water, we would have put this obstacle behind us if we could. But though the little river was not above five or six poles in width it was exceeding swift and deep; so impassable, in truth, that we were moved to wonder how the captive party had made shift to cross.

We guessed at it a while, Richard and I, and then gave it up until we might have the help of better daylight. But the old borderer's curiosity was not so readily postponed. Cutting a slim pole from a sapling thicket, he waded in cautiously, anchoring himself by the drooping branches of the willows whilst he prodded and sounded and proved beyond a doubt that the current was over man-head deep, and far too rapid for swimming.

Satisfied of this, he came out, dripping, and with a monitory word to us to keep a sharp lookout, disappeared up-stream in the growing dusk, his long rifle at the trail, and his body bent to bring his keen old eyes the nearer to the ground.

CHAPTER XXII

HOW THE FATES GAVE LARGESS OF DESPAIR

Ephraim Yeates was gone a full hour. When he returned he gave us cause to wonder at his lack of caution, since he filled his earthen Indian pipe and coolly struck a light wherewith to fire it. But when the pipe was aglow he told us of his findings.

"'Twas about ez I reckoned; them varmints waded in the shallows a spell to throw us off, and then came out and forded higher up."

"That will be a shrewd guess of yours, I take it, Ephraim?" said I; for the night was black as Erebus.

"Ne'er a guess at all; I've had 'em fair at eyeholts," this as calmly as if we had not been for ten long days pinning our faith to an ill-defined trace of foot-prints. "Ez I was a-going on to say, they're incamped on t'other bank ruther eenside o' two sights and a horn-blow from this. I saw 'em and counted 'em: seven redskins and the two gals."

"Thank God!" says Richard, as fervently as if our rescue of the women were already a thing accomplished. Then he fell upon the scout with an eager question: "How does she look, Ephraim?—tell me how she looks!"

"Listen at him!" said the old man, cackling his dry little laugh. "How in tarnation am I going to know which 'she' he's a-stewing about? There's a pair of 'em, and they both look like wimmin ez have been dragged hilter-skilter through the big woods for some better 'n a week. Natheless, they're fitting to set up and take their nourishment, both on 'em. They was perching on a log afore the fire, with ever' last idintical one o' them redskins a-waiting on 'em like they was a couple of Injun queens. I reckon ez how the hoss-captain gave them varmints their orders, partic'lar."

Dick was upon his feet, lugging out the great broadsword.

"Show us the way, Eph Yeates!" he burst out impatiently. "We are wasting a deal of precious time!"

But the old man only puffed the more placidly at his pipe, making no move to head a sortie.

"Fair and easy, Cap'n Dick; fair and easy. There ain't no manner o' hurry, ez I allow. Whenst I've got to tussle with a wheen o' full redskins, and me with my stummick growed fast to my backbone, I jest ez soon wait till them same redskins are asleep. Bime-by they'll settle down for the night, and then we'll go up yonder and pizen 'em immejitly, *if* not sooner. But there ain't no kind o' use to spile it all by rampaging 'round too soon."

There was wisdom undeniable in this, and, accordingly, we waited, taking turns at the hunter's terrible pipe in lieu of supper, and laying our plan of attack. This last was simple enough, as our resources, or rather our lack of them, would make it. At midnight we would move upon the enemy, feeling our way along the river till we should discover the ford by which the captive party had crossed. The stream safely passed, we would deploy and surround the camp of the Indians, and at the signal, which was to be the report of Yeates's rifle, we were to close in and smite, giving no quarter.

The old borderer dwelt at length upon the need for this severity, saying that a single Cherokee escaping would bring the warriors of the Erati tribe down upon us to cut off all chance of our retreat with the women.

"Onless I'm mightily out o' my reckoning, this here spot we're a-setting on ain't more than a day's Injun-running from the Tuckasege Towns. With them gals to hender us we ain't a-going to be in no fettle for a skimper-scamper race with a fresh wheen o' the redskins. Therefore and wherefore, says I, make them chopping-knives o' your'n cut and come again, even to the dividing erpart of soul and marrer."

Dick laughed, and, speaking for both of us, said between his teeth that we were not like to be over-merciful.

But now the old wolf of the border gave us a glimpse of an unsuspected side of him, taking Jennifer sharply to task and reading him a homily on the sin of vengeance for vengeance's sake. In this harangue he evinced a most astonishing tongue-grasp of Scripture, and for a good half-hour the air was thick with texts. And to cap the climax, when the sermon paused he laid his pipe aside, doffed his cap, and went upon his knees to pour forth such a militant prayer as brought my father's stories of the grim old fighting Roundheads most vividly to mind.

Here, being as good a place as any, I may say frankly that I never fully understood this side of Ephraim Yeates. Like all the hardy borderers, he was a fighter by instinct and inclination; and I can bear him witness that when he smote the "Amalekites," as he would call them—red skin or red coat—he smote them hip and thigh, and was as ruthless as that British Captain Turnbull who slew the wounded. Yet withal, on the very edge of battle, or mayhap fair in the midst of it, he was like to fall upon his knees to pray most fervently; though, as I have hinted, his prayers were like his blows—of the biting sort, full of Scriptural anathema upon the enemy.

Richard Jennifer, carelessly profane as all men were in that most godless day, would say 'twas the old borderer's way of swearing; that since he left out the oaths in common speech,—as, truly, he did,—he would fetch up the arrears and wipe out the score in one fell blast upon his knees. Be this as it may, he was a good man and a true, as I have said; and his warlike supplication that our blades should be as the sword of the Lord and of Gideon in the coming onfall was no whit out of place.

It wanted yet a full hour of midnight when Richard began again to plead piteously for instant action. Yeates thought it still over-early; but when Jennifer pressed him hard the old borderer left the casting vote to me.

"What say ye, Cap'n John? Your'n will be the next oldest head, and I reckon it hain't been turned plumb foolish rampaging crazy by this here purty gal o' Gilbert Stair's."

Now you have read thus far in my poor tale to little purpose if you have not yet discovered the major weakness of an old campaigner, which is to weigh and measure all the chances, holding it to the full as culpable to strike too soon as too late. This weakness was mine, and in that evil moment I gave my vote for further waiting, arguing sapiently that my old field-marshal would never set a night assault afoot till well on toward the dawn.

Jennifer heard me through and yielded, perforce, though with little good-will.

"I can not compass it alone, or, by the gods, I'd go!" he asserted, angrily. "Mark you, John Ireton, this delay is a thing you'll rue whilst you live. Your cold-cut pros and cons mouth well enough, and I'm no soldier-lawyer to argue them down. But something better than your damnable reasons tells me that the hour has struck—that these very present seconds are priceless." Whereupon he flung himself face down in the grass and would not speak again until the waiting time was fully over and Yeates gave the word to fall in line for the advance.

Having learned the lay of the land in his earlier reconnaissance, the old borderer shortened the distance for us by guiding us across the neck of a horseshoe bend in the stream; and a half-hour's blind groping through the forest fetched us out upon the river bank again, this time precisely opposite the Indians' lodge fire on the other side.

Here there was a little pause for three of us while Ephraim Yeates crept down the bank to try with his sounding-pole what chance we had of crossing.

Measured by what could be seen from our covert, the narrow width of quick water seemed the last of the many obstacles.

Lulled to security, as we guessed, by the apparent success of their ruse to throw us off the scent, six of the Cherokees were lying feet to fire like the spokes of a wheel for which the fitful blaze was the hub. The seventh man was squatted before a small tepee-lodge of dressed skins, which, as we took it, would be the sleeping quarters of the captives. Whilst all the others lay stiff and stark as if wrapped in soundest sleep, this sentry guard, too, it seemed, was scarcely more than half awake, for as we looked, his gun was slipping from the hollow of his arm and he was nodding to forgetfulness.

Richard was a-crouch beside me in this peeping reconnaissance, and I could feel him trembling in impatient eagerness.

"It should be easy enough—what think you?" he whispered; and then, with a sudden grasp upon my wrist: "You are cool and steady-nerved, John Ireton; I swear you do not love her as I do!"

"Nay, I grant you that, Dick," said I, making sure that his excitement would obscure the double meaning in the admission. And then I added, sincerely enough: "She has never given me the right to love her at all."

"God help her at this pass!" he said, more to himself than to me; and then he would go in a breath from blessing Margery to cursing Ephraim Yeates for this fresh delay.

It was Uncanoola who broke in upon the muttered malediction.

"Wah! Captain Jennif' cuss plenty heap, like missionary medicine-man. Look-see! Uncanoola no can find white squaw horse yonder. Mebbe Captain Jennif' see 'um, hey?"

At his word we both looked for the horses, marking now that they were nowhere to be seen within the circle lighted by the lodge fire. The Catawba grunted his doubt that the enemy was as in alert as he appeared to be; then he set the doubt in words. "Chelakee heap slick. Sleep only one eye, mebbe, hey? Injun warrior no hide horse and go sleep *both* eye on war-path!"

Here our scout came gliding back, so noiselessly that he was within arm's reach before we heard him. Dick had said I was over-cool, but the old man's ghostlike reappearance gave me such a start as made me prinkle to my fingers' ends.

"How will it be, Eph?" Dick queried, hotly eager to be at work. "We can make it across? Never say we can't pass that bit of still water, man!"

But Ephraim Yeates did say so in set terms.

"I reckon ez how we've got to cross, but not jest here-away, Cap'n Dick. She ain't making any fuss about it, but she's a-slipping along like greased lightning, deep and mighty powerful. I ain't saying we mought n't swim her and come out somewheres this side o' Dan'l Boone's country; but we'll make it a heap quicker by projec'ing 'round till we find the ford where them varmints made out to cross."

"God!" said Dick, deep in his throat; "more time to be killed! By—"

The old man was parting the bushes to have a better sight of the encampment opposite, but at Dick's outbreak he fell back quickly and clapped a hand on the lips of cursing.

"Hist! Lookee over yonder, will ye!" he cut in. And then in a whisper meant for no ear but mine: "The Lord be marciful to that little gal, Cap'n John; we've fooled our chance away—the game's afoot, and we ain't in it!"

I looked and saw nothing save that the sentry guard had risen to throw a handful of dry branches on the dying fire. But on the instant the dry wood blazed up, and in the wider circle of firelight I saw what the keener eyes of Ephraim Yeates had descried the sooner. In the shadowy background of the surrounding forest a dozen horsemen were converging in orderly array upon the encampment, and at the blazing up of the dry branches their leader gave the command to charge.

What sham battle there was, or was meant to be, was over in the briefest space. The troopers galloped in with shouts and aimless pistolings, raising a clamor that was instantly doubled by the yells of the Indians. As for resistance, the charging troop met with nothing worse than the yellings and a scattering fusillade in air. Then the ring of horsemen narrowed in to closer quarters and there was some flashing of bare steel in the firelight, at which the Cherokee kidnappers melted away and vanished as if by magic.

With the shouts and the firing Margery and her maid had burst out of the sleeping-lodge to find themselves in the thick of the sham battle; and it was but womanlike that they should add their shrieks to the din, being as well terrified as they had a right to be. But now the leader of the attacking troop speedily brought order with a word of command; and when his men fell back to post themselves as vedettes among the trees, the officer dismounted to uncover courteously and to bow low to the lady.

"The hoss-captain!" muttered Ephraim Yeates, under his breath; but we did not need his word for it. 'Twas but a child's pebble-toss across the barrier stream, and we could both see and hear.

"I give you joy of your escape, Mistress Margery," said the baronet, mouthing his words like a player who had long since conned his lines and got them well by heart and letter-perfect. "These slippery savages have given us a pretty chase, I do assure you. But you are trembling yet, calm yourself, dear lady; you are quite safe now."

I was watching her intently as he spoke. 'Twas now hard upon two months since I had seen her last in that fateful upper room at Appleby Hundred, and the interval—or mayhap it was only the hardships and distresses of the captive flight—had changed her woefully. Yet now, as when we had stood together at the bar of Colonel Tarleton's court, I saw her pass from mood to mood in the turning of a leaf, her natural terror slipping from her like a cast-off garment, and a sweet dignity coming to clothe her in a queenlier robe, making her, as I would think, more beautiful than ever.

"I thank you, Sir Francis—for myself and for poor Jeanne," she said. "You have come to take us back to my father?"

He bowed again and spread his hands as a friend willing but helpless.

"Upon my honor, my dear lady, nothing would give me greater pleasure. But what can I say? We are upon the king's business, as you well know, and our mission will not brook an hour's delay—indeed, we are here only by the good chance which led your captors to choose our route for theirs. I have no alternative but to take you and your woman with us to the west; but I do assure you—"

She stopped him with an impassioned gesture of dissent, and darting a despairing glance around that minded me of some poor hunted thing hopelessly enmeshed in the net of the fowler, she clasped her hands and wrung them, breaking down piteously at the last, and begging him by all that men hold sacred to send her and her maid back to her father, if only with a single soldier for a guard.

'Twas then we had to drag my dear lad down and hold him fast, else he had flung himself into the torrent in some mad endeavor to spend his life for her. So I know not in what false phrase the baronet refused her, but when I looked again she was no longer pleading as his suppliant; she was standing before him in the martyr steadfastness of a true, clean-hearted woman at bay.

"Then you will not by so much undo the wrong you have done me, Captain Falconnet?" she said.

"A wrong? How then; do you call it a wrong to rescue you from these brutal savages, Mistress Margery?"

She took a step nearer, and though the dry-stick blaze was dying down and I could no longer see her face distinctly, I knew well how the scornful eyes were whipping him.

"Listen!" she said. "When you set Tallachama and his braves upon us in the road that night, you were not cautious enough, Captain Falconnet. I saw and heard you. More than that, Tallachama and the others have spoken freely of your plans in their own tongue, not knowing that my poor Jeanne had been three years a captive among the Telliquos."

The attack was so sudden-sharp and so completely a surprise that he was taken off his guard, else I made sure he would not at such a time have dropped the gentlemanly mask to stand forth the confessed ravisher.

"So ho? Then you have been playing fast and loose with me as you did with the handsome young planter and that beggarly captain of Austrians? 'Twas a bold game, *ma petite*, but you have lost and I have won, for my game was still bolder than yours. What I need, I take, Mistress Madge, be it the body of a woman or the life of a man. *Savez-vous un homme désespéré, ma chérie?* I am that man. You pique me, and I need the dowry you will bring. If I could have killed your lover out of hand, I might have been content to leave you for a time. Since I could not, you go where I go; and when we return I shall do you the honor to make you Lady Falconnet!"

The effect of this fierce tirade, poured out in a torrent of hot words, was less marked upon his helpless captive than it was upon her four would-be defenders. It moved us variously, each after his kind; nevertheless, I think the same thought lighted instantly upon each of us. Though we might not reach and rescue her, her sharpest peril would be blunted upon the quieting of this fiend-in-chief.

So Ephraim Yeates stretched himself face downward in the damp grass and brought his long rifle to bear, while the Indian sprang up and poised his hatchet for the throw; but neither lead nor steel was loosed because the light was poor, and a hair's-breadth swerving of the aim might spare the man and slay the woman. As for the two of us who must needs come within stabbing distance, the same thought set us both to stripping coats and foot-clogs for a plunge into the barrier torrent. But when we would have broken cover, the old borderer dropped his weapon and gripped us with a hand for each.

"No, no; none o' that!" he whispered, hoarsely. "Ye'd drown like rats, and we can't afford no sech foolish sakerfices on the altar o' Baal. Hunker down and lie clost; if there's any dying to be done, ye've got a good half o' the night ahead of ye, and there's all o' to-morrow that ain't teched yet."

It takes a pitiless avalanche of words to spread these interlinear doings out for you; but you are to conceive that the pause is mine and not the action's. While the old man was yet pulling us down, my fearless little lady had drawn back a pace and was giving the villain his answer.

"I am glad I know you now for what you are, Captain Fal-connet," she said, coldly. And then: "You can take me with you, if you choose, having the brute strength to make good so much of your threat. But that is all. You can not take for yourself what I have given to another."

"Can not, you say?" He clapped his hat on smartly and whistled for his horse-holder; and when the man was gone to fetch the mounts for the women, he finished out the sentence. "Listen you, in your turn, Mistress Spitfire. I shall take what I list, and before you see your father's house again, you'll beg me on your knees, as other women have, to marry you for very shame's sake!"

It was then that Uncanoola did the skilfulest bit of jugglery it has ever been my lot to witness. Posturing like one of those old Grecian discus-throwers, he sent his scalping-knife handle foremost to glide snake-like through the grass to stop at Margery's feet. Though I think she knew not how it got there, she saw it, and the courage of the sight helped her to say, quickly:

"When it comes to that, sir, I shall know how to keep faith with honor."

His laugh was the harshest mockery of mirth. "You will keep faith with me, dear lady; do you hear? Otherwise—"

He turned to take the black mare from his man. At this my brave one set her foot upon the weapon in the grass.

"I have no faith to keep with you, Captain Falconnet," she said.

He struck back viciously. "Then, by heaven, you'd best make the occasion. It has happened, ere this, that a lady as dainty as you are has become a plaything for an Indian camp. It lies with me to save you from that, my Mistress."

She stooped to gather her skirts for mounting, and in the act secured and hid the knife. So her answer had in it the fine steadfastness of one who may make desperate terms with death for honor's sake.

"I thank you for the warning, Captain Falconnet," she said, facing him bravely to the last. "When the time comes, mayhap the dear God will give me leave to die as my mother's daughter should."

"Bah!" said he; and with that he whistled for his troopers; and while we looked, my dear lady and her tirewoman were helped upon their horses, and at the leader's word of command the escort formed upon the captives as a center. A moment later the little glade, with the smoldering embers of the lodge fire to prick out its limits in dusky red, was empty, and on the midnight stillness of the forest the minishing hoofbeats of the horses came fainter and fainter till the distance swallowed them.

Then it was that my poor lad, famine-mad and frenzied, rose up to curse me bitterly.

"Now may all the devils in hell drag you down to everlasting torments, John Ireton, for your cold-hearted caution that made us lose when we had good hope to win!" he cried. "One little hour I begged for, and that hour had fought her battle and set her free. But now—"

He broke off in the midst, choking with what miserable despair I knew, and shared as well; and throwing himself down in the wet grass, he would eke out the bitter words with such ravings and sobbings as bubble up in sheer abandonment of rage and misery.

CHAPTER XXIII

HOW WE KEPT THE FEAST OF BITTER HERBS

You may be sure that Richard Jennifer's bitter reproachings came home to me in sharpest fashion, the more since now I saw how we had lost our chance by neglecting the commonest precautions. Having determined to attack, the merest novice of a general would have moved his forces to the nearest point; would have had his scouts search out the ford beforehand; and, above all, would never have delayed the blow beyond the earliest moment of the enemy's unwatchfulness.

So now, when all was lost, I fell to kneading out this sodden dough of afterwit with Ephraim Yeates; but when I sought to carry off the blame as mine by right, the old borderer would not give me leave.

"Fair and easy, Cap'n John; fair *and* easy," he protested. "Let's give that old sarpent, which is the devil and Satan, his dues. Ez I allow, there was the whole enduring passel of us to ricollact all them things. To be sure, we had our warnings, mistrusting all along that this here dad-blame' hoss-captain had his finger in the pie. But, lawzee! we had ne'er a man o' God 'mongst us to rise up and prophesy what was a-going to happen if we didn't get up and scratch gravel immejitly, *if* not sooner; though I won't deny that Cap'n Dick did try his hand that-away."

"True; and I would now we had listened to him," said I, gloomily enough. "We have lost our chance, and God knows if we shall ever have another. Falconnet must have half a hundred men, red and white, in the powder train; and by this time he has learned from the Indian who reconnoitered us on the mountain that we are within striking distance. With the enemy forewarned, as he is, we might as well try to cut the women out of my Lord Cornwallis's headquarters."

The old man chuckled his dry little laugh, though what food for merriment he could find in the hopeless prospect was more than I could understand.

"Ho! ho! Cap'n John; I reckon ez how ye're a-taking that word from yonder down-hearted boy of our'n. Wait a spell till ye're ez old ez I be; then you'll never say die till ye're plumb dead."

Now, truly, though I was dismally disheartened, I could reassure him on the point of perseverance. 'Tis an Ireton failing to lose heart and hope when the skies are dark; but this is counterbalanced in some of us by a certain quality of unreasoning persistence which will go on running long after the race is well lost. My father had this stubborn virtue to the full; and so had that old Ironside Ireton from whom we are descended.

"That's the kind o' talk!" was the old man's comment. "Now we'll set to work in sure-enough arnest. Ez I said a spell back, my stummick is crying cupboard till I can't make out to hear my brain a-sizzling. Maybe you took notice o' me a-praying down yonder that the good Lord'd vouchsafe to give us scalps *and* provender. For our onfaithfulness He's seed fit to withhold the one; but maybe we'll find a raven 'r two, or a widder's mite 'r meal-bar'l, somewheres in this howling wilderness, yit."

So saying, he summoned the Catawba with a low whistle, and when Uncanoola joined us, told him to stay with Jennifer whilst we should make another effort to find the ford.

"There's nobody like an Injun for a nuss when a man's chin-deep into trouble," quoth this wise old woodsman, when we were feeling our way cautiously along the margin of the swift little river. "If Cap'n Dick rips and tears and pulls the grass up by the roots, the chief'll only say, 'Wah!' If he sits up and cusses till he's black in the face, the chief'll say, 'Ugh!' And that's just about all a man hankers for when his sore's a-running in the night season, and all Thy waters have gone over his head. Selah!"

Now you are to remember the sky was overcast and the night was pitchy dark, and how the old borderer could read a sign of any sort was far beyond my comprehension. Yet when we had gone a scant half-mile along the river brink he stopped short, sniffed the air and stooped to feel and grope on the ground like a blind man seeking for something he had lost.

"Right about here-away is where they made out to cross," he announced; "the whole enduring passel of 'em, ez I reckon—our seven varmints and the hoss-captain's powder train. Give me the heft o' your shoulder till we take the water and projec' 'round a spell on t'other side."

We squared ourselves, wholly by the sense of touch, with the river's edge, locked arms for the better bracing against the swift current, and so essayed the ford. It was no more than thigh deep, and though the water lashed and foamed over the shoal like a torrent in flood, there was a clean bottom and good footing. Once safe across, we turned our faces down-stream, and in a little time came to the deserted glade with the embers of the kidnappers' fire glowing dully in the midst.

Here a sign of some later visitants than Falconnet's horsemen set us warily on our guard. The tepee-lodge of dressed skins, which had been left undisturbed by the sham rescuers, had vanished.

"Umph! The redskins have been back to make sure o' what they left behind," said Yeates, in a whisper. "I jing! that's jest the one thing I was a-hoping they'd forget to do. I reckon ez how that spiles our last living chance o' finding anything that mought help slack off on the belly-pinch."

So he said, but for this once his wisdom was at fault and tricky fortune favored us. When we had found the covert in the bushes where the two horses had been concealed we lighted upon a precious prize. 'Twas a bag of parched corn in the grain; some share of the provision of the captive party overlooked by those who had returned to gather up the leavings.

With this treasure-trove we made all haste to rejoin our companions. And now behold what a miracle of reanimation may be wrought by a few handfuls of bread grain! In a trice the Catawba had found a water-worn stone to serve for a mortar, and another for a pestle. These and the bag of corn were carried back to a sheltered ravine which we had crossed on our late advance; and here the Indian fell to work to grind the corn into coarse meal, whilst Yeates and I kindled a fire to heat the baking-stones.

In these preparations for the breaking of our long fast even Richard bestirred himself to help; and when the cakes were baked and eaten—with what zestful sharp-sauce of appetite none but the famished may ever know—we were all in better heart, and better able to face the new and far more desperate plight in which our lack of common foresight had entangled us.

For now, since we knew the full measure of the peril menacing our dear lady, there was need for swift determination and a blow as swift and sure; a *coup de main* which should atone in one shrewd push for the sleeveless failure of the night. So we would grip hands around, even to the stolid Indian, and swear a solemn oath to cut the women out or else to leave our bones to whiten in the forest wilderness.

You'll laugh at all these vowings and handstrikings, I dare say, and protest there was a deal of such fustian heroics in your doddering old chronicler's day.

Mayhap there was. But, my dears, I would you might remember as you laugh that we of that simple-hearted elder time lived by some half-century nearer to that age of chivalry you dote on—in the story-books. Also, I would you might mingle with your merriment a little of the saving grace of charity; letting it hint that, perchance, these you call "heroics" were but the free, untrammeled folk-speech of that sincerer natural heart which you have learned to silence and suppress. For I dare affirm that now, as then and always, there will be some spark of the Promethean fire in every heart of man or maid, else this would indeed be a sorry world to live in.

So, as I say, we four struck hands anew on the desperate venture; and, after carefully burying the fire to the end that it might not betray us while we slept, we burrowed in the nearest leaf bed to snatch an hour or two of rest before the toils and hazards of the chase should begin afresh.

In the thick darkness following hard upon the douting of the fire, I saw not who my nearest bed-fellow might be. But ere I slept a hand was laid on my shoulder, and a voice that I knew well, said: "Are you waking yet, Jack?"

I said I was; and at that my poor lad would blurt out all his sorrow and shame for the mad fit of despair that had set him on to rail and curse me.

"You will say with good reason that I am but a sorry jockey for a friend—to fly out at you like a madman as I did," he added, by way of fitting epilogue; and to this I gave him the answer he wished, bidding him never let a thought of it spoil him of the rest he needed.

"The debt of obligation and forgiveness is all upon the other side, as you will some day know, Dick, my lad," said I, hovering, as a coward always will, upon the innuendo-edge of the confession he will never make.

He mistook the pointing of this protest, as he was bound to.

"Never say that, Jack. 'Twould be a dog-in-the-manger trick in me to blame you for loving her. And since you speak of debts, I do protest I owe you somewhat, too. With so fair a chance to cut a clean swath in that fair-weather month at Appleby Hundred, another man would have left me scant gleanings in the field, I'll be bound; whereas—"

"Damn you!" I broke in roughly, "will you never have done and go to sleep?" And so, taking surly harshness for a mask when my heart was nigh bursting with shame and grief, I turned my back and cut him off.

CHAPTER XXIV

HOW WE FOUND THE SUNKEN VALLEY

Looking back upon the hazards and chance-takings of our adventure in the wilderness, I recall no more promising risk than that we ran by sleeping unsentried within rifle-shot, for aught we knew, of the camp of the enemy.

But touching this, 'tis only on the mimic stage of the romances that the players rise to the plane of superhuman sagacity and angel-wit, never faltering in their lines nor betraying by slip or tongue-trip their kinship with common humankind. Being mere mortals we were not so endowed; we were but four outwearied men, well spent in the long chase, with never a leg among us fit to pace a sentry beat nor a decent wakeful eye to keep it company. So, as I have said, we took the risk and slept; would have slept as soundly, I dare say, had the risk been twice as great.

We were astir at the earliest graying of the dawn, Richard and I, and were the laggards of the company at that, since the old hunter was already out and away, and the Indian had kindled a fire and was grinding more of the parched corn for the morning meal. Dick sat up in his leaf litter, yawning like a sleepy giant.

"Lord, Jack," said he; "if ever we win out of this coil with a full day to spare, I mean to sleep the clock hands twice around at a stretch, I promise you. 'Twas but a catch, this cat-nap; no more than enough to leave a bad taste in the mouth."

"Aye; but the taste may be washed out," said I. "I am for a dip in the river; what say you?"

He took me at the word, and we had an eye-opening plunge in the spring-cold flood of the swift little river at the mouth of our ravine. 'Twas most marvelous refreshing; and with appetites sharp set and whetted by the stripping and plunging we were back at the fire in time to give good day to Ephraim Yeates, at that moment returned with the hindquarters of a fine yearling buck, fresh-killed, across his shoulders.

Seeing the deer's meat, we would think the old hunter's thrift of the dawn sufficiently accounted for; but when the cuts were a-broil, we were made to know that the buck was merely a lucky incident in the early morning scouting.

Taking time by the forelock, the old borderer had swept a circle of reconnaissance around our halting place, "to get the p'ints of the compass," as he would say. His first discovery was that the ford we had found in the darkness served as the river crossing of an ancient and well-used Indian trace. Along this trace from the eastward the powder train had come, no longer ago than mid-afternoon of yesterday; and arguing from this that the night camp of the band would be but a short march to the westward, Yeates had pushed on to feel out the enemy's position.

For a mile or more beyond the ford he had trailed the convoy easily. The Indian trace or path, well-trampled by the numerous horses of the cavalcade, followed the up-stream windings of the swift river straight into the eye of the western mountains. But in the eye itself, a rocky defile where the slopes on each hand became frowning battlements to narrow valley and stream, the one to a darkling gorge, the other to a thundering torrent, the trail was lost as completely as if the powder convoy had vanished into thin air.

Here was a fresh complication, and one that called for instant action. We had counted upon a battle royal in any attempt to rescue the women; but that Falconnet, impeded as he was by the slow movements of the powder cargo, could slip away, was a contingency for which we were wholly unprepared.

So, as you would guess, the hunter breakfast was hurriedly despatched; and by the time the sun was shoulder high over the eastern hills we had broken camp and crossed the river, and were pressing forward to the gorge of disappearance.

On each hand the mountains rose precipitous, the one on the left swelling unbroken to a bald and rounded summit, forest covered save for its tonsured head high in air, while that on the right was steeper and lower, with a line of cliffs at the top. As we fared on, the valley narrowed to a mere chasm, with the river thundering along the base of the tonsured mountain, and the Indian path hugging the cliff on the right.

In the gloomiest depths of this defile we came upon the hunter's stumbling-block. A tributary stream, issuing from a low cavern in the right-hand cliff, crossed the Indian path and the chasm at a bound and plunged noisily into the flood of the larger river. On the hither side of this barrier stream the trail of the powder convoy led plainly down into the water; and, so far as one might see, that was the end of it.

As we made sure, we left no stone unturned in the effort to solve the mystery. No horse, ridden or led, could have lived to cross the pouring torrent of the main river, or to wade up or down its bed; and if the cavalcade had turned up the barrier stream its progress must have ended abruptly against the sheer wall of the cliff at the entrance to the low-arched cavern whence the tributary came into being. But if Falconnet and his following had ridden neither up nor down the bed of the barrier stream, it seemed equally certain that no horse of the troop had crossed it. The Indian trace, which held straight on up the gorge and presently came out above into a high upland valley, was unmarked by any hoof print, new or old.

"Well, now; I'll be daddled if this here ain't about the beatin'est thing I ever chugged up ag'inst," was the old borderer's comment, when we had flogged our wits to small purpose in the search for some clue to the mystery. "What's your mind about it, hey, Chief?"

Uncanoola shook his head. "Heap plenty slick. No go up-stream, no go down, no cross over, no go back. Mebbe go up like smoke—w'at?"

The hunter shook his head and would by no means admit the alternative. "Ez I allow, that would ax for a merricle; and I reckon ez how when the good Lord sends a chariot o' fire after sech a clanjamfrey as this'n o' the hoss-captain's, it'll be mighty dad-blame' apt to go down 'stead of up."

We were standing on the brink of the barrier stream no more than a fisherman's cast from the black rock-mouth that spewed it up from its underground maw. While the hunter was speaking, the Catawba had lapsed into statue-like listlessness, his gaze fixed upon the eddying flood which held the secret of the vanished cav-alcade. Suddenly he came alive with a bound and made a quick dash into the water. What he retrieved was only a small piece of wood, charred at one end. But Ephraim Yeates caught at it eagerly.

"Now the Lord be praised for all His marcies!" he exclaimed. "It do take an Injun to come a-running whenst ever'body else is plumb beat out! Ne'er another one of us had an eye sharp enough to ketch that bit o' sign a-floating past. What say, Cap'n John?"

I shook my head, seeing no special significance in the token; and Dick asked: "What will it be, Ephraim, now that it is caught?"

The old man looked his pity for our dullard wit, and then set a moiety of it in words.

"Well, well, now; I'm fair ashamed of ye! What all d'ye reckon blackened the end o' this bit o' pine-branch?"

"Why, fire," says Richard, beginning, as I did, to see some glimmering of light.

"In course. And it come from yonder, didn't it?" pointing to the cavern under the cliff. "More than that, 'twas cut wi' a hatchet—this fresh end of it—no longer ago than last night, at the furdest; the pitch that the fire fried out'n it is all soft and gummy, yit. Gentlemen all: whenst we find where this here creek comes out into daylight again we're a-going to find the hoss-captain and the whole enduring passel o' redskins and redcoats, immejitly, *if* not sooner!"

What comment this startling announcement would have evoked I know not, for at the moment of its utterance the Catawba went flat upon the ground, making most urgent signs for us to do likewise. What he had seen we all saw a flitting instant later; the painted face of a Cherokee warrior as a setting for a pair of fierce basilisk eyes peering out of the low-arched cavern whence the stream issued, an apparition looking for all the world like a dismembered head floating on the surface of the outgushing flood.

'Twas the old borderer who took the initiative in the swift retreat, and we followed his lead like well-drilled soldiers. A crook in the stream, and the thickset underwood, screened us for the moment from the basilisk eyes; and in a twinkling we had rolled one after another into the mimic torrent and were quickly swept down to its mouth.

Here death lay in wait for us in the mad plungings of the main river; but we made shift to catch at the overhanging branches of the willows in passing, to draw ourselves out, to scramble up the gorge and to gain a great boulder on the mountain side whence we could look down upon the scene of our late surprisal.

By this we saw, from the wings, as it were, the setting of the stage for a tragedy which might have been ours. One by one a score of heads with painted faces floated silently out of the spewing rock-mouth. One by one the glistening, bronze-red bodies appertaining thereto emerged from the water, each to take its place in an ambuscade enclosing the stream-crossing of the Indian path in a pocket-like line of crouching figures, with the mouth of the pocket open toward the lower valley.

Ephraim Yeates chuckled under his breath and smote softly upon his thigh.

"They tell ez how the good Lord has a mighty tender care for chillern and simples," he whispered. "Whenst we was a-coming a-rampaging up the trace a hour 'r two ago, I saw the moccasin track o' that there spy, and was too dad-blame' biggity in my own consate to ax what it mought mean."

"What spy?" says Dick, matching the hunter's low whisper.

"Why, the varmint that tracked me back from here 'twixt dawn and daybreak, *to* be sure. He waited till we broke camp and then took out up here ahead of us to tell his chief 'twas e'ena'most time to set the trap for three white simples and a red one. Friends, I'm a-telling ye plain that the sperrit's a-moving me mighty powerful to get down on my hunkers and—"

"For heaven's sake, don't do it here and now!" gasped Dick. "Let's get out of this spider's-web while we may."

The old hunter postponed his prayerful motion, most reluctantly, as it would seem, and led the way in a silent withdrawal from the dangerous neighborhood of the ambushment. When we had pushed on somewhat higher up the gorge and stood on the confines of the upland valley for which it served as the approach, there was a halt for a council of war.

Since it was now evident that the powder convoy was encamped in some hidden gorge or valley to which the cavern of the underground stream was one of the approaches, 'twas plain that we must climb to some height whence we could command a wider view.

We were all agreed that the cavern entrance could not have been used by the entire company: this though the conclusion left the vanishing trail an unsolved riddle. For if the women could have been dragged through the low-springing arch of the waterway, we knew the horses could not—to say nothing of the certain destruction of the powder cargo in such a passage.

So we addressed ourselves to the ascent of the northern mountain; though Richard and I would first beg a little space in which to drain the water from our boots, and to wring some pounds' weight of it from our clothes. That done, we fell in line once more; and being so fortunate as to hit upon a ravine which led to the cliff-crowned summit, the climb was shorn of half its toil and difficulty. Nevertheless, by the sun's height it was well on in the forenoon before we came out, perspiring, like sappers in a steam bath, upon the mountain top.

As Yeates had guessed, this northern mountain proved to be a lofty table-land. So far as could be seen, the summit was an undulating plain, less densely forested than the valley, but with a thick sprinkling of pines to make the still, hot air heavy with their resinous fragrance. As it chanced, our ravine of ascent headed well back from the cliff edge, so we must needs fetch a compass through the pine groves before we could win out to any commanding point of view.

The old borderer took his bearings by the sun and laid the course quartering to bring us out as near as might be on the heights above the gorge. But when we had gone a little way, a thinning of the wood ahead warned us that we were approaching some nearer break in the table-land.

Five minutes later we four stood on the brink of a precipice, looking abroad upon one of nature's most singular caprices. Conceive if you can a segment of the table-land, in shape like a broad-bilged man o' war, sunk to a depth of, mayhap, six or seven hundred feet below the general level of the plateau. Give this ship-shaped chasm a longer dimension of two miles or more, and a breadth of somewhat less than half its length; bound it with a wall-like line of cliffs falling sheer to steep, forested slopes below; prick out a silver ribbon of a stream winding through grassy savannas and well-set groves of lordly trees from end to end of the sunken valley; and you will have some picture of the scene we looked upon.

But what concerned us most was a sight to make us crouch quickly lest sharp eyes below should descry us on the sky-line of the cliff. Pitched on one of the grassy savannas by the stream, so fairly beneath us that the smallest cannon planted on our cliff could have dropped a shot into it, was the camp of the powder train.

CHAPTER XXV

HOW UNCANOOLA TRAPPED THE GREAT BEAR

'Twas Richard Jennifer who first broke the noontide silence of the mountain top, voicing the query which was thrusting sharp at all of us.

"Now how in the name of all the fiends did they make shift to burrow from yonder bag-bottom into this?" he would say.

"Ez I allow, that's jest what the good Lord fotched us here for—to find out," was Yeates's rejoinder. "Do you and the chief, Cap'n John, circumambylate this here pitfall yon way, whilst Cap'n Dick and I go t'other way 'round. By time we've made the circuit and j'ined company again, I reckon we'll know for sartain whether 'r no they climm' the mounting to get in."

So when we had breathed us a little the circuiting was begun, Ephraim Yeates and Jennifer going toward the lower end of the sink, and the Catawba and I in the opposite direction.

Since we must examine closely every rift and crevice in the boundary cliff, it was a most tedious undertaking; and I do remember how my great trooper boots, sun-drying on my feet, made every step a wincing agony. They say an army goes upon its belly, but an old campaigner will tell you that you can march a soldier till he be too thin to cast a shadow if only he hath ease of his footgear.

Taking it all in all, it proved a slow business, this looping of the sunken valley; and when we had worked around to the eastern cliff and to a meeting point with the old hunter and Richard Jennifer, the sun was level in our faces and the day was waning.

Coming together again, we made haste to compare notes. There was little enough to add to the common fund of information, and the mystery of the lost trail remained a mystery. True, we, the Indian and I, had found a ravine at the extreme upper end of the valley through which, we thought, a sure-footed horse might be led at a pinch, up or down; but this ravine had not been used by the powder train, and apart from it there was no practicable horse path leading down from the plateau.

As for the hunter and Richard, they had made a discovery which might stand for what it was worth. At its lower extremity the sunken valley was separated from the great gorge without only by a ridge which was no more than a huge dam; and this diking ridge was evidently tunneled by the stream, since the latter had no visible outlet.

Inasmuch as the most favorable point of espial upon the camp below was the cliff whence we had first looked down into the sink, we harked back thither, passing around the lower end of the valley and along the barrier ridge. Plan we had none as yet, for the preliminary to any attempt at a rescue must be some better knowledge of the way into and out of Falconnet's cunningly chosen stronghold. True, we might win in and out again by the ravine which the chief and I had explored at the upper end, and Dick was for trying this when the night should give us the curtain of darkness for a shield. But the old hunter would hold this forlorn hope in reserve as a last resort.

"Sort it out for yourself, Cap'n Dick," he argued. "Whatsomedever we make out to do—four on us ag'inst that there whole enduring army o' their'n—has got to be done on the keen jump, with a toler'ble plain hoss-road for the skimper-scamper race when it *is* done. For, looking it up and down and side to side, we've got to have hosses—some o' their hosses, at that. I jing! if we could jest make out somehow 'r other to lay our claws on the beasteses aforehand—"

We had reached the cliff and were once more peering down at the enemy's camp. Though for the cliff-shadowed valley it was long past sunset and all the depths were blue and purple in the changing half-lights of the hour, the shadow veil was but a gauze of color, softening the details without obscuring them. So we could mark well the metes and bounds of the camp and prick in all the items.

The camp field was the largest of the savannas or natural clearings. On the margin of the stream the Indian lodges were pitched in a semicircle to face the water. Farther back, Falconnet's troop was hutted in rough-and-ready shelters made of pine boughs—these disposed to stand between the camp of the Cherokees and the tepee-lodge of the captive women which stood among the trees in that edge of the forest hemming the slope which buttressed our cliff of observation.

At first we sought in vain for the storing-place of the powder. It was the sharp eyes of the Catawba that finally descried it. A rude housing of pine boughs, like the huts of the troopers, had been built at the base of a great boulder on the opposite bank of the stream; and here was the lading of the powder train.

From what could be seen 'twas clear that the camp was no mere bivouac for the day; indeed, the Englishmen were still working upon their pine-bough shelters, building themselves in as if for a stay indefinite.

"'Tis a rest camp," quoth Dick; "though why they should

break the march here is more than I can guess."

"No," said Ephraim Yeates. "'Tain't jest rightly a rest camp, ez I take it. Ez I was a-saying last night, this here is Tuckasege country, and we ain't no furder than a day's running from the Cowee Towns. Now the Tuckaseges and the over-mounting Cherokees ain't always on the best o' tarms, and I was a wondering if the hoss-captain hadn't sot down here to wait whilst he could send a peace-offer' o' powder and lead on to the Cowee chiefs to sort o' smooth the way."

"No send him yet; going to send," was Uncanoola's amendment. "Look-see, Chelakee braves make haste for load horses down yonder now!"

Again the sharp eyes of the Catawba had come in play. At the foot of the great boulder some half dozen of the Cherokees were busy with the powder cargo, lashing pack-loads of it upon two horses. One of the group, who appeared to be directing the labor of the others, stood apart, holding the bridle reins of three other horses caparisoned as for a journey. When the loading was accomplished to the satisfaction of the horse-holding chieftain, he and two others mounted, took the burdened animals in tow, and the small cavalcade filed off down the stream toward the apparent *cul de sac* at the lower end of the valley.

Ephraim Yeates was up in a twinkling, dragging us back from the cliff edge.

"Up with ye!" he cried. "Now's our chance to kill two pa'tridges with one stone! If we can make out to get down into t'other valley in time to see how them varmints come out, we'll know the way in. More'n that, we can ambush 'em and so make sartain sure o' five o' the six hosses we're a-going to need, come night. But we've got to leg for it like Ahimaaz the son of Zadok!"

Thus the old borderer; and being only too eager to come to handgrips with the enemy, we were up and running faster than ever Joab's messenger ran, long before the old man finished with his Scriptural simile.

Not to take the risk of delay on any unexplored short cut, we made straight for the ravine of our ascent, found it as by unerring instinct, and were presently racing down to the Indian trace in the little upland valley above the gorge.

For all the helter-skelter haste I found time to remember that the gorge as we had last seen it had been well besprinkled with armed Cherokees lying in wait for us. If they were still there we should be like to have a hot welcome; and some reminder of this I gasped out to Yeates in mid flight.

"Ne'm mind that; if we run up ag'inst 'em anywhere, 'twon't

be there-away. They've took the hint and quit; scattered out to hunt us long ago," was his answer, jerked out between bounds. And after that I loosed the Ferara in its sheath and saved my breath as I might for the killing business of the moment.

'Twas a sharp disappointment that, for all the haste of our mad scramble down the mountain, we were too late to surprise the secret of the enemy's stronghold. The Catawba was leading when we dashed down into the valley, and one glance sent him flying back to stop us short with a dumb show purporting that the quarry was already out of the defile and coming up the Indian path.

Richard swore grievously, but the old backwoodsman took the checkmate placidly and began to set the pieces for the second game in which the horses were the stake, hiding his useless rifle in a hollow tree,—his powder had been soaked and spoiled in the early morning plunge for life,—and drawing his hunting-knife to feel its edge and point.

"Ez I allow, that fotches us to the hoss-lifting," he said, in his slow drawl. Then he laid his commands upon us. "Ord'ly, and in sojer-fashion, now; no whooping and yelling. If the hoss-captain's got scouts out a-s'arching for us, one good screech from these here varmints we're a-going to put out'n their mis'ry 'u'd fix our flints for kingdom come. I ain't none afeard o' your nerve,"—this to Richard and me—"leastwise, not when it comes to fair and square sojer-fighting. But this here cnfall has got to be like the smiting o' the 'Malekites—root *and* branch; and if ye're tempted to be anywise marciful, jest ricollect that for the sake o' them wimmen-folks *we've got to have these hosses!*"

You are not to suppose that he was holding us inactive while he thus exhorted us. On the contrary, he was posting us skilfully beside the trace like the shrewd old Indian fighter that he was, with a rare and practised eye to the maximum of cover with the minimum of thicket tangle to impede the rush or to shorten the sword-swing.

But when all was done we were at this disadvantage; that since the enemy was close at hand we dared not cross the path to give our trap a jaw on either side. To offset this, the Catawba dropped out of line and disappeared; and when the Cherokees were no more than a hundred yards away, Uncanoola came in sight a like distance in the opposite direction, running easily down the path to meet the up-coming riders.

Richard let slip an admiration-oath under his breath. "There's a fine bit of strategy for you!" he whispered. "That wily Jack-at-a-pinch of ours will befool them into believing that he is a runner from the Cowee Towns. 'Tis our cue to lie close; he will halt them just here, and there will be roving eyes in the heads of the two who have not to talk."

We had not long to wait. Our cunning ally timed his halting of the emissaries to a nicety, and when the three Cherokees drew rein they were within easy blade's reach. The powwow, lengthened by Uncanoola till we were near bursting with impatience, was spun out wordily, and presently we saw the pointing of it. The Catawba was affecting to doubt the protests of the emissaries and would have them dismount and prove their good faith by smoking the peace-pipe with him.

I give you fair warning, my dears, that you may turn the page here and skip what follows if you are fain to be tender-hearted on the score of these savage enemies of ours. It was in the very summer solstice of the year of violence; a time when he who took the sword was like to perish with the sword; and we thought of little save that Margery and her handmaiden were in deadliest peril, and that these Indians had five horses which we must have.

And as for my own part in the fray, when I recognized in the five-feathered chieftain of the three that copper-hued imp of Satan who had been the merciless master of ceremonies at the torturing of my poor black Tomas, the decent meed of mercy which even a seasoned soldier may cherish died within me, and I made sure the steel would find its mark.

So, when Uncanoola drew forth his tobacco pipe and made the three doomed ones sit with him in the path to smoke the peace-whiff all around, we picked out each his man and smote to slay. The scythe-like sweep of Jennifer's mighty claymore left the five-feathered chieftain the shorter by a head in the same pulse-beat that the Ferara scanted a second of the breath to yell with; though now I recall it, the gurgling death-cry of the poor wretch with the steel in his throat was more terrible to hear than any war-whoop. As for the old borderer, he was more deliberate. Being fair behind and within arm's reach of his man, he seized him by the scalp-lock, bent the head backward across his knee—but, faugh! these are the merest butcher details, and I would spare you—and myself, as well.

While yet this most merciless deed was a-doing, the Catawba bounded to his feet and made sure of the horses which were rearing and snorting with affright. That done, he must needs gloat, Indian-wise, over his fallen adversary, turning the headless body with his foot and gibing at it.

"Wah! Call hisself the Great Bear, hey? Heap lie; heap no bear; heap nothing, now. Papoose bear no let hisself be trap' that way.

No smoke peace-pipe—"

But now Ephraim Yeates, standing ear a-cock and motionless, like some grim old statue done in leather, cut him short with a sudden, "Hist, will ye!" and a twinkling instant later we had other work to do.

"Onto the hosses with this here Injun-meat, ez quick ez the loving Lord'll let ye!" was the sharp command. "There's a whole clanjamfrey o' the varmints a-coming down the trace, and I reckon ez how we'd better scratch gravel immejitly, *if* not sooner!"

CHAPTER XXVI

WE TAKE THE CHARRED STICK FOR A GUIDE

Luckily for us the new danger was approaching from the westward. So, by dint of the maddest hurryings we got the bodies of the three Cherokees hoist upon the horses, and were able to efface in part the signs of the late encounter before the band of riders coming down the Indian path was upon us. But there was no time to make an orderly retreat. At most we could only withdraw a little way into the wood, halting when we were well in cover, and hastily stripping coats and waistcoats to muffle the heads of the horses.

So you are to conceive us waiting with nerves upstrung, ready for fight or flight as the event should decide, stifling in such pent-up suspense as any or all of us would gladly have exchanged for the fiercest battle. Happily, the breath-scanting interval was short. From behind our thicket screen we presently saw a file of Indian horsemen riding at a leisurely footpace down the path. Ephraim Yeates quickly named these new-comers for us.

"'Tis about ez I allowed—some o' the Tuckaseges a-scouting down to hold a powwow with the hoss-captain. Now, then; if them sharp-nosed ponies o' their'n don't happen to sniff the blood—"

The hope was dashed on the instant by the sudden snorting and shying of two or three of the horses in passing, and we laid hold of our weapons, keying ourselves to the fighting pitch. But, curiously enough, the riders made no move to pry into the cause. So far from it, they flogged the shying ponies into line and rode on stolidly; and thus in a little time that danger was overpast and the evening silence of the mighty forest was ours to keep or break as we chose.

The old frontiersman was the first to speak.

"Well, friends, I reckon ez how we mought ez well thank the good Lord for all His marcies afore we go any furder," he would say; and he doffed his cap and did it forthwith.

It was as grim a picture as any limner of the weird could wish to look upon. The twilight shadows were empurpling the mountains and gathering in dusky pools here and there where the trees stood thickest in the valley. The hush of nature's mystic hour was abroad, and even the swiftly flowing river, rushing sullenly along its rocky bed no more than a stone's cast beyond the Indian path, seemed to pretermit its low thunderings. There was never a breath of air astir in all the wood, and the leaves of the silver poplar that will twinkle and ripple in the lightest zephyr hung stark and motionless.

Barring the old borderer, who had gone upon his knees, we stood as we were; the Catawba holding the pack horses, and Jennifer and I the three that bore the ghastly burdens of mortality. The bodies of the slain had been flung across the saddles to balance as they might; and to the pommel of that saddle which bore the trunk of the five-feathered chieftain, Uncanoola had knotted the grisly head by its scalp-lock to dangle and roll about with every restless movement of the horse—a hideous death-mask that seemed to mop and mow and stare fearsomely at us with its wide-open glassy eyes.

With this background fit for the staging of a scene in Dante Alighieri's tragic comedy, the looming mountains, the upper air graying on to dusk, and the solemn forest aisles full of lurking shadows, you are to picture the old frontiersman, bareheaded and on his knees, pouring forth his soul in all the sonorous phrase of Holy Writ, now in thanksgiving, and now in most terrible beseechings that all the vials of Heaven's wrath might be poured out upon our enemies.

His face, commonly a leather mask to hide the man behind it, was now ablaze with the fire of zealotry; and, truly, in these his spasm-fits of supplication he stood for all that is most awe-inspiring and unnerving, asking but a little stretch of the imagination to figure him as one of those old iron-hard prophets of denunciation come back to earth to be the herald of the wrath of God.

'Twas close upon actual nightfall when the old man rose from his knees and, with the rising, put off the beadsman and put on the shrewd old Indian fighter. Followed some hurried counselings as to how we should proceed, and in these the hunter set the pace for us as his age and vast experience in woodcraft gave him leave.

His plan had all the merit of simplicity. Now that we had the horses, Richard's notion of an approach from the head of the sunken valley became at once the most hopeful of any. So Ephraim Yeates proposed that we betake ourselves to the mountain top and to the head of that ravine which the Catawba and I had discovered. Here we should leave the horses well hidden and secured, make our way down the ravine, and, with the stream for a guide, follow the sunken valley to the camp at its lower end. Once on the ground without having given the alarm, we might hope to free the captives under cover of the darkness; and our retreat up the valley would be far less hazardous than any open flight by way of the unexplored road the powder train had used.

So said the old backwoodsman; but neither Dick nor I would agree to this *in toto*. Dick argued that while we were killing time in the roundabout advance we should be leaving Margery wholly at the mercy of the baronet, and that every hour of delay was full of hideous menace to her. Hence he proposed that three of us should carry out the hunter's plan, leaving the fourth to take the hint given by the charred stick and the swimming ambush crew, and so penetrating to the valley by the stream cavern, be at hand to strike a blow for our dear lady's honor in case of need.

"'Tis a thing to be done, and I am with you, Dick," said I. This before Ephraim Yeates could object. "Should there be need for any, two blades will be better than one. If it come to blows and we are killed or taken, Yeates and the chief must make the shift to do without our help."

As you would guess, the old hunter demurred to this halving of our slender force, but we over-persuaded him. If all went well, we were to rendezvous on the scene of action to carry out the plan of rescue. But if our adventure should prove disastrous, Yeates and Uncanoola were to bide their time, striking in when and how they might.

Touching this contingency, I drew the old man aside for a word in private.

"If aught befall us, Ephraim,—if we should be nabbed as we are like to be,—you are not to let any hope of helping us lessen by a feather's weight the rescue chance of the women. You'll promise me this?"

"Sartain sure; ye can rest easy on that, Cap'n John. But don't ye go for to let that rampaging boy of our'n upsot the fat in the fire with any o' his foolishness. He's love-sick, he is; and there ain't nothing in this world so ridic'lous foolish ez a love-sick boy— less'n 'tis a love-sick gal."

I promised on my part and so we went our separate ways in the gathering darkness; though not until the lashings of the packs had been cut and the powder and lead, save such spoil of both as Ephraim Yeates and Uncanoola would reserve, had been spilled into the river. As for the bodies of the dead Indians, the old hunter said he would let them ride till he should come to some convenient chasm for a sepulcher; but I mistrusted that he and the Catawba would scalp and leave them once we were safely out of sight.

At the parting we took the river's edge for it, Richard and I, keeping well under the bank and working our way cautiously down the gorge until we were stopped by the pouring cross-torrent of the underground tributary. Here we turned short to the left along the margin of the barrier stream, and tracing its course across the gorge came presently to the northern cliff at the lip of the spewing cavern mouth.

By now the night was fully come and in the wooded defile we could place ourselves only by the sense of touch.

"Are you ready, Dick?" said I.

"As ready as a man with a shaking ague can be," he gritted out. "This dog's work we have been doing of late has brought my old curse upon me and I am like to rattle my teeth loose."

"Let me go alone then. Another cold plunge may be the death of you."

"No," said he, stubbornly. "Wait but a minute and the fever will be on me; then I shall be fighting-fit for anything that comes."

So we waited, and I could hear his teeth clicking like castanets. Having had a tertian fever more than once in the Turkish campaigning, I had a fellow-feeling for the poor lad, knowing well how the thought of a plunge into cold water would make him shrink.

In a little time he felt for my hand and grasped it.

"I'm warm enough now, in all conscience," he said; and with that we slipped into the stream.

'Twas a disappointment of the grateful sort to find the water no more than mid-thigh deep. The current was swift and strong, but with the pebbly bottom to give good footing 'twas possible to stem it slowly. Laying hold of each other for the better breasting of the flood we felt our way warily to the middle of the pool; felt for the low-sprung cavern arch, and for that scanty lifting of it where we hoped to find head room between stone above and stream below.

We found the highest part of the arch after some blind groping, and making lowly obeisance to the gods of the underworld began a snail-like progress into the gurgling throat of the spewing rock-monster.

I here confess to you, my dears, that, had I loved my sweet lady less, no earthly power could have driven me into that dismal stifling place. All my life long I have had a most unspeakable horror of low-roofed caverns and squeezing passages that cramp a man for breath and for the room to draw it in; and when the suffocating madness came upon me, as it did when we were well jammed in this cursed horror-hole, I was right glad to have my love for Margery to make an outward-seeming man of me; glad, too, that my dear lad was close behind to shame me into going on.

Yet, after all, the passage through the throat of the rock dragon was vastly more terrifying than difficult. Once well within the closely drawn upper lip we could brace our backs against the roof and so have a purchase for the foothold. Better still, when we had passed a pike's-length beyond the lip the breathing space above the water grew wider and higher till at length we could stand erect and come abreast to lock arms and push on side by side.

From that the stream broadened and grew shallower with every step, and presently we could hear it on ahead babbling over the stones like any peaceful woodland brook. Then suddenly the dank and noisome air of the cavern gave place to the pine-scented breath of the forest; and, looking straight up, we could see the twinkling stars shining down upon us from a narrow breadth of sky.

CHAPTER XXVII

HOW A KING'S TROOPER BECAME A WASTREL

Dick pressed closer to me, and I could feel him drinking in deep drafts of the grateful outer air.

"What new wonder is this?" he would ask, with something akin to awe in his voice; but we must needs grope this way and that to feel out the answer with our finger-tips.

When the answer was found, the mystery of the lost trail was solved most simply. As we made out, we were in a deep crevice cut crosswise by the stream which, issuing from a yawning cavern in the farther wall, was quickly engulfed again by that lower archway we had just traversed. In some upheaval of the earthquake age a huge slice of the mountain's face had split off and settled away from the parent cliff to leave a deep cleft open to the sky. One end of this crevice chasm—that toward the upland valley—was choked and filled by the debris of later landslides; but the lower end was open.

Through this lower end, as we made no doubt, the powder train had come, turning from the Indian path in the gorge up the bed of the barrier stream, turning again at the outer cavern mouth to squeeze in single file between the thickly matted undergrowth and the cliff's face, and so to pass around the split-off mass and come into the crevice rift.

How the sharp eyes of the old hunter, and those of the Catawba as well, had missed the finding of this squeezing place where the cavalcade had left the stream-bed, we could never guess; but on the chance that we might yet need to know all the crooks and turnings of this outlet, we felt our way quite around the masking cliff and down to the stream's edge in the gorge.

That done we were ready for a farther advance, and clambering back into the crevice we once more took the stream for our guide and were presently deep in the natural tunnel piercing the mountain proper. This extension of the subterranean waterway proved to be a noble cavern, wide and high enough to pass a loaded wain, as we determined by tossing pebbles against the arching roof. None the less, 'twas full of crooks and windings; and in the sharpest elbow of them all, where we were like to lose our way by blundering into one of the many branching side passages, Richard stopped me with a hand thrust back.

"Softly!" he cautioned; "here are their vedettes!"

Just beyond the crooking elbow the dull red glow from a tiny fire gone to coals showed us two Indian sentries set to keep the pass. Dick drew his claymore, but he was chilling again and the hand that grasped the great blade was shaking as with a palsy. Yet he would mutter, as the teeth-chattering suffered him:

"What say you, Jack? Shall we rush them? There's naught else for it." And then, with a gritting oath: "Oh, damn this cursed chilling!"

I whispered back that we would wait till he was better fit. He was loath to admit the necessity, but, as it chanced, the momentary delay saved our lives in that strait. While we paused, hugging the shadows in the crooking elbow, the gloomy depths beyond the sentries were suddenly starred with flaring flambeaux lighting the way for a hasting rabble of savages; and had we been entangled in the struggle with the two sentinels we should have been taken red-handed.

As it was, we had to make the quickest play to save ourselves. In the same breath we both remembered the narrow side passage just behind in which we were nigh to losing our way, and into this we plunged, reckless of possible pitfalls. We were no more than safely out of the main corridor when the runners, some score of them, as we guessed, trooped past our covert in full cry, leaving us half smothered in the smoky trail of their pitch-pine flambeaux.

"Now what a-devil has set this hornet's nest of theirs abuzz so suddenly?" I whispered, when the smoke-choke gave us liberty to speak without coughing to betray ourselves.

"Our pony-riding Tuckaseges, doubtless," was Richard's ready answer. "By all the chances, they should have met the Great Bear and his peace-offering out yonder on the trace—which same they did not. So when they bring this tale to camp there is the devil to pay and no pitch hot. God help our tough old Ephraim and the Catawba if these bloodhounds win out in time to overtake them!"

"Aye," said I; and then we crept out of our dodge-hole and made ready to go about our business with the sentries.

But when we came to peer again around the crooking elbow it would seem that the hurrying search party had fought our battle for us. The watch-fire was there to light a little circle in the gloom, but the watchers were gone. We chanced a guess that they had joined the hue and cry, and so we pressed forward, past the handful of embers and into the pit-black depths beyond.

Twenty paces farther on it came to playing blind man's buff with the rocky walls again, and measured by the trippings and stumblings 'twas a long Sabbath day's journey to that final turn in the great earth-burrow whence we could see the glimmering of the enemy's camp-fires in the sunken valley.

"Now God be praised!" quoth Richard most fervently. "Another hour in this cursed kennel with the fever on me and I should be a yammering loose-wit." And I, too, was glad enough to see the stars again, and to be at large beneath them.

Emerging from the subterranean way, we held to the camp side of the stream, making an ample circuit to the left to come down upon the enemy's position from the wooded slope behind the encampment. We met no let or hindrance in this approach. Secure in their stronghold, the Indians had no patrols out; and as for the Englishmen, every mother's son of them, it seemed, was basking in the light of a great fire built before the pine-bough shelters.

Favored by a dense thicketing of laurel we made a near-hand reconnaissance of the little wigwam which held our dear lady. As I have said, this was pitched in the thinning of the forest which covered the steep slope behind the encampment, and so was the farthest removed from the stream, and from the Indian lodges disposed in a half-moon at the water's edge. Here all was quiet as the grave, and the clamor of the Indian camp came softened by the distance to a low monotonous humming like the buzzing of a bee-hive. The flap of the tepee-lodge was closely drawn, and the bit of fire before it had burned out to a heap of white-ashed embers.

"They are safe as yet, thank God!" says Richard, heaving a most palpable sigh of relief. Then, with the fever in his veins to whip his natural ardor into hasty action: "'Twill be hours before Eph and the Catawba can come in by your upper ravine, Jack, and we shall never have a better chance than this. Hold you quiet here, whilst I—"

But I laid fast hold of him and would not hear to any such a foolhardy marring of Ephraim Yeates's plan.

"Heavens, boy! are you gone clean mad?" I would say. "'Twill be risky enough with midnight in our favor; with the camp well asleep, and that great fire burned down to give us something less than broad daylight to work in!"

He turned upon me like a pettish child. "Oh, to the devil with your stumbling-blocks, John Ireton! You are always for holding back. By heaven! I'll swear you have no drop of lover's blood in your veins!"

"So you have said before. But let that pass, we must bide by our promise to Yeates, which was not to interfere unless Margery stood in present peril. Moreover, we should learn the lay of the land better while we have the firelight to help. When the time for action comes we must be able to make the play with our eyes shut, if need be. Come."

'Twas like pulling sound teeth to get him away, but he yielded at length and we crept on to have some better sight of the troop camp. We had it; had also a glimpse of the baronet-captain playing loo with his lieutenant and another. The tableau at the fire gave us better courage. The men had laid their arms aside and were sprawling at their ease; and while the arch scoundrel was in the gaming mood, Margery had less to fear from him.

I said as much to Dick, and for answer he pointed to the flask of usquebaugh which was at that moment making the round of the loo players.

"I know Frank Falconnet better than you do, Jack, for I have known him later. He is all kinds of a villain sober, but he is a fiend incarnate with the liquor in him. 'Tis lucky we are here. If he do but drink deep enough, Margery is like to have need—"

"Hist!" said I; "some of these lounging rascals may not be so drowsy as they look."

He nodded, and we backed away to make another circuit which fetched us out on the up-valley side of the encampment. Here we could look down into a smaller glade or bottom meadow on the stream where the horses of the band were cropping the lush grass. It was the sight of these, and of Margery's black mare among them, that set me thinking of a pickeering venture to the full as harebrained as that from which I had but now dissuaded Richard Jennifer.

"We shall need another mount, and Mistress Margery's saddle," I said. "Lie you close here whilst I play the horse-thief on these reavers."

But my dear lad was rash only for himself. "Now who is daft?" he retorted. "The Catawba himself could never run that gantlet and come through alive."

"Mayhap," I admitted. "But yet—"

He cut me off in the midst, winding an arm about my head by way of an extinguisher. One of the redcoat troopers lounging before the great fire had risen and was coming straight for our hiding place.

I saw not what to do; should have done nothing, I dare say, till the man had walked fair upon us. But Richard was quicker witted.

"Give me your sword!" he muttered; "mine will be too long to shorten upon," and when the Englishman's next stride would have kicked us out of hiding, Dick rose up before him like the devil in a play, gripped him by the collar and laid his sword's point at his throat.

"Follow me, step for step, or you are a dead man!" he commanded; and so, pacing backward, he led the fellow, with the hulking body of him for a shield and mask, out of the circle of fire-light and into the safer shadows of the forest.

When I had made a creeping detour to join him, he still had his man by the collar and was emphasizing the need for silence by sundry prickings with the Ferara.

"Say, quick! what to do with him, Jack?" he demanded, when I came up; and now my slower wit came into play.

"Out of this to some safer dressing-room, and I'll show you," said I; and forthwith we marched our prize up the valley a long musket-shot or more.

When the soldier had leave to speak he begged right lustily for his life, as you would guess; but we gave him a short shrift. If the plan I had in mind should have a fighting chance for success it must be set in train before this trooper should be missed.

So, having first gagged the poor devil with his own necker-chief, we stripped him quickly; and I as quickly donned the bor-rowed uniform and became, at least in outward semblance, a light-horse trooper of that king whose service I had once for-sworn. The items of small-clothes, waistcoat and head-gear fitted me passing well, but when it came to the boots we stuck fast, and I was forced to wear my own foot-coverings.

The change made,—and you may believe no play-house actor of them all ever doffed or donned a costume quicker,—we bound our luckless captive hand and foot, pinned him face downward in the sward, and so leaving him with only his boots for a mem-ento,—happily for him the night was no more than goose-flesh cool,—we raced back to our peeping-place on the skirting of the camp ground.

Here Dick wrung my hand, calling himself all the knaves unspeakable for letting me take a risk which he was pleased to call his own; and with that I stepped out into the firelight and was fair afoot in the enemy's camp.

CHAPTER XXVIII

IN WHICH I SADDLE THE BLACK MARE

Having so good a disguise, the thing I had set myself to do would seem to ask for little more than peaceful boldness held in check by common caution.

The point where I had broken cover to step into the circle of fire light was nearly equidistant from the Englishmen's camp on the right and the horse meadow on the left, so I had not to pass within recognition range of the great fire; indeed, I might have skulked in the laurel cover all the way, thus coming to the horses unseen by any, but that I was afraid Falconnet might miss his trooper. So I thought it best to show myself discreetly.

Copying our captive's lounging stride, I first held a sauntering course down to the stream's edge, keeping the great camp-fire and the droning Indian hive well to the right and far enough aloof to baffle any over-curious eye at either. Coming to the stream without mishap, I stopped and made a feint of drinking; after which I crossed and climbed slowly toward the makeshift powder magazine.

As I have said, the camp was pitched in a small savanna or natural clearing on the right bank of the little river. This clearing was hedged about by the forest on three sides, and backed by the densely wooded steeps and crags of the western cliff. I guessed the compass of it to be something more than an acre; not greatly more, since the fire at the troop camp lighted all its boundaries.

On the left or opposite bank of the stream there was no intervale at all. The ground rose sharply from the water's edge in a rough hillside thickly studded and bestrewn with boulders great and small; fallen cleavings and hewings from the crags of the eastern cliff. 'Twas at the foot of one of the boulders, a huge overhanging mass of weather-riven rock facing the camp, that the powder cargo was sheltered; so isolated to be out of danger from the camp-fires.

From the hillside just below this powder rock I could look back upon the camp *en enfilade*, as an artilleryman would say. Nearest at hand was the half-moon of Indian lodges with the hollow of the crescent facing the stream, and a caldron fire burning in the midst. Around the fire a ring of warriors naked to the breech-clout kept time in a slow shuffling dance to a monotonous chanting; and for onlookers there was an outer ring of squatting figures—the visiting Tuckaseges, as I supposed.

Beyond the Indian lodges, and a little higher up the gentle slope of the savanna, were the troop shelters; and beyond these, half concealed in the fringing of the boundary forest, was the tepee-lodge of the women.

On the bare hillside beneath the powder magazine I made no doubt I was in plainest view from the great fire, and the proof of this conclusion came shortly in a bellowing hail from Falconnet.

"Ho, Jack Warden!" he called, making a speaking-trumpet of his hands to lift the hail above the chanting of the Indian dancers. "Have a look at that shelter whilst you are over there and make sure 'twill shed rain if the weather shifts."

Now some such long-range marking down as this was what I had been angling for. So I came to attention and saluted in soldierly fashion, thereby raising a great laugh among my pseudo-comrades around the trooper fire—a laugh that pointed shrewdly to the baronet-captain's lack of proper discipline. But that is neither here nor there. Having my master's order for it, I climbed to the foot of the powder rock.

Here the bare sight of all the stored-up devastation set me athirst with a fierce longing for leave to snap a pistol in the well-laid mine. For if these enemies of ours had planned their own undoing they could never have given a desperate foeman a better chance. To hold the pine boughs of the rude shelter in place they had piled a great loose wall of stones around and over the cargo; and the firing of the powder, heaped as it was against the backing cliff of the boulder, would hurl these weighting stones in a murderous broadside upon the camp across the stream.

But since my dear lady would also share the hazard of such a broadside, I had no leave to blow myself and the powder convoy to kingdom come, as I thirsted to—could not, you will say, having neither pistol to snap nor flint and steel to fire a train. Nay, nay, my dears, I would not have you think so lightly of my invention. Had this been the only obstacle, you may be sure I should have found a way to grind a firing spark out of two bits of stone.

But being otherwise enjoined, as I say, I turned my back upon the temptation and held to the business in hand, which was to reach and recross the stream higher up and so to come among the horses.

As I had hoped to find them, the saddles were hung upon the branches of the nearest trees, Margery's horse-furnishings among them. At first the black mare was shy of me, but a gentling word or two won her over, and she let me take her by the forelock and lead her deeper into the herd where I could saddle and bridle her in greater safety.

My plan to cut her out was simple enough. Trusting to the darkness—the horse meadow was far enough from the fires to make a murky twilight of the ruddy glow—I thought to lead the mare quietly away up the stream and thus on to the foot of that ravine by which we hoped to climb to the old borderer's rendez-vous on the plateau. But when all was ready and I sought to set this plan in action, an unforeseen obstacle barred the way. To keep the horses from straying up the valley an Indian sentry line was strung above the grazing meadow, and into this I blundered like any unlicked knave of a raw recruit.

Had I been armed, the warrior who rose before me phantom-like in the laurel edging of the meadow would have had a most sharp-pointed answer to his challenge. As it was,—I had left my sword with Jennifer because the captured trooper whose under-study I was had left his sword in camp,—I tried to parley with the sentry. He knew no word of English, nor I of Cherokee; but that deadlock was speedily broken. A guttural call summoned others of the horse-keepers, and among them one who spoke a little Eng-lish.

"Ugh! What for take white squaw horse?" he demanded.

"'Tis the captain's order," I replied, lying boldly to fit the crisis.

At that they gave me room; and had I hastened, I had doubt-less gone at large without more ado. But at this very apex point of hazard I must needs play out the part of unalarm to the fool's *envoi*, taking time to part the mare's forelock under the head-stall, and looking leisurely to the lacings of the saddle-girth.

This foolhardy delay cost me all, and more than all. I was still fiddle-faddling with the girth strap, the better to impose upon my Indian horse-guards, when suddenly there arose a yelling hubbub of laughter in the camp behind. I turned to look and beheld a thing laughable enough, no doubt, and yet it broke no bubble of mirth in me. Half-way from the nearest forest fringe to the great fire a man, white of skin, and clothed only in a pair of trooper boots, was running swiftly for cover to the nearest pine-bough shelter, shouting like an escaped Bedlamite as he fled. It asked for no second glance, this apparition of the yelling madman; 'twas our captive soldier, foot-loose and racing in to raise the hue and cry.

Now you may always count upon this failing in a cautious man, that at a crisis he is like to do the unwisest thing that offers. This cutting out of Margery's mare was none so vital a matter that I should have risked the marring of Ephraim Yeates's plan upon it. Yet having done this very thing, I must needs make a bad matter infinitely worse.

Instead of mounting to ride a charge through the camp, and so to draw the pursuit after me toward the cavern entrance, as I should, I slapped the mare to send her bounding through the guard line, snatched a saddle from its oak-branch peg to hurl it in the faces of the sentry group, and darting aside, plunged into the laurel thicket to come by running where I could and creeping where I must to that place where I had left Richard Jennifer.

All hot and exasperated as I was, 'twas something less than cooling to find Dick a-double on the ground, holding his sides and laughing like a yokel at his first pantomime.

"Oh, ho, ho! did you—did you twig him, Jack?" he gasped. "Saw you ever such a mincing puss-in-boots since the Lord made you? Ah! ha! ha!"

"The devil take your ill-timed humor!" I cried. "Up with you, man, and let us vanish while we may!"

By this the camp was in a pretty ferment, as you would guess—our late captive having had space enough to tell his tale. Drunk or sober, Falconnet was afoot and alert, shouting his orders to the Englishmen who were scrambling for their arms, and to the Indians who came swarming up from the lodges.

Whilst we looked, the Cherokees scattered like a company of trained gillies to beat us out of cover; and when the hunt was fairly up, the baronet-captain set his men in marching order to surround the wigwam of the captives.

As yet there was time for a swift retreat up the valley, or at least for the choosing of some battle-field of our own where the enemy need not outnumber us twenty to one; and again I urged Richard to bestir himself. But it was the sight of Falconnet's troopers deploying to surround the tepee-lodge, and not any word of mine, that broke his merriment in the midst.

At a bound he was up and handing me my sword.

"Good by, Jack; go you whilst you can. You'll be like to meet Eph and the Catawba coming in; turn them back and tell them to bide their time."

"But you?" I would say.

"My place is inside of that soldier-cordon our friend is drawing about his dove-cote. I shall be at hand when she needs me, as I promised."

"Aye, so you may be; but not alone," said I; and with that we fell to running like a pair of doubling foxes through the wood on the steep slope behind the lodge, striving with might and main to gain the laurel thicket whence we had made our first reconnaissance before the converging lines of the redcoat cordon should close and shut us out.

We did it by the skin of our teeth, diving to cover through the closing gap not a second too soon. When we were in and hugging the bare ground under the scanty leafing of the laurel, I take no shame in saying that I would have given a king's ransom to be at large again. Had there been but one of us the covert would have been cramped enough; and I was painfully conscious that my borrowed coat of scarlet was but a poor thing to hide in.

To make it worse, Falconnet, who had lagged behind at the fire, was now heaping fresh fuel on, and this reviving of the blaze made the place as light as day. With the nearest links in the redcoat chain no more than a pike's-length at our backs, we dared not stir or breathe a word; and, all in all, we might have been taken like rats in a trap had any one of the sentries on our side of the circle chanced to look behind him.

Having repaired the fire to his liking, the troop-captain came up to pass a word or two with his lieutenant. They spoke guardedly, but we could hear—could not help hearing.

"You have seen nothing, Gordon?"

"Nothing, as yet."

"Make the round again and tell the men 'twill be ten gold joes and a double allowance of liquor to the man who first claps eyes on any one of the four."

The subaltern went to carry out the order, and Falconnet fell to pacing back and forth before the little wigwam. I could see his face at the turn where the firelight fell upon him; 'twas the face of a villain at his worst, namely, a villain half in liquor. There was a lurking devil of passion peering out of the sensuous eyes; and ever and anon he stopped as if to listen for some sound within the captives' lodge.

When the lieutenant returned to make his report, he was given another order to cap the first.

"Your line is too close-drawn and too conspicuous," said the captain, shortly. "Move the men out fifty paces in advance, and bid them take cover."

"They will scarce be within hail of each other at that," says the lieutenant.

"Near enough, with ten gold pieces to sharpen their eyesight. Go you with them and hold them to their work."

The line was presently extended as the order ran, each link in the cordon chain advancing fifty paces on its front into the forest. Dick fetched a deep sigh of relief; and I thought less of the thin-leafed cover and the scarlet coat of me.

Falconnet had resumed the pacing of his sentry beat before

the lodge, but when his men were out of sight and hearing he stopped short and stole on tiptoe to lay his ear to the flap.

"So, you are awake, Mistress Margery? Send your woman out. I would speak with you—alone."

There was no reply, but we could both hear the low anguished voice of our dear lady praying for help in this her hour of trial. Dick inched aside to give me room, freeing his weapon, as I did mine. We were not over-quiet about it, but the captain of horse was too hot upon his own devil's business to look behind him.

Having no answer from within, he stooped to loose the flap. It was pegged down on the inside. He rose and whipped out his sword; the firelight fell upon his face again and we saw it as it had been the face of a foul fiend from the pit.

"Open!" he commanded; and when there was neither reply nor obedience, he cut the flap free with his sword and flung it back.

The two women within the wigwam were on their knees before a little crucifix hanging on the lodge wall. So much we saw as we broke cover and ran in upon the despoiler. Then the battle-madness came upon us and I, for one, saw naught but the tense-drawn face of a swordsman fighting for his life—a face in which the hot flush of evil passion had given place to the ashen graying of fear.

We drove at him together, Dick and I, and so must needs fall afoul of each other clumsily, giving him time to spring back and so to miss the claymore stroke which else would have shorn him to the middle. Then ensued as pretty a bit of blade work as any master of the old cut-and-thrust school could wish to see; and through it all this king's captain of horse seemed to bear a charmed life.

There was no punctilio of the code of honor in this duel à outrance. Knowing our time was short, we fought as men who fight with halters round their necks; not to decide a nice point at issue, but to kill this accursed villain as we would kill a mad dog or a venomous reptile whose living on imperiled the life and honor of the woman we loved.

Thrice, whilst I held him in play, Dick rushed in to end it with a scythe-sweep of the broadsword; and thrice the Scottish death was turned aside by the flashing circle of steel wherewith the man striving shrewdly to gain time made shift to shield himself.

Yet it was not in flesh and blood to fend the double onslaught for more than some brief minute or two. Play as he would—and no *schlägermeister*, of my old field-marshal's picked troop could best him at this game of parry and defense—he must give ground step by step; slowly at the pressing of the Ferara, and in quick backward leaps when the great broadsword bit at him.

For the first few bouts he withstood us in grim silence. But now Richard cut in again and the claymore stroke, less skilfully turned aside, brought him to his knees. This broke his bull courage somewhat, and though he was afoot and on guard before my point could reach him, he began to bellow lustily for help.

As you would suppose, the call was all unneeded. At the first clash of steel the outlying troopers were up and swarming to the rescue; and now on all sides came the trampling rush of the in-closing cordon line.

Had Falconnet held his ground a moment longer he would have had us fast in the jaws of the trooper-trap; but 'tis the fatal flaw in mere brute courage that it will break at the pinch. No sooner did the volunteer captain catch a glimpse of his up-coming reinforcements than he must needs show us a clean pair of heels, running like a craven coward and shouting madly to his men to close with us and cut us down.

"After him!" roared Dick, who was by now as rage-mad as any berserker; and with a cut and thrust to right and left for the nipping trap-jaws we were out and away in chase.

Now you may mark this as you will; that whilst the devil hath need of his bond-servant he will come between with a miracle if need be to keep the villain breath of life in his vassal. Three bounds beyond the closing trap-jaws fetched us, pursued and pursuers, to the open camp field; and here the devil's miracle was wrought. Out of the forest fringe, out of the skirting of under-growth, out of the very earth, as it seemed, uprose a yelling mob of Cherokees—the detachment we had met in the cavern returned in the very nick of time to cut us off from the pursuit and to ring us in a whooping circle of death.

"Back to back, lad!" I shouted; and 'twas thus we met their onslaught.

In such a fray as that which followed 'tis the trivial things that leave their mark upon the memory. For one, I recall the curious thrill of master-might it gave me to feel the play of Jennifer's great shoulder muscles against my back in his plying of the heavy clay-more. For another, I remember the sickening qualm I had when the warm blood of my second—or mayhap 'twas the third—gushed out upon my sword hand, and I remember, too, how the impaled one, driven in upon the blade by the pressure of his fellows behind, would lay hold of the sharp steel and try in the death throe to withdraw it.

But after that sickening qualm I recall only this; that I could not free the sword for another thrust, and whilst I tugged and fought for space they dragged me down and buried me, these fierce tribesmen, piling so thick upon me that sight and sound and breath went out together, and I was but an atom crushed to earth beneath the human avalanche.

CHAPTER XXIX

IN WHICH, HAVING DANCED, WE PAY THE PIPER

Measured by the sense which takes cognizance of pauses it seemed no more than a moment between the stamping out of breath and its gasping recovery. But in the interval the scene had shifted from the open savanna to a thinly set grove of oaks with the stream brawling through the midst.

To the biggest of the trees I was tightly bound; and a little way apart a fire, newly kindled, smoked and blazed up fitfully. By the light of the fire a good score of the Cherokees were gathering deadfalls and dry branches to heap beside me; and from the camp below, the Indian lodges of which were in plain view beyond the intervening horse meadow, other savages were hurrying to join the wood carriers.

So far as these hasting preliminaries applied to me, their meaning was not difficult to read. I was to be burned at the stake in proper savage fashion. But Richard Jennifer—what had become of him? A sound, half sigh, half groan, told me where to look. Hard by, bound to a tree as I was, and so near that with a free hand I could have touched him, was my poor lad.

"Dick!" I cried.

He turned his head as the close-drawn thongs permitted and gave me a smile as loving-tender as a woman's.

"Aye, Jack; they have us hard and fast this time. I have been praying you'd never come alive enough to feel the fire."

"We were taken together?" So much I dared ask.

"In the same onset. 'Twas but a question of clock ticks in that back-to-back business. But they paid scot and lot," this with an inching nod toward a row of naked bodies propped sitting against a fallen tree; nine of them in all, one with its severed head between its knees, and three others showing the gaping hacks and hewings of the great broadsword.

"They've fetched them here to see us burn," he went on. "But by the gods, we have the warrant of two good blades and Ephraim Yeates's hunting-knife that the only fires they'll ever see are those of hell."

"Yeates?" I queried. "Then they have taken him and the Catawba, as well?"

"Not alive, you may be sure, else we should have them for company. But it has a black look for our friends that the flying column we met in the stream-cave came back so soon. Moreover, the bodies of the three peace-pipe smokers were found and brought in; that will be the Great Bear holding his head in his hands at the end of yonder bloody masquerade."

"I guessed as much. God rest our poor comrades!"

"Aye; and God help Madge! 'Tis no time for reproaches, but amongst us we have signed her death warrant with our bunglings."

"If it were only death!" I groaned.

"'Tis just that, Jack," said he; "no better, mayhap, but no worse. When we were downed by that screeching mob, she was out and on her knees to Falconnet, beseeching him to spare us. He put her off smoothly at first, saying 'twas the Indians' affair—that they would not be balked of their vengeance by any interference of his. But when she only begged the more piteously, he showed his true colors, rapping out that we should have as swift a quittance as we had meant to give him, and that within the hour she should be the mistress of Appleby and free to marry an English gentleman."

"Well?" said I, making sure that now at last he must know all.

"At that she stood before him bravely, and I saw that all the time she had had the Catawba's knife hidden in the folds of her gown. 'You have spoken truth for once, Captain Falconnet; I shall be free,' she said. 'Come and tell me when you have added these to your other murders.'"

"And then?"

"Then she went back to her prison wigwam, walking through the rabble of redcoats and redskins as proudly as the Scottish Mary went to the block."

"She will do it, think you?" I queried, fearful lest she would, but more fearful lest her courage should fail at the pinch.

"Never doubt it. Good Catholic as she is, there is martyr blood in her on the mother's side, and that will help her to die unsullied. And God nerve her to it, say I."

I said "Amen" to that; and thereupon we both fell silent, watching as condemned men on the gallows the busy preparations for our taking off.

Again, as in the late battle, it was the trivial things that moved me most. Chief among them the grinning row of dead Indians propped against the fallen tree is the constant background for all the memory pictures of that waiting interval, and I can see those stiffening corpses now, some erect, as if defying us; some lopping this way or that, as if their bones had gone to water at the touch of the steel.

I know not why these poor relics of mortality should have held me fascinated as they did. Yet when I would look away, through the vista to where the light of the great fire in the savanna camp played luridly upon the Indian lodges, or, nearer at hand, upon the savages gathering the wood to burn us with, this ghastly file of the dead drew me irresistibly, and I must needs pass the fearsome figures in review again, marking the staring eyes and unnatural postures, and the circular blood-black patches on the heads of the three peace-men whom Yeates and the Catawba had scalped.

While they were making ready for the burning, our executioners were strangely silent; but when the work was done they formed in a semicircle to front the row of corpses and set up a howling chant that would have put a band of Mohammedan dervishes to the blush.

"'Tis the death song for the slain," said Richard; and while it lasted, this moving tableau of naked figures, keeping time in a weird stamping dance to the rising and falling ululation of the chant, held us spellbound.

But we were not long suffered to be mere curious onlookers. In its dismalest flight the death song ended in a shrill hubbub, and the dancers turned as one man to face us.

I hope it may never be your lot, my dears, to meet and endure such a horrid glare of human ferocity as that these wrought-up avengers of blood bent upon us. 'Twas more unnerving than aught that had gone before; more terrible, I thought, than aught that could come after. Yet, as to this, you shall judge for yourselves.

The pause was brief, and when a lad ran up to cut the thongs that bound us from the middle up, the torture-play began in deadly earnest. Whilst the Indian youth was slashing at the deerskin, Richard gave me my cue.

"'Tis the knife and hatchet play; they are loosing us to give us freedom to shrink and dodge. Look straight before you and never flinch a hair, as you would keep the life in you from one minute to the next!"

"Trust me," said I. "We must eke it out as long as we can, if only to give our dear lady time for another prayer or two. Mayhap she will name us in them; God knows, our need is sore enough."

The lad ran back, and a warrior stood out, juggling his tomahawk in air. He made a feint to cast it at Richard, but instead sent it whizzing at me.

That first missile was harder to face unflinching than were all the others. I saw it leave the thrower's hand; saw it coming straight, as I would think, to split my skull. The prompting to dodge was well-nigh masterful enough to override the strongest will. Yet I did make shift to hold fast, and in mid flight the twirling ax veered aside to miss me by a hair's-breadth, gashing the tree at my ear when it struck.

"Bravo! well met!" cried Richard; and then, betwixt his teeth: "Here comes mine."

As he spoke, a second tomahawk was sped. I heard it strike with a dull crash that might have been on flesh and bone, or on oak-bark—I could not tell. I dared not look aside till Richard's taunting laugh gave me leave to breathe again.

The Indians answered the laugh with a yell; and now the marksmen stood out quickly one after another and for a little space the air was full of hurtling missiles. You will read in the romances of the wondrous skill of these savages in such diversions as these; how they will pin the victim to a tree and never miss of sticking knife or hatchet within the thickness of the blade where they will. But you must take these tales with a dash of allowance for the romancers' fancy. Truly, these Indians of ours threw well and skilfully; 'tis a part of the only trade they know—the trade of war—to send a weapon true to the mark. None the less, some of the missiles flew wide; and now and then one would nip the cloth of sleeve or body covering—and the flesh beneath it, as well.

Dick had more of the nippings than I; and though he kept up a running fire of taunts and gibing flings at the marksmen, I could hear the gritting oaths aside when they pinked him.

Notwithstanding, the worst of these miscasts fell to my lot. A hatchet, sped by the clumsiest hand of all, missed its curving, turned, and the helve of it struck me fair in the stomach. Not all the parting pangs of death, as I fondly believe, will lay a heavier toll on fortitude than did this griping-stroke which I must endure standing erect. 'Tis no figure of speech to say that I would have given the reversion of a kingdom, and a crown to boot, for leave to double over and groan out the agony of it.

Happily for us, there were no women with the band, so we were spared the crueler refinements of these ante-burning torments; the flaying alive by inch-bits, and the sticking of blazing splints of pitchwood in the flesh to make death a thing to be prayed for. There was naught of this; and tiring finally of the marksman play, the Indians made ready to burn us. Some ran to recover the spent weapons; others made haste to heap the wood in a broad circle about our trees; and the chief, with three or four to help, renewed the deer-thong lashings.

'Twas in the rebinding that this headman, a right kingly-looking savage as these barbarians go, thrust a bit of paper into my hand, and gave me time to glance its message out by the light of the fire. 'Twas a line from Margery; and this is what she said:

Dear Heart:

Though you must needs believe my love is pledged to your good friend and mine, 'tis yours, and yours alone, my lion-hearted one. I am praying the good God to give you dying grace, and me the courage to follow you quickly. Margery.

This by the hand of Tallachama.

For one brief instant a wave of joy caught and flung me upon its highest crest, and all these savage tormentors could do to me became as naught. Then the true meaning of this her brave *Ave atque vale* smote me like a space-flung meteor, and the joy-wave became an ocean of despair to engulf me in its blackest depths. The letter was never meant for me; 'twas for Richard Jennifer, who, as she would think, must know the story of her marriage to his friend and must believe her love went with the giving of her hand. And she named him Lion-Heart because he was brave, and true, and strong, like that first English Richard of the kingly line.

I thrust the message back upon the bearer of it, begging him in dumb show to give it quickly to my companion. I knew not at the time if he did it, being so crushed and blinded by this fresh misery. But when the Indians drew off to ring us in a chanting circle for the final act, I would not let the lad see my face for fear he might fathom the heart-break in me and know the cause of it.

'Twas at this crisis, when all was ready and one had run to fetch the fire, that I heard a smothered oath from Dick and saw the Indian who was coming up to fire the wood heaps drop his brand and tread upon it.

"Ecod!" said a voice, courtier-like and smoothly modulated. "'Tis most devilish lucky I came, Captain Ireton. Another moment and they would have grilled you in the king's uniform—a rank treason, to say naught of poor Jack Warden left without a clout to cover him."

It needed not the glance aside to name mine enemy. But I would not pleasure him with an answer. Neither would Richard Jennifer. He stood silent for a little space, smiling and nursing his chin in one hand, as his habit was. Then he spoke again.

"I came to bid you God-speed, gentlemen. You tumbled bravely into my little trap. I made no doubt you'd follow where the lady led, and so you did. But you'll turn back from this, I do assure you, if there be any virtue in an Indian barbecue."

At this Richard could hold in no longer.

"Curse you!" he gritted. "Do you mean that you kidnapped Mistress Stair to draw us out of hiding?"

"Truly," said this arch-fiend, smiling again. "Most unluckily for you, you both stood in my way,—you see I am speaking of it now as a thing past,—and I chanced upon this thought of killing two birds with the one stone; nay, three, I should say, if you count the lady in."

"Have done!" choked Richard, in a voice thick with impotent rage. "Give place, you hound, and let your savages to their work!"

"At your pleasure, Mr. Jennifer. I have no fancy for funeral baked meats, hot or cold, though they be made, as now, to furnish forth a marriage supper. I bid you good night, gentlemen. I'll go and make that call upon the lady which you were so rude as to interrupt a little while ago." And with that he turned his back upon us and strode away, forgetting to tell his redskinned myrmidons to strip me of that king's uniform he was so loath to have me burned in.

The Cherokees waited till the master-executioner was out of sight among the trees. Then they set up their infernal howling again, and the fire-lighter ran to fetch a fresh brand.

"Courage, lad! 'twill soon be over now," said I, hearing a groan from my poor Dick.

His reply was a chattering curse, not upon Falconnet or the Indians, but upon his malady, the tertian fever.

"Now, by all the fiends! I'm chilling again, Jack!" he gasped. "If these cursed wood-wolves mark it, they'll set it down to woman cowardice and that will break my heart!"

Again I bade him be of good courage, assuring him, not derisively, as it looks when 'tis written out, that the fire would presently medicine the chilling. In the middle of the saying the lighted brand was fetched and thrust among our fagotings, and the upward-curling smoke wreaths made me gasp and strangle at the finish.

For a little time after the sucking in of that first smoke-breath—nature's anodyne for any of her poor creatures doomed to die by fire—I saw and heard less clearly and suffered only by anticipation. But to this day the smell of burning pine-wood is like a sleeping potion to me; and the sleep it brings is full of dreams vaguely troubled.

So, while the Indians danced and leaped about us, brandishing their weapons and chanting the captives' death song, and while the blue and yellow tongues of flame mounted from twig to twig, climbing stealthily to flick at us like little vanishing demon whips, I saw and heard and felt as one remote from all the torture turmoil of the moment. Through the dimming haze of sleeping sensibility the dancing savages became as marionettes in some cunning puppet show; and the blood stained figures stiffening against their log took shapes less horrifying.

'Twas Dick's voice, coming, as it seemed, from a mighty distance, that broke the spell and brought me back to quickened agonies. He spoke in panting gasps, as the smoke would let him.

"One word, Jack, before we go—go to our own place. He said—he said she would be free to—to marry him. Tell me ... O God in Heaven!"

His agony was a lash to cut me deeper than any flicking demon whip of flame, yet I must needs add to it.

"Aye, Richard, I have wronged you, wronged you desperately; can you hear me yet? I say I have wronged you, and I shall die the easier if you'll forgive—"

Once more the smoke, rising again in denser clouds, cut me off, and through the blinding blue haze of it I saw the Indians running up with green branches to beat it down lest it should spoil their sport oversoon by smothering us out of hand.

With the chance to gasp and breathe again I would have confessed in full to Richard Jennifer and had him shrive me if he would. But when I called, he did not answer. His head was rolling from side to side, and his handsome young face was all drawn and distorted as in the awful grimaces of the death throe.

You will not wonder that I could not look at him; that I looked away for very pity's sake, praying that I might quickly breathe the flames, as I made sure he had, and so be the sooner past the anguish crisis.

There was good hope that the prayer would have a speedy answer. The fires were burning clearer now, leaping up in broad dragon's tongues of flame from the outer edges of the fagot piles to curtain off all that lay beyond. Through the luminous flame-veil the capering savages took on shapes the most weird and grotesque; and when I had a glimpse of the dead men's row, each hideous face in it seemed to wear a grin of leering triumph.

Thus far there had been never a puff of wind to fan the blaze. But now above the shrilling of the Indian chant and the crackling of the flames a low growl of thunder trembled in the upper air, and a gentle breeze swept through the tree-tops.

So now I would commend my soul to God, making sure that the breath He gave would go out on the wings of the first gust that should come to drive the fiery veil inward. But when the gust came it was from behind; a sweeping besom to beat down the leaping dragons' tongues; a pouring flood of blessed coolness to turn the ebbing life-tide and to set the dulled senses once more keenly alert.

With the wind came the rain, a passing summer-night's shower of great drops spattering on the leaves above and dripping thence to fall hissing in the fires. Then the thunder growled again; and into the monotonous droning of the Indian chant, or rather rising sharp and clear above it, came a sudden rattling fire of musketry from the camp in the savanna—this, and the sharp skirling of the troop captain's whistle shrilling the assembly.

While yet the flames lay flattened in the wind, I saw the Indians wheel and bound away to the rescue of their camp like a pack of hounds in full cry. In a trice they were wallowing through the stream at the foot of the powder boulder; and then, as the flames leaped up again, a dark form burst through the fiery barrier, my bonds were cut, and a strong hand plucked me out of the scorching hell-pit.

If I did aught to help it was all mechanical. I do remember dimly some fierce struggle to free my legs from the blazing tangle; this, and the swelling sob of joy at the sight of the faithful Catawba hacking at Dick's lashings and dragging him also free of the fire. And you may believe the welcome tears came to ease the pain of my seared eyes when my poor lad—I had thought him gone past human help—took two staggering steps and flung his arms about my neck.

Uncanoola gave us no time to come by easy stages to full-wit sanity. In a twinkling he had pounced upon us to crush us one upon the other behind the larger tree. And now I come upon another of those flitting instants so crowded with happenings that the swiftest pen must seem to make them lag. 'Twas all in a heartbeat, as it were: the Catawba's freeing of us; his flinging us to earth behind the tree; a spurt of blinding yellow flame from the foot of the powder-cliff, and a booming, jarring shock like that of an earthquake.

The momentary glare of the yellow flash lit up a scene most awe-inspiring. The spouting fountain of fire at the base of the great powder-rock was thick with flying missiles; and on high the very cliff itself was tottering and crumbling. So much I saw; then the Catawba sprang up to haul us afoot by main strength, and to rush us, with an arm for each, headlong through the wood toward the valley head.

But Dick hung back, and when the dull thunder of the falling rocks, the crash of the tumbling cliff and the shrill death yells of the doomed ones came to our ears, he fought loose from the Indian and flung himself down, crying as if his heart would break.

"O God! she's lost, she's lost!—and I have missed the chance to die with her or for her!"

CHAPTER XXX

HOW EPHRAIM YEATES PRAYED FOR HIS ENEMIES

However much or little the Catawba understood of Richard Jennifer's grief or its cause, the faithful Indian had a thing to do and he did it, loosing his grasp of me to turn and fall upon Dick with pullings and haulings and buffetings, fit to bring a man alive out of a very stiffening rigor of despair.

So, in a hand-space he had him up, and we were pressing on again, in midnight darkness once we had passed beyond the light of our grilling fires. No word was spoken; under the impatient urging of the Indian there was little breath to spare for speech. But when Richard's afterthought had set its fangs in him, he called a halt and would not be denied.

"Go on, you two, if you are set upon it," he said. "I must go back. Bethink you, Jack; what if she be only maimed and not killed outright. 'Tis too horrible! I'm going back, I say."

The Catawba grunted his disgust.

"Captain Jennif' talk fas'; no run fas'. What think? White squaw *yonder*—no yonder," pointing first forward and then back in the direction of the stricken camp.

Richard spun around and gripped the Indian by the shoulders. "Then she is alive and safe?" he burst out. "Speak, friend, whilst I leave the breath in you to do it!"

"Ugh!" said the chief, in nowise moved either by Jennifer's vehemence or by the dog-like shake. "What for Captain Jennif' think papoose thinks 'bout the Gray Wolf and poor Injun? Catch um white squaw *firs'*; *then* blow um up Chelakee camp and catch um Captain Jennif' and Captain Long-knife if can. Heap do firs' thing *firs'*, and las' thing *las'*. Wah!"

It was the longest speech this devoted ally of ours was ever known to make; and having made it he went dumb again save for his urgings of us forward. But presently both he and I had our hands full with the poor lad. The swift transition from despair to joy proved too much for Dick; and, besides, the fever was in his blood and he was grievously burned.

So we went stumbling on through the cloud-darkened wood, locked arm in arm like three drunken men, tripping over root snares and bramble nets spread for our feet, and getting well sprinkled by the dripping foliage. And at the last, when we reached the ravine at the valley's head, Dick was muttering in the fever delirium and we were well-nigh carrying him a dead weight between us.

'Twas a most heart-breaking business, getting the poor lad up that rock-ladder of escape in the darkness; for though I had come out of the fire with fewer burns than the roasting of me warranted, the battle preceding it had opened the old sword wound in my shoulder. So, taking it all in all, I was but a short-breathed second to the faithful Catawba.

None the less, we tugged it through after some laborious fashion, and were glad enough when the steep ascent gave place to leveler going, and we could sniff the fragrance of the plateau pines and feel their wire-like needles under foot.

By this the shower cloud had passed and the stars were coming out, but it was still pitch black under the pines; so dark that I started like a nervous woman and went near to panic when a horse snorted at my very ear, and a voice, bodiless, as it seemed, said; "Well, now; the Lord be praised! if here ain't the whole enduring—"

What Ephraim Yeates would have said, or did say, was lost upon me. For now my poor Dick's strength was quite spent, and when the chief and I were easing him to lie full length upon the ground, there was a quick little cry out of the darkness, a swish of petticoats, and my lady darted in to fall upon Richard in a very transport of pity.

"Oh, my poor Dick! they have killed you!" she sobbed; "oh, cruel, cruel!" Then she lashed out at us. "Why don't you strike a light? How can I find and dress his hurts in the dark?"

"Your pardon, Mistress Margery," I said; "'tis only that the fever has overcome him. He has no sore hurts, as I believe, save the fire-scorching."

"A light!" she commanded; "I must have a light and see for myself."

We had to humor her, though it was something against prudence. Ephraim found dry punk in a rotten log, and firing it with the flint and steel of a great king's musket—one of his reavings from the enemy—soon had a pine-knot torch for her. She gave it to the Catawba to hold; and while she was cooing over her patient and binding up his burns in some simples gathered near at hand by the Indian, I had the story of the double rescue from the old hunter.

Set forth in brief, that which had come as a miracle to Dick and me figured as a daring bit of strategy made possible by the emptying of the Indian camp at our torture spectacle.

Yeates and the Catawba, following out the plan agreed upon, had come within spying distance while yet we were in the midst of that hopeless back-to-back battle, and had most wisely held aloof. But later, when every Indian of the Cherokee band was busy at our torture trees, they set to work.

With no watch to give the alarm, 'twas easy to rifle the Indian wigwams of the firearms and ammunition. The latter they threw into the stream; the muskets they loaded and trained over a fallen tree at the northern edge of the savanna, bringing them to bear pointblank upon the light-horse guard gathered again around the great fire.

The next step was the cutting out of the women; this was effected whilst the baronet-captain was paying his courtesy call on us. Like the looting of the Indian camp, 'twas quickly planned and daringly done; it asked but the quieting of the two trooper guards on the forest side of the tepee-lodge, a warning word to Margery and her woman, and a shadow-like flitting with them over the dead bodies of their late jailers to the shelter of the wood.

Once free of the camp, Yeates had hurried his charges to a place of temporary safety farther up the valley, leaving the Catawba to cross the stream to lay a train of dampened powder to the makeshift magazine. When he had led the women to a place of safety, the old man left them and ran back to his masked battery of loaded muskets. Here, at an owl-cry signal from Uncanoola, he opened fire upon the redcoats.

The outworking of the *coup de main* was a triumph for the old borderer's shrewd generalship. At the death-dealing volley the Englishmen were thrown into confusion; whilst the Indians, summoned by the firing and the shrilling of the captain's whistle, dashed blindly into the trap. At the right moment Uncanoola touched off his powder train and cut in with a clear field for his rescue of Dick and me.

Of the complete success of these various climaxings, Ephraim Yeates had his first assurance when we three came safely to the rendezvous; for, after firing his masked battery, the old hunter lost no time in rejoining the women and in hastening with them out of the valley. Had these three been afoot we might have overtaken them; but Yeates had been lucky enough to stumble upon the black mare peacefully cropping the grass in a little glade; and with this mount for Margery and her tire-woman he had easily outpaced us.

All this I had from Yeates what time Margery was pouring the wine and oil of womanly sympathy into Richard's woundings; and I may confess that whilst the ear was listening to the hunter's tale, the eye was taking note of these her tender ministrations, and the heart was setting them down to the score of a great love which would not be denied. 'Twas altogether as I would have had it; and yet the thought came unbidden that she might spare a niggard moment and the breath to ask me how I did. And because she would not, I do think my burns smarted the crueler.

It was to have surcease of these extra smartings that I turned my back upon the trio under the flaring torch and took up with Ephraim Yeates the pressing question of the moment.

"As I take it, we may not linger here," I said. "Have you marked out a line of retreat?"

The old borderer was busied with his loot of the Indian camp—'twas not in his nature to come off empty-handed, however hard pressed he had been for time. In the raffle of it, guns and pistols, dressed skins and warrior finery, he came upon my good old blade and Richard's great claymore—trophies claimed by the head men of the Cherokees after our taking, as we made no doubt.

"Found 'em hanging in the lodge that usen to belong to the Great Bear," said the hunter, and then with grim humor: "'Lowed to keep 'em to ricollect ye by if so be ye was foreordained and predestinated to go up in a fiery chariot, like the good old Elijah." The weapons disposed of, he made answer to my query. "Ez for making tracks immejitly, *if* not sooner, I allow there ain't no two notions about that. But I'm dad-daddled if I know which-a-way to put out, Cap'n John, and that's the gospil fact."

"Why not strike for the Great Trace, and so go back the way the powder convoy came?" I asked.

It could be done, he said, but the hazard was great. 'Twas out of all reason to hope that there were no survivors left in the sunken valley to carry the news of the earthquake massacre. That news once cried abroad in the near-by Cowee Towns, the entire Tuckasege nation would turn out to run us down. Moreover, the avengers would look to find us in the only practicable horse-path leading eastward.

"Ez I'm telling you right now, Cap'n John, we made one more blunder in this here onfall of our'n, owin' to our having ne'er a seventh son of a seventh son amongst us to look a little ways ahead. Where we flashed in the pan was in not making our rendyvoo down yonder where you and Cap'n Dick got in. Ever' last one of 'em able to crawl is a-making straight for that crivvis dodge-hole right now, and if we was there we could do 'em like the Gileadites did the men o' Ephraim at the passages o' the Jordan."

Fresh as I was from the torture fire, I could not forbear a shudder at this old man's savagery.

"Kill them in cold blood?" I would say.

"Anan?" he queried, as not understanding my point of view;

and I let the matter rest. He was of those who slay and spare not where an enemy is concerned.

But when we came to consider of it there seemed to be no alternative to the eastward flitting by way of the Great Trace. To the west and south there was only the trackless wilderness; and to the north no white settlement nearer than that of the over-mountain folk on the Watauga. I asked if we might hope to reach this.

"'Tis a long fifty mile ez the crow flies, over e'enabout the mountainousest patch o' land that ever laid out o' doors," was the hunter's reply. "And there ain't ne'er a deer-track, ez I knows on, to p'int the way."

"Then we must ride eastward and run the risk of pursuit by the Tuckaseges," said I.

"Ez I reckon, that's about the long and short of it. And I do everlastedly despise to make that poor little gal jump her hoss and ride skimper-scamper again, when she's been fair living a-horse-back for a fortnight."

"She will not fail you," I ventured to say, adding: "But Jennifer is in poor fettle for making speed."

"It's ride or be skulped for him, and I allow he'll ride," quoth the old hunter, hastening his preparations for the start. "Reckon we can get him on a hoss right now."

I went to see. Margery rose at my approach, and even in the poor light I could see her draw herself up as if she would hold me at my proper distance.

"Your patient, Mistress Margery,—We must mount and ride at once. Is he fit?"

"No."

"But we must be far to the eastward before daybreak."

"I can not help it. If you make him ride to-night you will finish what those cruel savages began, Captain Ireton."

"We have little choice—none, I should say."

"Oh, you are bitter hard!" she cried, though wherein my offending lay just then I was wholly at a loss to know.

"'Tis your privilege to say so," I rejoined. "But as for making Dick ride, that will be but the kindest cruelty. We are only a little way from the nearest Indian towns, and if the daylight find us here—"

"Spare me," she broke in; and with that she turned shortly and asked Ephraim Yeates to put her in her saddle.

Richard was still in the fever stupor, but he roused himself at my urging and let us set him upon his beast. Once safe in the saddle, we lashed him fast like a prisoner, with a forked tree-branch at his back to hold him erect. This last was the old hunter's invention and 'twas most ingenious. The forked limb, in shape like a Y, was set astride the cantle, with the lower ends thonged stoutly to Dick's legs and to the girths. Thus the upright stem of the inverted Y became an easy back-rest for the sick man; and when he was securely lashed thereto there was little danger for him save in some stumbling of the beast he rode.

When all was ready we had first to find our way down from the mountain top; and now even the old borderer and the Indian confessed their inability to do aught but retrace their steps by the only route they knew: namely, by that ravine which we had twice traversed in daylight, and up which they had led the captured horses in the dusk.

This route promised all the perils of a gantlet-running, since by it we must take the risk of meeting the fleeing fugitives from the convoy camp, if the explosion had spared any fit to lift and carry the vengeance-cry. But here again there was no alternative, and we set us in order for the descent, with Yeates and the Catawba ahead, the women and Dick in the midst, and her Apostolic Majesty's late captain of hussars, masquerading as a British trooper, to bring on the rear.

Once in motion beneath the blue-black shadows of the pines, I quickly lost all sense of direction. After we had ridden in wordless silence a short half hour or less, and I supposed we should be nearing the head of our descending ravine, our little cavalcade was halted suddenly in a thickset grove of the pines, and Ephraim Yeates appeared at my stirrup to say:

' "H'ist ye off your nag, Cap'n John, and let's take a far'well squinch at the inimy whilst we can."

"Where? what enemy?" I would ask, slipping from the saddle at his word.

"Why, the hoss-captain's varmints, to be sure; or what-all the abomination o' desolation has left of 'em. We ain't more than a cat's jump from the edge o' the big rock where we first sot eyes on 'em this morning."

I saw not what was to be gained by any such long-range espial in the darkness. None the less, I followed the old man to the cliff's edge. He was wiser in his forecastings than I was in mine. There was a thing to look at, and light enough to see it by. One of the missile stones, it seems, had crashed into the great fire, scattering the brands in all directions. The pine-bough troop shelters were ablaze, and creeping serpents of fire were worming their way hither and yon over the year-old leaf beds in the wood. Ever and anon some pine sapling in the path of these fiery serpents would go up in a torch-like flare; and so, as I say, there was light enough.

What we looked down upon was not inaptly pictured out by Ephraim Yeates's Scripture phrase, the abomination of desolation. Every vestige of the camp save the glowing skeletons of the troop shelters had disappeared, and the swarded savanna was become a blackened chaos-blot on the fair woodland scene. I have said that the powder-sheltering boulder was a cliff for size; the mighty upheaval of the explosion had toppled it in ruins into the stream, and huge fragments the bigness of a wine-butt had been hurled with the storm of lighter debris broadcast upon the camp.

At first we saw no sign of life in all the firelit space. But a moment later, when three or four of the sapling torches blazed up together, we made out some half dozen figures of human beings—whether red or white we could not tell—stumbling and reeling about among the rocks like blind men drunken.

At sight of these the old hunter doffed his cap and fell upon his knees with hands uplifted to pour out his zealot's soul in the awful sentences of the Psalmist's imprecation.

"'Let God arise, and let His inimies be scattered; let them also that hate Him flee before Him. Like as the smoke vanisheth, so shalt thou drive them away; and like as the wax melteth at the fire, so let the ungodly perish at the presence of God. . . .'"

CHAPTER XXXI

IN WHICH WE MAKE A FORCED MARCH

It could have been but little short of midnight when we came down into the Great Trace near the ambush ground where we had set our trap for the peace men.

The night had cleared most beautifully, and overhead the stars were burning like points of white fire in the black dome of the heavens. As often happens after a shower, the night shrillings of the forest were in fullest tide; and a whip-will's-widow, disturbed by our approach, fluttered to a higher perch and set up his plaintive protest.

At our turning eastward on the trace, the old hunter massed our little company as compactly as the path allowed, and giving us the word to follow cautiously, tossed his bridle rein to the Catawba and went on ahead to feel out the way.

This rearrangement set me to ride abreast with Margery; and for the first time since that fateful night in the upper room at Appleby Hundred we were together and measurably alone.

Since death might be lying in wait for us at any turn in the winding bridle-path, I had no mind to break the strained silence. But, womanlike, she would not miss the chance to thrust at me.

"Are you not afire with shame, Captain Ireton?" she said, bitterly; and then: "How you must despise me!"

I knew not what she meant; but being most anxious for her safety, I begged her not to talk, putting it all upon the risk we ran in passing the outlet of the sunken valley. Now, as you have long since learned, my tongue was but a skilless servant; and though I sought to make the command the gentlest plea, she took instant umbrage and struck back smartly.

"You need not make the danger an excuse. I will be still; and when I speak to you again, you will be willing enough to hear me, I promise you!"

"Nay, then, dear lady; you must not take it so!" I protested. "'Tis my misfortune to be ever blundering."

But to this she gave me no answer at all; and barring a word or two of heartening for her serving woman, she never opened her lips again throughout the passage perilous.

By good hap we came to the crossing of the cavern stream without meeting any foeman; and on the farther side of the shallow ford we found the old borderer awaiting us.

"Ez I allow, we've smelt the bait in the trap and come off with whole bones, like Shadrach, Meshach and Abednego," he said, mixing metaphor, Scripture phrase and frontier idiom as was his wont. Then he put a leg over his horse and gave the stirrup-word: "From now on, old Jehu, the son o' Nimshi, is the hoss-whipper we've got to beat. Get ye behind, Cap'n John, and give the hoss that lags a half inch 'r so of your sword-p'int."

Then and there began a night flight long to be remembered. Down the valley of the swift river to the ford where Yeates and I had crossed after the mock rescue of Margery the night before, we let the horses pick the way as they could. But once beyond the ford, where the trace was wider and the footing less precarious, we plied whip and spur, pushing the saddle-beasts for every stride we could get out of them in the blind race.

I have marveled often that we came not once to grief in all this long night-gallop through the darkness. There was every chance for it. The over-arching trees of the great forest shut out all the starlight, and the trace was no more than a bridle-path, rougher than any cart road. Yet we held the breakneck pace steadily, save for the time it took to thread some steep defile to a stream crossing, or to scramble up its fellow on the opposite side; and when the dawn began to gray in the sky ahead, we were well out of the broken mountain region and into the opener forest of the hill country.

The sun was yet below the eastern horizon when we came to the fording of a larger stream than any we had crossed in the night. Its course was toward the sunrise, hence I took it for some tributary of the Catawba or the Broad.

"'Tis the Broad itself," said Ephraim Yeates, in answer to my asking; "and yit it ain't; leastwise, it ain't the one you know. 'Tis the one the Parley-voos claimed in the old war, and they call it the Frinch Broad."

"But that flows north and westward, if I remember aright," said I.

"So it do, so it do—in gineral. But hereabouts 'twill run all ways for Sunday, by spells."

"If this be the French Broad we are not yet out of the Tuckasege country, as I take it."

"Mighty nigh to it; nigh enough to make camp for a resting spell. I reckon ye're a-needing that same pretty toler'ble bad, ain't ye, little gal?" this last to Margery.

Weary as she was she smiled upon him brightly, as though he had been her grandsire and so free to name her how he pleased.

"I shall sleep well when we are out of danger. But you must not stop for me, or for Jeanne, till 'tis safe to do so."

"Safe? Lord love ye, child! 'safe' is a word beyond us yit, and will be till we sot ye down on your daddy's door-stone. But we'll make out to give ye a bite and sup and forty winks o' sleep immejitly, *if* not sooner, now."

So, on the farther side of the stream the hunter led the way aside, and when we were come to a small meadow glade with good grazing for the horses, he called a halt, lifted the women from their saddles and came to help me ease Dick down. The poor lad was stiff and sore, having no more use of his joints than if he were a bandaged mummy; but the fever delirium had passed and he was able to laugh feebly at the tree-limb contrivance rigged to hold him in the saddle.

"How did we come out of it, Jack?" he asked, when we had let him feel the comfort of lying flat upon his back on the soft sward.

"As you see. We are all here, and all in fair fettle, saving yourself. You're the heaviest loser."

He smiled, and his eyes languid with the fever sought out Margery, who would not come anigh whilst I was with him.

"That remains to be seen, Jack. If my dream comes true, I shall be the richest gainer."

"What did you dream?"

He beckoned me to bend lower over him. "I dreamed I was sore hurt, and that she was binding up my bruises and crying over me."

"'Twas no dream," I said; and with that I went to help Yeates make a bough shelter for the women while Uncanoola was grinding the maize for the breakfast cakes.

'Tis not my purpose to weary you with a day-by-day accounting for all that befell us on the way back to Mecklenburg. Suffice it to say that we ate and slept and rose to mount and ride again; this for five days and nights, during which Jennifer's fever grew upon him steadily.

At the close of the fifth day our night halt was in a deserted log cabin at the edge of an unfinished clearing in the heart of the forest. Here Richard's sickness anchored us, and for three full weeks the journey paused.

We nursed the lad as best we could for a fortnight, dosing him with stewings of such roots and herbs as the Catawba could find in the wood. Then, when we were at our wits' ends, and Yeates and I were casting about how we could compass the bringing of a doctor from the settlements, the fever took a turn for the better,— of its own accord, or for Uncanoola's physickings, we knew not which,—and at the end of the third week Dick was up and able to ride again, this time without the forked stick to hold him in the saddle.

After this we went on without mishap, and with no hardship greater than that of living solely upon the meat victual provided by the hunter's rifle; and you who know this plough-dressed region at this later day will wonder when I write it down that in all that long faring, or rather to the last day's stage of it, we saw never a face of any of our kind, or of the Catawba's.

You may be sure the month or more we spent thus in the heart of the wildwood was but a sorry time for me. While the excitement of the pursuit and rescue lasted, and later, when anxiety for Richard filled the hours of the long days and nights, I was held a little back from slipping into that pit of despair which I had digged for myself.

But when the strain was off and Dick was up and fit again, the misery of it all came back with added goadings. I had never dreamed how cutting sharp 'twould be to see these two together day by day; to see her loving, tender care of him, and to hear him babble of his love for her in his feverish vaporings. Yet all this I must endure, and with it a thing even harder. For, to make it worse, if worse could be, the shadow of complete estrangement had fallen between Margery and me. True to her word, given in that moment when I had besought her not to speak aloud for her own safety's sake, she had never opened her lips to me; and for aught she said or did I might have been a deaf-mute slave beneath her notice.

And as she drew away from me, she seemed to draw the closer to Richard Jennifer, nursing him alive when he was at his worst, and giving him all the womanly care and sympathy a sick man longs for. And later, when he was fit to ride again, she had him always at her side in the onward faring.

As I have said before, this was all as I would have it. Yet it made me sick in my soul's soul; and at times I must needs fall behind to rave it out in solitude, cursing the day that I was born, and that other more misfortunate day when I had reared the barrier impassable between these two.

What wonder, then, that, as we neared the fighting field of the great war, I grew more set upon seizing the first chance that might offer an honorable escape from all these heartburnings? 'Twas a weakness, if you choose; I set down here naught but the simple fact, which had by now gone as far beyond excusings as the underlying cause of it was beyond forgiveness.

'Twas on the final day, the day when we were riding tantivy to reach Queensborough by evening, that my deliverance came. I say deliverance because at the moment it had the look of a short shrift and a ready halter.

We had crossed our own Catawba and were putting our horses at the steep bank on the outcoming side, when my saddle slipped. Dismounting to tighten the girth, I called to the others to press on, saying I should overtake them shortly.

The promise was never kept. I scarce had my head under the saddle flap before a couple of stout knaves in homespun, appearing from I know not where, had me fast gripped by the arms, whilst a third made sure of the horse.

"A despatch rider," said the bigger of the two who pinioned me. "Search him, Martin, lad, whilst I hold him; then we'll pay him out for Tarleton's hanging of poor Sandy M'Guire."

I held my peace and let them search, taking the threat for a bit of soldier bullyragging meant to keep me quiet. But when they had turned the pockets of my borrowed coat inside out and ripped the lining and made it otherwise as much the worse for their mishandling as it was for wear, the third man fetched a rope.

"Did you mean that, friend?—about the hanging?" I asked, wondering if this should be my loophole of escape from the life grown hateful.

"Sure enough," said the big man, coolly. "You'd best be saying your prayers."

I laughed. "Were you wearing my coat and I yours, you might hang me and welcome; in truth, you may as it is. Which tree will you have me at?"

The man stared at me as at one demented. Then he burst out in a guffaw. "Damme, if you bean't a cool plucked one! I've a mind to take you to the colonel."

"Don't do it, my friend. Though I am something loath to be snuffed out by the men of my own side, we need not haggle over the niceties. Point out your tree."

"No, by God! you're too willing. What's at the back of all this?"

"Nothing, save a decent reluctance to spoil your sport. Have at it, man, and let's be done with it."

"Not if you beg me on your knees. You'll go to the colonel, I say, and he may hang you if he sees fit. You must be a most damnable villain to want to die by the first rope you lay eyes on."

"That is as it may be. Who is your colonel?"

"Nay, rather, who are you?"

I gave my name and circumstance and was loosed of the hand-grip, though the third man dropped the cord and stepped back to hold me covered with his rifle.

"An Ireton, you say? Not little Jock, surely!"

"No, big Jock; big enough to lay you on your back, though you do have a hand as thick as a ham."

He ignored the challenge and stuck to his text. "I never thought to see the son of old Mad-bull Roger wearing a red coat," he said.

"That is nothing. Many as good a Whig as I am has been forced to wear a red coat ere this, or go barebacked. But why don't you knot the halter? In common justice you should either hang me or feed me. 'Tis hard upon noon, and I breakfasted early."

"Fall in!" said the big man; and so I was marched quickly aside from the road and into the denser thicketing of the wood. Here my captors blindfolded me, and after spinning me around to make me lose the compass points, hurried me away to their encampment which was inland from the stream, though not far, for I could still hear the distance-minished splashing of the water.

When the kerchief was pulled from my eyes I was standing in the midst of a mounted riflemen's halt-camp, face to face with a young officer wearing the uniform of the colonelcy in the North Carolina home troops. He was a handsome young fellow, with curling hair and trim side-whiskers to frame a face fine-lined and eager—the face of a gentleman well-born and well-bred.

"Captain Ireton?" he said; by which I guessed that one of my capturers had run on ahead to make report.

"The same," I replied.

"And you are the son of Mr. Justice Roger Ireton, of Appleby Hundred?"

"I have that honor."

He gave me his hand most cordially.

"You are very welcome, Captain; Davie is my name. I trust we may come to know each other better. You are in disguise, as I take it; do you bring news of the army?"

"On the contrary, I am thirsting for news," I rejoined. "I and three others have but now returned from pursuing a British and Indian powder convoy into the mountains to the westward. We have been out five weeks and more."

He looked at me curiously. "You and three others?" he queried. "Come apart and tell me about it whilst Pompey is broiling the venison. I scent a whole Iliad in that word of yours, Captain Ireton."

"One thing first, if you please, Colonel Davie," I begged. "My companions are faring forward on the road to Queensborough. They know naught of my detention. Will you send a man to overtake them with a note from me?"

The colonel indulged me in the most gentlemanly manner;

and when my note to Jennifer was despatched we sat together at the roots of a great oak and I told him all that had befallen our little rescue party. He heard me through patiently, and when the tale was ended was good enough to say that I had earned a commission for my part in the affair. I laughed and promptly shifted that burden to Ephraim Yeates's shoulders.

"The old hunter was our general, Colonel Davie. He did all of the planning and the greater part of the executing. But for him and the friendly Catawba, it would have gone hard with Jennifer and me."

"I fear you are over-modest, Captain," was all the reply I got; and then my kindly host fell amuse. When he spoke again 'twas to give me a résumé in brief of the military operations North and South.

At the North, as his news ran, affairs remained as they had been, save that now the French king had sent an army to supplement the fleet, and Count Rochambeau and the allies were encamped on Rhode Island ready to take the field.

In the South the distressful situation we had left behind us on that August Sunday following the disastrous battle of Camden was but little changed. General Gates, with the scantiest following, had hastened first to Salisbury and later to Hillsborough, and had since been busy striving to reassemble his scattered forces.

A few military partizans, like my host, had kept the field, doing what the few might against the many to retard my Lord Cornwallis's northward march; and a week earlier the colonel with his handful of mounted riflemen had dared to oppose his entry into Charlotte.

"'Twas no more than a hint to his Lordship that we were not afraid of him," said my doughty colonel. "You know the town, I take it?"

"Very well, indeed."

"Well, we had harassed him all the way from Blair's Mill, and 'twas midnight when we reached Charlotte. There we determined to make a stand and give him a taste of our mettle. We dismounted, took post behind the stone wall of the court house green and under cover of the fences along the road."

"Good! an ambush," said I.

"Hardly that, since they were looking to have resistance. Tarleton was sick, and Major Hanger commanded the British van. He charged, and we peppered them smartly. They tried it again, and this time their infantry outflanked us. We abandoned the court house and formed again in the eastern edge of the town; and now, bless you! 'twas my Lord Charles himself who had to ride forward and flout at his men for their want of enterprise."

"But you could never hope to hold on against such odds!" I exclaimed.

"Oh, no; but we held them for a third charge, and beat them back, too. Then they brought up two more regiments and we mounted and got off in tolerably good order, losing only six men killed. But Colonel Francis Locke was one of these; and my brave Joe Graham was all but cut to pieces—a sore blow to us just now."

The colonel sighed and a silence fell upon us. 'Twas I who broke it to say: "Then we are still playing a losing hand in the South, as I take it?"

"'Tis worse than that. As the game stands we have played all our trumps and have not so much as a long suit left. Cornwallis will go on as he pleases and overrun the state, and the militia will never stand to front him again under Horatio Gates. Worse still, Ferguson is off to the westward, embodying the Tories by the hundred, and we shall have burnings and hangings and harryings to the king's taste."

I nursed my knee a moment and then said: "What may one man do to help, Colonel Davie?"

He looked up quickly. "Much, if you are that man, and you do not value your life too highly, Captain Ireton."

"You may leave that out of the question," said I. "I shall count it the happiest moment of my life when I shall have done something worth their killing me for."

Again he gave me that curious look I had noted before. Then he laughed.

"If you were as young as Major Joe Graham, and had been well crossed in love, I could understand you better, Captain. But, jesting aside, there is a thing to do, and you are the man to do it. Our spies are thick in Cornwallis's camp, but what is needed is some master spirit who can plot as well as spy for us. Major Ferguson moves as Cornwallis pulls the strings. Could we know the major's instructions and designs, we might cut him off, bring the Tory uprising to the ground, and so hearten the country beyond measure. I say we might cut him off, though I know not where the men would come from to do it."

"Well?" said I, when he paused.

"The preliminary is some better information than our spies can give us. Now you have been an officer in the British service, and—"

I smiled. "Truly; and I have the honor, if you please to call it so, of his Lordship's acquaintance. Also, I have that of Colonel Tarleton and the members of his staff, the same having tried and condemned me as a spy at Appleby Hundred some few weeks before this chase I have told you of."

His face fell. "Then, of course, it is out of the question for you to show yourself in Cornwallis's headquarters."

I rose and buttoned my borrowed coat.

"On the contrary, Colonel Davie, I am more than ever at your service. Let me have a cut of your venison and a feed for my horse, and I shall be at my Lord's headquarters as soon as the nag can carry me there."

CHAPTER XXXII

IN WHICH I AM BEDDED IN A GARRET

"Tis a very pretty hazard, Captain Ireton. But can it be brought off successfully, think you?"

"As I have said, it hangs somewhat upon the safety of my portmanteau. If that has come through unseized to Mr. Pettigrew at Charlotte, and I can lay hands on it, 'twill be half the battle."

"You say you left it behind you at New Berne?"

"Yes; Mr. Carey was to forward it as he could."

Colonel Davie had given me bite and sup, and I was ready to take the road. My plan, such as it was, had been determined upon, and to the furthering of it, the colonel had written me a letter to a friend in the town who might shelter me for a night and make the needed inquiry for my belongings. Also, he had given me another letter, of which more anon, and had pressed upon me a small purse of gold pieces—a treasure rare enough in patriot hands in that impoverished time.

When all was done, two of my late captors were ordered to set me straight in the road; and some half-hour past noon I had shaken hands with the big fellow in homespun who had been so bent upon hanging me without benefit of clergy, had crossed the river, and was making the first looping in a detour which should bring me into Charlotte from the westward.

'Twas drawing on toward evening, and I had recrossed the river a mile or more below Appleby Hundred, when I began to meet the outposts of the British army. I was promptly halted by the first of these; but my borrowed uniform and a ready word or two passed me within the lines as a courier riding post to headquarters from Major Ferguson in the west.

The lieutenant in command of the first vedette line was not over-curious. He asked me a few questions about the major's plans and dispositions,—questions which, thanks to Colonel Davie's information, I was able to answer glibly enough, swallowed my tale whole, and was so obliging as to give me the password for the night to help me through the inner sentry lines.

Thus fortified, I rode on boldly, and having the countersign the difficulties vanished. When I was come to town it was well past candle-lighting; and the patrol was out in force. But by dint of using the password freely I made my way unhindered to the house of the gentleman to whom Colonel Davie's letter accredited me.

Here, however, the difficulties began. Though the camp of the army lay just without the town to the southward, the officers were quartered in every house, and that of Colonel Davie's friend was full to overflowing. What was to be done we knew not, but at the last moment my friend's friend thought of an expedient and wrote a note for me whilst I waited, half in hiding, in the outer hall.

"'Tis a desperate chance, but these are desperate times," said my would-be helper. "I am sending you to the town house of one of our plantation seigneurs—a man who is fish, flesh or fowl, as his interest demands. I hear he came in to-day to take protection, and there is a chance that he will shelter you for the sake of your red coat and a gold piece or two. But I warn you, you must be what you appear to be—a soldier of the king—and not what this note of Colonel Davie's says you are."

Seeing a wide field of danger-chances in this haphazarding, I would have asked more about this trimming gentleman to whom I was to be handed on; but at that moment there came a thundering at the door, and my anxious host was fain to hustle me out through the kitchen as he could, catching up a black boy on the way to be my guide.

"God speed you," he said at parting. "Make your footing good for the night, if you can, and we'll see what can be done to-morrow. I'll send your portmanteau around in the morning, if so be Mr. Pettigrew has it."

With that I was out in the night again, turning and doubling after my guide, who seemed to be greatly afeard lest I should come nigh enough to cast an evil eye upon him.

'Twas but a little distance we had to go, and I had no word out of my black rascal till we reached the door-stone of a familiar mansion but one remove from the corner of the court house green. Here, with a stuttering "D-d-dis de house, Massa," he fled and left me to enter as I could.

Since the street was busily astir with redcoat officers and men coming and going, and any squad of these might be the questioners to doubt my threadbare courier tale, I lost no time in running up the steps and hammering a peal with the heavy knocker. Through the side-lights I could see that the wide entrance hall was for the moment unoccupied; but at the knocker-lifting I had a flitting glimpse of some one—a little man all in sober black—coming down the stair. There was no immediate answer to my peal, but when I would have knocked again the door was swung back and I stepped quickly within to find myself face to face with—Margery.

I know not which of the two of us was the more dumb-founded; but this I do know; that I was still speechless and fair witless when she swept me a low-dipped curtsy and gave me my greeting.

"I bid you good evening, Captain Ireton," she said, coldly; and then with still more of the frost of unwelcome in her voice: "To what may we be indebted for this honor?"

Now, chilling as these words were, they thrilled me to my finger-tips, for they were the first she had spoken to me since the night of my offending in the black gorge of the far-off western mountains. None the less, they were blankly unanswerable, and had the door been open I should doubtless have vanished as I had come. Of all the houses in the town this was surely the last I should have run to for refuge had I known the name of its master; and it was some upflashing of this thought that helped me find my tongue.

"I never guessed this was your father's house," I stammered, bowing low to match her curtsy. "I beg you will pardon me, and let me go as I came."

She laid a hand on the door-knob. "Is—is there any one here whom you would see?" she asked; and now her eyes did not meet mine, and I would think the chill had melted a little.

"No. I was begging a night's lodging of a friend whose house is full. He sent me here with a note to—ah—to your father, as I suppose, though in his haste he did not mention the name."

She held out her hand. "Give me the letter."

"Nay," said I; "that would be but thankless work. Knowing me, your father must needs conceive it his duty to denounce me."

"Give it me!" she insisted; this with an impatient little stamp of the foot and an upglance of the compelling eyes that would have constrained me to do a far foolisher thing, had she asked it.

So I gave her the letter and stood aside, hat in hand, while she read it. There were candles in their sconces over the mantel and she moved nearer to have the better light. The soft glow of the candles fell upon her shining hair, and upon cheek and brow; and I could see her bosom rise and fall with the quick-coming breath, and the pulse throbbing in her fair white neck. And with the seeing I became a fool of love again in very earnest, and was within a hair's breadth of sinking honor and all else in an outpouring of such words as a man may say once to one woman in all the world—and having said them may never unsay them.

'Twas a most practical little thing she did that saved me from falling headlong into this last ditch of dishonor. Twisting the letter into a spill she stood on tiptoe to light it at one of the candles, saying: "'Twas a foolish thing to put on paper, and might well hang the writer in such times as these. He says you are a king's man and well known to him, and you are neither." But when the letter was a crisp of blackened paper-ash she turned upon me, and once again the changeful eyes were cold and her words were stranger-formal.

"What is it you would have me do, Captain Ireton?"

"Nothing," I made haste to say; "nothing save to believe that I came here unwittingly—and to let me go."

"Where will you go? The town is alive with those who would—who would—"

"Who would show me scant mercy, you would say. True; and yet I came hither—to the town, I mean—of my own free will."

Her mood changed in the pivoting fraction of an instant, and now the beautiful eyes were alight and warm and pleadingly eloquent.

"Oh, why did you come? Are you—are you what they said you were?"

"A spy? If I am, you would scarce expect me to confess it, even to you."

"'Tis dishonorable—most dishonorable!" she cried. "I could respect a brave soldier enemy; but a spy—"

There was a clattering of hoofs in the street and a jingle of sword-scabbards on the door-stone. I wheeled to face the newcomers, determined now to front it boldly as a desperate man at bay. But before the fumbling hands without could find the door-knob Margery was beside me, all a-flutter in a trembling-fit of excitement.

"Up the stair, quickly, *pour l'amour de Dieu!*" she whispered; and we were at the clock landing when the great door opened and some half-dozen king's officers came in. We crouched together behind the balustrade till they should pass beyond the sight of us, and in the group I marked a man stout and heavy built, walking full solidly for his two-and-forty years. He wore his own hair dressed high in front in the fashion first set for the women by the Grand Monarque's loose-wife; and as he passed under the candles I saw that it was graying slightly. His face, high-browed, long-nosed, double-chinned, with the eyes womanish for bigness and marked with brows that might have been penciled by the hairdresser, I had seen before; but lacking this present sight of it, the orders on his breast would have named him the ranking general of the army in the field—Lord Charles Cornwallis. With all the houses in the town to choose among, I had blundered into this—my Lord's own headquarters.

I had but a passing glimpse of the incoming group, for when it was well beneath the turn of the stair, my lady had me up and running again, driving me on before her to the chamber floor above, along a dimly lighted corridor with many turnings, and so to a *cul-*

de-sac in the same—a doorless passage with a high dormer window in the end and no other apparent means of egress.

Margery had snatched a candle from one of the corridor holders in the flight, and now she bade me sit on the floor and draw my boots. I did it, shamefacedly enough, being but a foul and ragged vagabond unfit to have her come anigh me. But I might have spared my blushings for she had turned her back and was opening a secret door in the high wainscot.

Beyond the door lay a raftered garret half filled with cast-off house lumber and lighted and aired by two high roof windows. Into this she led me, with a finger on her lip for silence. A hum of voices, the clinking of glass, and now and again a hearty soldier laugh told me that my garret was above some living-room of the house.

While I stood, boots in hand, she found a makeshift candlestick and in a trice had spread me a pallet on an ancient oaken settle big enough to serve for a choir stall in a cathedral.

"You'll be safe here for the night, if so be you will make no more noise than a rat might make," she whispered. "*Mais, mon Dieu!* 'tis a terrible risk. How you will get off in the morning I do not know."

"Leave that to me," I rejoined. Then I remembered the portmanteau and the promise that it should be sent hither. Here was a further complication, and I must needs beg a boon of her. "A black boy will bring my portmanteau in the morning. I have a decent desire to be hanged in clean clothing; may I beg you to—"

She made a quick little gesture of impatience; at the further complication, or at my boldness in asking, I knew not which. But her whispered reply was of assent, and then she turned to leave me.

At that a sudden fierce desire to know why she had thus befriended me came to throttle prudence.

"One more word before you go, Mistress Margery. Will you tell me why you have done this for the man who can serve you only by thrusting his neck into the hangman's noose?"

She was silent for a little space, and I knew not what emotion it was that moved her to turn away and cover her face with her hands. But when she spoke her voice was low and tremulous with pent-up anger, as I thought.

"Truly, Captain Ireton, you have done a thing to make me hate you—and myself, as well. But I may not forget my duty, sir."

And with this cruel word she was gone.

CHAPTER XXXIII

IN WHICH I HEAR CHANCEFUL TIDINGS

You are not to suppose that the hazards of this hiding place in my Lord Cornwallis's headquarters would keep me from sleeping well and soundly. One of the things a soldier learns soonest is to take his rest when and as he can; and after peering curiously into the nooks and corners of my garret to make sure I was alone, I flung myself a-sprawl on the broad settle and was dropping off into forgetfulness when I heard a tapping at the wainscot.

It fetched me wide awake with a start, and I was up and weaponed instantly—having taken the precaution to lay my sword in easy reach before blowing out the candle. Groping my way cautiously to the secret door, I crouched and listened. All was silent save for the intermittent clamor of the wassailers in the room beneath. After waiting a full minute I opened the door and looked without. The high dormer window in the end of the corridor made the darkness something less than visible, and I could see that the passage was empty. But on the floor at my feet was my supper; a roasted fowl on a server, hot from the spit, with maize bread and garnishings fit for an epicure.

Since, as an appanage of Appleby Hundred, this was mine own house, and, by consequence, the fowl was mine, I ate as a hungry man should, making no scruple on the score of pride. Nor did I forget to be grateful to my lady; though when I remembered that this was doubtless but another leaf out of her duty-book, the meat was like to choke me. And it was this thought that made me resolve thrice over to loose her from the onerous burden of me so soon as ever the morning light should come to help me find the way out of my covert prison.

None the less, for all my fine resolves to be astir and off by daybreak, the sun was shining broadly in at my garret window when I awoke.

Seeing the sun, I tumbled out of my settle-bed, with a malediction on the sloth that had bound me so fast, and made for the door. But some one had been before me, entering whilst I slept. On a broken chair were a basin and ewer, with soap and towels; beside the chair was my portmanteau; and on a deal box, neatly covered with a linen cloth, was my breakfast.

You, my dears, who have your maid or man to tell you when your bath is ready, and to lay out the fresh, clean garments sweet from the laundering, may wonder that I put away the thought of flight and let the breakfast cool whilst I shaved and washed and scrubbed, and doffed the vagabond and donned the gentleman. I did it; did it leisurely, rolling the privilege as a sweet morsel under my tongue. They say the raiment never makes the man; 'tis a half-truth only. For in his own regard, at least, the man is vagabond or gentleman as he may dress the one part or the other. And I am sure of this; that when I drew up another of the cast-off chairs to sit at meat, freshly groomed, and clad in the field uniform of a captain of her Apostolic Majesty's Hussars, I was the fitter by many transmigrations to cope with fate or any other adversary.

And now, the claims of decency paid in full, and the keen edge of hunger somewhat dulled, I was free to think of my sweet lady's loving-kindness to one she hated—and to wonder what she would do and be for one she loved. As you would guess, there were dregs of bitterness in that cup; and I was once again set sharp upon relieving her of the burden of me.

Having my Austrian uniform, I was now ready to move in that venture outlined in part to Colonel Davie; but to set my plan in action I must first get free of the house unseen by my Lord or any of his suite. How to do this unaided I could not determine; and, since any fresh blundering would surely breed new trouble for Margery, I was forced to wait for her return.

I made sure she would come, if only to be the sooner quit of me; and so she did, tapping at the wainscot door whilst I was dallying with the breakfast leavings. 'Twas worth something to see her start of surprise when I opened to her; but she was far too true a lady to be one thing to the unwashed vagabond and another to the gentleman-clad.

I gave her good morning, and was beginning in some formal fashion to thank her for her thoughtful care, when she cut me short.

"'Tis my bounden duty, sir," she said, twanging once again upon that frayed string. "You are my guest and my—husband; though God knows I would you were neither."

"*Merci, Madame,*" said I; stung so sharply that the retort would out in spite of everything. "As once before, I am your poor misfortunate pensioner; but this time you are not less willing to give than I am to receive."

She gave me a look that I could not fathom, and for a flitting instant I could have sworn there was a mocking smile a-lurk at the back of the beautiful eyes. Then she went straight to the subject-matter of her errand, brushing aside the small passage at arms as if it had not been.

"You are in a most perilous situation, Captain Ireton; do you know it? News of your presence in Charlotte has got abroad, and at this very moment Tarleton's dragoons are making a house-to-house search for you."

"So; some one has betrayed me?"

She nodded.

"Do you know who it was?"

She nodded again.

I considered of it for a little time, and then said: "I must not be taken here. Will your—ah—*duty* stretch the length of showing me an unwatched door?"

"There are no doors unwatched. You must stay here till night-fall."

"Nay, that I will not. Will you tell me who it was set them on?"

"'Twas a man you hate—and who hates you heartily in return. He saw you come here last night; he knows you are here now—or guesses it."

I had no right to pry into her confidence as a thief would break into a house. But I was loath to fight my battle in the dark if she, or any one, could give me light.

"His name, if you may give it, Mistress Margery. It may point the way out of this coil."

"'Tis Owen Pengarvin. He was here last night when you came."

Now I remembered the little man in black whom I had seen coming down the stair whilst I knocked at the door. But this left me in a greater maze than ever.

"If he knows I am here, why does he let them search elsewhere?"

At this she looked away from me, and I made sure I saw the sweet chin quiver when she spoke.

"He has reasons of his own; reasons of—of—" but instead of telling me what they were she broke off to say: "But now you know why all the doors of this house are under guard."

"Truly," said I; and therewith I fell to pacing up and down the narrow clear-way in the garret, striving to see how I might come off with nothing worse than the loss of my burdensome life.

'Twas easy to guess how this shaveling lawyer had discomfited me. Forewarned is forearmed in any soldier camp; and through his blabbing, the plan by which I had hoped to lull resentment and forestall suspicion was nipped in the bud. I saw the far-reaching consequences, and was made to know how a trapped rat will turn and fight in sheer desperation whilst the terrier is shaking him to death.

When that leaven began to work in me I was fit for the daringest thing that offered; so I paused to ask if my Lord Cornwallis were yet in the house.

"He is writing letters in his bed-room," was her answer.

"If you will show me the way thither I shall be your poor debtor by that much more."

"I will not—unless you first tell me what you mean to do." She said it firmly, but now I was fronting death and could be as firm as she.

"If you will not show me the way, I shall find it for myself." So much I said; but as for telling her that I meant to save his Lordship and all the others the trouble of running me down, I could not do that.

"You are going to give yourself up," she said; and when I would not deny it, she darted before me and set her back against the wainscot door. "'Tis folly, folly!" she cried. "He would but pull the bell-cord and—"

"And give the order that Colonel Tarleton's sentence be executed upon me, you would say. Be it so. But in that event I can at least clear you and your father of any complicity in my hiding."

"I say you shall not go!"

What touch of savagery is it in a man that will not suffer him to let a woman, loved or unloved, stand in the last resort against his will? At any other time I would have pleaded with her; would have ended, mayhap, by weakly deferring to her wish. But now— well, you must remember, my dears, that I was the trapped rat. I took her gently in my arms, set her aside, and stepped out into the corridor.

I looked for nothing less than a volcano-burst of righteous indignation to pay me out for this piece of tyranny. But now, as twice or thrice before, my lady showed me how little a man may know of a woman's moods.

"You need not be so masterful rough with me," she said, with a pouting of the sweet lips that set me back upon that thought of a wayward child wanting to be kissed. "If you say I must, I am in duty bound to show you the way." And so she led on and I followed, in a deeper maze than any she had ever set me in.

Arrived at a pair of doors in the main passage, she showed me the one that opened to my Lord's bed-chamber and ran away; ran with her hands to her face as if to shut out a sight which would not bear looking upon.

I turned my back stiffly upon this newer wonder, pulled myself together and rapped on the door. A voice within bade me enter; the door opened under my hand and I stood in the presence of the man who, as I made no doubt, would shortly summon his guards and have me out to my rope and tree.

CHAPTER XXXIV

HOW I MET A GREAT LORD AS MAN TO MAN

The room in which I found myself was the guest-chamber, furnished luxuriously, for that day and place, in French-fashioned mahogany and gilt. The bed was high and richly canopied, as befitted a peer's resting place; there was a square of Turkish drugget on the floor, a cheerful fire burning in the chimney arch, and on the small table whereat the occupant of the guest-room had lately breakfasted, a goodly display of the Ireton silver.

My Lord was busy at his writing-desk when I entered; but when he looked up I saw the light of instant recognition in his eye. Never, I think, did another prisoner at the bar strive harder to read his sentence in his judge's eyes than I did in that moment of suspense. I liked not much the look he gave me; but his greeting was affable and kindly enough.

"Ah, Captain Ireton; 'tis you, is it? We are well met, at last. They told me you were gone to join the rebels, did they not?"

Here was an opening for a bold man, and in a flash I came to the right-about, choked down the defiance I had meant to hurl at him, and took quick counsel of cool audacity.

"Indeed, my Lord, I know not what they have told you. In times past, the king had no truer soldier than I; and when I came across seas 'twas not to fight against him. But that I have not joined the rebels is no fault of certain of your Lordship's officers."

"Say you so? But how is this? Surely I am not mistaken. I could be certain Colonel Tarleton reported your taking as a spy, and his trying of you. And was there not something about a rescue at the last moment by a band of these border bravos? But stay; let us have the colonel's story at first hands. Have the goodness to ring the bell for me, will you, Captain?"

The crisis was come. A pull at the bell-cord would summon the guard, and the guard would be sent after Colonel Tarleton. Well, said the demon Despair, 'tis time you were gone to make room for Richard Jennifer; and I laid a hand upon the tasseled rope. But when I would have rung, all the man-pride, of race and of soldier training, rose up to bid me fight for space to strike one good blow in freedom's cause by way of leave-taking.

So, as it had been an afterthought, I said: "A word further with you first, my Lord, and then, if you please, I will call the guard. All you remember is true, save as to the principal fact. So far from being a spy in intent, or even a partizan of either side, I was at the time but newly come into the province, knowing little of the cause of quarrel and caring still less. But Captain Falconnet and Colonel Tarleton did their earnest best to make a rebel of me out of hand."

"Ah? But the proof of all this, Captain Ireton."

"The best I can offer is the present fact of my coming to place myself at your Lordship's disposal, being moved thereto by your Lordship's own desire expressed in an order sent some weeks since to Sir Francis Falconnet."

"So?—then you knew of that order?"

"Captain Falconnet showed it to me after I was condemned and the firing squad was drawn up to snuff me out."

My Lord Charles gave me the courtier smile that so endeared him to his soldiers,—he was well-loved of his men,—and bade me sit.

"The plot thickens, as Mr. Richardson would say. Let me have your story, Captain Ireton. I would rejoice to know why Captain Sir Francis Falconnet saw fit to disobey his orders."

I was clear of the lee shore and the breakers at last, but I was fain to believe that not Machiavelli himself could hope to weather the storm in the open. How much or how little did Lord Cornwallis remember of Colonel Tarleton's report? How explicit had that report been?—was there any mention in it of my eavesdropping at the conference between Captain John Stuart and the baronet; of my attempt to warn the over-mountain men against the Indian-arming? Could I hope to tell his Lordship a tale so near the truth as to be unassailable by Tarleton and his officers, by Gilbert Stair and the spiteful little pettifogger, and yet so deftly garbled as to keep my neck out of the halter for the time being?

All these questions thronged upon me as a mob to pull cool reason from her seat, and I could only play the part of the trapped rat and snap back at them. Yet my Lord Cornwallis was waiting for his answer, and a single moment's hesitation might breed suspicion.

You must forgive me, my dears, if I confess it beyond me to set down here in measured words the tale I told his Lordship. A lie is a lie, be it told in never so good a cause; a thing deplorable and not to be glozed over or boasted of after the fact. So I beg you to let these quibblings to which I was driven rest in oblivion, figuring to yourselves that I used all the truth I dared, and that I strove through it all not wholly to sink the gentleman and the man of honor in the spy.

'Twas but a bridge of glass when all was said; a bridge that carried me safely over for the moment into my Lord's confidence, yet one which a pebble flung by any one of a dozen hands might shiver in the dropping of an eyelid.

"Truly, you have had a most romantic experience," said his Lordship, when I had made an end. Then he lay back in his chair and laughed till the stout body of him shook again. "And all about a little wench of the provincials. Well, well; Sir Francis was always a sad dog with the women. But all this was in the early summer, you say; where have you been since?"

Here was a chance for more romancing, this time of a sort less dangerous. So I drew breath and plunged again, telling how I had been carried off by my captor-rescuers; how I had fallen into the hands of the Indians—not all of whom, I would remind his Lordship, were friendly to the king; and lastly how I had but lately escaped from the mountain fastnesses back of Major Ferguson's camp at Gilbert Town. At this point my Lord interrupted the taletelling.

"So you know of the major and his doings? I would you had brought me late news of him. 'Tis a week since his last courier reached us."

This was the moment for the playing of my trump card—the only one I held. I rose, bowed, took from my pocket that other letter given me by Colonel Davie and handed it to his Lordship. 'Twas Major Ferguson's last report, intercepted by one of Davie's vigilant scouting parties.

"Ah!" said my Lord; and I strolled to the window whilst he read the letter.

When I turned to front him again he was all affability; and I knew I was safe—for the time, at least.

"The major commends you highly as a good man and a true, Captain Ireton," he said, and truly the letter did contain a warm-hearted commendation of "the bearer," whose name, for safety's sake, was omitted; and not only this, but the writer desired to have his man back again. Then my Lord added: "You are here to take your old service again, I assume?"

I hesitated. There be things that even a spy may balk at; and the taking of the oath of allegiance to the other side I conceived to be one of them. So I said:

"I have worn many uniforms since I doffed that of King George, my Lord, and—"

He laughed cheerily. "'But me no buts,' Captain Ireton; once an Englishman, always an Englishman, you know. I shall assign you to duty in my own family."

At this I made a bold stroke. "Let it be then as an officer of her Apostolic Majesty's service, and your Lordship's guest for the time. Believe me, it is thus I may best serve your—ah—the cause."

"As how?" he would ask.

I smiled and touched the braided jacket of my hussar uniform.

"As an Austrian officer on a tour of observation in the campaign I may go and come where others may not, and see and hear things which your Lordship may wish to know. Does your Lordship take me?"

He laughed and rose and clapped me on the shoulder.

"You may call the guard now, Captain, and I will turn you over—not to a firing squad, but to the tender mercies of our old rascal host who is a 'trimmer' of the devil's own school. If he tries to screw a penny's pay out of you, as he is like to, put him in arrest."

"It is your Lordship's meaning that I should be quartered here?—in this house?" I gasped.

"And why not? Ah, my good Captain of Hussars, I have made you my honorary aide-de-camp and a member of my family so that I may keep an eye on you. *Comprenez-vous?*"

He said it with a laugh and another hearty hand-clap on my shoulder, and I would fain take it for a jest. Yet there be playful gibes that hint at gibbets; and I may confess to you here, my dears, that I left my Lord's presence with the conviction that my acquittal was but a reprieve conditioned upon the best of future good behavior. So it took another turn of the audacity screw to tune me up for the battle royal with Gilbert Stair and the pettifogger, Owen Pengarvin.

CHAPTER XXXV

IN WHICH I FIGHT THE DEVIL WITH FIRE

With the house guard for a guide I found my host in a box-like den below stairs; a room with a writing-table, two chairs and a great iron strong-box for its scanty furnishings.

The old man was sitting at the table when I looked in, his long nose buried in a musty parchment deed. The light from the single small window was none too good, but it sufficed to help him recognize me at a glance, despite the hussar uniform. In a twinkling he put the breadth of the oaken table between us, hurled the parchment deed into the open strong-box, slammed to the cover and gave a shrill alarm.

"Ho! you devils without, there! Here he is—I have him! Help! Murder!"

The guard, a burly, bearded Darmstädter, turned on his heel and stood at attention in the doorway, looking stolidly for his orders, not to the shrilling master of the house, but to the man who wore a uniform.

"'Tis naught," I said, speaking in German. "He mistakes me for a *rittmeister* of the rebels. *Verstehen Sie?*"

The soldier saluted, wheeled and vanished; and I sat down to wait till the old man's outcry should pause for lack of breath. When my chance came, I said:

"Calm yourself, Mr. Stair. You are in no present danger greater than that which you may bring upon yourself. Blot out all the past, if you please, and consider me now as a member of Lord Cornwallis's military family seeking quarters in your house by my Lord's express command."

"Quarters in my house?—ye're a damned rebel spy!" he cried. "I'll denounce ye to my Lord for what ye are. Ho! ye rascals, I say!"

"Peace!" I commanded, sternly; "this is but child's folly. No man in the British army would arrest me at your behest. Ring the bell and summon your factor lawyer. I would have a word or two in private with both of you."

He dropped into a chair, and I could see the sweat standing in great beads on his wrinkled forehead.

"D' ye—d' ye mean to kill us both?" he gasped.

"Not if I can help it. But some better understanding is needful, and we will have it here and now, once for all. Will you ring, or shall I?"

He made no move to reach the bell-cord, and I rang for him. A grinning black boy came to the door, and seeing that Mr. Gilbert Stair was beyond giving the order, I gave it myself.

"Find Master Pengarvin and send him here quickly. Tell him Mr. Stair wants him."

There was a short interval of waiting and then the lawyer came. Being but a little wisp of a man, all malignance and no courage, he would have fled when he saw me. But I caught him by the collar and sent him scurrying around the table to keep his master company.

"Now, then; how much or how little have you two blabbed of the doings at Appleby Hundred some weeks since?" I demanded. "Speak out, and quickly."

'Twas the lawyer who obeyed, and now he was the trapped rat to snap blindly in despair.

"You will hang higher than Haman when the dragoons find you," he gritted out.

"On your information?"

"On mine and Mr. Stair's."

"Ye lie!" shrieked the miser. "I tell't ye to keep hands off, ye bletherin' little deevil, ye!"

"Never mind," said I; "what's done is done. But it must be undone, and that swiftly and thoroughly. Lie out of it to Colonel Tarleton and the others as you will; Captain John Stuart and the baronet are not here to contradict you, and you are the only witnesses. Knock together some story that will hold water and lose no time about it. Do you understand?"

Seeing he was not to be put to the wall and spitted on the spot, the lawyer recovered himself.

"'Tis not the criminal at the bar who dictates terms, Captain Ireton," he said, with his hateful smirk. "You are under sentence of death, and that by a court lawful enough in war time."

"You refuse?" I said.

He shrugged.

"Speaking for myself, I shall leave no stone unturned to bring you to book, Captain,—when it suits my purpose."

I was loath to go to extremities with either of them; but my bridge of glass must be defended at all hazards.

"You would best reconsider, Mr. Pengarvin. At this present moment I am of my Lord Cornwallis's military family and I have his confidence. A word from me will put you both in arrest as persons whose loyalty in times past has been somewhat more than blown upon."

"Bah!" said the pettifogger. "Bluster is a good dog, but Holdfast is the better. You can prove nothing, as you well know. Moreover, with your own neck in a noose you dare not mess and meddle with other men's affairs."

"Dare not, you say? I'll tell you what I may dare, Master Attorney. If you are not disposed to meet me half way in this matter, I shall go to my Lord, tell him how I have been cheated out of my estate, declare the marriage with Mistress Margery, and see that you get your just deserts. And you may rest assured that this soldier-earl will right me, come what may."

'Twas a bold stroke, the boldest of any I had made that morning; but I was wholly unprepared for its effect upon the lawyer. His rage was like that of some venomous little animal, a thing to make an onlooker shudder and draw back.

"Never!" he hissed; "never, I say! I'll kill her first—I'll—" He choked in the very exuberance of his malignance, and his face was like the face of a man in a fit.

'Twas then that I saw the pointing of his villainy and knew what Margery had meant when she said that for reasons of his own he was holding my betrayal in abeyance. He was Falconnet's successor and my rival. This little reptile aspired to be the master of my father's acres and the husband of my dear lady! And his holding off from denouncing me at once was also explained. Taking it for granted that the wife would bargain for the husband's life, he had made a whip of his leniency to flog Margery into subjection.

My determination was taken upon the instant. There was no safety for Margery whilst this plotting pettifogger was at large, and I stepped to the door and called the sentry. The Darmstädter came back and I pointed to the lawyer. Then, indeed, the furious little madman found his tongue and shrilled out his defiance.

"Curse you!" he yelled. "I'll be quits with you for this, Master Spy! 'Tis your hearing now, but mine will come, and you shall hang like a dog! I'll follow you to the ends of the earth—I'll—"

I made a sign and the soldier brought his musket into play and pricked his prisoner with the bayonet in token that time pressed. So we were rid of the lawyer in bodily presence, though I could hear his snarlings and spittings as the big Darmstädter ran him out at the bayonet's point.

During this tilt between his factor and me, Mr. Gilbert Stair had stood apart, watchful but trembling. When we were alone I said:

"Now, Mr. Stair, I shall trouble you to billet me somewhere in your house, as a member of my Lord's family. Lead on, if you please, and I'll follow."

He went before me without a word, out of the little den and up the broad stair, doddering like a man grown ten years older in a breath, and catching at the balustrade to steady himself as we ascended. The room he gave me was at an angle in one of the crookings of the corridor, and pointing me to the door he went pottering away, still without a word or a look behind him.

The door was on the latch, but it gave reluctantly, letting me in suddenly when I set my shoulder to it. There was a quick little cry, half of anger, half of affright, from within. I drew back hastily, with a muttered curse upon the old man's spite, and in the act my spur caught the door and slammed it shut behind me.

For reasons known only to Omniscience and to himself, Gilbert Stair had shown me to my lady's chamber; she was standing, with her bodice off, before the oval mirror on the high dressing case.

CHAPTER XXXVI

HOW I RODE POST ON THE KING'S BUSINESS

If a look might be a leven-stroke to do a man to death, I warrant you my lady's flashing eyes would have crisped me to a cinder where I stood fumbling with one hand behind me for the latch of the slammed door. Scorn, indignation, outraged maiden modesty, all these thrust at me like air-drawn daggers; and it needed not her, "Fie, for shame, Captain Ireton!—and you would call yourself a gentleman!" to set me afire with prinklings of abashment.

What could I say or do? The accursed door-latch would not find itself to let me fly; and as for excusings, I could not tell her that her own father had thrust me thus upon her. Yet, had she let me be, I hope I should have had the wit to find the door fastening and the grace to run away; in truth, I had the latch in hand when she lashed out at me again, and my tingling shame began to give place to that master-devil of passion which is never more than half whipped into subjection in the best of us.

"How are you better than the man you warned me of?" she cried. And then, in a tempest of grief: "Oh! you would not leave me the respect I bore you; you must even rob me of that to fling it down and trample it under foot!"

Figure to yourselves, my dears, that I was wholly blameless in this unhappy breaking and entering, and so, mayhap, you may find excuse for me. For now, though I could have gone, I would not. Her glorious beauty, heightened beyond compare by the passionate outburst, held me spellbound. And at my ear the master-devil whispered: She is your wedded wife; yours for better or worse, till death part you. Who has a better right to look upon her thus?

So it was that the love-madness came upon me again, and that thin veneering wherewith the Christian centuries have so painfully overlaid the natural man in us was cracked and riven, and the barbarian which lies but skin-deep underneath bestirred himself and winked and blinked himself awake in giant might, as did the primal man when he rose up to look about him for his mate.

Before I knew what I would do, I was beside her, and honor, or what may stand therefor betwixt a man and his friend, was flung away. But when I would have crushed her sweetness in my arms she went upon her knees to me.... Ah, God! she knelt to me as she had knelt to that other would-be ravisher and begged me for mine own honor's sake to bethink me of what I would do.

"Oh, Monsieur John! be merciful as you are strong!" she pleaded. "Think what it will mean to you, and how you will loathe me and yourself as well when this madness is overpast! Oh, go; go quickly, lest I, too, forget—"

And so it was that I found sudden strength to turn and leave her kneeling there; turned to grope blindly for the door with all the pains of hell aflame within me.

For now I had put honor under foot; now I knew that I had truly earned her scorn and loathing. I could no longer plead that I was the puppet of fate flung against my will between this maiden and my dear lad. I was the wilful offender; false to my love, false to my friend, a recreant to every oath wherewith I had bound myself to be true and loyal to these two.

With such a flaming sword to drive me forth, I stumbled from the room, thinking only how I should quickest rid me of myself. Hastening to my garret sleeping-place I buckled on my sword, found my shako, and went straight to my Lord's bed-chamber. My rap at the door went unanswered, and a broad-shouldered young fellow in a lieutenant's uniform, lounging on a settle in the clock landing of the stair, told me Lord Cornwallis was gone out.

I was face to face with this young lieutenant before I recognized him; being so bent upon haste I should have passed him on the landing without a second glance had he not risen to grip me by the shoulders.

"By the Lord Harry!" he cried, "is it thus you pass an old friend without a word, Captain Ireton?"

'Twas my good death-watch; that Lieutenant Tybee of the light-horse who had sunk the British officer in the man in that trying night at Appleby Hundred. I returned his hearty greeting as well as I might, and would have explained my present state and standing but that I was loath to lie to him. But as to this, he saved me the shame of it.

"I could have sworn you were no rebel, Captain Ireton; indeed, I made bold to say as much to our colonel, after it was all over. I told him a soft word or two would have won you back to your old service. You see I knew better than the others what lay beneath all your madnesses that night."

"You knew somewhat, but not all," I said; and thereupon, lest he should involve me deeper and detain me longer when I was athirst to be gone, I hastened to ask where I might hope to find his Lordship and Colonel Tarleton.

"'Tis the hour for parade; you will find them at the camp," he replied. And then, out of the honest English heart of him: "Have you made your peace, Captain? Do you need a friend to go with you?"

I said I had been granted a hearing by Lord Cornwallis but a little while before; that by my Lord's appointment I was now a sort of honorary aide-de-camp.

"Good!" said the lieutenant, gripping my hand in a way to make me wince for the lie-in-effect hidden in the simple statement of fact. Then he roared at the soldier standing guard at the house door below: "A mount for Captain Ireton—and be swift about it!"

He held me in talk till the horse was fetched, happily doing most of the talking himself, and when I was in the saddle gave me a hearty God-speed. Being so sick with self-despisings, I fear I made but a poor return for all this good comradeship; but at the time I could think of nothing but the hell that flamed within me, and of how I could soonest quench the fires of it.

The town, which I had not seen since early summer, was but little changed by the British occupation, save in the livening of it by the near-at-hand camp of an armed host. Being but a halt-point *en route* in the northward march, it was not fortified; indeed, for the matter of that, the camp proper was a little way without the town, as I have said.

I rode slowly across the common, skirting the commissary's quarters and making mental notes of all I saw; this from soldier habit solely, for at the time I had little thought of living on to make a spy's use of them. Arrived at the parade ground, I found my Lord galloping through the lines on inspection, and so I must draw rein in the background and wait my opportunity.

The pause gave space for some eye-sweep of the scene, and all the soldier blood in me was stirred by the sight, the first I had had in many a day, of a well-ordered army, fit, disciplined, machine-drilled to move like the parts of a wondrous mechanism.

At the back of Lord Cornwallis and his galloping suite, Tarleton's famous light-horse legion was drawn up; and fronting it was the infantry, rank on rank, the glittering bayonets slanting in the October sunlight as the regiments moved into place, or standing in rigid groves of steel at the command to halt and port arms.

What was there in all our poor raw land to stand against this well-trained host, armed—as we were not—with the deadly bayonet, and moving as one man at the word of command? Not the bravest home guard or militia troop, I thought; and this seeing of what he had had to front on the field of Camden made me think less scornfully of Horatio Gates.

Riding presently around the field to be the nearer to the general when my time should come, I missed the mark completely. It so chanced that as the parade was ended my Lord and his suite were at the extreme right; and when the regiments broke ranks I was forced to skirt the entire camp to come into the road. By this time those I sought were gone into the town, so I must needs turn about and follow, with the thing I had to say still unspoken.

I need not drag you back and forth with me on the search I made to find Lord Cornwallis again. 'Tis enough to say that after missing him here and there, I ran him to earth at the court house, where, it was told me, my Lord was sitting in council with his staff officers.

Thinking it worse than useless to try to force my way into the council chamber, I waited in the raff of soldiery without, cursing the delay which gave my despairing resolution time to cool. When I had closed the door of my dear lady's chamber behind me I was resolved to fling myself upon that fate which needed but a word from me to make my calling and election to a gibbet swift and sure. Had I found my Lord Cornwallis in his bed-room the word would have been spoken; but now the iron of resolution cooled in spite of me.

'Twas not that I was less willing to pay the price of expiation; that must be done in any case. But I had seen the enemy, and all the soldier in me rebelled at the thought of dying like a noosed bullock in the shambles. Could I but strike that one good blow.

The old court house of our greater Mecklenburg was such as some of you may remember; a stout wooden building raised upon brick pillars to leave a story underneath. In the time of the British occupation this lower story served as a market house, and the public entrance to the court room above was reached by steps on the outside. In my boyhood days this outer stair was the only one; but now in wandering aimlessly through the market-place beneath I found another flight in a corner; the "jury stair," they called it, since it provided the means of egress from the jury box above.

The sight of this inner stair set me plotting. Could I make use of it to come unseen into the council chamber of Lord Cornwallis and his officers?

The market-place was well thronged with venders and soldier buyers; the patriotic Mecklenburgers were not averse to the turning of an honest penny upon the needs of their oppressors, as it seemed. I watched my chance, and when there were no prying eyes to mark it, made the dash up the steps.

Happily for the success of the adventure there was an angle in the narrow stair to hide me whilst I lifted the trap door in the court-room floor a scant half-inch and got my bearings. As I had hoped, the trap opened behind the jury box, and I was able to raise it cautiously and so to draw myself up into the room above, unseen and unheard.

A peep around the corner of the high jury stalls showed me my Lord and his suite gathered about the lawyers' table in front of the bar. Of the staff I recognized only Stedman, the commissary-general; Tarleton, looking something the worse for his late illness; Major Hanger, his second in command, and the young Irishman, Lord Rawdon.

At the moment of my espial, Cornwallis was speaking, and I drew back to listen, well enough content to be in earshot. For if my good angel had timed my coming I could not have arrived at a more opportune moment.

"What we have to consider now is how best to reach Ferguson with an express instantly," his Lordship was saying. "This rising of the over-mountain men is likely to prove a serious matter—not only for the major, but for the king's cause in the two provinces. Lacking positive orders to the contrary, Ferguson will fight—we all know that; and if he should be defeated 'twill hopelessly undo his work among the border loyalists and set us back another twelvemonth."

"Then your Lordship will order him to come in with what he has?" said a voice which I knew for Colonel Tarleton's.

"Instanter, had I a sure man to send."

"Pshaw! I can find you a hundred amongst the late royalist recruits." 'Twas young Lord Rawdon who said this.

"Damn them!" said his Lordship shortly; "I would sooner trust this new aide of mine. He comes straight from the major and can find his way back again."

Tarleton laughed. "I fear we shall never agree upon him, my Lord. I know not how he has made his peace with you, but I do assure you he is as great a rascal as ever went unhung. 'Tis true, as you say, I did not go into the particulars; but were Captain Stuart or Sir Francis Falconnet here, either of them would convince your Lordship in a twinkling."

There was silence for a little space following the colonel's denunciation of me, and then my Lord broke it to say: "I may not be so credulous as you think, Colonel. Rebel spy or true-blue loyalist, he is safe enough for the present. In the meantime in this matter of reaching Ferguson we may make good use of him."

"In what manner, your Lordship?" asked one whose voice I did not recognize.

"He has come straight from Major Ferguson, as I say; and, loyalist or rebel, he can find his way back to Gilbert Town."

"But you'll never be trusting him with despatches!" said Lord Rawdon.

"There is no need to trust him. He can be given the despatches with some hint of their purport, and of how much the king's cause will profit by their safe delivery."

Again a silence fell upon the group around the lawyers' table, and then some one—'twas Major Hanger, as I thought—said: "'Tis an unread riddle for me as yet, my Lord."

Cornwallis laughed. "Where are your wits this morning, gentlemen? If he be loyal and true, the despatches will go safe enough. If, on the other hand, he be a rebel and a spy, he will doubtless tamper with them; but in that case he will none the less ride straight enough to Major Ferguson's headquarters in the West."

"H'm; your Lordship is still too deep for me," said Tarleton's second in command. "If he be a rebel and a spy, why, in God's name, should he carry your Lordship's letters to any but some rag-tag colonel of his own kidney?"

My Lord laughed again. "Truly, Major, you should go to a dame's school and learn diplomacy. If we tell him beforehand what our object is, how could any rebel of them all defeat it more surely than by going to Ferguson with a garbled message that would make him stand and fight a losing battle?"

"But, my Lord—the risk!" cut in the commissary-general.

"There need be none. An hour after he sets out we shall send a mounted detail after him with an Indian tracker to nose out his trail. The lieutenant in command will carry duplicate despatches. At the worst, Ireton will guide these followers to Ferguson's rendezvous; and, so far as we know, he is the only man who knows exactly where to find the major."

I had heard enough. Under cover of the chorus of bravos raised by Lord Cornwallis's explication of his plot within a plot, I lifted the trap-door and made my exit as noiselessly as I had come.

Guessing that no time would be lost in putting the plan into action, I made haste to be found inquiring hither and yon for the commander-in-chief when my Lord and his suite came down the outer stair; and when we were met I was quickly told of my assignment to courier duty.

"Make your preparations to take the road within the hour, and report to me at Friend Stair's," said my Lord, most affably. "We shall put your new-found loyalty to the test, Captain Ireton, by entrusting you with a most important mission. Go with the commissary-general and he will find you your mount and equipment."

Thus dismissed, I went with Stedman, and was accorded a

more gentlemanly welcome than my overhearings had given me leave to expect.

On the way to the horse paddock the commissary-general told me of his plan to write a history of the campaign; a bit of confidence which set me laughing inwardly and wondering if he would put one John Ireton, sometime of the Scots Blues, and late captain in her Apostolic Majesty's Hussars, between the covers of his book. 'Tis small wonder that he did not. I have since had the pleasure of reading his history of the great war, and I find it curiously lacking in those incidents which did not redound to the honor and glory of the king's cause and army in the field.

Not to digress, however, my makeshift mount was soon exchanged for a better; I was allowed to draw what I would of accoutrements and provender from the king's stores; and so, to cut it short, I was presently at the door of my Lord's headquarters fully equipped and ready for the road.

I did hope in those last few moments that I might have a chance to exchange a word with my dear lady; might ask her forgiveness, or, failing so much grace of her, might at least have another sight of her sweet face.

But even this poor boon was denied me. I was scarce out of the saddle when an aide came to conduct me to the general, and I saw no one in the house save my Lord himself.

As you would guess, my instructions conformed exactly to the plan outlined by Lord Cornwallis in the council. I was entrusted with a sealed packet for delivery to Major Ferguson, and, for safety's sake, as my Lord explained, I was given the meat of the message to deliver verbally should the need arise. Ferguson was to be ordered to come in instantly by forced marches, if necessary, and he was on no account to risk a battle with the over-mountain men.

You may be sure, my dears, that I scarce drew breath till I was a-horse and out of the town and galloping hard on the road to that ford of Master Macgowan's which afterward became famous in our history under the misspelling "Cowan's Ford." 'Twas too good to be true that I should be thrust thus into the very gaping mouth of opportunity, and now and again I would feel the packet buttoned tight beneath my hussar jacket to make sure 'twas not a dream to vanish at a touch.

In the mad joy of it the spirit of prophecy came upon me, and I saw as if the thing were done, how at last I held the fate of the patriot cause in all our west country in the hollow of my hand.

CHAPTER XXXVII

OF WHAT BEFELL AT KING'S CREEK

Skipping lightly over the happenings of the two days following my departure from Charlotte on the king's errand, I may say that after passing the British outposts at the crossing of the Catawba, I met neither friend nor foe; and from noon on I rode to the westward through a pitiless drizzling rain, splashed to the belt with the mire of the road, and having little chance to inquire my way.

This last lack grew with the passing hours to the size of a threatening hazard. As you may have guessed, I knew no more than a blind man the route I should take; knew no more of the whereabouts of Gilbert Town and Major Ferguson's rendezvous than that both were some eighty miles to the westward.

At the outset I had thought to feel out the way in general by cautious inquiry along the road; but when I came to consider of this, the risk of betraying my ignorance to those who followed me was too great to let me turn aside to any of the wayside houses; and as for chance passers-by, there were none—the rain kept all within doors.

So I was constrained to gallop on without pause; and throughout that comfortless afternoon and the scarce less miserable day which followed, there were no incidents to break the dull monotony of the blind race save these two; that once the clouds lifted enough to give me a glimpse of my pursuers in a far reach to the eastward; and once again I had a sight of an awkward horseman in the road before me—saw him and tried to overtake him, and could not, for all his clumsy riding.

Now I was curious about this lone horseman ahead for more reasons than one, but chiefly because my glimpse of him seemed to show me the back of a man whom I made sure I had left safe behind in the British guard-house in Charlotte, to wit: the scoundrelly little pettifogger.

At first I scoffed at the idea. Saying he were free to leave Charlotte, how should he be riding post on my haphazard road to the westward? 'Twas against all reason, and yet the tittuping figure of which I had but a rain-veiled glimpse named itself Owen Pengarvin in spite of all the reasons I could bring to bear.

'Twas close on eventide of the second day, the early evening gloaming of a chill autumnal rain-day, and I had been since morning dubiously lost in the somber trackless forest, when an elfish cry rose, as it would seem, from beneath the very hoofs of my horse.

"God save the king!"

The bay shied suddenly, standing with nostrils a-quiver; and I had to look closely to make out the little brown dot of humanity clad in russet homespun crouching in the path, its childish eyes wide with fear and its lips parted to shrill again: "God save the king!"

I threw a stiff leg over the cantle and swung down to go on one knee to my stout challenger. I can never make you understand, my dears, how the sight of this helpless waif appearing thus unaccountably in the heart of the great forest mellowed and softened me. 'Twas a little maid, not above three or four years old, and with a face that Master Raphael might have taken as a pattern for one of his seraphs.

"What know you of the king, little one?" I asked.

"Gran'dad told me," she lisped. "If I was to see a soldier-man I must say, quick, 'God save the king,' or 'haps he'd eat me. Is—is you hungry, Mister Soldier-man?"

"Truly I am that, sweetheart; but I don't eat little maids. Where is your grandfather?"

"Ain't got any gran'favver; I said 'gran'*dad*.'"

"Well, your gran'dad, then; can you take me to him?"

"I don't know. 'Haps you'd eat *him*."

"No fear of that, my dear. Do I look as if I ate people?"

She gave me a long scrutiny out of the innocent eyes and then put up two little brown hands to be taken. "I tired" she said; and my sore heart went warm within me when I took her in my arms and cuddled her. After a long-drawn sigh of contentment, she said: "My name Polly; what's yours?"

"You may call me Jack, if you please—Captain Jack, if that comes the easier. And now will you let me take you to your gran'dad?"

She nodded, and I spoke to the bay and mounted, still holding her closely in my arms.

"Tell me quickly which way to go, Polly," I said; for besides being, as I would fear, far out of the way to Gilbert Town, the last hilltop to the rear had given me another sight of my shadowing pursuers riding hard as if they meant to overtake me.

The little maid sat up straight on the saddle horn and looked about her as if to get her bearings.

"That way," she said, pointing short to the right; and I wheeled the horse into a blind path that wound in and out among the trees for a long half mile, to end at a little clearing on the banks of a small stream.

In the midst of the clearing was a rude log cabin; and in the open doorway stood a man bent and aged, a patriarchal figure with white hair falling to his shoulders and a snowy beard such as Aaron might have worn. At sight of me the old watcher disappeared within the house, but a moment later he was out again, fingering the lock of an ancient Queen's-arm.

I drew rein quickly, and the little maid sat up and saw the musket.

"Don't shoot, gran'dad!" she cried. "He's Cappy Jack, and he doesn't eat folkses."

At this the old man came to meet us, though still with the clumsy musket held at the ready.

"These be parlous times, sir," he said, half in apology, I thought. And then: "You have made friends with my little maid, and I owe you somewhat for bringing her safe home."

"Nay," said I; "the debt is mine, inasmuch as I have the little one for my friend. 'Tis long since I have held a trusting child in my arms, I do assure you, sir."

He bowed as grandly as any courtier. "I hope her trust is not misplaced, sir; though for the matter of that, we have little enough now to take or leave."

"You have given it all to the king?" said I, feeling my way as I had need to.

His eyes flashed and he drew himself up proudly.

"The king has taken all, sir, as you see," this with a wave of the hand to point me to the forlorn homestead. "There is naught left me save this poor hut and my little maid."

"'Taken,' you say? Then you are not of the king's side?"

He came a step nearer and faced me boldly. "Listen, sir: two of my sons were left on the bloody field of Camden, and the butcher Banastre Tarleton slew the other two at Fishing Creek. A month since a band of roving savages, armed with King George's muskets, mind you, sir, came down upon us at Northby, and this little maid's mother—"

He stopped and choked; and the child looked up into my face with her blue eyes full of nameless terror. "Oh, I want my mammy!" she said. "Won't you find her for me, Cappy Jack?"

I slipped from the saddle, still clasping the little one tightly in my arms.

"Enough, sir," I said, when I could trust myself to speak. "This same King George's minions have made me a homeless outcast, too. I live but to give some counter stroke, if I may."

"Ha!" said the old man, starting back; "then you are for our side? But your uniform—"

"Is that of an Austrian officer, my good sir, which I should right gladly exchange for the buff and blue, but that I can serve the cause better in this."

He dropped the Queen's-arm, took the child from me and bade me welcome to his cabin and all it held. But I was not minded to make him a sharer in my private peril.

"No," said I. "Tell me how I may find Gilbert Town and Major Ferguson's rendezvous, and I will ride whilst I can see the way."

He looked at me narrowly. "Ferguson left Gilbert Town some days since. If 'tis the place you seek, you are gone far out of your way; if 'tis the man—"

"'Tis the man," I cut in hastily.

The patriarch shook his head.

"If you be of our side, as you say, he will hang you out of hand."

"So I can make my errand good, I care little how soon he hangs me."

"And what may your errand be? Mayhap I can help you."

"It is to bring him to a stand till the mountain men can overtake him."

The old man trembled with excitement like a boy going into his first battle.

"Ah, if you could—if you could!" he cried. "But 'tis too late, now. Listen: his present camp is but three miles to the westward on Buffalo Creek. I was there no longer ago than the Wednesday. I—I made my submission to him—curse him—so that I might mayhap learn of his plans. He told me all; how that now he was safe; that the mountaineers were gone off from the fording of the Broad on a false scent; that Tarleton with four hundred of the legion would soon be marching to his relief.

"I stole away when I could, and that night took horse and rode twenty miles to Tom Sumter's camp at Flint Hill—all to little purpose, I fear. Poor Tom is still desperately sick of his Fishing Creek wounds, and Colonel Lacey was the only officer fit to go after Shelby and the mountain men to set them straight. I should have gone myself, but—"

"Stay, my good friend," said I; "you go too fast for me. If Ferguson is still out of communication with the main at Charlotte, we may halt him yet."

The old man made a gesture of impatience.

"'Tis a thing done because it is as good as done. The major will break camp and march to-morrow morning, and he can reach Charlotte at ease in two days. What with their losing of his trail, the mountain men are those same two days behind him."

"None the less, we shall halt him," said I. "Have you ever an inkhorn and a quill in your cabin?"

"Both; at your service, sir. But I can not understand—"

"We may call it the little maid's judgment on those who have made her fatherless. But for her stopping of me I should have come unprepared into the camp of the enemy. I am the bearer of a letter from Lord Cornwallis to this same Major Ferguson."

"You?—a bearer of Lord Cornwallis's despatches?" The old man put a blade's length between us and held the little one aloft as if he feared I might do her a mischief. I laughed and bade him be comforted.

"'Tis a long story, and I may not take the time to tell it now. But a word will suffice. Like yourself, I made my submission—and for the same purpose. My Lord accepted it and made me his despatch-bearer because he thought I knew the way to Ferguson when no one else knew it. But enough of this; time presses. Let me have ink and the quill."

The old man led the way into the cabin and put his writing tools at my disposal. Left to myself, I should have broken the seal of the packet; but my wise old ally, cool and collected now, showed me how to split the paper beneath the wax. Opened and spread before us on the rude slab table, the letter proved to be the briefest of military commands: a peremptory order to Ferguson to rejoin the main body at once, proceeding by forced marches if needful, and on no account to risk engagement with the over-mountain men.

How to change such an order to reverse it in effect, I knew no more than a yokel; but here again my ancient ally showed himself a man of parts. Dressing the pen to make it the fellow of that used by my Lord Cornwallis, he scanned the handwriting of the letter closely, made a few practice pot-hooks to get the imitative hang of it, and wrote this *postscriptum* at the bottom of the sheet.

> Since writing the foregoing I have your courier, and his despatches. Lieutenant-colonel Tarleton, with four hundred of the legion, will take the road for you to-night. If battle is forced upon you, make a stand and hold the enemy in check till reinforcements come.
>
> Cornwallis.

The old man sanded the wet penstrokes and bade me say if it would serve. 'Twas a most beautiful forgery. My Lord's crabbed handwriting was copied to a nicety, and of the two signatures I doubt if the earl himself could have told which was his own; 'twas the same circle "C," the same printing "r," the same heavy precision throughout.

"Capital!" said I. "Now, if the lightning would but strike these pursuers of mine, we should have the Scotsman at bay in a hand's turn."

"How?" said the patriarch; "are you followed?"

I told him I was; told him of my Lord's plot within a plot—that three light-horse riders, one of them a lieutenant bearing duplicate despatches, had been hard upon my heels all the way from Charlotte.

At this the old warhorse—I learned afterward that he had fought through the French and Indian war—wagged his beard and his eye flashed.

"We must stop them," he said. "Three of them, do you say?"

"Three white men and an Indian trailer."

"Ha! If it were not for the little maid.... Let me think."

He fell to pacing up and down before the fire on the hearth, and I took the small one on my knee to let her chatter to me. 'Twas five full minutes before my ancient gave me the worth of his cogitations, but when he did speak it was much to the purpose.

"These marplot rear-guards of yours will spoil it all if they come to Ferguson's camp either before or after you. Do they know the major's present whereabouts?"

"No more than I did an hour ago. As I take it, they are depending on me to show them the way."

"Well, then; dead men tell no tales."

"But, my good friend, you forget there are four of them and only two of us! We should stand little chance with them in fair fight."

Again the old man's eyes snapped and glowed as if pent-fires were behind them.

"Was it fair fight when Tarleton's men rode in upon Tom Sumter's rest camp at Fishing Creek and cut down this little maid's father whilst he was naked and bathing in the stream? Was it fair fight when King George's Indian devils came down in the dead of night upon our defenseless house at Northby? Never talk to me of fairness, sir, whilst all this bloody tyranny is afoot!"

I thought upon it for a little space. 'Twas none so easy to decide. On one hand, stern loyalty to the cause I had espoused passed instant sentence on these four men whose lives stood in the way; on the other, common humanity cried out and called it murder.

Never smile, my dears, and hint that I had found me a new

heart of mercy since that ambush-killing of the three Cherokee peace-men in the lone valley of the western mountains. We did but give the savages a dole out of their own store of cruel cunning and ferocity. But as for these my trackers, three of them, at least, were soldiers and men of my own race. I could not do it.

"No," said I, firmly. "These followers of mine must be stopped, as you say, else there is no need of my going on. But there must be no butcher's work."

The patriarch frowned and wagged his beard again.

"A true patriot should hold himself ready to give his own life or take another's," quoth he.

"Truly; and I am most willing on both heads. But we have had enough and more than enough of midnight massacre."

Where this argument would have led us in the end, I know not, since we were both waxing warm upon it. But in the midst the little maid came running from the open door, her blue eyes wide in childish terror.

"Injun man!" was all she could say; but that was enough. At a bound I reached the door. An Indian was at my horse's head, loosing the halter, as I thought. Before he could twist to face me the point of the Ferara was at his back.

Luckily, he had the wit not to move. "No kill Uncanoola," he muttered, this without the stirring of a muscle. Then, as if he were talking to the horse: "White squaw, she send 'um word; say 'good by.'"

My point dropped as if another blade had parried the thrust.

"Mistress Margery, you mean? Do you come from her?"

"She send 'um word; say 'good by,'" he repeated.

"What else did she say?" I demanded.

"No say anyt'ing else: say 'good by.'" He turned upon me at that and I saw why he had kept his face averted. He had on the war paint of a Cherokee chief.

"Uncanoola good Chelakee now," he grinned. "Help redcoat soldier find Captain Long-knife. Wah!"

I saw his drift, and though I knew his courage well, the boldness of the thing staggered me. He, too, had penetrated to the inner lines of the British encampment at Charlotte; and when they had sought an Indian tracker to lift my trail, 'twas he who had volunteered. But now my spirits rose. With this unexpected ally we might hope to deal forcefully and yet fairly with my rear-guard.

"Where are your masters now?" I asked.

He spat upon the ground. "Catawba chief has no master," he said, proudly. "Redcoat pale-faces yonder," pointing back the way I had come. "Make fire, boil tea, sing song, heap smoke pipe."

"We must take them," said I.

He nodded. "Kill 'um all; take scalp. Wah!"

The bloodthirstiness of my two allies was appalling. But I undertook to cool the Indian's ardor, explaining that the redcoat soldiers were the Long-knife's brothers, in a way, not to be slain save in honorable battle. I am not sure whether I earned the Catawba's contempt, or his pity for my weakness; but since he was loyal to the son of his old benefactor first, and a savage afterward, he yielded the point.

So now I made him known to my patriarchal host, who all this time had been standing guard at the cabin door with the old Queen's-arm for a weapon. So we three sat on the door-stone and planned it out. When the night was far enough advanced, we would stalk the soldiers in their camp, sparing life as we could.

When all was settled, the old man gave us a supper of his humble fare, after which we went into the open again to sit out the hours of waiting. The rain had ceased, but the night was cloudy and the darkness a soft black veil to shroud the nearest objects. High overhead the autumn wind was sighing in the tree-tops, and now and again a sharper gust would bring down a pattering volley of lodged rain-drops on the fallen leaves.

Uncanoola sat apart in stoical silence, smoking his long-stemmed pipe. The old man and I talked in low tones, or rather he would tell me of his past whilst I sat and listened, holding the little maid in my arms.

After a time the child fell asleep, and I craved permission to put her in the little crib bed in the chimney corner. The flickering light of the fire fell upon her innocent face when I loosed the clasp of the tiny hands about my neck and laid her down. Again the wave of softness submerged me and I bent to leave a kiss upon the sweet unconscious lips.

Ah, my dears, you may smile again, if you will; but at that moment I had a far-off glimpse of the beatitude of fatherhood; I was no longer the hard old soldier I have drawn for you; I was but a man, hungering and thirsting for the love of a wife and trusting, clinging little children like this sweet maid.

I rose, turning my back upon the chimney corner and its holdings with a sigh. For now the time was come for action, and I must needs be a man of blood and iron again.

Lacking the Catawba to guide us, I doubt if either the old man or I could have found my rearguard's bivouac near the trail I had left. But Uncanoola led us straight through the pitchy darkness; and when we were come upon the three soldiers we found them all asleep around the handful of camp-fire.

'Twould have been murder outright to kill them thus; and now I think the old patriarch forgot his wrongs and was as merciful as I. But not so the Catawba. He had armed himself with a stout war-club, and before I was free to stop him he had knocked two of the three sleepers senseless, and would have battered out their brains but for the old man's intervention.

As for the officer, I had flung myself upon him in the rush and was having a pretty handful of him. But though he was broad in the shoulders, and as agile as a cat, he was taken at a sleeping man's disadvantage, and so I presently had the better of him.

"Enough, man! 'tis as good as a feast!" he cried, when I had him fast pinioned; and thereupon I let him have breath and freedom to sit up. In the act he had his first good sight of me, as I had mine of him. 'Twas Tybee and no other.

"Gad! my Captain," he said, feeling his throat. "If you have a grip like that for your friends, I'm damned glad I'm not your enemy."

"But you are," I rejoined, rather shamefacedly, yet thankful to the finger-tips that I had not consented to a massacre. "I am for the Congress and the Commonwealth, Lieutenant, and you are my prisoner. May I trouble you for the despatches you carry?"

He looked up at me with a queer grimace on his boyish face.

"The devil! but you're a cool hand, Captain Ireton! Whatever you were in that coil at Appleby, you've led the spy's long suit this time. And I'm not sure whether I like you any the worse for it, if so be you must be a rebel." And with that, he gave me the sealed packet and asked what I would do with him.

His query set me thinking. As for the two stunned troopers, I meant to turn them over to the old man for safe keeping; but I was loath to make it harder than need be for this good-natured youngster. So I put him upon his honor.

"Do you know what this packet contains?" I asked.

He laughed. "My Lord did not honor me with his confidence. I was to follow you in to Major Ferguson's camp, deliver the despatches, and vanish."

"Good; then you need tell no lies. When the Indian has fetched my horse, I shall ride to Ferguson's camp, and you may ride with me. I shall ask no more than this; that you do not fight again till you are exchanged; and that you will not tell Major Ferguson whose prisoner you are. Do you accept the terms?"

"Gad! I'd be a fool not to. But what's in the wind, Captain? Surely you can tell me, now that I am safely out of the running."

"You will know in a day or two; and in the meantime ignorance is your best safety. You can tell Major Ferguson that you were waylaid on the road by a party of the enemy, and that you were paroled and fell in with me."

He looked a little rueful, as a good soldier would, but was disposed to make the best of a bad bargain.

"Here's my hand on it," he said; and a little later we had dragged the two troopers to the cabin, where the old man became surety for their safe keeping, and were feeling our way cautiously westward at the heels of the Catawba who had taken his directions from our patriarch.

We pressed forward in silence through the shadowy labyrinth of the wood for a time, but at the crossing of a small runlet where we would stop to let the horses drink, Tybee burst out a-laughing.

"'Tis as good as a play," he said. "Three several times I've had to change my mind about you, Captain Ireton, and I'm not cocksure I have your measure yet. But I'll say this: if you've strung my Lord successfully, you'll be the first to do it and come off alive in the end."

"The end is not yet, my good friend; and I may not come off better than the others," I rejoined. And with that we fared on again till we could see the camp-fires of Ferguson's little army twinkling between the tree trunks.

CHAPTER XXXVIII

IN WHICH WE FIND THE GUN-MAKER

As you may be sure, Major Patrick Ferguson was far too good a soldier to leave his camp unguarded on any side, and whilst we were yet a far cannon-shot from the glimmering fires a sentry's challenge halted us.

To the man's "Halt! Who goes there?" I gave the word "Friends," salving my conscience for the needful lie as I might.

"Advance, friends, and give the countersign."

I confessed my ignorance of the night-word, saying that we were a paroled prisoner and a bearer of despatches, and asking that we be taken to Major Ferguson's headquarters. There was some little cautious demurring on the part of the sentry, but finally he passed the word for the guard-captain and we were escorted to the tent of the field commander.

I marked the encampment as I could in passing through it. The little army was three-fourths made up of Tory militia; and there was drinking and song-singing and a plentiful lack of discipline around the camp-fires of these auxiliaries. But a different air was abroad in the camp of the regulars; you would see a soldierly alertness on the part of the men, and there was no roistering in that quarter.

Major Ferguson's tent was on a hillock some distance back from the stream, and thither we were conducted; we, I say, meaning Tybee and myself, for Uncanoola had disappeared like a whiff of smoke at our challenging on the sentry line.

Late as it was, the major was up and hard at work. His tent table, transformed for the time into a mechanic's work-bench, was littered with gun-barrels and tools and screws and odd-shaped pieces of mechanism—the disjointed parts of that breech-loading musket of which the ingenious Scotchman was the inventor.

Being deep in the creative trance when we came upon him, the major gave us but an absent-minded greeting, listening with the outward ear only when Tybee reported his mission, and his capture and parole.

"From my Lord, ye say? I hope ye left him well," was all the answer the Lieutenant got, the inventor fitting away at his gun-puzzle the while.

Tybee made proper rejoinder and stood aside to give me room. I drew a sealed inclosure from my pocket and laid it on the work-bench table.

"I also have the honor to come from my Lord Cornwallis, bringing despatches"—so far I got in my cut-and-dried speech, and then my tongue clave to the roof of my mouth and I could no more finish the sentence than could a man suddenly nipped in a vise. Instead of the carefully doctored original, I had given the major the duplicate despatch taken from Tybee.

Ah, my dears, that was a moment for swift thought and still swifter action; and 'tis the Ireton genius to be slow and sure and no wise "gleg at the uptak'," as a Scot would say. Yet for this once my good angel gave me a prompting and the wit to use it. In that clock-tick of benumbing despair when the success of the hazardous venture, and much more that I wist not of, hung suspended by a hair over the abyss of failure, I minded me of a boyish trick wherewith I used to fright the timid blacks in the old days at Appleby Hundred. So whilst the major was reaching for the packet—nay, when he had it in his hand—I started back with a warning cry, giving that imitation of the ominous *skir-r-r* of a rattlesnake which had more than once got me a cuffing from my father.

In any crisis less tremendous I should have roared a-laughing to see the doughty major and my good friend the lieutenant vie with each other in their skippings to escape the unseen enemy. But it was no laughing moment for me. At a flash my sword was out and I was hacking hither and yon at the imaginary foe. In the hurly-burly I contrived to sprawl all across the work-bench table, and the packet which would have killed my plot—and, belike, the plotter as well—was secured and quickly juggled into hiding.

"Damme! see now what you've done; you've spilt my breech-charger all about the place!" rasped the major, when all was over. And then: "Who the devil are ye, anyway; and what do ye want wi' me?"

I clicked my heels, saluted, and gave him the express from my Lord—the right one, this time. He tore off the wrapping, swore a hearty soldier oath when he read the fore part of the letter and clapped his leg joyfully, like the brave gentleman that he was, when he came to the *postscriptum*.

"Ye're a fine fellow, Captain; ye've brought me good news," he said; then he bade an aide call Captain de Peyster, his second in command, and in the same breath gave Tybee and me in charge to an ensign for our billeting for the night.

You will conceive that I was overjoyed at this seemingly safe and easy planting of the petard which was to blow my Lord Cornwallis's plans into the air; and in anticipation I saw the tide-turning battle and heard the huzzas of the mountaineer victors. But 'tis a good old saw that cautions against hallooing before you are out of the wood. Captain de Peyster was come, and Tybee and I were taking our leave of the major, when there was a sudden commotion among the guards without, and a little man in black, his wig awry and his clothing torn by the rough man-handling of the sentries, burst into the tent.

"Seize him! seize him! he is a rebel spy!" he shrieked, pointing at me.

As you would guess, all talk paused at this dramatic interruption, and all eyes were turned upon me. Had the little viper been content to rest his charge upon the simple accusation, I know not what might have happened. But when he got his breath he burst out in a tirade of the foulest abuse, cursing me up one side and down the other, and ending in a gibbering fit of rage that left him pallid and foaming at the lips—and gave me my cue.

"'Tis the little madman of Queensborough," I said, coolly, explaining to the bluff major. "His mania takes the form of a curious hatred for me, though I know not why. Two days since, he was put in arrest by my Lord's authority for threatening my life and that of his master's daughter. Now, it would seem, he has broken jail and followed me hither."

"A lunatic, eh? He looks it, every inch," said the major; and the blackguard lawyer, hearing my counter accusation, was doing his best to give it a savor of likelihood by fighting frantically with the two soldiers who had followed him into the tent.

"Out wi' him!" commanded the major. "We've no time to foolish away wi' a Bedlamite. Take him away and peg him out, and gi' him a dash o' water to cool his head."

Pengarvin fought like a fury, and his venomous rage defeated all his attempts to say calmly the words which might have got him a hearing. So he was haled away, spitting and struggling like a trapped wildcat; and when we were rid of him the major bade us good night again.

Tybee held his peace like a good fellow till we had rolled us in our blankets before one of the camp-fires. But just as I was dropping asleep he broke out with, "I would you might tell me what piece of rebel villainy this is that I've been a winking accomplice to."

I laughed. "'Tis a thing to make Major Ferguson rejoice, as you saw. And surely, it can be no great villainy to give a man what he's thirsting for. Bide your time, Lieutenant, and you shall see the outcome."

CHAPTER XXXIX

THE THUNDER OF THE CAPTAINS
AND THE SHOUTING

The camp was astir early the next morning, and it soon became noised about that we were to fall back, but only so far as might be needful to find a strong position. From this it was evident that a battle was imminent, though as yet there were no signs of the approach of the patriots.

From the camp talk we, Tybee and I, gleaned some better information of the situation. A fortnight earlier Major Ferguson had captured two of the over-mountain men of Clark's party and had sent them to the settlement on the Watauga with a challenge in due form—or rather with the threat to come and lay the over-mountain region waste in default of an instant return of the pioneers to their allegiance to the king.

This challenge, so our scouts told us, had been immediately accepted. Sevier and Shelby had embodied some two hundred men each from the Watauga and the Holston settlements, and Colonel William Campbell, the stout old Presbyterian Indian fighter, had joined them with as many more Virginians.

Crossing the mountain these three troops had fallen in with other scattered parties of the border patriots under Benjamin Cleaveland, Major Chronicle and Colonel Williams, of South Carolina, until now, as the scouts reported, the challenged outnumbered the challengers. Learning this, Ferguson, who was as prudent as he was brave, thought it best to make his stand at some point nearer the main body of the army; and so the withdrawal from Gilbert Town had fallen into a retreat and a pursuit.

From what Captain de Peyster has since told me, there would seem to be little doubt that the major meant to fight when he had manoeuvered himself into a favorable position; this in spite of Lord Cornwallis's commands to the contrary. In his despatches he was continually urging the need for a bold push in his quarter, and asking for Tarleton and a sufficient number of the legion to enable him to cope with a mounted enemy. But be this as it may, the garbled letter I had brought him turned whatever scale there was to turn. He had now with him some eleven hundred regulars and Tories, the latter decently well drilled; he had every reason to expect the needed help from Cornwallis; and, on the night of my arrival, he had word that another Tory force under Major Gibbs would join him in a day or two, at farthest.

For his battle-ground Major Ferguson chose the top of a forest-covered hill, the last and lowest elevation in the spur named that day King's Mountain.

In some respects the position was all that could be desired. There was room on the flat hilltop for an orderly disposition of the fighting force; and the slopes in front and rear were steep enough to give an attacking enemy a sharp climb. Moreover, there was a plentiful outcropping of stone on the summit, scantiest on the broad or outer end of the hill, and this was so disposed as to form a natural breastwork for the defenders.

But there were disadvantages also, the chief of these being the heavy wooding of the slopes to screen the advance of the assaulting party; and while the major was busy making his dispositions for the fight, I was on tenter-hooks for fear he would have the trees felled to belt the breastwork with a clear space.

He did not do it, being restrained, as I afterward learned, by his uncertainty as to whether or no the mountain men had cannon. Against artillery posted on the neighboring hillocks the trees were his best defense, and so he left them standing.

As you would suppose, my situation was now become most trying, and poor Tybee's was scarcely less so. Knowing my name and circumstance, and having, moreover, a high regard for my old field-marshal's genius, Major Ferguson was very willing to make use of my experience. These askings from one whom I knew for a brave and honorable gentleman let me fall between two stools. As a patriot spy, it was my duty to turn the major's confidence as a weapon against him. But as an officer and a gentleman I could by no means descend to such depths of perfidy.

In this dilemma I sought to steer a middle course, saying that I must beg exemption because my long hard ride had re-opened my old sword wound—as indeed it had. So the major generously let me be, thus heaping coals of fire upon my head; and I kept out of his way, consorting with Tybee, who, like myself, must be an onlooker in the coming fray.

As for the lieutenant, he was all agog to learn more than I dared tell him, and it irked him most nettlesomely to have a fight in prospect in the which he was in honor bound not to take a hand. Time and again he begged me to release him from his parole; and when I would not, he was for fighting me a duel with his freedom for a stake.

"Consider of it, Captain Ireton," he pleaded. "For God's sake, put yourself in my place. Here am I, in the camp of my friends, gagged and bound by my word to you whilst your infernal plot, whatever it may be, works out to the *coup de grâce*. Ye gods! it

242 ∞ FRANCIS LYNDE

would have been far more merciful had you run me through in our wrestling match last night!"

"Mayhap," said I, curtly. "'Twas but the choice between two evils. Nevertheless, in time to come I hope you may conclude that this is the lesser of the two."

"No, I'm damned if I shall!" he retorted, fuming like a disappointed boy, and minding me most forcibly of my hot-headed Richard Jennifer. And then he would repeat: "I thought you were my friend."

"So I am, as man to man. But this matter concerns the welfare of a cause to which I have sworn fealty. Take your own words back, my lad, and put yourself in my place. Can I do less than hold you to your pledge?"

"No, I suppose not," he would say, grumpily. "Yet 'tis hard; most devilish hard!"

"'Tis the fortune of war. Another day the shoe may be upon the other foot."

The baggage wagons had been massed across the broad end of the hill to eke out the stone breastwork, and the last of these arguing colloquies took place beneath one of the wagons whither we had crept for shelter from the rain, which was now pouring again. In the midst of our talk, Major Ferguson dived to share our shelter, dripping like a water spaniel.

"Ha! ye're carpet soldiers, both of ye!" he snorted, and then he began to swear piteously at the rain.

"'Twill be worse for the enemy than for us," said Tybee. "We can at least keep our powder dry."

"Damn the enemy!" quoth the major, cheerfully. "So the weather does not put the creeks up and hold Tarleton and Major Gibbs back from us, 'tis a small matter whether the rebels' powder be dry or soaked."

"You have made all your dispositions, Major?" Tybee asked.

The major nodded. "All in apple-pie order, no thanks to either of ye. 'Tis a strong position, this, eh, Captain Ireton? I'm thinking not all the rebel banditti out of hell will drive us from it."

"'Tis good enough," I agreed; and here the talk was broken off by the major's diving out to berate some of his Tory militiamen who were preparing to make a night of it with a jug of their vile country liquor.

The rain continued all that Friday night and well on into the forenoon of the Saturday. During this interval we waited with scouts out for the upcoming of the mountain men. At noon Major Ferguson sent a final express to Lord Cornwallis, urging the hurrying on of the reinforcements, not knowing that his former despatch had been intercepted, nor that Tarleton had not as yet started to the rescue. A little later the scouts began to come in one by one with news of the approaching riflemen.

There was but a small body of them, not above a thousand men in all, so the spies said, and my heart misgave me. They were without cannon and they lacked bayonets; and moreover, when all was said, they were but militia, all untried save in border warfare with the Indians. Could they successfully assault the fortified camp whose defenders—thanks to the major's ingenuity—had fitted butcher-knives to the muzzles of their guns in lieu of bayonets? Nay, rather would they have the courage to try?

'Twas late in the afternoon before these questions were answered. The rain had ceased, and the chill October sunlight filtered aslant through the trees. With the clearing skies a cold wind had sprung up, and on the hilltop the men cowered behind the rock breastwork and waited in strained silence. At the last moment Major Ferguson sent Captain de Peyster to me with the request that I take command of the Tory force set apart to defend the wagon barricade—this if my weariness would permit. I went with the captain to make my excuses in person.

"Say no more, Captain," said this generous soldier, when I began some lame plea for further exemption; "I had forgot your sword-cut. Take shelter for yourself, and look on whilst we skin this riffraff alive."

And so he let me off; a favor which will make me think kindly of Patrick Ferguson so long as I shall live. For now my work was done; and had he insisted, I should have told him flatly who and what I was—and paid the penalty.

I had scarce rejoined Tybee at the wagons when the long roll of the drums broke the silence of the hilltop, and a volley fire of musketry from the rock breastwork on the right told us the battle was on. Tybee gave me one last reproachful look and stood out to see what could be seen, and I stood with him.

"Your friends are running," he said, when there was no reply to the opening volley; and truly, I feared he was right. At the bottom of the slope, scattering groups of the riflemen could be seen hastening to right and left. But I would not admit the charge to Tybee.

"I think not," I objected, denying the apparent fact. "They have come too far and too fast to turn back now for a single overshot volley."

"But they'll never face the fire up the hill with the bayonet to cap it at the top," he insisted.

"That remains to be seen; we shall know presently. Ah, I

thought so; here they come!"

At the word the forest-covered steep at our end of the hill sprang alive with dun-clad figures darting upward from tree to tree. Volley after volley thundered down upon them as they climbed, but not once did the dodging charge up the slope pause or falter. Unlike all other irregulars I had ever seen, whose idea of a battle is to let off the piece and run, these mountain men held their fire like veterans, closing in upon the hilltop steadily and in a grim silence broken only by the shouting encouragements of the leaders—this until their circling line was completed.

Then suddenly from all sides of the beleaguered camp arose a yell to shake the stoutest courage, and with that the wood-covered slopes began to spit fire, not in volleys, but here and there in irregular snappings and cracklings as the sure-shot riflemen saw a mark to pull trigger on.

The effect of this fine-bead target practice—for it was naught else—was most terrific. All along the breastwork, front and rear, crouching men sprang up at the rifle crackings to fling their arms all abroad and to fall writhing and wrestling in the death throe. At our end of the hill, where the rock barrier was thinnest, the slaughter was appalling; and above the din of the firearms we could hear the bellowed commands of the sturdy old Indian fighter, Benjamin Cleaveland, urging his men up to still closer quarters. "A little nearer, my brave boys; a little nearer and we have them! Press on up to the rocks. They'll be as good a breastwork from our side as from theirs!"

You will read in the histories that the Tory helpers of Ferguson fought as men with halters round their necks; and so, indeed, a-many of them did. But though they were most pitiless enemies of ours, I bear them witness that they did fight well and bravely, and not as men who fight for fear's sake.

And they were most bravely officered. Major Ferguson, boldly conspicuous in a white linen hunting-shirt drawn on over his uniform, was here and there and everywhere, and always in the place where the bullets flew thickest. His left hand had been hurt at the first patriot gun fire, but it still held the silver whistle to his lips, and the shrill skirling of the little pipe was the loyalist rallying signal. Captain de Peyster, too, did ample justice to the uniform he wore; and when Campbell's Virginians gained the summit at the far end of the hilltop, 'twas de Peyster who led the bayonet charge that forced the patriot riflemen some little way down the slope.

But these are digressions. No man sees more of a battle than that little circle of which he is the center; and the fighting was hot enough at the wagon barricade to keep both Tybee and me from knowing at the time what was going on beyond our narrow range of sight or hearing. You must picture, therefore, for yourselves, a very devils' pandemonium let loose upon the little hilltop so soon as the mountain men gained their vantage ground at the fronting of the rock breastwork; cries; frantic shouts of "God save the king!" yells fierce and wordless; men in red and men in homespun rushing madly hither and yon in a vain attempt to repel a front and rear attack at the same instant. 'Twas a hell set free, with no quarter asked or given, and where we stood, the Tory defenders of the wagon barrier were presently dropping around us in heaps and windrows of dead and dying, like men suddenly plague-smitten.

In such a time of asking you must not think we stood aloof and looked on coldly. At the first fire Tybee stripped off his coat and fell to work with the wounded, and I quickly followed his lead, praying that now my work was done, some one of the flying missiles would find its mark in me and let me die a soldier's death.

So it was that I saw little more of the battle detail, and of that fierce frenzy-time I have memory pictures only of the dead and dying; of the torn and wounded and bleeding men with whom we wrought, striving as we might to stanch the ebbing life-tide or to ease the dying gently down into the valley of shadows.

And as for my prayer, it went all unanswered. Once when I had a dying Tory's head pillowed on my knee I saw a rifleman thrust his weapon between the wheel-spokes of the outer wagon and draw a bead on me. I heard the crack of the Deckard, the *zip* of the bullet singing at my ear, and the man's angry oath at his missing of me. Once again a rifle-ball passed through my hair at the braiding of the queue and I felt the hot touch of it on my scalp like a breath of flame. Another time a mountaineer leaped the rock barrier to beat me down with the butt of his rifle—and in the very act Tybee rose up and throttled him. I saw the grapple, sprang to my feet and whipped out my sword.

"Stop!" I commanded; "you have broken your parole, Lieutenant!"

The freed borderer glared from one to the other of us. "Loonies!" he yelled; "I'll slaughter the both of ye!" And so he would have done, I make no doubt, had we not laid hold of him together and heaved him back over the breastwork.

These are but incidents, points of contact where the fray touched us two at the wagon barricade. I pass them by with the mention, as I have passed by the sterner horrors of that furious killing-time. These last are too large for my poor pen. As we could gather in the din and tumult, the mountain men rushed again and again to the attack, and as often the brave major, or De Peyster, led the bayonet charges that pushed them back. Yet in the end the unerring bullet outpressed the bayonet; there came a time when flesh and blood could no longer endure the death-dealing cross-fire from front and rear.

I saw the end was near when the major ordered the final charge, and Captain de Peyster formed his line and led it forward at a double-quick. The mountaineers held more than half the hilltop now, and this forlorn hope was to try to drive them down the farther slopes. On it went, and I could see the men pitch and tumble out of the line until at bayonet-reach of the riflemen there were less than a dozen afoot and fit to make the push.

De Peyster fought his way back to the wagons, gasping and bloody. Some of the Tories crowding around us raised a white flag. The major, sorely wounded now and all but disabled, swore a great oath and rode rough-shod into the ruck of cowering militiamen to pull down the flag. Again the white token of surrender was raised, and again the major rode in to beat it down with his sword. At this Captain de Peyster put in his word.

"'Tis no use, Major; there is no more fight left in us! Five minutes more of this and we'll be shot down to a man!"

Ferguson's reply was a raging oath broad enough to cover all the enemy and his own beaten remnant as well; and then, before a hand could be lifted to stay him, he had wheeled his horse and was galloping straight for the patriot line at the farther extremity of the hilltop.

What he meant to do will never be known till that great day when all secrets shall be revealed. For that furious oath was this brave gentleman's last word to us or to any. A dozen bounds, it may be, the good charger carried him; then the storm of rifle-bullets beat him from the saddle. And so died one of the gallantest officers that ever did an unworthy king's work on the field of battle.

I would I might forget the terrible scene which followed this killing of the British commander. 'Twas little to our credit, but I may not pass it over in silence. De Peyster quickly sent a man to the front with a white flag, and the answer was a murderous volley which killed the flag-bearer and many others. Again the flag was raised on a rifle-barrel, and once more the answer was a storm of the leaden death poured into the panic-stricken crowd huddled like sheep at the wagons.

"God!" said de Peyster; and with that he began to beat his men into line with the flat of his sword in a frenzy of desperation, being minded, as he afterward told me, to give them the poor chance to die a-fighting.

I saw not what followed upon this last despairing effort, for now Tybee was down and I was kneeling beside him to search for the wound. But when I looked again, the crackling crashes of the rifle-firing had ceased. A stout, gray-headed man, whom I afterward knew as Isaac Shelby's father, was riding up from the patriot line to receive Captain de Peyster's sword, and the battle was ended.

CHAPTER XL

VAE VICTIS

If my hand were not sure enough to draw you some speaking picture of this our epoch-marking battle of King's Mountain, it falters still more on coming to the task of setting forth the tragic horrors of the dreadful after-night. Wherefore I pray you will hold me excused, my dears, if I hasten over the events tripping upon the heels of the victory, touching upon them only as they touch upon my tale.

But as for the stage-setting of the after-scene you may hold in your mind's eye the stony hilltop strewn with the dead and dying; the huddle of cowed prisoners at the wagon barricade; the mountaineers, mad with the victor's frenzy, swarming to surround us. 'Twas a clipping from Chaos and Night gone blood-crazed till Sevier and Isaac Shelby brought somewhat of order out of it; and then came the reckoning.

Of the seven hundred-odd prisoners the greater number were Tories, many of them red-handed from scenes of rapine in which their present captors had suffered the loss of all that men hold dear. So you will not wonder that there were knives and rifles shaken aloft, and fierce and vengeful counsels in which it was proposed to put the captives one and all to the cord and tree.

But now again Sevier and Shelby, seconded by the fiery Presbyterian, William Campbell, flung themselves into the breach, pleading for delay and a fair trial for such as were blood guilty. And so the dismal night, made chill and comfortless by the cold wind and most doleful by the groans and cries of the wounded, wore away, and the dawn of the Sunday found us lying as we were in the bloody shambles of the hilltop.

With the earliest morning light the burial parties were at work; and since the stony battle-ground would not lend itself for the trenching, the graves were dug in the vales below. Captain de Peyster begged hard for leave to bury the brave Ferguson on the spot where he fell, but 'twas impossible; and now, I am told, the stout old Scotsman lies side by side with our Major Will Chronicle, of Mecklenburg, who fell just before the ending of the battle.

The dead buried and the wounded cared for in some rough and ready fashion, preparations were made in all haste for a speedy withdrawal from the neighborhood of the battle-field. Rumor had it that Tarleton with his invincible legion was within a few hours' march; and the mountain men, sodden weary with the toils of the flying advance and the hard-fought conflict, were in no fettle to cope with a fresh foe.

As yet I had not made myself known to the patriot commanders, having my hands and heart full with the care of poor Tybee, who was grievously hurt, and being in a measure indifferent to what should befall me.

But now as we were about to march I was dragged before the committee of colonels and put to the question.

"Your uniform is a strange one to us, sir," said Isaac Shelby, looking me up and down with that heavy-lidded right eye of his. "Explain your rank and standing, if you please."

I told my story simply, and, as I thought, effectively; and had only black looks for my pains.

"'Tis a strange tale, surely, sir,—too strange to be believable," quoth Shelby. "You are a traitor, Captain Ireton—of the kind we need not cumber ourselves with on a march."

"Who says that word of me?" I demanded, caring not much for that to which his threat pointed, but something for my good name.

Shelby turned and beckoned to a man in the group behind him. "Stand out, John Whittlesey," he directed; and I found myself face to face with that rifleman of Colonel Davie's party who had been so fierce to hang me at the fording of the Catawba.

This man gave his testimony briefly, telling but the bare truth. A week earlier I had passed in Davie's camp for a true-blue patriot, this though I was wearing a ragged British uniform at the moment. As for the witness himself, he had misdoubted me all along, but the colonel had trusted me and had sent me on some secret mission, the inwardness of which he, John Whittlesey, had been unable to come at, though he confessed that he had tried to worm it out of me before parting company with me on the road to Charlotte.

I looked from one to another of my judges.

"If this be all, gentlemen, the man does but confirm my story," I said.

"It is not all," said Shelby. "Mr. Pengarvin, stand forth."

There was another stir in the backgrounding group and the pettifogger edged his way into the circle, keeping well out of hand-reach of me. How he had made shift to escape from Ferguson's men, to change sides, and to turn up thus serenely in the ranks of the over-mountain men, I know not to this day, nor ever shall know.

"Tell these gentlemen what you have told me," said Shelby, briefly; and the factor, cool and collected now, rehearsed the undeniable facts: how in Charlotte I had figured as a member of Lord Cornwallis's military family; how I had carried my malignancy to the patriot cause to the length of throwing a stanch friend to the commonwealth, to wit, one Owen Pengarvin, into the common jail; how, as Lord Cornwallis's trusted aide-de-camp, I had been sent with an express to Major Ferguson. Also, he suggested that if I should be searched some proof of my duplicity might be found upon me.

At this William Campbell nodded to two of his Virginians, and I was searched forthwith, and that none too gently. In the breast pocket of my hussar jacket they found that accursed duplicate despatch; the one I had taken from Tybee and which had so nearly proved my undoing in the interview with Major Ferguson.

Isaac Shelby opened and read the accusing letter and passed it around among his colleagues.

"I shall not ask you why this was undelivered, sir," he said to me, sternly. "'Tis enough that it was found upon your person, and it sufficiently proves the truth of this gentleman's accusation. Have you aught further to say, Captain Ireton?—aught that may excuse us for not leaving you behind us in a halter?"

Do you wonder, my dears, that I lost my head when I saw how completely the toils of this little black-clothed fiend had closed around me? Twice, nay, thrice I tried to speak calmly as the crisis demanded. Then mad rage ran away with me, and I burst out in yelling curses so hot they would surely dry the ink in the pen were I to seek to set them down here.

'Twas a silly thing to do, you will say, and much beneath the dignity of a grown man who cared not a bodle for his life, and not greatly for the manner of its losing. I grant you this; and yet it was that same bull-bellow of soldier profanity that saved my life. Whilst I was in the storm of it, cursing the lawyer by every shouted epithet I could lay tongue to, a miracle was wrought and Richard Jennifer and Ephraim Yeates pushed their way through the ever-thickening ring of onlookers; the latter to range himself beside me with his brown-barreled rifle in the hollow of his arm, and my dear lad to fling himself upon me in a bear's hug of joyous recognition and greeting.

"Score one for me, Jack!" he cried. "We were fair at t'other end of the mountain, and 'twas I told Eph there was only one man in the two Carolinas who could swear the match of that." Then he whirled upon my judges. "What is this, gentlemen?—a court martial? Captain Ireton is my friend, and as true a patriot as ever drew breath. What is your charge?"

Colonel Sevier, in whose command Richard and the old borderer had fought in the hilltop battle, undertook to explain. I stood self-confessed as the bearer of despatches from Lord Cornwallis to Major Ferguson, he said, and I had claimed that the orders had been so altered as to delay the major's retreat and so to bring on the battle. But they had just found Lord Cornwallis's letter in my pocket, still sealed and undelivered. And the tenor of it was precisely opposite to that of an order calculated to delay the major's march, as Mr. Jennifer could see if he would read it.

While Sevier was talking, the old borderer was fumbling in the breast of his hunting-shirt, and now he produced a packet of papers tied about with red tape.

"'Pears to me like you Injun-killers from t'other side o' the mounting is in a mighty hot sweat to hang somebody," he said, as coolly as if he were addressing a mob of underlings. "Here's a mess o' billy-doos with Lord Cornwallis's name to 'em that I found 'mongst Major Ferguson's leavings. If you'll look 'em over, maybe you'll find out, immejitly *if* not sooner, that Cap'n John here is telling ye the plumb truth."

The papers were examined hastily, and presently John Sevier lighted upon the despatch I had carried and delivered. Thereat the colonels put their heads together; and then my case was re-opened, with Sevier as spokesman.

"We have a letter here which appears to be the original order to Ferguson, Captain Ireton. Can you repeat from memory the *postscriptum* which you say was added to it?"

I gave the gist of my old patriarch's addendum as well as I could; and thereupon suspicion fled away and my late judges would vie with one another in hearty frontier hand-grasps and apologies, whilst the throng that ringed us in forgot caution and weariness and gave me a cheer to wake the echoes.

'Twas while this burst of gratulation was abuzz that Ephraim Yeates raised a cry of his own.

"Stop that there black-legged imp o' the law!" he shouted, pushing his way out of the circle. "He's the one that ought to hang!"

There was a rush for the wagon barricade, a clatter of horse-hoofs on the hillside below, and Yeates's rifle went to his face. But the bullet flew wide, and the black-garbed figure clinging to the horse's mane was soon out of sight among the trees.

"Ez I allow, ye'd better look out for that yaller-skinned little varmint, Cap'n John," quoth the old man, carefully wiping his rifle preparatory to reloading it. "He's rank pizen, he is, and ye'll have to break his neck sooner 'r later. I 'lowed to save ye the trouble, but old Bess got mighty foul yestiddy, with all the shoot-ings and goings on, and I hain't got no lead-brush to clean her out."

Now that I was fully exonerated I was free to go and come as I chose; nay, more, I was urged to cast in my lot with the over-mountain partizans. As to this, I took counsel with Richard Jennifer whilst the colonels were setting their commands in order for the march and loading the prisoners with the captured guns and ammunition.

"What is to the fore, Dick?" I asked; "more fighting?"

The lad shook his head. "Never another blow, I fear, Jack. These fellows crossed the mountain to whip Ferguson. Having done it they will go home."

I could not forego a hearty curse upon this worst of all militia weaknesses, the disposition to disperse as soon as ever a battle was fought.

"'Tis nigh on to a crime," said I. "This victory, smartly followed up, might well be the turning of the tide for us."

But the lad would not admit the qualifying condition. "'Twill be no less as it is," he declared. "Mark you, Jack; 'twill put new life into the cause and nerve every man of ours afresh. And as for the redcoats, if my Lord Cornwallis gets the news of it in a lump, as he should, Gates will have plenty of time to set himself in motion, slow as he is."

'Twas then I had an inspiration, and I thought upon it for a moment.

"What are your plans, Richard?"

He shook his head. "I have none worth the name."

"Then you are not committed to Colonel Sevier for a term of service?"

"No; nor to Cleaveland, nor McDowell, nor any. We heard there was to be fighting hereaway,—Ephraim Yeates and I,—and we came as volunteers."

"Good! then I have a thought which may stand for what it is worth. To make the most of this victory over Major Ferguson, Gates should be apprised at once and by a sure tongue; and his Lordship should have the news quickly, too, and in a lump, as you say. Let us take horse and ride post, we two; you to Gates at Hillsborough, and I to Charlotte."

"I had thought of my part of that," he said in a muse. Then he came alive to the risk I should run. "But you can't well go back to Cornwallis now, Jack: 'tis playing with death. There will be other news-carriers—there are sure to be; and a single breath to whisper what you have done will hang you higher than Haman."

I shrugged at this. "'Tis but a war hazard."

He looked at me curiously. I saw a shrewd question in his eyes and set instant action as a barrier in the way of its asking.

"Let us find Colonel Sevier and beg us the loan of a pair of horses," said I; and so we were kept from coming upon the dangerous ground of pointed questions and evasive answers.

Somewhat to my surprise, both Sevier and Shelby fell in at once with our project, commending it heartily; and I learned from the lips of that courtliest of frontiersmen, "Nolichucky Jack," the real reason for the proposed hurried return of the over-mountain men. The Cherokees, never to be trusted, had, as it seemed, procured war supplies from the British posts to the southward, and were even now on the verge of an uprising. By forced marches these hardy borderers hoped to reach their homes in time to defend them. Otherwise, as both commanders assured us, they would take the field with Gates.

"We have done what we could, Captain Ireton, and not altogether what we would," said Sevier in the summing-up. "It remains now for General Gates to drive home the wedge we have entered." Then he looked me full in the eyes and asked if I thought Horatio Gates would be the man to beetle that wedge well into the log.

I made haste to say that I knew little of the general; that I was but a prejudiced witness at best, since my father had known and misliked the man in Braddock's ill-fated campaign against the French in '55. But Richard spoke his mind more freely.

"'Tis not in the man at this pass, Colonel Sevier," he would say; "not after Camden. I know our Carolinians as well as any, and they will never stand a second time under a defeated leader. If General Washington would send us some one else; or, best of all, if he would but come himself—"

"George Washington; ah, there is a man, indeed," said Sevier, his dark-blue eyes lighting up. "Whilst he lives, there is always a good hope. But we must be doing, gentlemen, and so must you. God speed you both. Our compliments to General Gates, Mr. Jennifer; and you may tell him what I have told you—that but for our redskin threateners we should right gladly join him. As for Lord Cornwallis, you, Captain Ireton, will know best what to say to him. I pray God you may say it and come off alive to tell us how he took it."

We made our acknowledgments; and when I had bespoken good care for Tybee, we took leave of these stout fighters, and of old Ephraim as well, since the borderer was to serve as a guide for the over-mountain men, at least till they were come upon familiar ground to the westward.

'Twas now hard upon ten of the clock in the forenoon, and we had our last sight of the brave little army whilst it was wending its way slowly down the slopes of King's Mountain. Of what became of it; how its weary march dragged on from day to day; how it was hampered by the train of captives, halted by rain-swollen torrents, and was well-nigh starved withal; of all these things you may read elsewhere. But now you must ride with Richard Jennifer and me, and our way lay to the eastward.

All that Sunday we pressed forward, hasting as we could through the stark columned aisles of the autumn-stripped forest, and looking hourly to come upon Tarleton's legion marching out to Ferguson's relief.

Since Richard Jennifer had ridden to the hounds in all this middle ground from boyhood, we were able to take my blind wanderings in reverse as the arrow flies; and by nightfall we were well down upon the main traveled road leading to Beattie's fording of the Catawba.

As your map will show you, this was taking me somewhat out of my way to the northward; but it was Richard's most direct route to Salisbury and beyond, and by veering thus we made the surer of missing Colonel Tarleton, who, as we thought, would likely cross the river at the lower ford.

Once in the high road we pushed on briskly for the river, nor did we draw rein until the sweating beasts were picking their way in the darkness down the last of the hills which sentinel the Catawba to the westward.

At the foot of this hill a by-road led to Macgowan's ford some six miles farther down the river, and here, as I supposed, our ways would lie apart. But when we came to the forking of the road, Richard pulled his mount into the by-path, clapping the spurs to the tired horse so that we were a good mile beyond the forking before I could overtake him.

"How now, lad?" said I, when I had run him down. "Would you take a fighting hazard when you need not? There is sure to be a British patrol at the lower ford."

He jerked his beast down to a walk and we rode in silence side by side for a full minute before he said gruffly: "You'd never find the way alone."

I laughed. "Barring myself, you are the clumsiest of evaders, Dick. I am on my own ground here, and that you know as well as I."

"Damn you!" he gritted between his teeth. "When we are coming near Appleby Hundred you are fierce enough to be rid of me."

I saw his drift at that: how he would take all the chance of capture and a spy's rope for the sake of passing within a mile of Mistress Margery, or of the house he thought she was in.

"Go back, Dick, whilst you may," said I. "She is not at Appleby Hundred."

He turned upon me like a lion at bay.

"What have you done with her?"

"Peace, you foolish boy. I am not her keeper. Her father took her to Charlotte on the very day you saw her safe at home."

He reined up short in the narrow way. "So?" he said, most bitingly. "And that is why you take the embassy to Lord Cornwallis and fub me off with the one to Gates. By heaven, Captain Ireton, we shall change rôles here and now!"

Ah, my dears, the love-madness is a curious thing. Here was a man who had saved my life so many times I had lost the count of them, feeling for my throat in the murk of that October night as my bitterest foeman might.

And surely it was the love-demon in me that made me say: "You think I am standing in your way, Richard Jennifer? Well, so I am; for whilst I live you may not have her. Why don't you draw and cut me down?"

'Twas then Satan marked my dear lad for his very own.

"On guard!" he cried; "draw and defend yourself!" and with that the great claymore leaped from its sheath to flash in the starlight.

What with his reining back for space to whirl the steel I had the time to parry the descending blow. But at the balancing instant the brother-hating devil had the upper hand, whispering me that here was the death I coveted; that Margery might have her lover, if so she would, with her husband's blood upon his head.

So I sat motionless while the broadsword cut its circle in air and came down; and then I knew no more till I came to with a bees' hive buzzing in my ears, to find myself lying in the dank grass at the path side. My head was on Richard's knee, and he was dabbling it with water in his soaked kerchief.

CHAPTER XLI

HOW I PLAYED THE HOST AT MY OWN FIRESIDE

You may be sure that by now the anger gale had blown itself out, that the madness had passed for both of us; and when I stirred, Richard broke out in a tremulous babblement of thanksgiving for that he had not slain me outright.

"I was mad, Jack; as mad as any Bedlamite," he would say. "The devil whispered me that you would fight; that you wanted but a decent excuse to thrust me out of the way. And when I saw you would not stir, 'twas too late to do aught but turn the flat of the blade. Oh, God help me! I'll never let a second thought of that little Tory prat-a-pace send me to hell again."

"Nay," said I; "no such rash promises, I pray you, Richard. We are but two poor fools, with the love of a woman set fair between us. But you need not fight me for it. The love is yours—not mine."

"Don't say that, Jack; I'm selfish enough to wish it were true; as it is not. I know whereof I speak."

"No," I denied, struggling to my feet; "it has been yours from the first, Dick. I am but a sorry interloper."

For a moment he was all solicitude to know if my head would let me stand; but when I showed him I was no more than clumsily dizzy from the effects of the blow, he went on.

"I say I know, and I do, Jack. She has refused me again."

I groaned in spirit. I knew it must have come to that. Yet I would ask when and where.

"'Twas on our last day's riding," he went on; "after we had had your note saying you would undertake a mission for Colonel Davie."

I took two steps and groped for the horse's bridle rein.

"Did she tell you why she must refuse you?"

He helped me find the rein for my hand and the stirrup for my foot.

"There was no 'why' but the one—she does not love me."

"But I say she does, Dick; and I, too, know whereof I speak."

He flung me into the saddle as a strong man might toss a boy, and I understood how that saying of mine had gone into his blood.

"Then there must be some barrier that I know not of," he said. Whereupon he put hand to head as one who tries to remember. "Stay; did you not say there was a barrier, Jack?—when we were wrestling with death in the Indian fires? Or did I dream it?"

"You did not dream it. But you were telling me what she said."

"Oh, yes; 'twas little enough. She cut me off at the first word as if my speaking were a mortal sin. And when I would have tried again, she gave me a look to make me wince and broke out crying as if her heart would burst."

I steadied myself as I could by the saddle horn and waited till he was up and we were moving on. Then I would say: "Truly, there is a barrier, Richard; if I promise you that I am going to Charlotte to remove it once for all, will you trust me and go about your affair with General Gates?"

"Trust you, Jack? Who am I that I should do aught else? When I am cool and sane, I'm none so cursed selfish; I could even give her over to you with a free hand, could I but hear her say she loves you as I would have her love me. But when I am mad.... Ah, God only knows the black blood there is in the heart at such times."

We rode on together in silence after that, and were come to the bank of the river before we spoke again. But here Dick went back to my warning, saying, whilst we let the horses drink: "'Tis patrolled on the other bank, you say?"

"It was when I passed it a few days agone."

"Then I will turn back and cross at Beattie's. 'Twill make you a risk you need not take—to have me with you."

But I thought now that the upper ford might be guarded as well; and if there must be a cutting of a road through the enemy's outpost line for Dick, two could do it better than one. So I said:

"No; we are here now, and if need be I can lend you the weight of a second blade to see you safe through."

"And you with your head humming like a basket of bees, as I make no doubt it will?"

I laughed. "I should be but a sorry soldier and a sorrier friend if I should let a love-tap with the flat of a blade make me fail you at the pinch."

He reached across the little gap that parted us and grasped my hand.

"By God!" he swore, most feelingly, "you are as true as the steel you carry, Jack Ireton!"

"Nay," said I, in honest shame; "I do confess I was thinking less of my friend than of the importance of the errand he rides on."

"But if there should be a fight, you will spoil your chance of coming peaceably to Charlotte and my Lord's headquarters."

"If I am recognized—yes. But the night is dark, and a brush with the outpost need not betray me."

At this he consented grudgingly, and we pushed on to the

crossing. Now since this fording place of Master Macgowan's has marched into our history, you will like to know what the historians do not tell you: namely, how it was but a makeshift wading place, armpit deep over a muddy bottom from the western bank to the bar above an island in mid-stream, and deflecting thence through rocky shallows to a point on the eastern bank some distance below the island. 'Twas here that Lord Cornwallis got entangled some months later—but I must not anticipate.

We made the crossing of the main current in safety and were a-splash in the rocky shallows beyond the island when we sighted the camp-fires of the outpost. To ride straight upon the patrol was to invite disaster, and though Jennifer was for a charging dash, a hurly-burly with the steel, and so on to freedom beyond, he listened when I pointed out that our beasts were too nearly outworn to charge, and that the noise we must make would rouse the camp and draw the fire of every piece in it long before we could reach the bank and come to blade work.

"What for it, then?" he asked, impatiently. "My courage is freezing whilst we wait."

"There is nothing for it but to hold straight on across," I said.

"That we can not; 'twill be over the horses' ears. The beasts will drown themselves and us as well."

How we should have argued it out I do not know, for just then Jennifer's horse, scenting the troop mounts on the farther shore, cocked tail and ears, let out a squealing neigh, and fell to curveting and plunging in a racket that might have stood for the splashings of an advancing army.

In a twinkling the outpost camp was astir and a bellowing hail came to us across the water. Having no answer, the troopers began to let off their pieces haphazard in the darkness; and with the singing *zip* of the first musket ball, Richard went battle-mad, as he always did in the face of danger.

"At them!" he thundered, clapping spurs to his jaded beast and whipping out the great claymore; and so we charged, the forlornest hope that ever fell upon an enemy.

How we came ashore alive through the gun-fire is one of those mysteries to which every battle adds its quota; but the poor beasts we rode were not so lucky. Jennifer's horse went down while we were yet some yards from the bank; and mine fell a moment later. To face a score of waiting enemies afoot was too much for even Richard's rash courage; so when we were free of the struggling horses we promptly dove for shelter under the upstream bank.

Here the darkness stood our friend; and when the redcoat

troopers came down to the river's edge with torches to see what had become of us, we took advantage of the noise they made and stole away up-stream till a shelving beach gave us leave to climb to the valley level above.

Richard shook himself like a water-soaked spaniel and laughed grimly.

"Well, here we are, safe across, horseless, and well belike to freeze to death," he commented. "What next?"

I made him a bow. "You are on my demesne of Appleby Hundred, Captain Jennifer, and it shall go hard with us if we can not find a fire to warm a guest and a horse to mount him withal. Let us go to the manor house and see what we can discover."

He entered at once into the spirit of the jest, and together we trudged the scant mile through the stubble-fields to my old roof-tree. As you would guess, we looked to find the manor house turned into an outpost headquarters; but now we were desperate enough to face anything.

Howbeit, not to rush blindly into the jaws of a trap, we first routed out the old black majordomo at the negro quarters; and when we learned from him that the great house was quite deserted, we took possession and had the black make us a rousing fire in the kitchen-arch. Nay, more; when we had steamed ourselves a little dry, we had old Anthony stew and grill for us, and fetch us a bottle of that madeira of my father's laying in.

"A toast!" cried Richard, when the bottle came, springing to his feet with the glass held high. "To the dear lady of Appleby Hundred, and may she forgather with the man she loves best, be it you, or I, or another, Jack Ireton!"

We drank it standing; and after would sit before the fire, havering like two love-sick school-boys over the charms of that dear lady to whom one of us was less than naught, and to whom the other could be but naught whilst that first one lived.

You will smile, my dears, that we should come to this when, but a short hour before, one of us had been bent upon slaying the other for Mistress Margery's sake. But the human heart is many-sided; notably that heart the soldier carries. And though I looked not to live beyond the setting of another sun, I was glad to my finger-tips to have this last loving-cup with my dear lad. I thought it would nerve me bravely for what must come—and so it did, though not as I prefigured.

We were still sitting thus before the kitchen-arch when the dawn began to dim the firelight, and the work of the new day confronted us. Pinned down, old Anthony confessed that some two or three horses of the Appleby Hundred stables had escaped the hands of the foragers of both sides; and two of these he fetched for us. Of the twain one chanced to be Blackstar, the good beast which had carried me from New Berne in the spring; and so I had my own horse betwixt my knees when I set Dick a mile on the road to Salisbury, and bade him farewell.

His last word to me was one of generous caution.

"Remember, Jack; 'haste, haste, post haste' is your watchword. There will be other couriers in from the battle-field at King's Mountain; and you must hang and fire your news-petard and vanish before they come to betray you."

"Trust me," said I, evasively; and so we parted, he to gallop eastward, and I to charge down peaceably upon that British outpost we had set abuzz in the small hours of the night.

CHAPTER XLII

IN WHICH MY LORD HAS HIS MARCHING ORDERS

Though I had passed out of the British lines less than a week before in decent good odor, save for Colonel Tarleton's ill word, I met with nothing like the welcome at the outpost camp that a king's courier had a right to expect.

The captain in command was not the one who had passed me out. He was a surly brute of the Yorkshire breed; and when he had heard that I was an express rider from Major Ferguson, he was pleased to demand my papers.

To this I must needs make answer that I carried no written despatches; that my news was for the commander-in-chief's private ear. This I told my Yorkshire pig, demanding to be sent, under guard if he chose, to the headquarters in Charlotte.

But Captain Nobbut would hear to no such reasonable proposal. On the contrary, he would hold me in arrest till he could report me and have instructions from his colonel.

Knowing what a stake it was I rode for, you may imagine how this day in durance ate into me like a canker. With ordinary diligence the trooper who carried the news of me should have gone to Charlotte by way of Queensborough and returned by noon. But being of the same surly breed with his captain, 'twas full three of the clock before he came ambling back with an order to set me forthwith upon the road to headquarters.

Once free of the camp of detention you may be sure I put Blackstar to his best paces; but hasten as I would it was coming on to evening when I passed the inner safety line and galloped down the high street of the town.

As luck would have it, the first familiar face I saw was that of Charles Stedman, the commissary-general. On my inquiry he directed me straight.

"My Lord is at supper at Mr. Stair's. Have you news, Captain?"

I drew breath of relief. Happily the loss of the day had not made me the bearer of stale tidings. So I made answer with proper reticence, saying that I had news, but it was for Lord Cornwallis's ear first of all. None the less, if the commissary-general were pleased to come with me—

He took the hint at once; and he it was who procured me instant admittance to the house, and who took on himself the responsibility of breaking in upon the party in the supper-room.

I shall not soon forget the scene that fronted us when we came into my Lord's presence. The supper was in some sort a gala feast held in honor of my Lord's accession to his earldom. The table, lighted by great silver candelabra which I recognized as Ireton heirlooms, was well filled around by the members of the commander-in-chief's military family, with the earl at the head, and Mistress Margery, bedight as befitted a lady of the quality, behind the tea-urn at the foot.

At our incoming all eyes were turned upon us, but it required my Lord's sharp question to make me leave off dwelling upon my sweet lady's radiant beauty.

"How now, Captain Ireton? Do you bring us news from the major?"

I broke the fascinating eyehold and turned slowly to face my fate.

"I do, my Lord."

"Well, what of him? You left him hastening to rejoin with his new loyalist levies, I hope?"

I drew my sword, reversed it and laid it upon the table.

"May all the enemies of the Commonwealth be even as he is, my Lord," I said, quietly.

Now, truly, I had hanged my petard well and 'twas plain the shock of it had gone far to shatter the wall of confidence our enemies had builded on the field of Camden and elsewhere. Had a hand-grenade with the fuse alight been dropped upon the table, the consternation could scarce have been greater. To a man the tableful was up and thronging round me; but above all the hubbub I heard a little cry of misery from the table-foot where my lady sat.

"How is this, sir?—explain yourself!" thundered my Lord, forgetting for once his mild suavity.

"'Tis but a brief tale, and I will make it as crisp as may be in the telling," I replied. "I came upon the major some miles this side of the crossing of the Broad. He was marching to rejoin you, in accordance with his orders. But when he had your Lordship's command to stand and fight, he obeyed."

"My command?—but I gave him no such order!"

"Nay, truly, you did not—neither in the original nor in the duplicate, my Lord. But when we had waylaid Lieutenant Tybee and quenched the duplicate, and had so amended the original as to make it fit our purpose, the brave major thanked you for what you had not done and made his stand to await the upcoming of the over-mountain men."

For a moment I thought they would hew me limb from limb, but my Lord quelled the fierce outburst with a word.

"Put up your swords, gentlemen. We shall know how to deal with this traitor," he said. And then to me: "Go on, sir, if you please; there has been a battle, as I take it?"

"There has, indeed. The mountain men came up with us in the afternoon of the Saturday. In an hour one-third of the major's force was dead or dying, the major himself was slain, and every living man left on the field was a prisoner."

Again a dozen swords hissed from their scabbards, and again I heard the little cry of misery from the table-foot. I bowed my head, looking momently to pay the penalty; but once more my Lord put the swords aside.

"Let us have a clean breast of it this time, Captain Ireton," he said. "You know well what you have earned, and nothing you can say will make it better or worse for you. Was this your purpose in making your submission to me?"

"It was."

"And you have been a rebel from the first?"

I met the cold anger in the womanish eyes as a condemned man might.

"I have, my Lord—since the day nine years agone when I learned that your king's minions had hanged my father in the Regulation."

"Then it was a farrago of lies you told me about your adventures in the western mountains?"

"Not wholly. It was your Lordship's good pleasure to send succors of powder and lead to your allies, the western savages. I and three others followed Captain Falconnet and his Indians, and I have the honor to report that we overtook and exploded them with their own powder cargo."

"And Captain Sir Francis Falconnet with them?"

"I do so hope and trust, my Lord."

He turned short on his heel, and for a moment a silence as of death fell upon the room. Then he took the Ferara from the table and sought to break it over his knee; but the good blade, like the cause it stood for, bent like a withe and would not snap.

"Put this spy in irons and clear the room," he ordered sharply. And this is how the little drama ended: with the supper guests crowding to the door; with my Lord pacing back and forth at the table-head; with two sergeants bearing me away to await, where and how I knew not, the word which should efface me.

CHAPTER XLIII

IN WHICH I DRINK A DISH OF TEA

Being without specific orders what to do with me, my two sergeant bailiffs thrust me into that little den of a strong-room below stairs where I had once found the master of the house, and one of them mounted guard whilst the other fetched the camp armorer to iron me.

The shackles securely on, I was left to content me as I could, with the door ajar and my two jailers hobnobbing before it. Having done all I had hoped to do, there was nothing for it now but to wait upon the consequences. So, hitching my chair up to the oaken table, I made a pillow of my fettered wrists and presently fell adoze.

I know not what hour of the night it was when the half-blood Scipio, who was Mr. Gilbert Stair's body-servant, came in and roused me. I started up suddenly at his touch, making no doubt it was my summons. But the mulatto brought me nothing worse than a cold fowl and a loaf, with a candle-end to see to eat them by, and a dish of hot tea to wash them down.

I knew well enough whom I had to thank for this, and was set wondering that my lady's charity was broad enough to mantle even by this little my latest sins against the king's cause. None the less, I ate and drank gratefully, draining the tea-dish to the dregs—which, by the by, were strangely bitter.

I had scarce finished picking the bones of the capon before sleep came again to drag at my eyelids, a drowsiness so masterful that I could make no head against it. And so, with the bitter taste of the tea still on my tongue, I fell away a second time into the pit of forgetfulness.

When I awakened from what seemed in the memory of it the most unresting sleep I ever had, it was no longer night, and I was stretched upon the oaken settle in that same lumber garret where I had been bedded through that other night of hiding. So much I saw at the waking glance; and then I realized, vaguely at first, but presently with startling emphasis, that it was the westering sun which was shining in at the high roof windows, that the shackles were still on, and that my temples were throbbing with a most skull-splitting headache.

Being fair agasp with astoundment at this new spinning of fate's wheel, I sprang up quickly—and was as quickly glad to fall back upon the pallet. For with the upstart a heaving nausea came to supplement the headache, and for a long time I lay bat-blind and sick as any landsman in his first gale at sea.

The sunlight was fading from the high windows, and I was deep sunk in a sick man's megrims, before aught came to disturb the silence of the cobwebbed garret. From nausea and racking pains I had come to the stage of querulous self-pity. 'Twas monstrous, this burying a man alive, ill, fettered, uncared-for, to live or die in utter solitude as might happen. I could not remotely guess to whom I owed this dismal fate, and was too petulant to speculate upon it. But the meddler, friend or foe, who had bereft me of my chance to die whilst I was fit and ready, came in for a Turkish cursing—the curse that calls down in all the Osmanli variants the same pangs in duplicate upon the banned one.

It was in the midst of one of these impotent fits of malediction that the wainscot door was opened and closed softly, and light footsteps tiptoed to my bedside. I shut my eyes wilfully when a voice low and tender asked: "Are you awake, Monsieur John?"

I hope you will hold me forgiven, my dears, if I confess that what with the nausea and the headache, the fetters and the solitude, I was rabid enough to rail at her. 'Twas so near dusk in the ill-lighted garret that I could not see how she took it; but she let me know by word of mouth.

"*Merci, Monsieur,*" she said, icily. And then: "Gratitude does not seem to be amongst your gifts."

At this I broke out in all a sick man's pettishness.

"Gratitude! Mayhap you will tell me what it is I have to be grateful for. All I craved was the chance to die as a soldier should, and some one must needs spoil me of that!"

"Selfish—selfish always and to the last," she murmured. "Do you never give a moment's thought to the feelings of others, Captain Ireton?"

This was past all endurance.

"If I had not, should I be here this moment?" I raved. "You do make me sicker than I was, my lady."

"Yet I say you are selfish," she insisted. "What have I done that you should come here to have yourself hanged for a spy?"

"Let us have plain speech, in God's name," I retorted. "You know well enough there was no better way in which I could serve you."

"Do I, indeed, *mon ami*?" she flashed out. "Let me tell you, sir, had she ever a blush of saving pride, Margery Stair—or Margery Ireton, if you like that better—would kill you with her own hand rather than have it said her husband died upon a gallows!"

A sudden light broke in upon me and I went blind in the

horror of it.

"God in Heaven!" I gasped; "'twas you, then? I do believe you poisoned me in that dish of tea you sent me last night!"

She laughed, a bitter little laugh that I hated to think on afterward.

"You have a most chivalrous soul, Captain Ireton. I do not wonder you are so fierce to shake it free of the poor body of clay."

"But you do not deny it!" I cried.

"Of what use would it be? I have said that I would not have you die shamefully on the gallows; so I may as well confess to the poppy-juice in the tea. Tell me, Monsieur John; was it nasty bitter?"

"Good Lord!" I groaned; "are you a woman, or a fiend?"

"Either, or both, as you like to hold me, sir. But come what might, I said you should not die a felon's death. And you have not, as yet."

"Better a thousand times the rope and tree than that I should rot by inches here with you to sit by and gird at me. Ah, my lady, you are having your revenge of me."

"*Merci, encore.* Shall I go away and leave you?"

"No, not that." A cold sweat broke out upon me in a sudden childish horror of the solitude and the darkness and the fetters. And then I added: "But 'twould be angel kindness if you would leave off torturing me. I am but a man, dear lady, and a sick man at that."

All in a flash her mood changed and she bent to lay a cool palm on my throbbing temples.

"Poor Monsieur John!" she said softly; "I meant not to make you suffer more, but rather less." Then she found water and a napkin to wring out and bind upon my aching head.

At the touch and the word of womanly sympathy I forgot all, and the love-madness came again to blot out the very present memory of how she had brought me to this.

"Ah, that is better—better," I sighed, when the pounding hammers in my temples gave me some surcease of the agony.

"Then you forgive me?" she asked, whether jestingly or in earnest I could not tell.

"There is none so much to forgive," I replied. "One hopeless day last summer I put my life in pledge to you; and you—in common justice you have the right to do what you will with it."

"Ah; now you talk more like my old-time Monsieur John with the healing sword-thrust. But that day you speak of was not more hopeless for you than for me."

"I know it," said I, thinking only of how the loveless marriage must grind upon her. "But it must needs be hopeless for both till death steps in to break the bond."

Again she laughed, that same bitter little laugh.

"Indeed, it was a great wrong you did that night, sir. I could wish, as heartily as you, that it might be undone. But this is idle talk. Let me see if this key will fit your manacles. I have been all day finding out who had it, and I am not sure it will be the right one, after all."

But it did prove to be the right one; and when the irons were off I felt more like a man and less like a baited bear.

"That is better," said I, drawing breath of unfeigned relief. "I bear my Lord Charles no malice, but 'twas a needless precaution, this ironing of a man who was never minded to run away."

"But you are going to run away," she said, decisively; "and that as soon as ever you are able to hold a horse between your knees. Shall I bring you another dish of tea? Nay, never look so horrified; I shall not poison you this time."

"Stay," I cried. "You mean that you are going to help me escape? 'Tis a needless prolonging of the agony. Go and tell the guards where they can find me."

She stopped midway to the wainscot door and turned to give me my answer.

"No; you are a soldier, and—and I will not be a gallows-widow. Do you hear, sir? If you are so eager to die, there is always the battle-field." And with that she left me.

I may pass over the two succeeding days in the silence I was condemned to endure through the major part of them. After that first visit, Margery came only at stated intervals to bring me food and drink, and my nurse was an old black beldame, either deaf and dumb, or else so newly from the Guinea Coast as to be unable to twist her tongue to the English.

And in the food-bringings I could neither make my lady stay nor answer any question; this though I was hungering to know what was going on beyond the walls of my garret prison. Indeed, she would not even tell me how I had been spirited away from the two sergeants keeping watch over me in her father's strong-room below stairs. "That is Scipio's secret," she would say, laughing at me, "and he shall keep it."

But in the evening of the third day the mystery bubble was burst, and I learned from Margery's lips the thing I longed to know. Lord Cornwallis had decided to abandon North Carolina, and in an hour or two the army would be in motion for withdrawal to the southward.

"Now, thanks be to God!" I said, most fervently. "King's

Mountain has begun the good work, and we shall show Farmer George a thing or two he had not guessed."

On this, my lady drew herself up most proudly and her lip curled.

daughter."

"True," said I; "I did forget. We are at cross purposes in this, as in all things else. I crave your pardon, Madam."

Her eyes were snapping by now. Never tell me, my dears, that eyes of the blue-gray can not flash fire when they will.

"How painstakingly you will go about to make me hate you!" she burst out. And then, all in the same breath: "But you will be rid of me presently, for good and all."

"Nay, then, Mistress Margery, you are always taking an ell of meaning for my inch of speech. 'Tis I who should do the ridding."

"*Mon Dieu!*" she cried, in a sudden burst of petulance; "I am sick to death of all this! Is there no way out of this coil that is strangling us both, Captain Ireton?"

"I had thought to make a way three days ago; did so make it, but you kept me from walking in it. Yet that way is still open—if you will but drop a word in my Lord's ear when you go below stairs."

"Oh, yes—a fine thing; the wife betray the husband!" This with another lip-curl of scorn. "I have some shreds and patches of pride left, sir, if you have not."

"Then free me of my obligation to you and let me do it myself. I am well enough to hang."

"And so make me a consenting accomplice? Truly, as I have said before, you have a most knightly soul, Captain Ireton."

I closed my eyes in very weariness.

"You are hard to please, my lady."

"You have not to try to please me, sir. I am going away—to-night."

"Going away?" I echoed. "Whither, if I may ask?"

"My father has taken protection and we shall go south with the army. As Lord Cornwallis says, Mecklenburg is a hornets' nest of rebellion, and in an hour or two after we are gone you will be amongst your friends."

She made to leave me now, but I would not let her go without trying the last blunt-pointed arrow in the quiver of expedients.

"Stay a moment," I begged. "You are leaving the untangling of this coil you speak of to a chance bullet on a battle-field. Had you ever thought that the Church can undo what the Church has done?"

Again I had that bitter laugh which was to rankle afterward in memory.

"You are a most desperate, pertinacious man, Captain Ireton. Failing all else, you would even storm Heaven itself to gain your end," she scoffed; then, at the very pitch-point of the scornful out-burst she put her face in her hands and fell a-sobbing as if her heart would break.

I knew not what to say or do, and ended, man-like, by saying and doing nothing. And so, still crying softly, she let herself out at the wainscot door, and this was our leave-taking.

CHAPTER XLIV

HOW WE CAME TO THE BEGINNING OF THE END

It was on the third day of December, a cheerless and comfortless day at the close of the most inclement autumn I ever re"You forget, sir, you are speaking to Mr. Gilbert Stair's member, that the patriot Army of the South was paraded on the court-house common in Charlotte to listen to the reading of General Gates's final order, the order announcing the arrival of Major-general Greene from Washington's headquarters to take over the command of the field forces in the Carolinas.

As members of Colonel William Washington's light-horse, Richard Jennifer and I were both present at this installation of the new field commander; and it was here that we both had our first sight of Nathaniel Greene, the "Hickory Quaker."

Now the historians, as is their wont, have pictured Greene the general to the complete effacement of Greene the man, and it is in my mind that you may like to see the new commander as we saw him, making his first inspection of Horatio Gates's poor "shadow of an army" on that dismal December day in Charlotte.

In years he was rising forty; and as weight goes he was a heavy man, pressing hard upon fifteen stone with the knuckle of it under his waistcoat. None the less, though his great bulk made him sit his horse more like a farmer than a soldier, he had the muscular shoulders and arms of the anchor-smiths, to which trade he had been bred.

The hint of grossness which his figure gave was not borne out by his face. Like my Lord Cornwallis's, his eyes were womanish large, and nose and mouth and the lift of the brow were cast in a mold to match; yet there was that in his face which made it the mask of a soul thoughtful and serene; and his ruddy complexion and fair hair gave him a look of openness that a dark man is like to miss.

' A skilled soldier, with a good promise of strenuous patience, was my summing up of him, and Dick saw him as I did, though with a more prophetic eye.

"He will make his mark, Jack, look you; not in stubborn infighting at the barrier, mayhap, like Dan Morgan, nor in a brilliant dash, like our colonel, but in his own anchor-smith's way—a heat at a time, and a blow at a time," said Jennifer; and I nodded.

Stirrup to stirrup with the new commander as he passed down the line rode Daniel Morgan, big, strong, masterful, handsome, the very pick and choice of leaders for his rough and ready riflemen. Like most of his men, he scorned to wear a uniform, appearing on parade, as in the field, in a neat-fitting hunting-shirt of Indian-tanned buckskin with fringings of the same—a costume that set off his gigantic figure as no tailor-fine coat could have set it off.

When he pulled his horse down to make it keep step with the sedater pacings of the general's, we could hear him declaring, with an oath, that his Eleventh Virginia alone would give a good account of all the Tories between the Catawba and the Broad; and when the cavalcade passed the rifle corps, the men flung their hats and cheered their leader in open defiance of all discipline.

Ah me! they tell me that in after years this stout Daniel, the "Lion-bearder," as we used to dub him, became a doddering old man, even as thy old tale-teller is now; that he put off all his roistering ways and might be found any Lord's Day shouting, not curses, as of yore, but psalm tunes, in the church whereof he was a pillar! But 'twas the other Daniel we knew; the bluff, hearty man of his two hands, who could pummel the best boxer in his own regiment of fisticuffers; who could out-curse, out-buffet and out-drink the hardiest frontiersman on the border.

Next conspicuous in the general's suite was our colonel, the pink of light-horse commanders, with only Harry Lee in all the patriot rank and file for his peer. 'Tis a thousand pities that William Washington, "the Marcellus of the army," has had to suffer the eclipse which must dim the luster of all who walk in the shadow of a greater of the same name. For surely there never was a finer gentleman, a truer friend, a nobler patriot, or, according to his opportunities, an abler officer than was our beloved colonel of the light dragoons.

But this is all beside the mark, you will say; and you will be chafing restively to know how Dick and I had come together in this troop of Colonel Washington's; to know this in a word and to pass on at a gallop to the happenings which followed. Nay, in fancy's eye I can see you turning the page impatiently, wondering where and when and how this tiresome old word-spinner will make an end.

As Margery had promised, I passed out of my garret prison and out of door on that memorable evening of October fourteenth to find the British gone from Charlotte and the town jubilant with patriotic joy.

Having nothing to detain me, and being bound in honor by the wish of my dear lady not to follow and give myself up to the retreating British general, I took horse and rode to Salisbury, where I had the great good fortune to find Dick, already breveted a captain in Colonel Washington's command, hurrying his troop southward to whip on the British withdrawal.

Here was my chance to drown heartburnings in an onsweeping tide of action, and then and there I became a gentleman volunteer in Dick's company, asking nothing of my dear lad save that I might ride at his stirrup and share his hazards.

Touching the hazards, there were plenty of them in the seven weeks preceding and the month or more following our new general's coming to take the field, as you may know in detail if you care to follow the gallopings of Colonel Washington's light-horse troop through the pages of the histories. But these have little or naught to do with my tale, and I pass them by with the word you will anticipate; that in all the dashes and forays and brushes with the enemy's foraging parties and outposts, no British or Tory bullet could find its billet in the man who was enamored of death.

As for my most miserable entanglement, the lapse of time made it neither better nor worse, nor greatly different; and there was little in all the skirmishings and gallopings to beat off the bandog of conscience, or that other and still fiercer wild beast of starved love, that gnawed at me day and night.

Though the hope for some easement would now and then lift its head, I was reminded daily that hope itself was hopeless; and when the days lengthened into weeks and the weeks into months, bringing no salving for the double hurt, I knew that time could only make me love Margery the more; that there be wounds that heal, and others that open afresh at each remembrance of the hand that gave them.

One grain of comfort I had in all these dreary weeks. 'Twas whilst we were quartering in Charlotte, and I had chanced to fall upon the half-blood Scipio who had been left by Gilbert Stair to be the caretaker of the deserted town house.

As you will remember, 'twas he who had brought me the drugged tea, and the word I had from him made me hot with shame for the cruel imputation I had put upon my dear lady. "Yas, sar; gib um sleep-drop to make buckra massa hol' still twell we could tote 'im froo de window an' 'roun' de house an' up de sta'r. Soljah gyards watch um mighty close dat night; yes, sar!" And thus this nightmare thought of mine was turned into another thorn to prick me on the self-accusing side. 'Twas her keen woman's wit, and no cold-blooded plan to cheat the gallows, that made her give me the sleeping draft. Having the object-lesson of my late surrender before her, she had no mind to let me mar the rescue by waking to forbid it. And when I taxed her, 'twas natural pride that drove her to let me go on thinking the unworthy thought, if so I would.

I did penance for my disloyalty as a despairing lover might, and I do think it made me tenderer of Dick, whose bearing to me through all these tempestuous weeks was most nobly generous and forgiving. I say forgiving because I was often but the curstest of companions, as you would guess. For when I was not bent upon finding that wicket gate of death which would let me from the path of these two, I was in a wicked tertian of the mind whose chill was of despair, and whose fever was a hot desire to look once more into the eyes of my dear lady before the wicket gate should open for me.

'Twas this desire that finally drew me to her—the desire and another thing which shall have mention in its place. The new year was now come, and the Southern Army, as yet too weak to cope with the enemy, was cut into two wings of observation; one under General Greene himself at Cheraw Hill, the other and lesser in the knoll forests of the Broad with Daniel Morgan for its chief; both watching hawk-like the down-sitting of my Lord Cornwallis, who seemed to have taken root at Winnsborough.

As you will know, Washington's light-horse was with Morgan; and we ate, drank and well-nigh slept in the saddle. But for all our scoutings and outridings, and all Dan Morgan's hearty cursings at the ill success of them, we could come by no sure inkling of Lord Cornwallis's designs. As I have said, the British commander seemed to have taken root and was now waiting to sprout and grow.

It was at this lack-knowledge crisis that I volunteered to go to the British camp at Winnsborough in my old quality of spy; did this and had my leave and orders before Dick learned of it.

Left to my own devices, I fear I should have slipped away without telling Jennifer. But, as so many times before, fate intervened to drive me where I had not meant to go. On the morning set for my departure I woke to find a letter pinned to the ground beside me with an Indian scalping-knife thrust through it.

Dick was sitting by the newly-kindled fire, nursing his knees and most palpably waiting for me to wake and find my missive.

"What is it?" I asked, eying the ominous thing distrustfully.

"'Tis a letter, as you see. Uncanoola left it." Then, most surlily: "'Tis from Madge, and to you. There is your name on the back of it."

At this I must needs read the letter, with the lad looking on as if he would eat me. 'Twas dated at Winnsborough, and was brief and to the point.

Monsieur:

"When last we met you said the Church might undo what the Church had done. I have spoken to the good Père Matthieu, and he has consented to write to the Holy Father at Rome. But it is necessary that he should have your declaration. Since the matter is of your own seeking, mayhap you can devise a way to communicate with Père Matthieu, who is at present with us under our borrowed roof here."

That was all, and it was signed only with her initial. I read it through twice and then again to gain time. For Dick was waiting.

"'Tis a mere formal matter of business," said I, when I could put him off no longer.

"Business?" he queried, the red light of suspicion coming and going in his eye. "What business can you have with Mistress Madge Stair, pray?"

"'Tis about—it touches the title to Appleby Hundred," said I, equivocating as clumsily as a schoolboy caught in a fault. "Of course you know that the confiscation act of the North Carolina Congress re-established my right and title to the estate?"

"No," said he; "you never told me." Then: "She writes you about this?"

"About a matter touching it, as I say."

"As you did not say," he growled; after which a silence came and sat between us, I holding the open letter in my hand and he staring gloomily at the back of it.

When the silence grew portentous I told him of my design to go a-spying. He looked me in the eye and his smile was not pleasant to see.

"You are lying most clumsily, Jack; or at best you are telling me but half the truth. You are going to see Mistress Margery."

"That is altogether as it may happen," I retorted, striving hard to keep down the flame of insensate rivalry which his accusings always kindled in me.

"It is not. Winnsborough is neither London nor yet Philadelphia, that you may miss her in the crowd. And you do not mean to miss her."

"Well? And if I do chance to see her—what then?"

"Don't mad me, Jack. You should know by this what a fool she has made of me."

"'Tis your own folly," I rejoined hotly. "You should blame neither the lady nor the man to whom she has given nothing save—"

"Save what?" he broke in savagely.

I recoiled on the brink as I had so many times before. The months of waiting for the death I craved had hardened me.

"Save a thing you would value lightly enough without her love. Let us have done with this bickering; find the colonel and ask his leave to go with me, if you like. Then you may do the love-making whilst I do the spying."

"No," said he; "not while you stand it upon such a leg as that."

I reached across and gripped his hand and wrung it. "Shall we never have the better of these senseless vaporings?" I cried. "'Tis as you say; I can neither live sane nor die mad without another sight of her, Dick, and that is the plain truth. And yet, mark me, this next seeing of her will surely set a thing in train that will make her yours and not mine. Get your leave and come with me on your own terms. Mayhap she will show you how little she cares for me, and how much she cares for you."

So this is how it came about that we two, garbed as decent planters and mounted upon the sleekest cobs the regiment afforded, took the road for Winnsborough together on a certain summer-fine morning in January in the year of battles, seventeen hundred and eighty-one.

CHAPTER XLV

IN WHICH WE FIND WHAT WE NEVER SOUGHT

'Tis fifty miles as a bird would fly it from the grazing uplands of the Broad known as the Cowpens to the lower plantation region lying between that stream and the farther Catawba or Wateree; and Richard Jennifer and I ambled the distance leisurely, as befitted our mission and disguise, cutting the journey evenly in half for the first night's lodging, which we had at the house of one Philbrick—as hot a Tory as we pretended to be.

From our host of the night we learned that within two days the British outposts on the Wateree and the Broad had been advanced; and there were rumors in the air that Lord Cornwallis, who was hourly expecting General Leslie with two thousand of Sir Henry Clinton's men from New York, would presently move on to the long-deferred conquest of North Carolina.

"Has Cornwallis lost his wits?" Dick would say, when we were a-jog on the southward road again. "'Tis a braver lordling than I gave him credit for being—if he will put his head in a trap that will close behind him and cut him off from his line and base."

I laughed. "You may wager Jennifer House against an acre of the Cowpens that Lord Charles will do no such unsoldierly thing. If this rumor be true, we have heard only the half of it."

"And the other half will be?—"

"That my Lord Cornwallis will do his prettiest to pull the teeth of one or the other of the trap-jaws before he trusts himself within them."

Jennifer was silent for an ambling minute or two. Then he said: "'Twill be our teeth he'll try to pull, then. The Broad is nearer than the Pedee; and ours is the weaker of the two jaws."

"Right you are," said I. "And now we know what we have to discover."

"Anan?" he queried.

"We must learn by hook or crook who is to be sent against Dan Morgan, and when."

"That should be easy—if the use of it afterward be not choked out of us at a rope's end."

"We can divide the rope's-end chance of failure by two. We may work together as the opportunity offers, but once within the lines we must pass as strangers to each other, or at most as chance acquaintances of the road."

"Good," said he; and then his jaw dropped. "But what if one

of us be taken? Never ask me to stand by stranger-wise and see you hanged, Jack!"

"I shall both ask it and promise to do the same by you. Your hand on it before we go a step farther, if you please."

"'Tis out of all reason," he demurred.

"'Tis the only reasonable course. Bethink you, this is no knight-errant venture; we are two of Dan Morgan's soldiers bent upon doing a thing most needful for the welfare of the country and its cause. 'Tis a duty higher than any obligation friendship lays on Richard Jennifer or John Ireton."

At this he yielded the point, though I could see that the proposal jumped little with the promptings of his generous heart.

"'Tis a scurvy trap you have set for me," he grumbled. "The risk is chiefly yours, and you know it. You are known to Lord Cornwallis, and to God knows how many more of them, and belike—"

The interruption came in the shape of a troop of redcoat horsemen galloping in the road to meet us, and we were shortly surrounded and put sharply to the question. We answered each for himself. Dick was a loyalist from Yorkville way, eager to be set in arms against the bandit Daniel Morgan. I was a refugee from "hornets'-nest" Mecklenburg, also bent upon revenge.

The troop officer passed us on, something doubting, as I suspected. But we were riding in the right direction, and he was unwilling to clog himself with a pair of plain country gentlemen held in leash as prisoners.

A few miles farther down the road the same brace of lies got us safely through the loosely drawn vedette line, and by evening we were in sight of our goal.

Viewing it from the rising ground of approach, Winnsborough appeared less as a town than as a partly fortified camp. The few houses of the village were lost in the field of tents, huts and troop shelters, and measuring by the spread of these, it would seem that my Lord Cornwallis's army had been considerably augmented since I had last seen it in Charlotte. I spoke of this, but Dick was intent upon the business of the moment.

"Aye; there are enough of them, God knows. But tell me, Jack—I'm new to this game—what's to do first when we are among them?"

I laughed at him. "You are my troop commander, Captain Jennifer. 'Tis for you to make the dispositions."

"Have your joke and be hanged to you. There are no captains here."

"If you leave it to me, we shall ride boldly to the tavern, put up as travelers, and listen to the gossips, each for himself," I replied; and this is what we did.

The village tavern, servilely bearing the king's arms thinly painted over the palmetto tree of South Carolina on its swinging sign-board, was a miserable doggery, full to overflowing with a riffraff of carousing soldiery. Separating by mutual consent in the public tap-room, Richard and I presently drifted together again at a small table in a corner, with a black boy in attendance to set before us such poor entertainment as the hostelry afforded.

"Well, what luck?" asked Dick, mumbling it behind his hand, though he might safely have shouted it aloud in the din and clamor of the place.

I shook my head. "Nothing as yet, save that I overheard a tipsy corporal telling his tipsier sergeant that the officers would be holding a revel to-night at a Tory manor house situate somewhere beyond the camp confines to the northward; the house of one Master Marmaduke Harndon, if I heard the name aright." Then I added: "This rabble is too drunken to serve our purpose. 'Tis only the common soldiery, and we shall learn nothing here."

"There was at least one who was not a ranker," said Dick, and there was something akin to awe in his voice. Then he leaned across the table to whisper. "Jack, I've fair had a fright!"

I smiled. Fear, of God, man or the devil, was not one of the lad's weaknesses.

"You may grin as you please," he went on; "but answer me this; do the dead come back to life?"

"Not this side of the resurrection reveille, if we may believe the dominies."

"Then I have seen a ghost—a most horrible mask of a man we both know to our cost."

"Name him and I will tell you whether he be a ghost or no."

"'Tis the ghost of Frank Falconnet; or else it is what of the man himself the fire hath left," said Dick, and I marked his shiver at the word.

"No!" said I.

"I tell you yes."

I sprang up, but the lad reached across the table and smote me back into the chair.

"Softly, old firebrand; 'twas you who said the public matter must take precedence of the private. Moreover, if this be Francis Falconnet whom I have seen, your sweetest revenge on him will be to let him live—as he is."

"I will kill him as I would a wild beast," I raged, thinking of that midnight scene in the great forest when my sweet lady had gone on her knees to this fiend in human guise. "And so should you," I added, "if you care aught for the honor of the woman who loves you."

But now it was this hot-headed Richard I have drawn for you who saw farthest and clearest.

"All in good time," he said, coolly. "At this present we have Dan Morgan's fish to fry, and sitting here saucing this devil's mess of a supper with thoughts of private revenge will never fry it. Set your wits at work; Falconnet's ghost has put mine hopelessly out of gear. Ye gods! but 'twas a most fearsome thing to look at!"

I did not answer him at once, and whilst I plied knife and fork for the sake of appearances, I would think upon what he had discovered. This reappearance of Francis Falconnet was not to be passed over lightly. What would he do, or seek to do? Nay, what devilish thing was it he might not do? If the fire had burned his passion out, it had doubtless kindled a feller blaze of revenge. And if his thirst was for vengeance, how could he quench it in a deeper draft than by harrying the woman we both loved? 'Twas only by a mighty effort that I could drag myself back to Dick's urging and the needs of the hour.

"To have some chance of hearing gossip to our purpose, we must make shift to gain admittance to this officers' rout at the manor house," I said.

"The devil!" quoth Dick, "I venture that's easier said than done—for two plain country gentlemen."

"Never fear; there will be others there lacking fine clothes, and so the throng be great enough, we may pass current in it."

Richard pushed his plate back with a grimace of disgust.

"Let us be at it, then. Another grapple with this pig-bait will finish me outright."

A half-hour later we were tethering our cobs at the already crowded hitching-rail in front of a goodly mansion some mile or more beyond the camp limits on the northward road; a rambling manor house to the full as large as Appleby Hundred, with a shaven lawn in front, and within, lights and music and sounds of revelry.

"By the Lord Harry! but this Master Harndon would seem to be a man of substance," says Dick. And then: "Can you pick out a good horse in the dark, Jack? It may come to a race for our necks, by and by, and these cobs of ours are too broad-backed for speed."

I said I could, and so we went deeper into the cavalcade at the hitch-rail and marked out two clean-limbed chargers, a gray and a sorrel; this before we gave the final touches to our plan of action and passed up the broad avenue to the manor house.

CHAPTER XLVI

HOW OUR PIECE MISSED FIRE AT HARNDON ACRES

For a doorkeeper some one or another of the officer guests had set a sergeant on guard; but though the night was yet young the man passed us into the great entrance hall with a hiccough and a wink that spoke thus early of an open house and freely flowing good cheer.

As we had hoped to find it, this rout at Master Harndon's was a stifling jam, and a good half of the guests were in civilian plain clothes, neither Paris nor London having as yet reached so far into the Carolina plantations to proscribe homespun and to prescribe the gay toggeries of the courts. This for the men, I hasten to add; for then, as now, our American dames and maids would put a year's cropping of a plantation on their backs, thinking nothing of it; and there was no lack of shimmering silks and stiff brocades, of high-piled *coiffures*, paint, patches and powder at this merry-making at Harndon Acres.

Lacking an introducer, and wanting, moreover, nothing save the leave to have standing-room in the throng as lookers-on, we gave Mr. Marmaduke Harndon, a sleek, rotund little gentleman, smirking and bowing and tapping the lid of his silver snuff-box, a wide berth; and with an agreement to meet later for the comparing of notes, Jennifer and I went apart at the door of the ball-room, each to lose himself in the assembled company as an otter slips into a pool, namely, without ruffling it.

'Twas easily done. Winnsborough had by this time become a refuge camp for all the loyalists in the region roundabout, and there were many in the present company who were strangers one to another, uneasy, shifting figures in the gay throng, beneath the notice alike of haughty dames and prinking dandy officers. Beneath the notice, I say; yet I would qualify this, for more than one of the epauletted macaronis trod upon my toes or bustled me rudely in the crush till I trembled, not for my own self-control, but for Richard's, making sure that the lad was having no more gentlemanly welcome than I.

'Twas with some notion of finding ampler room for my feet that I edged away through the fringing wall-crowd in the dancing-room toward a curtained archway at the back. As yet I had overheard naught save the silly persiflage of the belles and beaux—a word here and another there—and I was beginning to fear that this was as poor a place to look for information as was the pot-house, when a thing befell to set me a-quiver with all the thrillings the human heart-strings can thrum to in one and the same instant of time.

I had shouldered my way out of the ball-room medley and into the less crowded room at the back. This proved to be a rear withdrawing-room serving for the nonce as a refectory. There were little groups and knots of chatterers standing about; fair maids, each with her ring of redcoated courtiers, laughing and jesting or picking daintily at the viands on the great oaken table in the midst.

Rounding the promontory of the table's-end to come to anchor in some quiet eddy where I could listen unnoticed for the word I was thirsting for, I must needs entangle the button of my coat-cuff in the delicate lace of a lady's sleeve in passing.

The wearer of the sleeve had her back to me, and I saw the white shoulders go up in a little shrug of petulance whilst I sought to disentangle the button. Then she turned to face me and the words of apology froze on my lips. 'Twas Mistress Margery, standing at ease with—good heavens! with Richard Jennifer and Colonel Banastre Tarleton for her company!

Here was a halter, with a double snaffle at the end of it, was the thought that flashed upon me; and I was gathering my wits to brazen it out in some such manner as to leave Jennifer untainted, when my lady give a little start and a shriek.

"La, Mr. Septimus; how you startled me!" she cried. Then, without a tremor of the lip or a pause for breath-taking, she presented me: "Colonel Tarleton; Mr. Septimus Ireton, of Iretondene in Virginia." And next to Dick: "Mr. Richard; my very good friend, Mr. Ireton."

'Twas done so cleverly and with such an air that even Dick, who had known her from childhood, was struck dumb with admiration, as his face sufficiently advertised. And, indeed, I had much ado to play my own part with any decent self-possession, though I did make shift to bow stiffly, and to say: "I see I should have brought the Iretondene title deeds with me to make you sure that I am not my rebel cousin John, Mistress Margery. Your servant, Colonel Tarleton; and yours, Mr. Richard."

Dick's bow was an elaborate hiding of his tell-tale face; but the colonel's was the slightest of nods, and I could feel the sloe-black eyes of him boring into my very soul.

Had my lady given him but a moment's time I make no doubt he would have come instantly at the truth and the little farce would have been turned into a tragedy on the spot. But she gave him no time. The spinet in the ball-room alcove was tinkling out the overture to a minuet, and she laid the tips of her dainty fingers on the colonel's arm.

"This will be ours to walk through, will it not, Colonel Tarleton?" she said, playing the sprightly minx to the very climax of perfection. Then she dipped us a curtsy. "*Au revoir*, gentlemen. 'Tis a thousand pities you had not joined sooner and so had the red coat and small-sword to grace you here."

When they were gone, Dick laughed sardonically.

"Saw you ever such a cool-blood little jade in all your life? 'Twas with me as it was with you; I, too, stumbled upon them, and the colonel bustled me and set his heel on my foot. I daresay I should have had myself in irons in another moment but for Madge. She slipped in between and introduced us as sweetly as you please."

"Nevertheless," said I, "the colonel recognized us both."

"No! Think you so?"

"'Tis certain enough to play upon. What we do now must be done quickly or not at all. What have you overheard?"

He swore softly. "Never a cursed word; less than nothing of any interest to Dan Morgan."

"We must try again. 'Twill surely be talked of here if the army is about to move. Do you take a turn in the anteroom and meet me in a quarter of an hour at the outer door."

At the word, Dick promptly lost himself in the throng whilst I made a slow circuit of the refreshment table. Once I thought I had the clue when a girl hanging on the arm of an infantry lieutenant said: "Will it be true that you will presently go out to hunt the rebels down, Mr. Thornicroft?" But the prudent lieutenant smiled and put her off cleverly, leaving his fair questioner—and me— none the wiser.

I went on, drifting aimlessly from group to group and dallying of set purpose. If I had read Colonel Tarleton's glance aright, the moments were growing diamond-precious; but as yet neither half of my errand was done. Come what might, I must see Margery again and have her tell me where and how to find the priest; and 'twas borne in upon me that she would come back to seek me as soon as she could be free of her partner in the dance.

The forecast as to my lady had its fulfilment while yet the spinetter was striking out the final chords of the minuet. A lady dropped her kerchief, and I was before her swain in stooping to pick it up. As I bowed low in returning the bit of lace to its owner, a voice that I had learned to know and love whispered in my ear.

"Make your way to the clock landing of the stair; I must have speech with you," it said; and for a wonder I was cool enough to obey with no more than a sidelong glance at my lady passing on the arm of another epauletted dangler.

She was before me at the meeting place, and there was no laughing welcome in the deep-welled eyes. Instead, they flashed me a look that made me wince.

"What folly is this, sir?" she demanded. "Will you never have done taking my honor and your own life into your reckless hands?"

I bowed my head to the storm. With the dagger of my miserable errand sticking in my heart there was no fight in me.

"I am but come to do your bidding," I said, slowly, for the words cost me sorely in the coin of anguish. "I had your letter, and if you will say how I may find Father Matthieu—"

She broke me in the midst. "*Mon Dieu!*" she cried. "Could I guess that you would come here, into the very noose of the gallows? Oh, how you do heap scorn on scorn upon me! Once you made me give silent consent to a falsehood you told; twice, nay, thrice, you have made me disloyal to the king; and now you come again to make me look the world in the face and tell a smiling lie to shield you! O Holy Mother, pity me!" And with this she put her face in her hands and began to sob.

Now we were only measurably isolated on the stair, and some sense of the hazard we took—a hazard involving her as well as Richard and myself—steadied me with a sudden shock.

"Control yourself," I whispered. "What is done, is done; and the misery is not all yours to suffer. Tell me how I may find the priest, and I will do my errand and begone."

"You can not stay to find him now—you must not," she insisted, coming out of the fit of despair with a rebound. "He is in the town—indeed, I know not where he is just now. Can you not endure it a little longer, Captain Ireton?"

"No," said I, sullenly. "I have been living a lie all these months to the friend I love best, and I will not do it more."

Could I be mistaken? Surely there was a flash not of anger in the eyes that were lifted to mine, and a tremulous note of eagerness in the voice that said: "Then Dick does not know?—you have not told him?"

"No; I have told no one."

"Poor Dick!" she said softly. "I thought he knew, and I—"

She paused, and in the pause it flashed upon me how she had wronged my dear lad; how she had thought he would make brazen love to her knowing she was the wife of another. I thanked God in my heart that I had been able to right him thus far.

After a time she said: "Why did you make me marry you,

Monsieur John? Oh, I have racked my brain so for the answer to that question. I know you said it was to save my honor. But surely we have paid a heavier penalty than any that could have been laid upon me had you left me as I was."

"I was but a short-sighted fool, and no prophet," I rejoined, striving hard to keep the bitterness of soul out of my words. "At the moment it seemed the only way out of the pit of doubt into which my word to Colonel Tarleton had plunged you. But there was another motive. You saw the paper I signed that night, with Lieutenant Tybee and your father's factor for the witnesses?"

"Yes."

"Do you know what it was?"

"No."

"'Twas the last will and testament of one John Ireton, gentleman, in which he bequeathed to Margery, his wife, his estate of Appleby Hundred."

"Appleby Hundred?" she echoed. "But my father—"

"Your father holds but a confiscator's title, and it, with many others, has been voided by the Congress of North Carolina. Richard Jennifer is my dear friend, and you—"

"I begin to understand—a little," she said, and now her voice was low and she would not look at me. Then, in the same low tone: "But now—now you would be free again?"

"How can you ask? As matters stand, I have marred your life and Dick's most hopelessly. Do you wonder that I have been reckless of the hangman? that I care no jot for my interfering life at this moment, save as the taking of it may involve you and Richard?"

"No, surely," she said, still speaking softly. And now she gave me her eyes to look into, and the hardness was all melted out of them. "Did you come here, under the shadow of the gallows, to tell me this, Monsieur John?"

"There shall be no more half-confidences between us, dear lady. I had my leave of General Morgan on the score of our need for better information of Lord Cornwallis's designs; but I should have come in any case—wanting the leave, my commission as a spy, or any other excuse."

"To tell me this?"

"To do the bidding of your letter, and to say that whilst I live I shall be shamed for the bitter words I gave you when I was sick."

"I mind them not; I had forgotten them," she said.

"But I have not forgotten, nor ever shall. Will you say you forgive me, Margery?"

"For thinking I had poisoned you? How do you know I did not?"

"I have seen Scipio. Will you shrive me for that disloyalty, dear lady?"

"Did I not say I had forgotten it?"

"Thank you," I said, meaning it from the bottom of my heart. "Now one thing more, and you shall send me to Father Matthieu. 'Tis a shameful thing to speak of, but the thought of it rankles and will rankle till I have begged you to add it to the things forgotten. That morning in your dressing-room—"

She put up her hands as if she would push the words back.

"Spare me, sir," she begged. "There are some things that must always be unspeakable between us, and that is one of them. But if it will help you to know—that I know—how—how you came there—"

She was flushing most painfully, and I was scarce more at ease. But having gone thus far, I must needs let the thought consequent slip into words.

"Your father's motives have ever been misunderstandable to me. What could he hope to gain by such a thing?"

I had no sooner said it than I could have bitten my masterless tongue. For in the very voicing of the wonder I saw, or thought I saw, Gilbert Stair's purpose. Since I had not made good my promise to die and leave the estate to Margery, he would at least make sure of his daughter's dowry in it by putting it beyond us to set the marriage aside as a thing begun but not completed. So, having this behind-time flash of after-wit, I made haste to efface the question I had asked.

"Your pardon, I pray you; I see now 'tis a thing we must both bury out of sight. But to the other—the matter which has brought me hither; will you put me in the way of finding Father Matthieu?"

We had talked on through the measures of a cotillion, and the dancers, warm and wearied, were beginning to fill the entrance hall below. Our poor excuse for privacy would be gone in a minute or two, and she spoke quickly.

"You shall see Father Matthieu, and I will help you. But you must not linger here. In a few days the army will be moving northward—Oh, heavens! what have I said!"

"Nothing," I cut in swiftly; "you are speaking now to your husband—not to the spy. Go on, if you please."

"We shall return to Appleby Hundred within the fortnight. There, if you are still—if you desire it, you may meet the good *curé*, and—"

A much-bepowdered captain of cavalry was coming up the stair to claim her, and I was fain to let her go. But at my passing of her to the step below, I whispered: "I shall keep the tryst—my first and last with you, dear lady. Adieu."

So soon as she was gone I made haste to find Richard, having, as I feared, greatly overstayed my appointment to meet him at the door. He was not among the promenaders in the hall, so I began to drift again, through the ball-room and so on to where the spread table stood ringed with its groups of nibblers. I had made no more than half the round of the refectory when I saw Margery standing in the curtained arch, looking this way and that, with anxious terror written plainly in her face.

"What is it?" I asked, when she had found me out.

"'Tis the worst that could happen," she whispered. "You are discovered, both of you. Colonel Tarleton was too shrewd for us. He has let it be known among the officers that there are two spies in the house, and now—Hark! what is that?"

We were standing in a deep window-bay and I drew the curtain an inch or two. The air without was filled with the trampling of hoofbeats on greensward. A light-horse troop was surrounding the manor house.

I drew her arm in mine and led her back to the ball-room; 'twas now come to this, that open publicity was our best safeguard. "We must find Dick," said I. "Have you seen him?"

"No."

Together we made the slow circuit of the dancing-room, but Jennifer was not to be found. Out of the tail of my eye I saw a soldier slipping in here and there to stand statue-like against the wall. This brought it to a matter of minutes, of seconds, mayhap, and still we looked in vain for Dick.

"Oh, why did you bring him here? He will surely be taken!" Her voice was tremulous with fear, and I answered as I could, being sore at heart, in spite of all, that her chief concern should be for Richard.

But by now my purpose was well taken, and though it appeared that Richard Jennifer was more than ever my successful rival, I pledge you, my dears, I had no thought of leaving him behind. So we made another slow round of the rooms, and whilst we were looking for Dick I spoke in guarded whispers to warn my lady of Falconnet's return. But the warning was not needed.

Her shudder of loathing shook the hand on my arm. "That man! Oh, Monsieur John! I fear him day and night! If I could but run away; but we are not finding Dick—we *must* find him quickly!"

There was no other place to look save in the entrance hall, and at the door one of the statue-like soldiers took two steps aside and barred the way. I faced about and we plunged once again into the throng, but not before I had had a glimpse of Richard in the hall beyond. When the chance offered, I bent to whisper.

"Dick is in the hall, looking for me, go you to him and warn him. I may not pass the door, as you have seen."

"He will not escape without you," she demurred.

"Tell him he must. Tell him I say he must!"

She glanced over her shoulder with a look in her eyes that made me think of a wounded bird fluttering in the net of the fowler.

"Oh, 'tis hard, hard!" she murmured.

I snatched the word from her lips. "To choose between love and wifely duty? Then I make it a command. Go, quickly!"

She went at that, and I made my way slowly to the far side of the ball-room, taking post in a deep-recessed window giving upon the lawn. Though it was January and the night was chill and raw, the rooms were summer warm with the breath of the crush, and some one had swung the casement.

Without, I could hear the horses of the waiting troop champing restlessly at their bits, and now and again the low gentling words of the riders. Why the colonel did not spring his trap at once I could not guess; though I learned later that he had magnified our two-man spying venture into a patriot foray meant to capture the whole houseful of British officers at a swoop, and was taking his measures accordingly.

'Twas while I was listening to the champing horses that I heard my name whispered in the darkness beyond the open casement; I turned slowly, and the nearest of the soldier watchers began to edge his way toward my window.

"'Tis I—Dick Jennifer," whispered the voice without. "Swing the casement a little wider and out with you. Be swift about it, for God's sake!"

"I am fair trapped," I whispered back. "Make off as you can."

"And leave you behind?" So much I heard; and then came sounds of a struggle; the breath-catchings of two men locked in a strangler's hold, a smothered oath or two, a fall on the turf under the window, followed by the soft thudding of fist blows. I could bear it no longer. The edging soldier had come within arm's reach, and when I swung the casement a little wider, he laid a hand on my shoulder.

"In the name of the king!" he said; and this was all he had time or leave to say. For at the summons I drove my fist against the point of his wagging jaw, to send him plunging among the dancers, and the recoil of the blow carried me clear of the window-seat with what a din and clamor of a hue and cry to speed the parting guest as you may figure for yourselves.

The alighting ground of the leap was the body of Dick's late antagonist lying prone beneath the window ledge; but the lad himself was up and ready to catch me when I stumbled over the vanquished one.

"'Tis legs for it now," he cried. "Make for the avenue and the horses at the hitch-rail!"

At rising twenty a man may run fast and far; at rising forty he may still run far if the first hundred yards do not burst his bellows. So when we had darted through the thin line of encircling horsemen and were flying down the broad avenue with all the troopers who had caught sight of us thundering at our heels, Dick was the pace-setter, whilst I made but a shifty second, gasping and panting and dying a thousand deaths in the effort to catch my second wind.

"Courage!" shouted Dick, flinging the word back over his shoulder as he ran. "There is help ahead if we can live to reach the gate!"

But, luckily for me, the help was nearer at hand. Half way down the box-bordered drive, when I was at my last gasp, the shrill yell of the border partizans rose from the shrubbery on the right, and a voice that I shall know and welcome in another world cried out:

"Stiddy, boys! stiddy till ye can see the whites o' their eyes! Now, then; give it to 'em hot *and* heavy!"

A haphazard banging of guns followed and the pursuit drew rein in some confusion, giving us time to reach the great gate and the horse-rail, and to loose and mount the gray and the sorrel we had marked out.

Whilst we were about this last, Ephraim Yeates came loping down the avenue and through the gate to vault into the saddle of the first horse he could lay hands on; and so it was that we three took the northward road in the silver starlight, with the pursuit now in order again and in full cry behind us.

'Twas not until we had safely run the gantlet of the vedette lines by a by-path known to the old hunter, and had shaken off the troopers that were following, that I found time to ask what had become of the men who had formed the ambush in the shrubbery.

The old man gave me his dry chuckle of a laugh.

"'Twas the same old roose de geer, as the down-country Frenchers 'u'd say. I stole the drunken sergeant's gun and two others, and let 'em off one to a time. As for the screechin', one bazoo's as good as a dozen, if so be ye blow it fierce enough."

"'Twas cut and dried beforehand," Dick explained. "I had an

inkling of what was afoot from Ephraim, here, whom I stumbled on when I dropped from the stair window that Madge opened for me. He went to set his one-man ambush whilst I was trying to warn you."

"So," said I. "Our skins are whole, but after all we have come off with never a word to take back to Dan Morgan—unless you have the word."

"Not I," Dick said, ruefully.

The old man chuckled again.

"Ye ain't old enough, neither one o' ye, ez I allow. It takes a right old person to fish out the innards of an inimy's secrets. Colonel Tarleton, hoss, foot and dragoons, with the seventh rigiment and a part o' the seventy-first, will take the big road for Dan Morgan's camp to-morrow at sun-up. And right soon atterwards, Gin'ral Cornwallis 'll foller on. Is that what you youngsters was trying to find out?"

CHAPTER XLVII

ARMS AND THE MAN

In that book he wrote—the book in which he never so much as names the name of Ireton—my Lord Cornwallis's commissary-general, Charles Stedman, damns Colonel Tarleton in a most gentlemanly manner for his ill-success at the Cowpens, and would charge to his account personal the failure of Cornwallis's plan to crush in detail the patriot Army of the South.

Now little as I love, or have cause to love, Sir Banastre Tarleton,—they tell me he has been knighted and now wears a major-general's sword-knot,—'tis but the part of outspoken honest enmity to say that we owed the victory at the Cowpens to no remissness on the part of the young legion commander who, if he were indeed the most brutal, was also the most active and enterprising of Lord Cornwallis's field officers.

No, it was no remissness nor lack of bravery on the part of the enemy. 'Twas only that the tide had turned. King's Mountain had been fought and won, and there were to be no more Camdens for us.

In the affair at the cow pastures, which followed hard upon Richard's and my return from our flying visit to Winnsborough, the very elements fought for us and against the British. As for instance: Tarleton, with his famous legion of horse, and infantry enough to make his numbers exceed ours, began his march on the eleventh and was rained on and mired for four long days before he had crossed the Broad and had come within scouting distance of us.

Left to himself, Dan Morgan would have locked horns with the enemy at the fording of the Pacolet; but in the council of war, our colonel and John Howard of the Marylanders were for drawing Tarleton still deeper into the wilderness, and farther from the British main, which was by this moved up as far as Turkey Creek. So we broke camp hastily and fell back into the hill country; and on the night of the sixteenth took post on the northern slope of a low ridge between two running streams.

For its backbone our force had some three hundred men of the Maryland line and two companies of Virginians. These formed our main, and were posted on the rising ground with John Howard for their commander. A hundred and fifty paces in their front, partly screened in the open pine, oak and chestnut wooding of the ground, were Pickens's Carolinians and the Georgians;

militiamen, it is true, but skilled riflemen, and every man of them burning hot to be avenged on Tarleton's pillagers.

Still farther to the front, disposed as right and left wings of outliers, were Yeates and his fellow borderers and some sixty of the Georgians set to feel the enemy's approach; and in the reserve, posted well to the rear of the Marylanders and Virginians, was our own colonel's troop guarding the horses of the dismounted Georgians.

'Twas when we were all set in order to await the sun's rising and the enemy's approach that Dan Morgan rode the lines and harangued us. He was better at giving and taking shrewd blows than at speech-making; but we all knew his mettle well by now, and I think there was never a man of us to laugh at his unwonted grandiloquence and solemn periods. In the harangue the two battle lines had their orders: to be steady; to aim low; and above all to hold their fire till the enemy was within sure killing distance.

"'Tis a brave old Daniel," said Dick, whilst the general was sawing the air for the benefit of the South Carolinians. "'Twill not be his fault if we fail. But you are older at this business than any of us, Jack; what think you of our chances?"

I laughed, and the laugh was meant to be grim. I knew the temper of the British regulars, and how, when well led, they could play the hammer to anybody's anvil.

"Any raw recruit can prophesy before the fact," said I. "We have Tarleton, his legion, the Seventh, a good third of the Seventy-first, and two pieces of artillery in our front. If they do not give a good account of themselves, 'twill be because Tarleton has marched them leg-stiff to overtake us."

Dick fell silent for the moment, and when he spoke again some of Dan Morgan's solemnity seemed to have got into his blood.

"I have a sort of coward inpricking that I sha'n't come out of this with a whole skin, Jack; and there's a thing on my mind that mayhap you can take off. You have had Madge to yourself a dozen times since that day last autumn when I asked her for the hundredth time to put me out of misery. As I have said, she would not hear me through; but she gave me a look as I had struck her with a whip. Can you tell me why?"

The morning breeze heralding the sunrise was whispering to the leafless branches overhead, and there was nothing in all Dame Nature's peaceful setting of the scene to hint at the impending war-clash. Yet the war portent was abroad in all the peaceful morning, and my mood marched with the lad's when I gave him his answer.

"Truly, I could tell you, Richard; and it is your due to know it from no other lips than mine. Mayhap, a little later, when restitution can go hand in hand with repentance and confession—"

"No, no;" he cut in quickly. "Tell me now, Jack; your 'little later' may be all too late—for me. Does she love you?—has she said she loves you?"

"Nay, dear lad; she despises me well and truly, and has never missed the chance of saying so. Wait but a little longer and I pledge you on the honor of a gentleman you shall have her for your very own. Will that content you?"

At my assurance his mood changed and in a twinkling he became the dauntless soldier who fights, not to die, but to win and live.

"With that word to keep me I shall not be killed to-day, I promise you, Jack; and that in spite of this damned queasiness that was showing me the burying trench." And then he added softly: "God bless her!"

I could say amen to that most heartily; did it, and would have gone on to add a benison of my own, but at the moment there were sounds of galloping horses on our front, and presently three red-coated officers, one of them the redoubtable Colonel Tarleton himself, rode out to reconnoitre us most coolly.

I doubt if he would have been so rash had he known that Yeates and his borderers were concealed in easy pistol-shot; but the simultaneous cracking of a dozen rifles warned and sent the trio scuttling back to cover.

Dick swore piteously, with the snap-shot skirmishers for a target. "The fumblers!" he raged. "'Twas the chance of a life-time, and they all missed like a lot of boys at their first deer stalking!"

"They will have another chance, and that speedily," I ventured; and, truly, the chance did not tarry.

From our view point on the rising ground we could see the enemy forming under cover of the wood; and as we looked, the two pieces of cannon were thrust to the front to bellow out the signal for the assault.

'Twas a sight to stir the blood when the enemy broke cover into the opener wooding of the field to the tune of the roaring cannon, the volleyings of small arms and the defiant huzzaings of the men. The sun was just peering over the summit of Thicketty Mountain, and his level rays fell first upon the charging line sweeping in like a tidal wave of red death to crumple our skirmishers before it.

"Lord!" says Richard; "if Yeates and the Indian come alive out of that—"

But the outliers closed upon our first line in decent good order, firing as they could; and in less time than it takes to write it down the onsweeping wave of red was upon the Carolinians. We looked to see the militia fire and run, home-guard fashion; but these men of Pickens's were made of more soldierly stuff. They took the fire of the assaulting line like veterans, giving ground only when it came to the bayonet push.

"That fetches it to us," said Richard, most coolly; drawing his claymore when the Carolinians began to come home like spindrift ahead of the wave of red. Then he had a steadying word for the men of his company, and a hearty shout and a curse for some of the Georgians who had cut around the flanks of our main to come at their horses in the rear.

But the lad's assertion that our time was come was only a half prophecy. The Marylanders, with the Virginians on either flank, stood firm, giving the onrushing wave a shock that went near to breaking it. But the British were better bayoneted than we, and when it came to the iron our lads must needs give ground sullenly, fighting their way backward as a stubborn assault fights its way inch by inch forward.

"Here come their reserves," said Dick, pointing with his blade to a second red line forming in the farther vistas of the wood. "Lord! shall we never get into it?"

'Twas just here that an order sent by Colonel Howard to his first company, directing it to charge by the flank, came near costing us a rout. The order was misunderstood,—'twas received at the precise moment of the upcoming of the British reserves,— and the Marylanders fell back. In the turning of a leaf our entire fighting front gave way, and what of the Georgians there were left in the mellay made a frantic dash for the horses.

At this crisis John Howard saved the day for us by shrewdly executing the most difficult manoeuver that is ever essayed by a field officer in the heat of battle. Suffering his men to drift backward until the enemy, sure now of success, were rushing on in disorder to give the *coup de grâce*, he gave the quick command: "About face! Fire! Charge!"

I saw the volley delivered in the faces of the redcoats at pike's length range; saw the Virginians on the flanks bend to encircle the enemy; saw the rout transfer itself at the roar of the muskets from our side to the recoiling British. Then I heard Dick's shouted command. "Charge them, lads! they're sabering the Georgians!"

A section of Tarleton's horse had hewed its way past our flank and was at work on the militiamen scrambling for their mounts. At it we went, with our brave colonel a horse's length ahead of the best rider in the troop, pistols banging and sword blades whistling, and that other curious sound you will hear only when the cavalry engages—the heavy dunch of the horses coming together like huge living missiles hurled from catapults.

'Twas soon over, and the enemy, horse and foot, was flying in hopeless confusion through the open wood. Our troop led the pursuit; and this brings me to an incident in which thy old chronicler—figuring in the histories as an unnamed sergeant—had his share.

It was in the hot part of the chase, and Colonel Tarleton—a true Briton in this, that he would be first in the charge and last in the retreat—was galloping with two of his aides in rear of the dragoons. Since many of us knew the British commander by sight, there was a great clapping-to of spurs to overtake and cut him off. In this race three horses outdistanced all the others; the great bay ridden by Colonel Washington, a snappy little gray bestridden by the colonel's boy bugler, and my own mount.

When the crisis came, our colonel had the wind of the boy and me and was calling on Colonel Tarleton to surrender at discretion. For answer the three British officers wheeled and fell upon him. Never was a man nearer his death. In a whiff, Tarleton was foining at him in front whilst the two aides were rising in their stirrups on either hand to cut him down.

'Twas the little bugler boy who saved his colonel's life, and not the unnamed "sergeant," as the histories have it. Having neither a sword nor the strength to wield one, the boy reined sharp to the left and pistoled his man as neatly as you please. Seeing his fellow *sabreur* drop his weapon and clap his hand to the pistol-wound, my man hesitated just long enough to let me in with the clumsiest of upcuts to spoil the muscles of his sword arm. This transferred the duel to the two principals, who were now at it, hammer and tongs. Both were good swordsmen, but of the twain our colonel was far the cooler. So when Tarleton made to end it with a savage thrust in tierce, Washington parried deftly and his point found his antagonist's sword hand.

At this, Tarleton dropped his blade,—it hangs now over the chimney-piece in Mr. Washington's town house in Charleston,—gave the signal for flight, and the three Britons, each with a wound to nurse, wheeled and galloped on. But in the act Tarleton snatched a pistol from his holster and let drive at our colonel, wounding him in the knee, so we did not come off scatheless.

This pistoling of Colonel Washington by the British commander skimmed a little of the cream from our great and glorious victory. 'Twas no serious hurt, but wanting it I make no doubt we should have ridden down the flying dragoons, adding them, and their doughty colonel to boot, to the five-hundred-odd prisoners we took.

The battle fought and won,—'twas over and done with two full hours before noon,—Dan Morgan knew well what must befall, lacking the swiftest after-doing on our part. With Greene near a hundred miles away, and my Lord Cornwallis less than three hours' gallop to the southward on Turkey Creek, the time was come for the hastiest welding of our little army with that of the general-in-command; if, indeed, the promptest running would take us to the upper fords of the Catawba before Cornwallis should intervene and cut us off.

Accordingly, Jennifer and I were detailed to carry the news of the victory to Greene's camp at Cheraw Hill; and when we rode away on the warm trail of the flying British, we left Dan Morgan's men hard at it, burning the heavy impedimenta of the capture, and otherwise making ready for the swiftest of forced marches to the north.

'Twould be a thankless task to take you with us stage by stage on our cross-country gallop to advertise General Greene of the victory at the cow pastures. Suffice it to say that we made shift to turn the head of the advancing British main, now in motion and hastening with all speed to cut Dan Morgan off; that we were by turns well soaked by rain and stream, deep mired in bogs, chased times without number by the enemy's outriders, and hardshipped freely for food and horse provender before we saw the camp on the Pedee. All this you may figure for yourselves, the main point being that we came at length to the goal, weary, mire-splashed and belted to the last buckle-hole to pinch down the hunger pains, but sound of skin, wind and limb.

Having our news, which set the camp in a pretty furor of rejoicing, I promise you, General Greene lost not an hour in making his dispositions. Leaving Isaac Huger and Colonel Otho Williams in command at Cheraw, the general sent Edward Stevens with the Virginians by way of Charlotte to Morgan's aid, and himself took horse, with a handful of dragoons in which Dick and I were volunteers, to ride post haste to a meeting with Morgan at the upper fords.

Again I may pass lightly over an interval of three days spent hardily in the saddle, coming at once to that rain-drenched thirty-first of January, cold, raw and dismal, when we drew rein at Sherrard's Ford and found Dan Morgan and his men safe across the Catawba with his prisoners, and my Lord Cornwallis quite as safely flood-checked on the western bank of the stream.

Having done our errand, Dick and I reported at once to our colonel. 'Twas of a piece with William Washington's goodness of heart to offer us leave to rest.

"You have had weary work of it, I doubt not, gentlemen," he would say. "Your time is your own until General Greene sets us in order for what he has in mind to do."

I looked at Dick, and he looked at me.

"May we count upon twenty-four hours, think you, Colonel?" I asked.

"Safely, I should say."

"Then I shall ask leave of absence for Captain Jennifer and myself till this time to-morrow," I went on. "This is our home neighborhood, as you know, and we have a little matter of private business which may be despatched in a day."

"Will this business take you without the lines?"

"That is as it may be, sir. I do not know the bounds of the outposting."

The colonel wrote us passes to come and go at will past the sentries, and I drew Dick away.

"What is it, Jack?" he asked, when we were by ourselves.

"'Tis the fulfilling of my promise to you, Richard. Get your horse and we will ride together."

"But whither?" he queried.

"To Appleby Hundred—and Mistress Margery."

CHAPTER XLVIII

HOW WE KEPT TRYST AT APPLEBY HUNDRED

'Twas late in the afternoon of the last day of January when we set out together, Jennifer and I, from the camp of conference at Sherrard's Ford.

The military situation, lately so critical for us, had reached and passed one of its many subclimaxes. Morgan's little army, with its prisoners still safe in hand, was on its way northward to Charlottesville in Virginia, and only the officers remained behind to confer with General Greene.

For the others, Huger and Williams were hurrying up from Cheraw to meet the general at Salisbury; and General Davidson, with a regiment of North Carolina volunteers, was set to keep the fords of the Catawba.

As for the British commander's intendings, we had conflicting reports. Two days earlier, Lord Cornwallis had burned his heavy baggage at Ramsour's Mill, and so we had assurance that the pursuit was only delayed. But whether, when he should break his camp at Forney's plantation, he would go northward after Morgan and the prisoners, or cross the river at some nearhand ford to chase our main, none of our scouts could tell us.

We were guessing at this, Richard and I, as we jogged on together down the river road, and were agreed that could my Lord cross the flooded river without loss of time, his better chance would be to fall upon our main at Salisbury or thereabouts. But as to the possibility of his crossing, we fell apart.

"Lacking another drop of rain, we are safe for forty-eight hours yet," Dick would say, pointing to the brimming river rolling its brown flood at our right as we fared on. "And with two days' start we shall have him burning more than his camp wagons to overtake us."

"Have it so, if you will," said I, to end the argument. "But this I know: were Dan Morgan or General Greene, or you or I, in Lord Cornwallis's shoes, the two days would not be lost."

Jennifer laughed. "Leave the rest of us out, Sir Hannibal Ireton, and tell what you would do," he said, mocking me.

We were at that bend in the road where Jan Howart and his Tories had sought to waylay us in the cool gray dawn of a certain June morning when we were galloping this same road to keep my appointment with Sir Francis Falconnet. A huge rock makes a promontory in the stream just here, and I pointed to a water-worn cavity in it where the flood lapped in and out in gurgling eddies.

"You've been sharp to take me up on my forgetting of the landmarks, but there is one I've not forgot," said I. "One day, about the time you were getting yourself born, I was passing this way with my father and a company of the county gentlemen. 'Twas in the Seven Years' War, and the Cherokees were threatening us from the other side. The river was in flood as it is now; and I mind my father saying that when you could see that hole in the rock, Macgowan's Ford would be no more than armpit deep."

"So?" said Richard; "then it behooves us to—" He stopped in mid sentence, drew rein and shifted his sword hilt to the front.

"What is it?" I asked.

For reply he pointed me to a canoe half hidden in the bushes where roadside and river-edge came together.

I laughed. "An empty pirogue. Shall we charge and run it through?"

"Hist!" said he; "that canoe was afloat a minute since. Mark the paddle—'tis dripping yet."

As he spoke an Indian stood up in the bushes beside the pirogue, holding out his empty hands in token of amity. We rode up and were presently shaking hands with our old-time ally, the Catawba.

"How!" said he; "heap how! Chief Harris glad; wah! Make think have to go to Sal'bury to find Captain Long-knife and Captain Jennif'. Heap much glad!"

"Chief Harris?" I queried. "Who may he be?"

The Catawba drew himself up and drummed upon his breast.

"Chief Harris here," he answered, proudly. "The Great War Chief," by which we understood he meant General Greene, "say all Catawba take war-path 'gainst redcoat; make Uncanoola headman; give um new name. Wah!"

At this we shook hands with him again, well pleased that our stanch ally should have recognition at the hands of the general. Then I would ask if he were on the way to raise his tribesmen to fight with us.

"Bimeby; no have time now; big thing over yonder," pointing across the river. "Manitou Cornwally fool Great War Chief, mebbe, hey?"

"How is that?" said Dick; and the query elicited a bit of news to make us prick our ears. The Catawba had been in the British camp at Forney's, posturing again as a Cherokee friendly to the king's side. Some sudden movement had been determined upon, though what it was to be he could not learn. At the end of his own resources he had crossed the river in a stolen pirogue to find and warn us.

"What say you, Dick?" I asked, when we had heard the Catawba through.

The lad was holding his lip in his hand and scowling as one who pits duty against inclination.

"'Tis our cursed luck!" he gloomed. Then he swore it out by length and breadth, and, when the air was cleared, let me have what was in his mind.

"After all, 'tis like enough we should find Appleby house deserted. Gilbert Stair will cling to Lord Cornwallis's coat-skirt as long as he can for sheer safety's sake. At all events, our business must wait; the country's weal comes first." Then to the Indian: "If we can make the beasts take the water, will you ferry us across, Chief?"

The Catawba nodded, and made the nod good by setting us dry-shod on the farther bank of the brown flood. By the time we had the horses rubbed down and resaddled 'twas twilight in the open and night dark in the wood; but we were on our own ground and knew every by-path through the forest.

So, when we had sent the Indian back to carry news of us to General Davidson at the lower ford, and to advertise him of our purpose, we mounted to begin a scouting jaunt, keeping to the wood paths and bearing cautiously northward toward the enemy's camp at Forney's plantation.

At times we were close upon the British sentries, with every nerve strained tense for fight or flight; anon we would be making wide detours through bog and fen, or beneath the black network of wet branches with the rain-soaked leaf beds under foot to make the horses' treadings as noiseless as a cat's.

None the less, in the fullness of time—'twas near about midnight as we guessed it—we had our patience well rewarded. Hovering on the confines of the camp we heard the muffled drum-tap of the reveille, and soon there was the stir of an army making ready for the march.

"Which way will it be, north or south?" whispered Dick, when we had dismounted to cloak the heads of the horses.

"We shall know shortly," said I; and truly, we did, being well-nigh enveloped and ridden down by the fringe of light-horse deploying to pioneer the way. When we had sheered off to let this skirmish cloud blow by, Dick struck a spark into his tinder-box to have a sight of his compass needle.

"South and by east," he announced; "that will mean Beattie's Ford, I take it."

"Not unless they swim, horse and foot," I objected. "'Twill be

Macgowan's, more likely."

Having this uncertainty to resolve, we must hang upon the skirts of the British advance till we could make sure, and this proved to be a most perilous business. Yet by riding abreast of the moving main we did resolve the uncertainty; heard the orders passed from man to man, and later saw a small feinting detachment split off to take the road for Beattie's, whilst the main body held on for Macgowan's; all this before we were discovered in the gloaming of the dawn by some of Tarleton's men.

Then, I promise you, my dears, it was neck or nothing, with the devil to take the hindmost. Away we sped toward the near-by river, spurring our wearied beasts as men who ride for life, with a dozen troopers so close upon us that when I glanced over my shoulder the foremost of the redcoat riders was having his face well bespattered with the mud from my horse's heels.

'Twas touch and go, but happily, as I have said, the river was at hand. We came to the high bank some hundred yards above the fording place, and lacking Dick's example to shame me to the braver course, I fear I should have recoiled at the brink. But when the lad sent his horse without the missing of a bound far out over the eddying flood, I shook the reins on the sorrel's neck, gave him the word and shut my eyes.

After all, it was nothing worse than a cold plunge, with a few pistol bullets to spatter harmlessly around us when we came up for air. Moreover, there were the camp-fires of Davidson's men on the farther bank to encourage us; and so swimming and wading by turns we got across in time to give the alarum.

As you would guess, there was a mighty stir on our side of the river when we had splashed ashore and got our news well born. As it turned out, General Davidson's main camp was a good half-mile back from the river in one of the outfields of Appleby Hundred. So it chanced there were upon the spot only brave Joe Graham and his fifty riflemen to dispute the passage of an army.

What was done at Macgowan's Ford in the gray of the morning of February first, 1781, has become a page in our history. But I protest that not any of the chroniclers do even-handed justice to the little band of patriot riflemen doing their utmost to hold a hundred-to-one outnumbering host in check.

'Twas a fine sight, be the onlooker Whig or Tory. The Guards, led by the fiery Irishman, O'Hara, took the water first, the men crowding shoulder to shoulder to brace against the sweep of the current which, on the western side of the stream, was little less than a mill-tail for swiftness. After them came the foot and horse in solid squares, and always with more to follow. None the less, our little handful did not blanch; and when the Guards in mid-stream held straight across instead of bearing to the right as the ford ran, a shout went up on our side and the fifty hastened up from the ford-head as one man to face the enemy squarely.

Now it was that the brown-barreled rifles began to crack and spit fire; and I do think if we had had our other two hundred and fifty out of that back field on the manor lands, we might at least have made the wading redcoats hurry a little. Indeed, as it was, the van of the Guards broke here and there, and we could hear O'Hara berating his men as only a battle-mad Irishman can, with blarneyings and curses intermingled.

Having no firearms save our wetted pistols, Jennifer and I crouched in cover, waiting to do what two swordsmen might when the blade's length should bridge the fast-narrowing distance between us and the advancing host.

'Twas in this little interval of forced inaction that we heard a most familiar voice issuing from a clump of holly just below our covert; a voice lifted now in fervent prayer and again in Scriptural anathema on the foe.

"'Let God arise and let His inimies be scattered.... Let them be as the chaff upon a threshing-floor'—"

The sharp crack of the old borderer's rifle filled the momentary pause, and a British officer in a colonel's uniform swayed drunkenly in his saddle and plunged headlong in the stream.

"'Let them be as the children of Amalek before the Mighty One of Israel: make them and their princes like Oreb and Zeeb; yea, make all their princes like as Zebah and Zalmunna.... O my God, make them like unto a wheel, and as the stubble before the wind; like as the fire that burneth up the wood, and as the flame that consumeth the mountains.'"

Crack! went the long-barreled piece again, and again an officer hallooing on his floundering battalion bent to his saddle horn and slipped into the turbid flood.

My gorge rose. This picking off of officers has always seemed to me the savagest of war's barbarities. How Richard divined my thought and purpose, I know not; but when I would have slipped down to Yeates's holly bush he laid a detaining hand on my arm.

"Let be," he said; "'tis murder, if you like, but all war is that. When old Eph's turn comes, they will kill him as relentlessly as he is killing them."

By this time the British vanguard was storming ashore through the shallows below the tree fringe which served as cover for Graham's men, and the king's muskets, silent hitherto, began to roar and belch by platoon and volley fire. Jennifer craned his neck and took a swift view of the situation.

"By the Lord Harry!" he cried, "'tis high time Joe Graham was getting his lads in order for a foot race. Once those fellows come ashore they'll play hare and hounds with us to the king's taste. Keep your eye on the nags, Jack. It may chance us to do what two men can to cover a belated retreat."

We had tethered our horses in a thicket of scrub oak where they would be out of bullet-reach until the enemy gained the bank. As I looked to make sure of them, the sorrel gave a shrill neigh to welcome the pounding of hoofs on the Appleby road. I made sure this would be General Davidson bringing in the reserves; and so, indeed, it was; but he came too late. O'Hara's men were already climbing the bank; and Joe Graham was rallying his little company for flight in the face of an onset that made the tree fringe sing with musket balls.

"'Tis our cue to run away!" Dick shouted, dragging me to my feet. "To the horses!"

But now we were too late. Davidson's men were between us and the scrub oak thicket, and we must wait till the column swept by.

Dick swore fervently and put his face to the foe and his back to a tree. Whereupon I dragged him down as promptly as he had just now dragged me up, telling him his broadsword would make but a poor shift parrying musket-balls.

What followed after was over and done with in a dozen fluttering heart-beats. Seeing the case was desperate, General Davidson gathered Graham's fifty into his flying column, flogged his rear into the retreat, and was pitched out of his saddle by a Tory rifle-bullet whilst he was doing it. And when the way to our horses was clear of the galloping Carolinians, and we would have run to mount and ride after them, the swarming redcoat van was upon us.

"Up with you and out of this!" cried Jennifer, setting me the example. "We must e'en gallop as we can. Quick, man!"

But in the gathering and the retreat our old sharpshooter under his holly bush had been left behind; and now we heard him again, chanting his terrible imprecations on the enemy.

Dick saw the meaning in my look, and together we pounced to drag the old man out of hiding. When we burst down upon him, Yeates had his piece to his face and was drawing a bead on a stout man in cocked hat and plain regimentals whose horse was curveting and sidling in the nearer shallows; no less a figure, in truth, than my Lord Cornwallis himself, cheering his men on to the attack.

We had scarce made out the old hunter's target when the rifle spat fire, the curveting charger reared in its death plunge, and the British commander-in-chief, unhurt, as it seemed, was dragged from the entanglement of his stirrups by his aides.

The old marksman sprang up in a fury of wrath. "Dad blast ye for a pair of aim-sp'ilin'—"

A roar of musketry cut the rebuke in half, and a storm of bullets smote through the branches overhead. A falling bough knocked my hat off, and I stooped to recover it. When I rose, Dick was clipping the old man tightly in his arms. Yeates's belt was cut, and a little oozing well-spring of red was slowly soaking the fringe of his hunting-shirt.

"Ease me down, Cap'n Dick; ease me down. The old man's done for, this time, ez I allow—spang in the innards. Ease me down and get off for yerselves, if so be ye can, im—me—jit—"

The wagging jaw dropped and the keen old eyes went dim and sightless. Dick's oath was more a sob than an imprecation; and now it was I who said: "Come on—the living before the dead!" and so we made the well-nigh hopeless dash for the horses.

How we rode free out of that hurly-burly at the ford-head you must figure for yourselves, if you can. The men of the British vanguard were all about us when we got to the scrub oak thicket and mounted, but no one of them raised a hand to stay us. I have thought since that mayhap they took us for a pair of their own Tory allies who were not above wearing the stolen uniforms of the dead. Be that as it may, we rode away unhindered, Dick in all the bravery of his captain's slashings, and I in light-horse buff and blue, taking the road toward the manor house because that was the only one open to us, and ambling leisurely till we were beyond the sight and sound of the victors at the ford.

But once at large, we put spurs to our horses in true *ritter* fashion; and we had galloped half way to Appleby house before Dick said:

"Now we are well out of that, what next? We can not go to Margery with the whole British army at our heels."

"Nay, but we shall, if only for a short half-hour," I asserted. Then, as once before, I gave him my best bow. "For the last time, it may be, let me play the lord of the manor. You are very welcome to my father's demesne, Richard, and to all of its holdings."

"All?" said he, giving me a quick eye-shot as we pressed on side by side.

"Yes, all," said I; and I meant it in good faith. He should have the lady, too; that precious holding of the old manse without whom my father's acres would be but a bauble to be lost or won indifferently.

"Then you do not love Madge more?" he queried, his eye kindling.

"Nay, I did not say that. But I did say the other; that you should have the house and all its holdings."

We were cantering up the oak-sentried avenue to that door which Gilbert Stair had once sought to keep against us with his bell-mouthed blunderbuss. There was no sign of any living thing about the place; and when we had no answer to our sword-hilt knockings on the door, the lad turned upon me with a flash of anger in his eyes and his lip a-curl.

"You knew full well what you were promising, John Ireton!" he said. "She is not here."

CHAPTER XLIX

IN WHICH A LAWYER HATH HIS FEE

What Richard's most natural resentment would have led to, in what new tangle of the net of bitterness we might have been enmeshed, we were spared the knowing. For when he said, "She is not here," two happenings intervened to give us both other things to think of.

The first was the advent, at the far end of the oak-lined avenue, of a troop of British light-horse, trotting leisurely; the second was the swinging inward of the door of unwelcome, with old Anthony grinning and bowing behind it.

Now when you have fairly surprised a fox in the open, he asks nothing more than a hole to hide him in. There were the hunters coming up the avenue; and here was our dodge-hole gaping before us. So, as hunted things will, we took earth quickly; though, truly, 'twas an ostrich-trick rather than a fox's, since we left the horses standing without to advertise our presence to all and sundry.

It was Richard who first found the wit to realize the ostrich-play.

"The horses!—we may as well have left the town crier outside to ring his bell and tell the redcoats we are here," he would say; and before I knew what he would be at he had snatched the door open and was whistling softly to the big gray.

Hearing his master's call, the gray pricked his ears and came obediently, with the sorrel tagging at his heels. A moment later, when the up-coming troop was hidden by a turn in the avenue, we had the pair of them in the hall with the door shut and barred behind them.

"So far, so good," quoth Dick. Then to the old black, who had stood by, saucer-eyed and speechless, the while: "Anthony, do you be as big a numbskull as you were born to be, and hold these redcoat gentlemen in palaver till we can win out at the back."

The old majordomo nodded his good-will, but now my slow wit came in play. "We've done it now," said I. "The horses will go out as they came in, or not at all. Had you forgotten the stair at the back?"

Judge for yourselves, my dears, if this were the time, place or crisis for a man to fling himself upon the hall settle, grip his ribs and laugh like any lack-wit. Yet this is what Richard Jennifer did.

It was in the very midst of his gust of ill-timed merriment, while the horses were nosing niftily at their strange surroundings, and the hoof-strokes of the redcoat troop could be plainly heard on the gravel of the avenue, that I chanced to lift my eyes to the stair. There, looking down upon us with speechless astoundment in the blue-gray eyes, stood our dear lady.

Another instant and she was with us, stamping her foot and crying: "*Mon Dieu!* what is this? Are you gone mad, both of you?"

Dick's answer was another burst of laughter, loud enough, you would think, to be heard by those beyond the door.

"Behold four witless brute beasts, Mistress Madge—two horses and two asses," he said. And then to old Anthony: "Open the door, Tony, and invite the gentlemen in."

But Margery was before him. Ah, my dears, a man's wit is like a matchlock, fizzing and sputtering its way noisily to find the powder whilst the enemy hath time to ride up and saber the musketeer; but a woman's is like the spark in a tinder-box—a quick snip of flint and steel and you have your fire. In a flash my lady had torn down the heavy curtains from an inner doorway and was carpeting a horse path for us to the rear.

"Quick!" she cried; "lead them gently, for the love of heaven!"

She went before us, padding the way with whatever came first to hand, rugs, curtains, table-coverings, and I know not what besides; and by the time the British troopers were hammering at the outer door, we were deep within the old mansion and had made shift to drag the unwilling horses by one and two-step descents to a room half under and half out of ground, which served as a sort of ante-dungeon to the wine cellar.

Here I thought we might be safe for the moment, but not so my lady. Calling Dick to help her—in all the fierce haste of it I marked that she called to Dick and not to me—she unlocked and opened the door to the wine vault, and in a trice we two and the luckless horses were safely jailed in pitchy darkness, with the stout oaken door slammed behind us, the bolt shot in the lock, and the key withdrawn, as we could see by the spot of light which came through the keyhole.

Richard was the first to break the grave-like silence of our dungeon.

"Lord!" said he; "did ever you see such sharp-wit work in all your adventures? What a soldier's wife she'd make!"

I smiled at that, being safe to smile in the darkness. For was she not a soldier's wife? I hugged that saying as we cling to the thing that is slipping from us. True, I was here to give her freely over to another and a better soldier; but while she was mine I would claim her, in my heart, at least.

The excitement of the narrow escape somewhat overpast, we sat long on the edge of a wine-bin, speculating in whispers as to what would befall, and listening vainly for the footsteps which would forecast our release or our capture by the enemy. But when no sounds, threatening or encouraging, came from the upper world, we groped about till we found the cellar candle, lighted it with flint and steel and tinder-box, and took a survey of our jail.

'Twas the same old cavernous wine vault of my youthful remembrance, such an one as has not its mate in all Carolina to this good day, as I firmly believe. My father's hobby was to build for all eternity; and this stone-arched cellarage was more like a cathedral crypt than a store-room for a country gentleman's table-stock of wines.

Dick held the candle aloft and scanned the bottle racks, none so greatly depleted as they might have been, had any hand but that close-fisted one of Gilbert Stair's taken the key in charge after my father.

"There is no lack of potables," says my candle-bearer; "but, unhappily, there is never so much as a dry crust to soak in them. And as for the horses, I'll venture they'd give it all, pint for pint, for a good feeding of oats."

"Truly," said I; and then we fell to stripping the straw casings from the bottles of madeira to give the poor beasts a feed of rye-stalks which had grown and ripened their grain many a year before either the sorrel or the gray was foaled.

Having no time-measure save our own impatience, it seemed a weary while before we heard the key rasping in the lock of our prison door.

"'Tis Madge," said Dick, with a true lover's gift of second sight; and 'twas he who went to help her swing the thick-slabbed oak.

What passed between them I did not hear, nor want to hear. But when the door was swung to and locked again I knew we were not free to go abroad.

Richard came back to me in the inner vault bearing gifts; the better part of a boiled ham with bread to match, a jug of water from the well, and more candles.

"We are not to starve, but that is our best news, thus far," he said. "Of all the houses on our side of the river, Lord Cornwallis must needs pitch upon this manor of Appleby for his rallying headquarters. Madge can not guess when he and the army will be gone, and she is frighted stiff for our sakes."

This was sober news, indeed, but we could do naught but make the best of it. As for me, I was most anxious to know if the good priest were at Appleby, and what of my chance for seeing him; but of this I could say no word to Richard.

So, when we had done full justice to my lady's bounty, we stowed the horses in the deepest of the vaults and stripped more of the bottle coverings for them. But having only the jug of water, we could do no more than swab their mouths out with a wetted kerchief in lieu of giving them a drink.

When all was done we sat ourselves down to wait as we must; and when the silence and solitude had wrought their perfect work, we fell to talking in low tones to match the place and circumstance; and I do think in those quiet hours, walled in as we were from all the disturbments of the outer world, we came closer than we had come for many months.

And while we sat and talked the long day wore on to evening and a storm came on, as we could determine, though no otherwise than by the muffled rolling of the thunder which, since we could not see the lightning nor hear the rain, we took at first for the booming of distant cannon.

I can not tell you all we spoke of in that day-long immurement. There was some talk of the great struggle for independence, now, though we knew it not, drawing near to its close; and there was much of reminiscence, harking back to the exciting and tragic scenes in which we two had had our entrances and our exits. Also, there was a tribute paid to the memory of our true old friend and trusted comrade in arms, Ephraim Yeates, so lately gone to his own place. 'Twas at this time I learned what of the old man's gifts and peculiarities I have hereinbefore set down; for Richard had known him long and well.

From speaking of old Ephraim and his sudden taking-off we came to things more nearly present; and at length Dick would lay a finger gently upon the mystery in which he was as yet walking as one blindfolded.

"'Tis not a shameful thing; don't tell me it is that, Jack," he would say; and I gave him speedy assurance upon that head.

"No,'tis never shameful; so much I may lay an oath to."

"Yet you said once—in that black night when I went mad and would have killed you—that your life lay between Madge and me."

"So it did—and does. And God will bear me witness, dear lad, that I have worn that life upon my sleeve."

"Nay," he said, very gently; "you need not go so high for a witness; have I not seen?"

We fell silent upon that, and there, in the candle-yellowed gloom of our dungeon harbor, I fought the fellest battle of my life; fought it and won it, too, my dears, once and for all. There was a cold sweat on my brow when I began in low tones to tell him the story of that fateful night in June. At rising forty 'tis no light thing to lose a friend—nay, to turn a friend's love into scorn and loathing and bitter hatred.

He heard me through without a word; and at the end, when I looked to see him spring up and bid me draw and let him have his one poor chance for satisfaction, he still sat motionless, winking and staring at the guttering candle. And when he spoke 'twas with a quivering of the lip that was not of anger.

"Dear God," said he; "'tis I who stand in the way."

"No; for she loves you, Richard, as dearly as she hates me. And 'tis not so hopeless now, else I had never screwed together the courage to tell you all this. She has at last consented to the Church's undoing of the incomplete marriage—'twas this she wrote me about when we were at the Cowpens, and 'twas her letter that set me upon going to Winnsborough to see the priest. I missed him there, as you know; but I am here now by her own appointment to meet him in her father's house."

He shook his head slowly. "You've killed the hope in me, Jack. I do think you are all at sea; 'tis you she loves—not me."

I could afford to smile at that.

"If you could see how she has ever gone about to prove that she did not love me, you would rest easy on that score, dear lad."

But he would only shake his head again.

"'Twas to save your life she rode in on us that morning under the oaks in the glade."

"'Twas a womanly horror of a duel and bloodshed, more belike," said I.

"But she has saved your life thrice since then, as you confess."

"Yes; from a strained sense of wifely duty, as she took good care to tell me."

"None the less—ah, Jack, you do not know her as I do; she would never have consented to stand before the priest with you had there not been something warmer than hatred in her heart."

"'Twas a bitter necessity, fairly forced upon her. Tell me; had there been a spark of love for me in her heart, would she have treated me as the dust beneath her feet on that long infaring from the western mountains? She never spoke a word to me, Dick, in all those weeks."

"Which may prove no more than that you said or did something to cut her to the quick. 'Twould be well in your way, Jack. She is as sensitive as she should be, and you are blunter than I—which is the worst I could say of you."

"No, no; you are far beside the mark. You forget that the

breaking of the marriage is of her own proposing—at least, I should say I only hinted at it."

"There may be two sides to that, as well. Have you ever told her that you love her, Jack?"

"Surely not! I have been all kinds of a poltroon in this matter, as I have confessed, but this one thing I have not done."

"Well," said he, speaking slowly, as one who thinks the path out word by word, "what if she believes 'tis you who want your freedom? What if you have made her that bitterest thing in all the world—a woman scorned?"

I would not listen to him more.

"This is all the merest folly, Richard, as I will prove to you beyond the question of a doubt. Do you mind that little interval in the Cherokees' torture-play when they came to bind us afresh for the burning?"

"I mind no more of that horror-night than I can help."

"Well, in that hour, when death was waiting for all three of us, she wrote a little farewell note to the man she loved. 'Twas for you, Dick, but her Indian messenger blundered and gave it me."

He got upon his feet at that and began to pace slowly back and forth under the gloomy archings. But ere long he paused to grasp and wring my hand most lovingly, saying, "Who am I, Jack, to buy my happiness at such a price?"

"Nay, lad; 'tis neither you nor I who should figure greatly in the matter; 'tis our dear lady. She must e'en have what she longs for, if you, or I, or both of us, should have to go above stairs and put our necks into my Lord Cornwallis's noose."

"Now, by heaven, Jack Ireton, 'tis you who are the true lover and the gentleman; and I am naught but a selfish churl with my face in my own trencher!" he burst out, wringing my hand yet again. "'Tis as you say; yet I will not be driven from this; for aught you have told me to prove it otherwise, Madge has yet to choose between us, and she shall have that choice, fairly and squarely, and knowing that you love her, before we three go apart again."

I smiled, and tried hard to keep the heart-soreness out of my reply.

"As for that, my lad, I have had my stirrup-cup long since, and have drained it to the dregs with a wry face, as an old man must when a young man brews for him. But if the priest—"

Jennifer had resumed his pacing sentry beat, and at this juncture a most singular thing happened. Though we were sealed in, as I have said, from all the outer world with no crack nor cranny for a peephole, a blinding flash of lightning, blue and ghastly, came suddenly to fill the whole cellar with its vivid glare.

"Good Lord!" says Richard, clapping his hands to his eyes; "where did that come from?"

I was wholly at a loss for a moment. Then I remembered that there was, or had been in my boyhood days, a narrow, iron-barred window in the farther end of the wine cellar, opening beneath that other window of the great south room where I had climbed to spy upon the conspirators on the night of Captain John Stuart's visit to Appleby. So it chanced that when another flash came I was looking straight over Dick's head at the place in the farther arching of the vault where the little window should be.

The momentary glare showed me the low square of the window opening, and framed for a flitting instant therein a face of most devilish malignity peering in upon me with foxy-fierce eyes; the face, to wit, of Gilbert Stair's lawyer-factor.

In a twinkling the vision was gone, and in the space between the flash and the crash there was a sound as of a wooden shutter slamming in place. Dick heard the noise without knowing the cause of it, being so far beneath the window as to see nothing but the lighting of the glare.

"What was that?" he demanded, when the thunder gave him leave.

"'Twas our trapper clapping the shutter on the window over your head," said I. "He was looking in to see if we were ripe for hanging."

"'Tis no time for riddles; what mean you?"

"I mean that we shall have a file of redcoats down upon us as soon as ever Mr. Owen Pengarvin can give the alarm."

"Oho!" said Dick; and then he pulled his sword from its scabbard, and I could see the battle-veins swelling in his forehead. "They can hang me when I am too dead to cut and thrust more—not sooner."

I got me up and went to find the sword which I had laid aside in the horse-baiting. 'Twas a poor blade—one of our captures at the Cowpens; and when I tried its temper it snapped in my hand.

"Never mind," said I; "give me the broadsword scabbard and I will play it as a cudgel, 'tis long enough and full heavy enough."

He laughed and clapped me on the shoulder, swearing out his love for me as if I had said something moving. "You are every inch a soldier, Jack; you would put heart into a worse craven than I am ever like to be." And he loosed the iron scabbard and gave it me.

Now ensued a most painful time of waiting and listening for the tramp of our takers. We posted us near the door, a little to the side, so that its inswing might not catch us; and so, bracing for the onset, we waited till the strain of suspense grew so great that we both started like frighted children, when finally the key was thrust into the lock and the bolt shot back.

But when the heavy door gave inward, as at the pushing of a weak or timid hand, we saw our dear lady standing in the half gloom of the ante-dungeon, breathless and trembling with excitement.

"Come!" she panted; "come quickly—there is not an instant to spare. The factor has betrayed you; he will be here directly with the dragoons!"

I cut in swiftly. "He has not seen Dick; does he know we are both here?"

She had one hand on her heart to still its tumultuous beating, and the other held behind her, and she could scarce speak more for her eagerness to have us out and away.

"No; it was you he saw; and my father heard Colonel Tarleton give the order. Lieutenant Tybee is to take a file of his troopers and hang without grace the man he will find hiding in the wine cellar; those were his very words. Oh, merciful heaven! will you never stir?"

Richard gave a low whistle.

"So Tybee has come alive in good time to square the old account with us," he would say; but my wonder was greater on the other head. "Your father?" I gasped. "And he sent you to save me?"

"Surely," she said. "Are you not once again his guest, Captain Ireton?" Then she stamped her foot, and though the candle-light was of the poorest, I could see her eyes flash. "Will you squander the last moment in silly questions?" she burst out. "Come, I say!"

I smiled. "Give me that sword you are hiding behind you and I will keep the door whilst you spirit Dick away. He is not to be in this."

She gave me the weapon, though not, as I made sure, in any consenting to my proposal. I could have cried out in sheer joy when I found the sword to be my own good blade of proof—the ancient Ferara willed me by my father.

Sharp as the crisis was, I make no doubt I should have asked her then and there how she came by the blade I had last seen when my Lord Cornwallis tried to break it over his knee; but the march of events suddenly became too swift for me. There was a sound of cautious footsteps in the inclined passage leading from the butler's pantry above, and our chance for escape that way was gone.

"Too late!" said Dick; and with an arm about Margery he whipped behind the great oaken door opened back against the cellar wall, whispering me to follow.

We were scarce in hiding, with the door well drawn back

to screen us, when the cautious footsteps came slowly into the out-cellar. Peeping through the crack behind the door we saw Pengarvin—alone.

What brought him there without his tale of armed men at his back no man will ever know; but since his ways were always crooked and devious, I guessed he would not wish to appear in the matter in his own proper person, and yet could not deny himself a 'forehand peep to see if the trap were still safe shut and secure.

'Twas evident he was much disconcerted at finding the door open and the wine vault apparently empty. At first he would start and dodge as if to run away; then his rage got the better of his caution and he had one of those senseless cursing fits I have before told you of, raving and swearing and promising all manner of fiendish recompense to Mistress Margery when he should have her in his power.

A little longer dwelling upon this variation of the cursing theme—ravings in which Dick learned for the first time of the factor's design to marry my widow and the estate—and I do think the lad would have gone out to make him sing another tune. But now the factor left off suddenly to cock his ear and listen, and afterward to come tiptoeing into the cellar, all eyes to spy and legs to run if a mouse should but squeak at him.

He was muttering to himself as he passed our hiding place.

"By all the devils, he must be here, some gait. The little jade would have warned him if she had known; but it is known only to the doddering old miser and me, and the girl is safe in her bedroom. Happen this devil of an Austrian captain has drunken himself sodden; ah, that would be a rare jest—to wake with the rope around his neck! If those cursed, slow-footed dragoons would but come! Damme! I'll have that bull-necked lieutenant cashiered if his high and mighty loitering balks me in this."

He stopped before the wine cask whereon the flickering candle stood and craned his neck to look beyond it. The candle was guttering smokily, and he reached a shaking thumb and finger to pluck the "dead man" from the wick. At that we heard him muttering again.

"'Twas a play to make the very devil envious; and to have it marred by that pig of a lieutenant! No one knew me in it save the legion colonel, and could we have sprung the trap fair and softly, not even Mistress Margery herself could have laid this swashbuckler's death at my door. But now he's gone—vanished like a straw bailee, and all because that damned understrapper of Colonel Tarleton's must needs turn up his nose at a bit of sheriff's work. Curse him!"

The candle was burning brightly now, and he crept catlike around the cask to peer into the bin beyond it. Just then the shutter to the little window of espial fell open with a shrill creaking of its rusty hinges, and a blue glare of lightning came to prick out every nook and corner of the cellar. Being almost within a blade's length of the factor, I saw him plainly; saw him start back and put his hands to his face and drop down all of a tremble on the bin's edge, where I had been sitting when he discovered me.

To second the flash a prolonged drum-roll of thunder dinned upon the still air of the vault, and mingled with the thunder came other flashes, searing the eye and making the candle flame appear as a sickly orange halo in the blue-white glare. What with the play of the storm artillery we could neither see nor hear for the moment; but when the candle-light came to its own again the scene had changed as if by magic. Under cover of the thunder din a squad of dragoons had come to ring the factor in where he sat upon the edge of the wine bin.

"So-ho!" said my good friend Tybee, with a little strident laugh, "'tis you I am to take out and hang, is it, Master Lawyer? I thought mayhap you'd double on your track once too often, and so it seems you have. Up with you and come along."

All in a flash Pengarvin was up and bursting out in a trembling frenzy-fit of protestation.

"Oh, 'tis all a mistake, my good sir—a devil's own trap! I—I am not the man; I pledge you my sacred word! I—hands off, you cursed villains, or I'll have the law on you!" this last when one of the men cast the noose of a rope over his head whilst a second drew his arms to his sides in the looping of another cord. "By God! you shall all smart for this; all, I say! Take me to Colonel Tarleton. The king has no stancher friend in all the province than I. Why, damme,'twas I who—"

A trooper came behind and gagged him with the loose end of the rope; and Tybee held the candle to light the knotting of it. And so they marched him out, with Tybee muttering between his teeth that it was rat-catcher's work, and no soldier's, this killing of vermin, and bidding his men make haste.

CHAPTER L

HOW RICHARD COVERDALE'S DEBT WAS PAID

For some breathless moments after we three were left alone in the Stygian darkness of the wine cellar, no word was spoken. The rolling of the thunder drum was muffled now, as it were booming out the dirge of the man who had digged a pit and had himself fallen therein; and the lightning flashes coming at longer intervals served but to intensify the gloom they lit up for the instant.

It was a minced oath from Richard that first broke the spell that bound us.

"'Twas too much for Madge," said he, "she has fainted. Swing the door, and light another candle."

I did both as quickly as might be, and we bedded her on the floor, stripping our coats to soften the stone flagging for her and trying by all the means known to two unskilled soldier leeches to bring her to.

"Water!" said Dick; but when we had laved her face with that, and with wine as well, without effect, we were well dismayed, I do assure you. For all our efforts she lay as one dead; and neither of us could be cold enough to pry her lips apart to play the drenching doctor with the wine.

"Lord!" cried Dick, the sweat standing out upon his face in great drops; "this is terrible! What shall we do?"

"Jeanne will know what to do," I asserted. "We must get her out of this and up to her chamber."

Richard started to his feet and stooped to gather the dear body of her in his arms. But in the act he paused and straightened himself to look fixedly at me.

"Do you take her, Jack; she is—she is—your wife."

"Nay," said I, drawing back. "You are her own true lover; and could she choose her bearer—"

"A murrain on your finickings!" he burst out. "She may die whilst we are haggling over the right to help her. Take her up quick, man, and begone!"

"But bethink you, Dick," I urged; "if you are taken, you have one chance in ten of faring as an officer and a prisoner of war. For me 'tis a spy's death as swift as they can drag me to it."

Now you will know, my dears, how much I loved these two when I could twist a cord of such mean fiber to bind them closer together. Richard's eyes flashed and his lip curled.

"Overlook it in me, if you can," he said, with fine scorn. "I had not thought upon the peril of it." And with that he took her in his arms as she had been a child to be carried, and I swung the door for him. But on the threshold he gave me back my sorry little subterfuge. "Once more, your forgiveness, Jack. I knew well you were but lying to give me precedence. Can you trust me with her?"

"Aye, dear lad; now and ever," said I; and so I pushed him out.

After he was gone I made shift to lead the horses through the narrow passage and out by a rear door, giving them a friendly slap to point them toward the stables.

This done I went back to my immurement, and I know not how long it was that I paced a weary sentry beat up and down the narrow limits of the wine cellar, alone with such thoughts as go to make the sum of that despair which follows hard upon the heels of some climaxing catastrophe. But I do know that, as the hours dragged on leadenshod, a slow fever of impatience came to dry the blood in my veins; to make me hunger and thirst for leave to say the final word to Father Matthieu, and so to be set at liberty to find the bottom of the pit into which a mocking fate had plunged me.

'Twas all over now. My dear lad was told, and he had forgiven me; the persecuting, plotting factor was effaced, and he could never trouble my sweet lady more. Between the two I loved there stood only the shadow of the marriage, and this the good priest would presently help me to dispel.

And after that ... I dared not look beyond. There is a way beset with lions, and any man who bears the name of man in honor may draw his sword and fix his eye upon the goal and hew his path to it, joying in the conflict. But there is also another way, a desert trail owning no peril more affrighting than its own dread waste and limitless monotony; and when his eyes behold the dismal prospect, and his feet have pressed the hitherward sands of this desert of despair, a man may well pause to gird his loins, to cross himself and patter such a prayer for strength and fortitude as his creed hath taught him.

To such a faring through all the days and nights of this grim desert of a future these lonely hours in the wine vault were a fitting vigil, as I conceived; and when I had hugged my misery close, and a sort of monstrous self-pity had come to make a seeming virtue of the hard necessity, I was best pleased to be alone. In such a frame of mind the sound of footsteps in the out-cellar, warning me that more company was coming, sent a wave of sullen anger to submerge me, and I do think 'twas in me to turn my back upon a friend who should come to tell me I was free to go at large.

Since I had led forth the good horses the great oaken door had stood ajar. So I wondered why my visitor made so much ado rattling the key in the lock. Then it came to me suddenly that the noise and delay were meant to give me timely warning; and at the scent of threatening peril—a peril I might cope with and grapple soldierwise—I became a man again. A sweep of my hat sent the sputtering candle flying from its barrel head to the farther corner of the vault, and I dropped quickly behind a row of empty wine-butts to await what should befall.

Had she been a ghost, Mistress Margery would scarce have startled me more when she swung the door to let me see her. She was gowned in her best; there was a heightened color in her cheek; her eyes were like stars. Truly, I do think I never saw her so beautiful as she appeared at that moment, standing under the massive arch of the doorway with her candle held high to light the inner gloom.

"This way, Scipio," she said, tripping ahead of the mulatto to point out the madeira bin. "We shall give my Lord and his gentlemen the best the Appleby cellar holds to speed their parting." Wherewith she stood aside to wait whilst he filled his basket with the straw-cased bottles.

At this I saw why she had come. Lord Cornwallis and his gentlemen were about to take the road, and the wine was wanted for the stirrup-cup. Trusting my fate to no hand less loyal than her own, she had come herself with Scipio to stand betwixt me and possible discovery. And her word to the serving man was also a word to me to let me know my prisonment was near an end.

I thought it a most generous thing in her; the last of all her many wifely loyalties; and I would have given much for leave to stand forth and tell her so. Indeed, when the mulatto had poised his basket upon his head and vanished, and she was lingering to take a last look around before she followed him, I was upon the point of speaking.

But whilst I hesitated I saw her start back with a little cry of terror. Standing in the arched doorway through which the mulatto had but now passed was a man cloaked, hatted, booted and spurred as for the road. At her cry he doffed his hat and ...

My dears, I shall never be able to draw for you the hideous death-mask this man was wearing for a face. Seamed and scarred, shriveled and livid in purple and crimson welts, you would think a nine-thonged whip of fire had scourged out every semblance of comeliness, leaving only the skeleton frame on which to hang this ghastly caricature of a human face. Fearing him not at all, I could scarce forbear a shudder at the sight of this walking death-mask of the libertine, Sir Francis Falconnet.

And if his face were terrifying in repose, 'twas fair demoniac when he laughed.

"Ha!" he said, bowing again in a mockery of politeness. "You are surprised, Mistress Margery; you heard my Lord's order and thought I would be by now some miles on the road to Salisbury?"

"If you were the loyal soldier you should be, sir," she said, drawing herself up proudly, "you would be at the head of your troop, as his Lordship directed." And then, with a gesture that was most queenly: "Stand aside, Sir—Libertine, and let me pass."

His answer was another mocking laugh, and he stepped within to close the door and lock it. When he turned to front her again his face was the face of a tormented devil.

"By God! you think too lightly of me, Mistress Margery. Before ever this day dawned I owed you much, but like a spiteful little hellicat you must needs add to the score by making me a target for your wit at the supper-table. 'Twill cost a life to more than one of them who laughed with you, my lady, but 'twill cost you dearer still."

He came nearer as he spoke, thrusting that horrible face farther into the circle of candle-light; but she would not draw back nor flinch a hair, and I marked that the hand that held the candlestick was as steady as a rock. But when he made an end she flung a quick glance over her shoulder and my heart leaped for joy. For then I knew she was leaning upon me.

"Once more, Captain Falconnet, will you let me pass?" she said.

"No!" he snarled, adding a horrid blasphemy. "'Twas passion in me once, and I am none so sure there was not a time when you could have cooled it into love. But now 'tis hatred and revenge." He snapped his fingers in her face. "The thing they'll find here in the morning—"

He fell face downward at her feet and I set my heel in the small of his back to hold him whilst I could drive the point of the Ferara between his ribs. But my dear lady would not have it so.

"No, no! for the love of heaven, not that, Monsieur John!" she cried; and for the moment her fine courage was all swallowed up of pity and she became a compassionate woman pleading for a life.

But now my blood was up. "You are my wife," I said, coldly. "If he had a dozen lives I should take them all for that which he said to you."

"But not that way—oh, not that way, I do beseech you!" she begged. "Think of what it will mean to you—and—and to me. For your own sake, Monsieur John."

I took my heel from the man's back.

"Your wish is law to me, dear lady. But your way is clear now; you may go."

She took a step toward the door.

"You will not kill him when I am gone, Monsieur John?"

"By the name he bears he was doubtless born a gentlemen; since you wish it, he shall die like one."

I saw she did not take my meaning; that when she was gone I should let him have his chance to die sword in hand.

"Remember, I have your promise," she said, turning to go. "The army is on the march for Salisbury, and in a little while your friends will be here to—"

The sentence ended in a very womanly shriek of terror. Watching his chance, my dastard enemy had bounded to his feet to make a quick lunge, not at me, but at her.

Of course I came between to parry the murderous thrust, and after that it was life for one of us and death for the other. I looked to see my lady run, shrieking; indeed, I called to her to go; but she stood fast as if her terror had frozen her; and so it was her candle that lighted the grim vault for the duel.

As you will know full well, I was not minded to give this thrice-accursed fiend more than the gentleman's chance I had promised to give him. But now, as twice before, he fought most desperately, trying by every trick of fence to come between me and the silent little figure holding the candle aloft. As I have often said, he was a pretty swordsman, and at this crisis, with life at stake, and all the fury of the seven devils of disappointed vengeance to nerve his arm, his sword play was most masterly.

Yet twice in his stamping rushes I found my opening; once the Ferara's point passed his blade, and but for the ringed guard of the German long-sword that stopped it when his parry failed, the steel would have passed through him. After this he grew warier, having in mind, as I supposed, that other time when I had shown him that my wrist and arm could outweary his. Yet his savage onset never flagged for an instant; and when the light fell upon his hideous face, I could see the fierce eyes glinting like a basilisk's, with no sign in them that my time was come to press him home.

None the less, I did press him, inch by inch, driving him at each new clash of the steel a little deeper into the gloom that crowded close upon the narrow circle of candle-light. He saw my object—to push him to unfamiliar ground where he might trip and stumble in the darkness—and he strove furiously to defeat it. Yet he had no choice, and presently I had him among the empty wine-butts, foining and parrying for his life and pouring out such blasphemies as would make your blood run cold.

Here the end came quickly. Being entangled among the broached butts he had no room to play skilfully. So presently it chanced that he caught his point in the chine of a cask and his blade snapped short at the hilt. With a yelling oath, hissing hot from the devil's thumb-book, he snatched up the broken blade to fling and stick it javelin-wise in my shoulder; and then I saw the dull gleam of the candle-light on the barrel of a pistol.

Had he aimed the pistol at me, I trust I should still have given him his gentleman's chance. But when I saw him level the weapon at my dear lady ... they came in one and the same heart-beat; the sword-thrust that found his life and took it; the crash of the pistol-shot echoing like a clap of thunder in the close vault, and pitchy darkness to draw its curtain over all.

I know not how I reached her, pulling the broken sword-blade from my shoulder as I ran; nor can I tell you how an upgushing spring of thankfulness choked me when I found her unharmed by the bullet which had snuffed the candle out.

She was in a most piteous state, now it was all over; and though I charged it all where I supposed it should belong—to the account of a natural womanly passion to cling to something in her moment of weakness—yet the blood ran quick in my veins when she suffered me to lead her out of that dismal, smoking death-pit, she clinging to me the while so close that I could feel the warmth of her and the fluttering of her dear heart beneath my hand.

She said no word, nor did I, till we were come above stairs. We found the rooms on the main floor deserted by all save the blacks, who were clearing away the debris of the feast of leave-taking. In the hall we came upon old Anthony, putting on the chain of the outer door. Here my lady drew apart from me.

"Is my Lord gone?" she asked.

"Yis, Missa. He say tell yo' he gwine tek it mighty hawd yo' no come ter gib him de sti'up-cup."

"And my father?"

"Gone to de lib'ry to wait fo' Massa Pengarbin; yis, Missa."

She turned away, shuddering at this mention of the factor for whose coming the master would wait long and in vain, and I heard her murmur: "Oh, the horror of this night!" But in a moment she came back to me, and was her cool, calm self again.

"For that I am here, alive and well, I thank you, Captain Ireton. Need I say more?"

I can not tell you what was in the words to make me hot with anger, as I had but now been hot with love. But the new wound in my shoulder was bleeding freely, and I would not let her see I was hurt; and if aught will stanch a wound, 'tis anger.

"You need not say so much," I retorted, bowing low. "You have spoken now and then of certain duties binding upon those who are knotted up, ever so loosely, in the marriage bond; I have my part in these as well as you, Mistress Margery."

She bit her lip and was upon the edge of tears. I saw what I had done and would curse the masterless tongue that must needs add its word-thong to the night's whip of scourgings.

When she spoke again it was to say: "This is your own house, Captain Ireton; what will you do?"

"One question first, is Richard Jennifer safe?"

"He is."

"Then, by your good leave, I shall do what I came to do."

She bent her head in acquiescence.

"You will find the—the person whom you wish to see in your old room in the north gable. Shall I have Anthony light you up?"

"No; I can find the way."

My hand was on the stair rail when the cruel irony of it struck me like a blow. She had planned the loosing of the bond in the very room where we had knelt to take the good father's blessing upon it.

I stepped back, stumbled, I should say, for a curious weakness had come upon me, and drew her arm in mine.

"We will go together, if you please, my lady. 'Tis only just to me that you should hear what I must say to Father Matthieu."

And so, dear heart! she bore with me to the last; and together we climbed the stair to come into the upper corridor with the room of destiny at its farther end.

We came as far as the door; I mind it perfectly, for I remember marking that the wooden bar my father had put upon it was gone, and the iron brackets as well. But whilst I was groping for the latch there came a taste of blood in my mouth, and I heard my dear lady's voice as if she were calling to me across the eternal abysses. "Monsieur John!—you are hurt!" And then, from a still remoter distance: "Oh, Father Matthieu—Dick! come quickly! He is dying!"

CHAPTER LI

IN WHICH THE GOOD CAUSE GAINS A CONVERT

Which one of you, my dears, faring across the frontier of the shadow land of dreams into the no less mysterious country of the real, can not recall the struggle of the waking senses to knot up the gossamer filament of the night's fantasies with the coarser web of reality?

For a time, longer or shorter as the dream thread holds, the vagaries of the night are shuttled into the warp of life. But presently comes the master-weaver Reason to point out this or that fantastic pattern; to bid the ear listen to the measured clacking of the day-loom, and the eye to mark that the web of reality has grown never an inch for all the shuttlings of the sleeping-time. Whereupon, full-blood consciousness regains her sway, and you sigh, gladly or sorrowfully, and say, "Dear God, 'twas but a dream I dreamed!"

Some such awakening came to me on a day whereof I knew not the name or its number in the calendar.

I was lying in bed in my old room at Appleby Hundred. The armored soldier was glowering down upon me from his frame over the chimney piece; the great blackened clothes-press loomed darkly in its corner; the show of curious china filled the shelves where my boyhood books had rested; and there was the same faint smell of lavender in the bed linen that once—was it yesterday or months ago?—had minded me of my mother.

When I sought to move me on the pillows the dream seemed more than ever dream-sure. The pain of a sword wound was grinding at my shoulder, and I was bandaged stiff as I had been that other day.

So I said, as you have said in like awakenings, "Dear God,'twas but a dream!" and saying it, would turn my head to see if Mistress Margery were sitting where I last remembered her.

She was there, in very deed and truth, deep in the hollow of the great chair of Indian wickerwork; and as before, the soft graying of the evening sky was mirrored in her eyes.

I sighed, and there was a catching of the breath at the bottom of it. Truly, the wondrous dream had had its agonies, but there were also beatitudes to tip the scale the other way. For I had dreamed this sweet-faced watcher was my wife—in name, at least.

'Twas while I looked, minding not the eye-ache the effort cost, that she rose and came softly to the bedside. She said no word, but, as once in the dream-time, she laid a cool palm on my forehead. Weak as I was—and surely King David was not weaker when he wrote his bones were gone to water—the old love-madness of that other day came to thrill me at her touch, and I made as if I would take her hand and press it to my lips.

"Nay, sir," she said, with a swift return to sick-room discipline, "you must not stir; you have been sorely hurt."

"Aye," said I; "I do remember; 'twas in a duel with one Francis Falconnet. He said he would make you his—"

Now the soft palm was laid on my lips, and I kissed it till she snatched it away.

"*Ma foi!*" she cried; "I think you are in a hopeful way to recover now, Captain Ireton. I do protest I shall go and send old Anthony to sit with you."

"Anthony?" said I; "he was in the dream, too, putting up the chain on the hall door."

"Ah, *mon Dieu!*" she said softly, as if to herself, "he is wandering yet." At which, as if to try to help me: "'Twas no dream; you did see him putting on the chain."

"Did I? I made sure I dreamed it. But tell me another thing; was it not yesterday that I met Sir Francis Falconnet under the oaks in the wood field and got this pair of redhot pincers in my shoulder?"

She turned away, and if I ever saw a tear there was one trembling in her eyelashes.

"'Twas three full weeks ago," she said. "And it was not in the wood field—'twas in the wine cellar. Never tell me you do not remember; I—I could never—ah, Mother of Sorrows! that would be worse than all."

Here was a curious coil, but I could break one strand of it, at least, and so I did.

"I remember well enough," I hastened to say. "But being here, and seeing you there in the great chair, carried me back to that other time, making all the interval stand as a dream. Have I been ailing?"

"You have been terribly near to death, Monsieur John; so near that Doctor Carew has twice given you over."

"No," said I; "there was no fear of that. I am like that man in the old German folk tale who made a compact with the Evil One, selling thereby his chance to die. Death would not take me as a gift, Mistress Margery; I have tried him too often."

"Hush!" she said; "'tis an ill thing to jest about. Why should you want to die?"

"Rather ask why I should choose to live. But this is beside the mark. You should have let me die, dear lady; but since you did not, we must e'en make the best of it."

She faced me with a smile that struggled with some deeper stirring of the heart; I knew not what.

"'Tis a monstrous doleful alternative, *n'est-ce pas*? And I must not let you talk of doleful things; indeed, I must not let you talk at all—'tis Doctor Carew's order."

So saying, she smoothed the counterpane and straightened my pillows; and after giving me a great spoonful of some cordial that first set a pleasant glow alight in me and afterward made me drowsy, she took post again in the hollow of the big chair and was so sitting when I fell asleep.

This day's awakening was the first of many so nearly of a piece that I lost the count of them; and sleep, deep and dreamless for the better part, stole away the hours till the memory of that inch-by-inch return to health and strength is itself like the memory of the vaguest of dreams.

By times when I awoke it was the bluff Doctor Carew bending over me to dress my wound; at other times it was Margery come to tempt me with a bowl of broth or some other kickshaw from the kitchen. Now and again I awoke to find Scipio or old Anthony standing watch at my bedside; and once—but that was after I was up and in my clothes and able to sit and drowse in the great chair—I opened my eyes to find that my company was the master of the house.

He was sitting as I had seen him sit once before, behind a lighted candle at the little table with a parchment spread out under his bony hands. He was mumbling over the written words of it when I looked, but at my stirring he gave over and sat back in his chair to cross his thin legs and match his long fingers by the ends, and wink and blink at me as though he had but now discovered that he was not alone.

"I give ye good even, Captain Ireton," he said, finally, rasping the greeting out at me as it had been a curse. "I hope ye've slept well."

I said I had, and thanked him, once for the wish, and again for his coming to see me. I know not how it was, but if there had been rancor in my former thoughts of him 'twas something abated now.

"Ye've had a nearhand escape this time, sir," he said, after a longish pause.

"One more or less of a good many since we were last met together in this room, Mr. Stair," I would say.

He muttered something to himself about the devil taking precious good care of his own; and I laughed.

"That is as it may be; but my being here this second time a pensioner on your bounty is by no good will of mine, I do assure you, sir."

He sat nodding at me as if I had said a thing to be most heartily agreed to. But his spoken word belied the nods.

"The ways of Providence are inscrutable—something inscrutable, Captain Ireton. I make no doubt ye are sufficiently thankfu' for all your mercies."

"Why, as to that, there may be two ways of looking at it. As a soldier, I may justly repine at a fate which ties me here when I should be in the field."

"Well said, sir; brawly said; 'tis the part of a good soldier to be ay wanting to be in the thick o' the fighting. But now that ye're a man of substance, Captain Ireton, ye will be owing other debts to our country than the one ye can pay with a hantle o' steel."

"'Our country,' did you say, Mr. Stair?" I asked, feigning a surprise which no one knowing him could feel in very truth.

"And what for no? 'Tis the birthland of some—yourself, for example, and the leal land of adoption for others—your humble servant, to wit. I've taken the solemn oath of allegiance to the Congress, I'd have ye to know."

At this I must needs laugh outright.

"Have you taken it one more time than you have forsworn it, Mr. Stair?"

"Laugh and ye will," he said, quite placably; "ye shall never laugh the peetriotism out o' me. 'Tis little enough an old man can do, but the precious cause o' liberty will never have to ask that little twice, Captain Ireton."

Since he would ever be on the winning side, this foreshadowed good tidings, indeed. So I would ask him straight what news there was.

"Have they not told ye? 'Tis braw news," he chuckled. "Whilst ye were on your back, General Greene led Lord Cornwallis a fine dance all across the prov—the state, I mean, crooking his finger at him and saying, 'Come on, ye led-captain of a tyrant king, and when I'm ready I'll turn and rend ye.' And by the same token, that is juist what he did the other day at Guilford Court House."

"A victory?" I would ask.

"Well, not precisely that, maybe; they're calling it a drawn battle. But I'm thinking 'tis Lord Cornwallis that's drawn. He's off to Wilmington, they say, and I'm fain to hope we've seen the last o' him and his reaving redcoats in these parts."

His words set me in a muse. I could never make out what he would be at, telling me all this. But he had an object, well-defined, and presently it showed its head.

"Ye're the laird o' the manor, now, Captain Ireton, with none to gainsay ye," he went on. "So I've come to give ye an account o' my stewardship. I made no doubt, all along, ye'd come back to your own when ye'd had your fling wi' the Old Worldies, and so I've kept tab o' the poor bit land for ye."

"Oh, you have?" said I, being so far out-brazened as to be incapable of saying more.

"I have that—every plack and bawbee. 'Tis ten years come Michaelmas since I took over the charge o' Appleby Hundred, and I'm ready to account to ye for every season's crop—when ye'll pay down the bit steward's fee."

"Truly," said I; "you are an honest man, Mr. Stair." Then, to humor him to the top of his bent: "Haphazarding a guess, now; would this accounting leave a balance in my favor, or in yours?"

He gave me a look like that of a costermonger weighing and measuring the gullibility of his customer.

"Oh, aye; I'm no saying there mightn't be a bit siller coming to me; a few hundred pounds, more or less—sterling, man, sterling; not Scots," he added hastily. And then, as if it were best to leave this nail as it was driven, he changed the subject abruptly. "I've brought ye that last will and testament ye signed," handing me the parchment. "No doubt you'll let it stand; but when the bairns come, ye'll want to be adding a codicil or two."

Leaving the matter of the estate, I thought it high time to cut to the marrow of the bigger bone. So I said: "Let us be frank with each other in this, Mr. Stair. How much has your daughter told you of the matter between us?"

"She's a jade!" he rasped, lapsing for a moment into his real self. But he recovered his self-control instantly. "Ye'd no expect a romantic bit lassie wi' French blood in her veins to be confidencing wi' her old dried-up wisp of a father, now, would ye? She's no tell't me everything, I daresay."

"Then I will tell you the plain truth of it," I said. "This marriage was never anything more than the form we all agreed it should be at the time; a makeshift to serve a purpose. If you think I would hold your daughter to it—"

"Hut, tut, man! what will ye be havering about! Ye'll never cast the poor bit lassie off that way! Ye canna, if ye would; her Church will have a word to say to that."

For all his aping the manner of the ignored father, I shrewdly suspected that he knew more about the ins and outs of our affair than he owned to. Nevertheless, I was forced to meet him on his own ground.

"There is no 'casting off' about it, Mr. Stair; and as to the Church, there is good ground for an appeal to Rome. The marriage as it stands is little more than a formal betrothal, as you well know, sound enough legally to make Mistress Margery my heir-at-law, mayhap, but still lacking everything of—"

He could not wait to let me finish.

"Lacking, d'ye say?" he rapped out, wrathfully. "And whose fault is that, ye cold-blooded stick? Tell me this; did I no bundle ye neck and heels into your own wife's bed-room? And how do you thank me? I'm to suppose ye quarrel wi' her like the dour-faced imp o' Sawtan that ye are, and presently ye come raging out, swearing most shamefully at a man old enough to be your father!"

'Twas far enough in the retrospect now so that I could smile at it. Yet I would not suffer him to bluster me aside.

"It was an ill thing for you to do, none the less, Mr. Stair; the more as you must have known that Mistress Margery's faith was plighted to Richard Jennifer long before all this came to pass."

"Did I know it?" he shrilled. "That lang-legged jackanapes of a Dickie Jennifer? Light o' love jade that she is, she never cared the snap of a finger for him."

"You are talking far enough beside the mark now," I retorted. "Your daughter loves Richard Jennifer well and truly; and with this entanglement brushed aside she will marry him when he comes back from the wars."

"She will, ye say? And what will become o' the braw acres of Appleby that gait, I'd like to know? But ye're daft, man; clean daft. Didn't I speir her giving him his quittance once for all that night when he rode away after they had pitten ye to bed? She tell't him flat she loved another man."

"Another man?" I echoed. "I—explain yourself, if you please, Mr. Stair. What other man—"

He was at the door by this, and he broke out upon me in such a blast of cursing as I hope never to hear from the lips of such an old man again.

"Ye cold-blooded, crusty devil!" he quavered, when all his breath was spent upon the bigger malisons. "Has it never come intil your thick numbskull that the poor fule lassie is sick wi' love for ye, ye dour-faced loon?"

And with that he let himself out and slammed the door behind him, and I heard him go pottering down the corridor, still cursing me by all the choice phrases he could lay tongue to.

CHAPTER LII

WHICH BRINGS US TO THE JOURNEY'S END

I may confess to you, my dears, that Mr. Gilbert Stair's parting tirade did not move me greatly, since I would set down everything he had said to the one account—the miser's.

Yet when I came to second thoughts upon it, this account balanced but indifferently. Why should he be so eager to make me think small of Margery's love for Richard Jennifer? And why, misliking me, as I made sure he did, should he be so hot to make the shadow marriage a thing of substance? From the miser-father's point of view, Richard, with his goodly heritage of Jennifer House, was a match to be angled for; yet here was the man in whose eye house and lands loomed largest flying into rage because I sought to put his daughter in the way of marrying them.

I was pondering thoughtfully on this, giving the pinching old man credit for any and every motive save that which he had so cursingly avowed, to wit, the furthering of his daughter's happiness, when there came a tap at the door and Mistress Margery entered.

"Dear heart! Do they limit you to a single candle when my back is turned?" she said, in mock pity; and saying it, went to light the candles in the mantel sconces.

The sight of her standing a-tiptoe to touch off the candles on the chimney breast set the old lovespell at work to make my heart beat faster. What if there were a hint of truth in Gilbert Stair's wrathful protest? What if, after all, she cared less for Richard and more for me?

Do not, I pray you, my dears, think too hardly of the man who thus lays bare the secret thoughts of his heart for you. 'Twas but a passing gust of the tempest of disloyalty, and I was not swept wholly from my moorings. Nay, when she came to sit on the hassock at my feet, as she used to do in that other halcyon-time of convalescence, I was myself again and could look upon her sweet face with eyes that saw beyond her to the camp or battle-field where my dear lad was spending himself.

For a time we sat in silence, and 'twas she who spoke first.

"My father has been with you," she said. "I hope you did not quarrel with him."

"No," I denied, salving my conscience with the remembering that it takes two to make a quarrel; and I had done none of the cursing. "He came to give me this," I added, handing her the will.

She opened the folded parchment, reading a line of it here and there softly to herself.

—"'Being of sound mind, doth bequeath and devise to his loving wife, Margery—' Ah, had you been writing it you would not have written it so, would you, Monsieur John?"

"'Tis but a form," I would say. "All wives are 'loving' in lawyers' speech."

She smiled up at me so like an innocent and fearless child that for the moment I could figure her no otherwise. Yet her rejoinder was a woman's.

"I say you would not have written it so; is not that the truth?"

I would not let her pin me down.

"If I should write it now, it should be written in great letters, dear lady. Though it is but a form, though that which followed was but another form, you have not failed in any wifely duty, Mistress Margery."

"Not once?"

"No, not once. Three times you have done what the lovingest wife could do to save a husband's life; and I do greatly suspect there was a fourth and earlier time. Tell me, little one; was it not you who sent the Indian to Captain Forney to tell him a patriot spy was to be executed at day-dawn in the oak glade?"

She would not answer me direct.

"'Twas I who brought you to that pass," she said, speaking soft and low. "But for my riding down upon you one other morning in that same oak glade, you would not have had Sir Francis Falconnet's sword in your shoulder. And but for that sword wound, nothing that followed would have followed."

Saying this she fell silent for a space, and when she spoke again she was become by some subtle transmutation my trusting little maid of the by-gone halcyon-time.

"Do you remember how you used to make a comrade of me in the old days, Monsieur John, telling me things my elder brother might have told me, had I had one?"

I said I remembered; that I was not likely to forget.

"Are you strong enough to stand in that elder brother's place again to-night?"

"Try me and see, dear lady."

"Not whilst you say 'dear lady,'" she pouted. "'Twas 'Margery' and 'Monsieur John' a year agone."

"Have it as you will; I will even call you 'Madge' if it pleases you better."

"No," she said; "that is Dick's name for me; and—and it is of Dick that I would speak. You love him well, do you not, Monsieur

John?"

I said I could never make her, or any woman, fully understand the bond there was between us.

"Truly?" There was the merest flavor of playful sarcasm in the uptilt of the word, but it was gone when she went on.

"Being so good a friend to Dick, then, you can advise me the better. Tell me, if you please, must I marry him—when—"

"When you are free to do it?" I finished for her. "Why should you not, my dear?"

She was pulling the threads from the lace edging of her kerchief and would not for a king's ransom let her eyes meet mine.

"You used to say—in that other time—that love should go before a marriage; did you not? Or do I remember badly?"

"You remember well. I said it then, and I say it again at this present. But Dick loves you well and truly, sweetheart; and you—"

She looked up quickly with the little laugh that used to mind me of happy children at play.

"And I?—now you will read a woman's heart for me, Monsieur John. Tell me; do I love him as his mistress should?"

"Nay, surely," said I, gravely, for somehow her laugh jarred upon me, "surely that is for you to say. But you have said it, long since."

"Have I?" she queried, with an arch lifting of the penciled brows that came straight from her French mother. "Mayhap you overheard me say it, Monsieur Eavesdropper?"

"God help me, little one—so I did," said I.

All in a flash her laughing mood was gone and she stood before me like an accusing goddess.

"You told me once the past was like a dream to you; you must have dreamed that part of it, sir. And yet you said a little while ago that I had not failed in any wifely duty!"

"The time and circumstance were their own best excuse. Sure I am far from blaming you, my dear. But let it pass, 'tis enough that I know you love him as he loves you."

Again her mood changed in the twinkling of an eye. She sank down upon the hassock, laughing merrily.

"O wise Monsieur John! how well you read a woman's heart! 'Tis you should be the lover, instead of Dick. He rides a-courting as he would charge a legion on a battle-field. But nothing would ever tempt you to be so masterful rough, would it, Monsieur John? You would look deep into your sweetheart's eyes and say—Tell me what you would say, *mon ami*?"

Ah, my dears, I hope no one of you will ever be tempted as I was tempted then. I forgot my dear lad, forgot honor, forgot everything save that I had leave to tell her how I had loved her from the first; how I should go on loving her to the end. So for a moment I hung trembling on the brink; and then she pushed me over.

"Is this how you would do, Monsieur—Monsieur Ogre?—sit stock still and glower at the poor thing as if you were between two minds as to loving her or eating her?"

I bent quickly, took her face between my hands and kissed her twice—thrice.

"That is what I should do. Now that you have made me what I was not before, are you satisfied?"

'Twas long before she gave me a word. And when she spoke it was only to say: "Are you not most monstrous ashamed, Monsieur John?"

"No!" said I. "I am but a man, and you have roused that part of me that knows neither shame nor remorse. I love you, Mistress Margery; do you hear? I have loved you since that day in June when I came back from death's door to find you sitting here to bear me company."

She locked her fingers across her knee and would not look at me.

"But by your own showing you should be ashamed, sir," she insisted. "What of the dear friend to whom you would give up even the love of your mistress?"

"You may flay me as you will; I shall neither flinch nor go back from my word. You are mine, and I shall give you up to no man. I know I have not your love—shall never have it. Also, I know that I have gained an enemy where once I had a loving friend. Richard Jennifer may kill me if he please—he shall have the chance to do it; but you are mine and shall be whilst I live to claim and hold you."

There was something less than anger in the blue-gray eyes when she let me see them; nay, I could have sworn there was a flash of playful mockery in them when she said: "Dear heart! how masterful rough you have grown, all in a moment, my Lord." And then the beautiful eyes filled and she said, "Poor Dick!" in a way to make me suffer all the torments of that old myth-king who could never quaff the water that was ever rising to his lips.

"Aye, you may love him, if you must and will," I gloomed. "God pity me! I know you do love him."

She looked up quickly. "So you have said a dozen times before. Tell me, Monsieur Oracle, how do you know it?"

"If I tell you, you will hate me more than you do now."

"That would be hard, indeed," she murmured. "Yet I would hear you say it."

"Listen, then: once, when we three were at the very door and threshold of death, you wrote the cry of your heart out on a bit of paper for a leave-taking and sent it to the man you loved. You said, 'Though you must needs believe my love is pledged to your dear friend and mine, 'tis yours, and yours alone.' Were not these your very words?"

Her "yes" was but the lightest whisper, but I heard it and went on. "That is all, save this; the Indian bearer of your letter blundered and gave it me instead of Dick."

She looked me full in the eyes and my soul went all afire. Then she laid her cheek against my knee and I heard her dear voice as it had been a chime of sweet-toned joy-bells:

"Ah, Monsieur John; how blind this thing called love can make us all. Suppose—suppose the Indian did not blunder, dear lord and master of me?"

THE END